AN AIR THAT KILLS

AN AIR
THAT KILLS

Andrew Taylor

Hodder & Stoughton
LONDON SYDNEY AUCKLAND

First published in Great Britain in 1994
by Hodder and Stoughton
A division of Hodder Headline PLC

10 9 8 7 6 5 4 3 2 1

British Library Cataloguing in Publication Data

Taylor, Andrew
Air That Kills
I. Title
823.914 [F]

ISBN 0-340-61713-6

Typeset by Keyboard Services, Luton

Printed and bound in Great Britain by
Mackays of Chatham PLC, Chatham, Kent

Published by Hodder and Stoughton Ltd
A Division of Hodder Headline PLC
338 Euston Road
London NW1 3BH

For Nick and Pippa

Into my heart an air that kills
  From yon far country blows:
What are those blue remembered hills,
  What spires, what farms are those?

A. E. Housman, *A Shropshire Lad*,
                                  XL

Part One

Wednesday

1

November is the month of the dead. Jill Francis acquired this scrap of information quite by chance and only minutes before she reached Lydmouth.

The train had rattled out of a tunnel and into the daylight. The wind drove the smoke from the engine at window level along the line of carriages. Jill coughed and put down her book. The window of the compartment was slightly open.

"Allow me," said the bearded man in the corner by the door.

"Thank you."

The compartment had been full when they left Paddington two and a half hours earlier. Now there were only the two of them. She thought that the beard gave the man an ostentatiously nautical air which did not fit with the rest of his appearance. Perhaps he had served in the Navy during the war and like so many men of his age was reluctant to leave the past behind.

He laid his own book on the seat between them and stood up. He was slightly built and wore a brown double-breasted pinstripe suit with a poppy in the buttonhole. The suit was badly cut and hung loosely on him. His beard was neatly trimmed and his complexion had the texture of candle wax.

The train swayed and he steadied himself by holding on to the luggage rack. When he closed the window he was careful not to brush against Jill's knees. He smelled powerfully of tobacco and eau de cologne.

"Thank you," she said again as he edged past her.

"My pleasure entirely." The man hesitated, which made Jill instantly wary. He waved towards the window and added, "It's a pretty sight, eh?"

She looked up again, first at him and then through the window. The train was running parallel to the river. On the farther bank was a rolling patchwork of fields which rose gradually towards a range of blue hills in the west. It was a grey day and mist blurred the outlines of the hills. The train was still in England, but the hills must be in Wales. She supposed that in normal circumstances it would strike her as a beautiful landscape. She wasn't quite sure what normal meant any longer.

"Super, eh?" the man said in a flat, unemotional voice.

Jill nodded and allowed her eyes to stray back to her book; she turned a page. A moment later, the man slid back the door of their compartment and disappeared into the corridor.

She was alone for the first time since this morning when the taxi had arrived to take her from the flat to Paddington station. As if on cue, her eyes began to smart with tears.

"Damn it," Jill said aloud.

In an attempt to distract herself, she glanced towards the book which her fellow passenger had been reading. It lay face upwards on the seat. She could see the pages without moving her head. Probably a detective novel, she thought, or perhaps a textbook on a subject like accountancy or surveying.

The running title at the top of the left-hand page dispelled this idea. It said 'Aspects of Common Culture'. Jill skimmed through the first few lines, gathering the sense even though the unshed tears made the lines of print buckle and blur.

> *. . . is often referred to as the month of the dead. The Dutch called November* Slaght-maand, *which means slaughter month. This clearly corresponds with the Anglo-Saxon* Blodmonath, *or blood month. It was the time of year when the beasts were slain and salted for the winter months.*
>
> *As so often happens, pagan usages, albeit much altered, have descended into the modern world. The Roman Catholic Church, for example, celebrates All Souls' Day on the 2nd November, when worshippers pray for the souls of those in Purgatory. Curiously enough, we mourn the millions who died in the Great War in November – on the eleventh hour of the eleventh day of the eleventh month. Strangeways and Foster have shown . . .*

A change in the light, a minute darkening of the page, alerted Jill to the fact that she was no longer alone. The door slid back. The bearded man came in and sat down. She wondered whether he had seen her prying. To her surprise she found that she didn't much care.

She couldn't concentrate on her own book. Since they left Paddington she had taken in hardly a word. Instead she stared out of the window. Now the train was running along the bottom of a wooded slope. The changing colours of the dying leaves brought a richness and a warmth to the dull landscape. The world seemed unreal, like a picture in a gallery or a film in a darkened cinema.

Jill looked at her watch. If the train were on time, they should be in Lydmouth within five minutes. She wished she were looking forward to getting there. It struck her, not for the first time, that perhaps she was making a mistake in coming. On the other hand, she could hardly have stayed at the flat in London. She had considered making her excuses to the Wemyss-Browns and going to a hotel by herself. But in that case there would have been no distractions, nothing to save her from her thoughts. Besides it would have forced her to make decisions. It was easier to drift.

In truth, whatever she did would feel wrong. Coming to Lydmouth could be no more of a mistake than any other course of action. The mistake had already been made – long before, when she had first allowed Oliver Yateley to take her out to dinner and feed her a heady mixture of compliments and inside information. Now there was nothing to be done except live through the consequences. She sat staring out of the window and seeing nothing. Instead, she remembered and wished with all her heart that she might forget.

The tears threatened again. She dug her nails into the palm of her hand and forced herself to concentrate on the view. The train rounded a bend. In front of her and to the right was a low hill covered with buildings. Near the highest point was a church with a spire. They had arrived.

The train began to slow. Turning towards the window so that the bearded man could not see her, Jill opened her handbag and dabbed her eyes with a handkerchief. She examined her face in the mirror inside the lid of her powder compact. It surprised and almost offended her that she should look so normal. There was no sign of the emotions churning so uncomfortably behind the mask of skin and bone. She put a dab of powder on the tip of her nose and shut the compact with a click.

The train hissed as it slid along the platform. Jill got up and put on her coat. She checked the angle of her hat in the brown-spotted mirror beside the fading prewar photograph of Tintern Abbey. Her fellow passenger showed signs of wanting to lift her suitcase down from the rack. She pretended not to notice.

As she lowered the case, the past sprang another of its boobytraps: she noticed that there was part of a blue label gummed to the lid, and it brought with it the memory of a hotel in Paris; and the memory had the sharpness of a knife. Her eyes blurred again. She blundered towards the door of their compartment.

The man with the beard slid back the door for her. She heard herself murmuring thank you. The train stopped with a jerk; Jill staggered and almost collided with him.

"Lydmouth!" a voice cried. "Lydmouth!"

Carrying the suitcase, she walked crabwise along the corridor and joined the little queue at the end. She would have to find a porter if Philip had not come to meet her; she was still weak, and the doctor had advised her not to exert herself physically. To her dismay, she heard footsteps behind her. The man with the beard was also getting out at Lydmouth.

There was a delay before the door opened. Then the first passengers, a mother with two toddlers in tow, took an interminable time getting off the train. Jill did not look round. She smelled tobacco and eau de cologne. Beneath it she thought there lurked the rank smell of sweat.

One by one the passengers spilled on to the platform. Jill and the man behind her were almost the last to get off the train. She glanced up and down the platform. To her dismay, there was no sign of Philip or Charlotte. Most of the passengers were already walking towards a staircase leading to a bridge over the lines.

Jill followed. The suitcase was heavy enough to make her feel lopsided. Unfortunately there was only one porter in sight, and he was crawling up the stairs laden with the luggage of an elderly lady. But Jill was determined not to show any hesitation, because the man with the beard might construe it as a request for him to carry her case. She did not want to show weakness. Nor did she want to accept favours, particularly from a man.

She climbed the stairs more quickly than she would otherwise have done. There were footsteps behind her. The man's shoes had nails in their soles which rang against the iron treads of the stairs. He was gaining on her.

She pushed herself to go faster. The footsteps behind her seemed to quicken their pace. Turning round was out of the question. She forced herself to go still faster. Her head hurt and her breathing was fast and ragged. There was a stab of pain deep in her groin which made her gasp. She stumbled and had to seize the handrail with her free hand to prevent herself from falling. Simultaneously her mind was pointing out that she was reacting inappropriately. The little man behind her had shown her nothing but kindness. But he was a man, and she didn't want kindness ever again.

She reached the top of the stairs. Her right arm felt as though it were on fire. The fingers were becoming numb. The last of the passengers in front had reached the head of the stairs down to the opposite platform. A moment later, she was alone on the bridge with the bearded man.

Her suitcase collided with one of the stanchions supporting the handrail. The impact jerked the handle from her fingers. The case scraped against her leg as it fell. She clung to the rail with both hands.

She felt sick. Part of her mind wondered if her stocking was laddered. A door slammed on the platform below and a whistle blew.

"Can I be of any assistance, miss?"

She felt the man's breath on her cheek. She smelled the eau de cologne and the stale tobacco.

"Jill!"

The train began to move. The bridge shook. Smoke billowed from the engine. She looked up. Philip was loping towards her, an anxious expression on his florid face. He was hatless and his overcoat flapped about him. A poppy glowed in his buttonhole like a spot of blood. He loomed over her – he was a good six inches taller than she was – and his size was enormously and shamefully reassuring.

"Are you all right?" he demanded.

"I – I dropped my case."

He pecked her cheek, and the warmth of his lips brought her nothing but comfort. She found it difficult to think of Philip as a man. He had more to do with childhood memories of large dogs and teddy bears.

"You look pale," he said accusingly. "*Is* everything all right?"

"Yes, fine." She watched the man with the beard disappearing down the stairs to the farther platform. Such a lot of fuss about nothing: she felt as though her emotions were no longer hers to control.

"Sorry I'm late. Got held up in some roadworks." Philip picked up her bag. "Have a good journey?"

"Yes, thanks. How's Charlotte?"

"I left her polishing the silver teapot in your honour." He glanced at her and smiled; but his eyes were serious. "She'll murder me if she finds out I was late."

They walked along the bridge and down the stairs to the platform below. The man with the beard had gone. Philip steered her through the ticket hall into the station yard. It had begun to rain – a fine drizzle that cast a grey, greasy pall over everything it touched. The Wemyss-Browns' Rover 75 was standing by the kerb. Philip opened the front passenger door for Jill and put her case on the back seat.

Jill stared through the windscreen. The rain trickled down the glass. To her dismay, she felt her eyes filling with tears. This time there was no holding them back.

Philip opened the driver's door. The car rocked under his weight.

"Jill – what is it?"

He moved towards her. He lifted his arm as if to put it round her shoulders. Before she could stop herself she jerked away.

"It's all right," Philip said. "I'm quite harmless, you know." He leant back in his seat, his hands safely in his lap, and cleared his throat.

"I'm sorry." Jill rummaged in her handbag for a handkerchief. "It's just that – it's been a bad week – I'm rather tired."

"Yes, yes of course."

She turned away to wipe her eyes and blow her nose.

"I always say November's a depressing month," he went on. "Nothing to look forward to. Even Christmas isn't what it used to be before the war."

"It's the month of the dead," Jill said. "November, I mean."

"What?"

"I read it somewhere." She felt she had to keep talking – partly for Philip's sake and partly for hers. "It's the time of year when they used to kill all the animals, and when the Roman Catholics pray for dead souls. And then there's Remembrance Day."

"I hadn't thought of it like that," Philip said. "Makes it seem even worse."

"I'm better now."

"Is there something wrong? Something it would help to tell me?"

Jill shook her head. She left it unclear which question she was answering. Philip seemed not to notice.

"You know – a trouble shared, eh?"

No. Jill thought. No, no, no.

"Overwork, that's what it is. And all those parties, of course."

"Philip – don't mention it to Charlotte, will you? Well, do if you want to. It's just that I don't want to make a fuss."

"Of course."

After a few seconds, Philip started the engine, drove slowly out of the station yard and turned left on to a main road rising gently towards the town centre. After fifty yards he was forced to stop.

"This is what made me late," he said. "There's a demolition job over there. They've had to cordon off part of the road for their vehicles."

A youthful policeman was directing the traffic. Jill glanced at the warren of buildings on the other side of the road. Some of them had lost their roofs. Most of the windows were broken. The brickwork of the warehouse at one end of the site was blackened, as if by fire.

"Bomb damage?"

"Natural wear and tear. The Rose in Hand has been falling apart for centuries."

"The what?"

"It used to be the name of an inn. See? That building with the tall gables. They're pulling down everything from there to the ware-house, and there are some yards and outbuildings behind and at the side. And that's just the first stage. The site's part of an area called Templefields which stretches up to the town centre. It's all very rundown. I imagine they'll eventually pull most of it down."

"What are they planning to do here?"

"There's going to be a car park and some council houses. All part of Lydmouth's contribution to our brave new world."

Jill glanced at him, catching the unfamiliar note of cynicism in his voice. "I'd have thought you'd approve of that."

His mouth twisted into a smile. "I do. But Charlotte feels the working classes have managed perfectly well without flush lavatories for centuries, so why start bothering now? Also, of course, she thinks it's vandalism to bulldoze the existing buildings out of existence. She's got a point. Some of them are very old."

Jill said nothing. She watched a file of workmen walking slowly along the narrow pavement from the warehouse. They were laden with tools and their heads were bowed. The rain fell steadily on them. They turned under an archway at the other end of the site.

"Not much of a job, eh?" Philip said.

The policeman turned and waved them on. Philip let out the clutch. The Rover moved forward.

"No," Jill said. "Not much of a life either."

2

There were four of them in the line. The three in the front were bunched tightly together. After a gap of a couple of yards, Charlie Meague followed. He had the ghost of a swagger and his eyes flickered from side to side. He was taller than the others, a dark, good-looking man wearing army boots and trousers below a shabby tweed jacket. He hadn't bothered to shave or wear a collar. His flat cap was pulled down low over his face.

Under the archway, Charlie hesitated. The other three walked on. He moved to the shelter of a doorway, rested the sledgehammer against the wall and took a half-smoked cigarette from the top pocket of his jacket. After he had smoothed it out, he lit it with a match. Staring at the traffic, he noticed the Wemyss-Browns' Rover going up the hill. He exhaled smoke and spat across the pavement into the roadway.

"Meague! Come on, you lazy bugger."

Charlie hoisted the sledgehammer on to his shoulder. With the cigarette in the corner of his mouth, he sauntered out from the archway and across the yard. The other men were picking their way through a ruined barn. Ted Evans, the foreman, beckoned impatiently. His mouth was pursed with irritation.

Charlie followed them into the barn. The roof had gone and the interior was heaped with rubble and charred beams. Evans pushed the left-hand leaf of the huge double doors on the far wall. It moved a few inches. There was a rending sound as the top hinge parted company with the gatepost.

"The wood's like wet cardboard. Give me the sledgehammer."

Charlie passed it to him. Evans swung it at the lower hinge. A spark flashed as metal collided with metal. The gate groaned and swayed. Evans swung the hammer again. Wood cracked. The door tore itself free from its one remaining hinge and fell outwards.

Beyond the barn was another yard. Heavy double gates, reinforced with iron and topped with spikes, were immediately opposite. To the left was a range of stabling. Other buildings, their original purpose harder to guess, had been reduced to mounds of stone, earth and

10

dead and dying weeds. A leafless elder tree stood on one of the mounds. The roofs and gables of the Rose in Hand were visible on the right.

"See that?" Evans waved at one of the ruins. "We're going to cut a trench through there."

"For God's sake," Charlie said. "Why can't they use the bloody digger? That's what it's for."

Evans stabbed a finger at Charlie. "Listen, Meague. You trying to tell me how to do my job?"

"Just asking a civil question."

The foreman came a step closer. He was several inches shorter than Charlie, but his bulk and his long arms made him formidable. When he was angry, he lowered his voice rather than raised it.

"A question? Then here are some civil answers. One, they're already using the digger over there." He gestured towards the inn, on the other side of which lay the warehouse. "Two, we're cheaper. Three, this is exploratory work, the sort of thing you need men for, not machines. The surveyor thinks there might be a culverted stream down there, and that's got implications for the foundations and the drainage. Four, you give me trouble and you'll be out on your ear. Got that, son?"

Charlie stamped his foot and shouldered the sledgehammer like a rifle. He came to attention. "Yes, sir!"

The rain pattered down from the grey sky. Evans stared up at Charlie's face and Charlie stared back. A lorry changed gear on the main road.

"Watch it," Evans said softly. "Just watch it." He turned to the others. "Right – we'll start by clearing the rubbish out. Frank, you'd better fetch a barrow. Get another shovel, too. We'll make a start in here."

Frank walked off the way they had come. Charlie flicked his cigarette away and followed the other two men through a low doorway into a small, stone-walled building which had lost its roof. A rat darted between his legs. He swore at it. The floor was visible at the end near the door, but a heap of rubbish had been thrown against the wall at the rear.

"We'll clear the bigger stuff first," Evans said. "Just pile it outside for now."

He picked up a pair of rusting jerry cans and lumbered into the yard with them. Charlie and the fourth man, Emrys Hughes, dragged a balk of timber from the pile and pulled it across the floor. Frank returned with the wheelbarrow, which they loaded with bricks and stones. Charlie worked mechanically, and also as slowly as he dared.

Slowly the pile of rubble diminished. After thirty minutes' work, they were almost down to floor level. Charlie tried to drive his shovel under a block of unsquared stone about the size of a car's wheel. The stone was slightly higher than the level of the floor and about four feet away from the rear wall of the building. It was pinning down one end of a sheet of rusting corrugated iron which extended back under what was left of the rubble.

The angle was wrong and Charlie couldn't get any leverage on the stone. He brought the shovel closer to the vertical and dug down with all his strength. The end of the sheet of corrugated iron disintegrated under the pressure. The blade of the shovel disappeared and he lurched forward.

"There's a hole in the floor, look," Charlie said. "The stream?"

Evans left the wheelbarrow by the doorway. The hole was no more than a crack. He squatted and tried to peer around the stone and the shovel.

"Damned if I know. Help me move it."

He and Charlie rocked the stone to and fro until they could ease it away from the shovel and back on to the nearest flagstone. Together they dragged out the sheet of corrugated iron which was still covered with bricks, smaller stones and earth. The sheet was larger than Charlie had expected: it stretched almost as far as the walls on either side of the building – about eight feet – and back to the rear wall. With the help of the others, they manoeuvred it into the yard.

Charlie went back inside. Evans was already there, staring at the place where the corrugated iron had been. There were no flagstones below: instead there was a shallow depression lined with earth, shards of china and clay, old bricks and fragments of timber. The hole was the full width of the building and it went back to the rear wall; it reminded Charlie of a large, half-filled grave. A pair of eyes gleamed at them from the darkest corner and then vanished. Evans picked up a half-brick and threw it where the eyes had been.

"What the hell was this place?" Charlie asked.

Evans ignored the question. Using the shovel, he scraped earth away from the edge of the last row of flagstones. Butting against the flagstones were the remains of wooden posts.

"You've found a shithouse, boy." Evans glanced up at Charlie. "That's an old earth closet, look, or maybe there was once a cesspool under all that. Those posts would have supported the seats. This was probably a two-seater. There'll be a chamber underneath us, but it'll be full of rubbish." He stooped and picked up a scrap of china. He brushed the dirt away: two flowers, one red and one green, appeared against a delicate grey background. He sucked his teeth. "That's been there for a while. Bit of an old teacup, that is. What they call Lowestoft ware."

12

"How do you know?"

"My dad used to be sexton up at St John's." Evans put the piece of china in his trouser pocket. "They were always turning up stuff like that. Old vicar used to say what it was sometimes."

He turned away and told Frank to bring the wheelbarrow in. Charlie thought Evans seemed embarrassed and annoyed – as if he'd made a confidence he hadn't intended to make.

"Come on," Evans said to no one in particular. "We'll have to dig it out. Let's get on with it."

"A shithouse?" Charlie said. "No wonder the rats like it."

"Not much here for them now. I reckon this place hasn't been used as a privy for years. Looks like they've been dumping builders' rubbish since the battle of Waterloo."

They shovelled earth, bricks and small stones into the wheelbarrow. At intervals, Frank pushed the barrow away and dumped the spoil in the corner of the yard. Charlie noticed that he was going through the contents of the heap with the tip of his spade.

"What are you looking for?"

"Never know your luck, eh?" Frank said. "Mate of mine in Bristol had a job digging out an old privy. Found a gold sovereign down there."

Emrys Hughes looked up sharply. "I reckon we should take turns with the barrow."

"You're paid to work," Evans said in a voice so soft it was almost a whisper. "If you want to look for buried treasure, you do it in your own time."

Frank shied away as though Evans had hit him. "Sorry. I didn't mean—"

"Just shut up." Evans turned away. He nodded to Charlie: "Get hold of the end of that beam."

They had uncovered a worm-eaten and roughly squared length of timber which lay diagonally across the opening to the chamber with one end against the rear wall. It was nearly a foot beneath the level of the flagstones. Charlie pushed his shovel underneath and used it to lever it out of its bed of earth. Another rat darted out and ran over the handle of the shovel. With sudden ferocity, Evans brought down his own shovel on the rat as it was running for the doorway. Charlie glanced down at the inert bundle of fur. It was beginning to ooze blood over the grey flagstone.

"That's old, that is," Evans said calmly, nodding towards the beam. "Cut by hand, look. Maybe it fell in there when the roof caved in."

He pushed his shovel under the beam. He and Charlie eased it away from its resting place.

13

"What's that?" Charlie said. He pointed at what looked like a wooden box, about eighteen inches long and twelve inches wide, which lay beside the wall. The beam had masked it completely. He scrambled over to the box: it was no more than six inches deep, and the wood was peppered with wormholes.

"Bring it here," Evans ordered.

Charlie shrugged, guessing that if there was anything worth finding, Evans intended to have a claim to it. He picked up the box and discovered that it had been lying upside down. The lid was still embedded in the earth. He passed the box to Evans and picked up the lid. There was a scrap of paper on it, some earth and a few fragments of bone.

"I'll have that too."

Holding the lid as though it were a tray, Charlie handed it to Evans. The foreman poked the collection of objects with a blunt finger. He picked up a handful of earth and crumbled it; inside was a piece of blackened and twisted metal which he tapped on the palm of his hand.

"Look," Evans said. "There's a pin on the back. Some kind of brooch, maybe."

He scraped at it with his fingernail and some more of the dry, powdery earth dropped away, revealing a shape like a squat figure of eight with a pair of prongs projecting from each of two opposite sides. The other three men had gathered round but, with a wave of his hand, he pushed them away.

"You're getting in my light. I think it's silver."

"What's it worth?" said Frank quickly.

"How do I know? I think it's a sort of knot pattern."

Frank laughed. "A true love's knot."

Charlie picked up the box itself and examined it. He frowned, because something nudged his memory. He turned the box over and over in his hands. At either end there were crudely made iron handles stapled to the wood. There had been no hinges – the lid had simply rested on the base.

He put the box down and crouched beside the lid and its contents. He picked up one of the little bones.

"What do you think they came from?" he asked. "A cat or something?"

"It *is* silver," Evans said. "Look, there's a hallmark. What did you say, Charlie?"

Charlie noticed that in the excitement of the moment Evans had called him by his Christian name. He said. "The bones – I wondered what they came from."

Evans glanced at them – at first without curiosity. Then his face

14

changed: the features sharpened, and he stared intently at the cluster of grubby little objects. Still clutching the brooch, he crouched beside the lid and picked up a bone. He looked up at Charlie. When he spoke his voice was unexpectedly gentle.

"I think they're human, son. I think you've found yourself a dead baby."

3

Charlotte Wemyss-Brown raised the silver teapot. China tea trickled from the spout. Most of the tea landed in the cup, but some of it dribbled down the curving spout and landed on the lace doily which covered the silver tray.

"Damn," she muttered.

"Why the hell do we use that pot?" Philip said. "It always does that."

Charlotte, who was sitting on a low armchair to the left of the fire, rotated the upper half of her substantial body towards her husband. The effect reminded Jill of a swivelling gun turret on a warship. Philip was standing behind the sofa with a cigarette box in his hand.

"But it's very pretty," Jill said. "Is it Georgian?"

Charlotte's attention swung back towards the visitor. "Yes – late Georgian. It was my grandmother's. Most of our silver came from her."

There was a good deal of silver on display in the drawing room at Troy House. The milk jug, the sugar bowl and the teaspoons were silver; so too was the cigarette box in Philip's hand and the frames of the photographs on the mantelpiece. Silver twinkled on the small, gilt-encrusted desk in the bay window. There was also a wall-mounted display cabinet containing an array of silver snuff boxes.

"Philip," Charlotte snapped. "Aren't you going to pass Jill her tea?"

Philip bustled forward and gave Jill her cup. "Trouble with silver is the cleaning," he said. "Mrs Meague was telling me all about it only the other day."

"That's one less cross you'll have to bear, dear." Charlotte said.

"Don't tell me we're getting rid of the silver?"

"I was referring to Mrs Meague."

"She's handed in her notice?"

"No, dear. I was obliged to ask her to leave."

"Whatever for?"

"First she wanted a loan. Came to me with some cock-and-bull

16

story about needing money for an operation. She had the nerve to insinuate that she'd leave me in the lurch if I couldn't help her. I said no, of course. Then later this morning I caught her slipping one of those snuff boxes into the pocket of her pinafore."

"What did you do?"

Charlotte left Philip's question hanging in the air and turned to Jill. "Mrs Meague has helped Susan with the heavy cleaning for the last few years. Not an ideal arrangement as far as I was concerned, but then it's so terribly difficult to get any sort of help in the house these days."

"Have you told the police?" Philip asked.

"No." Charlotte hesitated and covered her hesitation by turning to add hot water to the teapot. "I suppose I should have done. It's just that – she's having rather an awful time at present. What with that son of hers."

Philip lit a cigarette with the lighter on the mantelpiece. "Charlie Meague's one of our local ne'er-do-wells," he explained to Jill. "He moved to London after the war. But a couple of months ago, he decided to come back to Mum."

Charlotte glanced at her watch. "I must have a word with Susan about dinner. Would you excuse me?"

Jill smiled and nodded at her hostess. The smile felt devoid of warmth, a mere stretching of the lips. Charlotte seemed not to notice. She levered herself out of her chair and strode towards the door. She had been a sturdy woman when Philip married her nine years before, and since then she had grown steadily sturdier.

Philip leant on the mantel shelf and smoked. Jill stared at the flames. She knew that she should make conversation but her mind could think of nothing to say, and she could not put her tongue around words. She was discovering that misery ebbed and flowed according to some mysterious law of its own. At present it was flowing. It paralysed her.

It was partly the effect of seeing Philip and Charlotte at home for the first time. In the past, the three of them had always met in London, either in a public place like a restaurant or a theatre, or at Jill's flat. The problem was not so much seeing them as a couple, because Jill was used to that, but seeing them as a couple in their home, with family photographs on the mantelpiece.

"Well?" Philip said. "What do you think of it?"

Taken by surprise, Jill found that she could talk after all. "Think of what?"

Philip waved his cigarette around the big drawing room. "All this. Troy House."

She looked up at his face, which was closed and intent, as if he were concentrating on something that she couldn't see. He had put on a lot of weight in the last few years.

"It seems very nice," Jill said. "I know that's a silly thing to say. But it does. Solid. A home."

Philip grinned at her. "It's a shrine to respectability. A tomb haunted by the shade of Granny Wemyss."

"And why not? There's nothing wrong with a bit of respectability. Actually, it seems rather attractive."

He stared at her and opened his mouth to say something. But at that moment the door opened and Charlotte came into the room in a procession of one. She sank into her chair with a sigh of relief.

"Philip, give me a cigarette, would you?" She turned to Jill. "And what's this I hear about your new job? It sounds wonderful."

Jill looked at Charlotte and the panic rose inside her. She couldn't think of what to say or how to say it. Charlotte sat there, waiting and smiling. The smile seemed to grow wider and wider until the round, white face threatened to split in two.

Philip held open the cigarette box for Charlotte and cleared his throat noisily. "Quite a triumph, eh? Mark you, you'll have to keep it a deadly secret. You can imagine how all the old fogies would react if they found out that a woman was writing the Bystander column."

"Just think of it," Charlotte said, bending towards the flame which Philip held out to her. "In a hundred and fifty years you're the first woman to do that job. Good Lord." She blew out smoke and stared down her long thin nose at the glowing tip of her cigarette. "It must feel a heavy responsibility. Still, I'm sure you'll be equal to it."

Jill shook her head. "I'm not going to do the Bystander column after all."

Philip frowned. "But you said in your last letter that it was all settled. I don't understand. What happened? Did they change their minds?"

"No. They offered me the job. I turned it down."

Charlotte nodded. "Perhaps you're wise, dear." Her eyes gleamed in the firelight. "It would have been very difficult for a woman. I'm not sure how I would have felt if—"

"For God's sake, Jill," Philip interrupted. "You've been angling for that job for years. Play your cards right and you'd end up editor. What went wrong?"

Jill knotted her fingers together on her lap. "I told you. I decided not to take it in the end."

"But why not?" Philip said, and his voice was brusque, almost angry: it might have been his future which she had so wantonly discarded.

Jill forced herself to smile at him, and simultaneously felt irritated

18

that she should feel it necessary to propitiate him. "I felt I needed a change." she lied. The pain twisted and stabbed deep inside her. She glanced at the clock on the mantel shelf and turned to Charlotte. "If you don't mind, I'll go up to my room now and sort myself out."

4

"I appreciate you're not a local man, Thornhill, and you may not be entirely familiar with the way we like to do things in this neck of the woods. I'm a fair man, I hope, and I realise this is only your third day." Superintendent Williamson picked up his pipe and began to ream it with deliberation. "Still – I don't know how you fellows used to manage in the depths of Cambridgeshire, but here we like to get results and we like them quickly. You follow me?"

The superintendent rapped his pipe vigorously against the metal ashtray on his desk. Richard Thornhill surreptitiously pinched his thigh in a desperate attempt to make himself feel more alert. He had slept very badly for the last few nights and the superintendent's voice reminded him of a bass drone attached to a set of bagpipes: it rumbled on and on, never stopping, never changing. To make matters worse, the window was closed and the gas fire was on full.

"Yes, sir," he said, and clamped his lips together to prevent a yawn escaping.

"Attention to detail, Thornhill. No possibility is too small to be worth examining. Constant vigilance. Every CID officer should have those words engraved on his heart. Those are the standards I have in mind when I monitor and direct the work of this department."

Williamson opened his tobacco pouch, sniffed happily at its contents and glanced across the desk. Without warning, he switched from the general to the specific. "So what have you got for me on that Templefields case? The King's Head? Surely you've found out *something*?"

"Whoever it was broke in through a pantry window," Thornhill said. "The window opens on to an alley at the back of the pub. He probably went in at about one o'clock. Mrs Halleran, the landlady, tells me he lifted a case of Scotch and about two thousand cigarettes. But I'm not sure that I believe her."

"Why not?"

"I don't believe she'd keep that much in stock at one time. She's running the place on a shoestring. Besides, he'd have to be a cool customer to run off with a case of whisky under his arm once she started yelling."

Williamson grunted. "Go on."

"And then he went upstairs. Mrs Halleran keeps the takings under the bed apparently."

"So he knew that?"

"Just as likely he couldn't find anything else worth stealing downstairs and thought he'd have a look upstairs. Unfortunately for him, she's a fairly light sleeper. She heard the stairs creak. Then the bedroom door opened. There's a streetlight outside the landing window. She saw his silhouette."

"Anything useful?"

Thornhill shook his head. "She said he was enormous. She thought he was carrying a revolver. Which is more or less what they all say. Anyway, she let out a scream and the man ran off. By the time Mrs Halleran's son came down from the next floor, he was well away."

"Fingerprints?"

"He wore gloves."

"Ten to one it's someone local." The superintendent filled his pipe with stubby fingers.

"Mrs Halleran mentioned a man named Meague. One of her customers, apparently."

"Charlie Meague? Currently living in Minching Lane, about three doors down from the King's Head. He's got a record. We did him for nicking a car once. He was only about eighteen."

"She claims he's got it in for her."

"More than likely." Williamson patted his pockets until he located his matches. "But it doesn't follow that it was him. Wouldn't foul his own nest. But that reminds me. It's a small world, I always say, and especially small in Lydmouth. I had a call from a friend of mine at the Met this afternoon. He'd picked up a whisper that Genghis Carn is heading for this part of the world."

"Who?" Thornhill watched with irritation as a layer of condescension spread over Williamson's face.

"I'd have thought you'd have heard of Genghis Carn even in the Fens. Used to be into the black market in a big way. But they sent him down a few years back for a neat little confidence trick – letting the same flat to umpteen different people. Amazing how stupid you can be when you're desperate for a roof over your head."

Thornhill made a quick recovery: "Yes, of course. My old boss always used to call him Jimmy Carn. He had him up before the war for street betting."

Williamson scowled at this attempt to regain the advantage. "I understand he's just out of prison."

"Why would he want to come here?"

"That's just it. There's a rumour that Charlie Meague used to work for him in London."

"But do we know that Carn's actually making for Lydmouth?"

Williamson scraped a match along the side of the box. He lit his pipe with loving deliberation. "Just a possibility to bear in mind," he said between puffs. "I don't like it when people like him come heading for my patch. Bloody foreigners."

In Lydmouth, Thornhill had already learned, anyone from outside the county ranked as a foreigner. Williamson pulled a folder towards him, opened it and lowered his head over its contents. Smoke billowed around him. Thornhill stood up, assuming that he was dismissed.

"And another thing," the superintendent said without looking up. "Ninety per cent of the crime we get in Lydmouth has something to do with Templefields. That place sets alarm bells ringing up here." He prodded his forehead with his index finger.

"Yes, sir."

"So get it sorted."

Thornhill nodded and turned to go.

"Not so fast. I notice you haven't got yourself a poppy yet."

"No, sir. Not yet."

"I like my officers to wear them. It's the least we can do, I think. Such a small token of respect."

"Yes, sir."

Thornhill closed the door of the superintendent's office quietly behind him and walked down the corridor towards his own room. When he got there, he didn't bother to turn on the light. He put on his hat and shrugged himself into his overcoat. The phone on his desk began to ring. He was tempted to leave it. He should have gone off duty hours ago. No one would ever know that he'd been here. Except himself.

He sighed and picked up the receiver. "Thornhill here."

"This is Sergeant Fowles, sir. We've just had a call from the contractors down at the Rose in Hand site in Templefields. They were digging a drain or something and they found some bones."

"Human?"

"They don't rightly know. There's an old brooch too, it seems."

"It doesn't sound very urgent. Have you tried to get Sergeant Kirby? He can deal with it."

"He's already left, sir. The thing is, I don't know if it's relevant, but one of the men who found the bones is Ted Evans."

"Who?"

There was a pause as Sergeant Fowles assimilated the inadequacy of Thornhill's local knowledge. Then Fowles went on: "Ted Evans – the point is, he knows about bones on account of his dad being a gravedigger. Used to help him when he was a lad. Ted reckons those bones come from a baby."

Thornhill said nothing. A few old bones, possibly human, possibly a baby's – certainly old. Any sane police officer would accept that in the circumstances further investigation could safely be left until the morning.

Thornhill sighed. "Have you put out a call for Dr Bayswater?"

"No, sir. Thought I'd better have a word with you first."

"See if you can get him to meet me there in half an hour. I'll go down now."

Thornhill broke the connection. He got an outside line and dialled his own number. The phone rang for some time before Edith answered.

"Darling, it's me – I'm afraid I won't be back for a while."

"Will you be in time to read the stories?"

"I don't know. Probably not."

"David, don't do that," Edith shouted. "He's got mashed potato all over his hair," she added in her ordinary voice. "I must go."

"Yes. Goodbye."

Thornhill dropped the receiver back on its rest and left the office. He went downstairs to the car park behind police head-quarters. It was only four thirty, but it was already almost dark. As he walked towards his car, he glanced up at the brightly lit windows of the rear façade of the building. In Victorian times it had been a private house with a large garden, a coach house and stables. Now the garden was devoted either to car parking or to workshops, temporary offices and storage sheds. The house itself had sprouted extensions in unexpected places. Fire escapes criss-crossed the back of the building, giving it the appearance of a badly fastened parcel.

The Austin started immediately. It was Thornhill's own car, a recent purchase, though of course second hand; the novelty had not yet worn off, and he was secretly rather proud of it -- and of himself for being able to afford it. He drove carefully out of the car park and up to the High Street. The pavements were full of hurrying figures. He loathed this time of year when the nights were longer than the days.

A policeman was directing the traffic near the Templefields site. To avoid the queue of vehicles going towards the station Thornhill steered into the kerb and drove with his nearside wheels on the pavement. The policeman blew his whistle and waved. He had not recognised the car, which did not improve Thornhill's temper. He rolled down his window.

"Just what do you think you're doing?" the young constable began, pink-faced with righteous indignation.

Thornhill scowled and thrust his warrant card out of the window. The constable's features registered first shock, and then fear. Hurriedly, he waved the Austin on.

Thornhill reached the makeshift barrier erected by the building contractors. A Jaguar was parked on the other side of the barrier. As Thornhill turned off his engine, its doors opened. From the driver's seat emerged a tall figure wearing a heavy tweed overcoat with a poppy in the buttonhole. A sturdy, broad-chested man dressed as a workman got out from the passenger side.

The two men watched while Thornhill got out of his car and locked the door. The one in the overcoat took a couple of steps forward and pulled aside the barrier to allow Thornhill to come into the enclosure.

"You are the police, I assume?" he said.

"Yes. Inspector Thornhill, CID."

"I'm Cyril George. What I really want to know is whether this is going to cause any delay. Time's money, you know."

"I'm afraid I can't comment on that until we know a little bit more."

George stamped his feet, perhaps from cold, perhaps from irritation. He was a big, fleshy man in his forties. "We're already running behind schedule. In any case, it's not a good time of year for this type of work. And the longer we leave it, the worse it will get."

"Is this Mr Evans?" Thornhill asked.

The other man nodded.

"You found the bones, I understand."

Evans came a step nearer Thornhill. "In a manner of speaking. There were four of us there altogether."

"I sent the others home," George said. "No point in keeping them hanging on."

Thornhill wondered if keeping them hanging on would have involved George's having to pay them overtime. He said to Evans, "Are the bones still where you found them?"

"No. I took them along to the site office."

"It was the obvious thing to do," George snapped, though Thornhill had said nothing to the contrary. "It's not as if Evans was disturbing the scene of the crime, is it? Frankly don't really understand why you're here. These bones – they've probably been here for centuries."

"I appreciate that, sir. But when human remains are reported to us we have to investigate. Standard procedure."

George shrugged. "Well, come on. We might as well get this over with, I suppose."

He led the way along the cordoned-off part of the pavement towards a pair of gates set in an archway big enough to admit a small lorry. He opened a wicket in the right-hand leaf and stepped into a darkened yard.

"I was having a drink with Superintendent Williamson only the other evening," he said over his shoulder. "Give him my regards, won't you?"

Thornhill nodded, registering the oblique threat, and followed George across the cobbles to a doorway in the range of buildings on the right. Behind him he heard a click as the wicket closed and the hobnailed soles of Evans's boots scraping on the stones. The doorway had lost its door, which lay against the wall of the dimly lit corridor beyond.

"Mind the steps," George said.

Thornhill sniffed. He smelled damp, decaying vegetable matter, dry rot and – faint but unmistakable – urine. The building was dying.

George stopped at a door. Keys rattled. A moment later the three of them were inside what had once been a large kitchen. The plaster was coming adrift from the walls and the old cooking range was a tangle of rust and soot; but the room was at least warm. It smelt of the two paraffin heaters which stood behind the larger of the two desks. There was also a filing cabinet, three hard chairs and an easel on which had been pinned a plan of the site. The office was as comfortless as a military command post.

"There you are." George waved towards the smaller desk. "There's your corpse."

He sat down behind the larger desk, opened a file and began to study its contents. Thornhill glanced at Evans who met his gaze and did not look away. The man's face was reserved but not necessarily hostile. He stood patiently by the door, his cap clasped in his hands. In another man the pose might have seemed subservient.

Thornhill went up to the smaller desk, Utility furniture scarred by mistreatment. On it stood a roughly made wooden box with rusty handles at either end made of squared hand-made nails bent to shape and stapled to the wood.

"It was upside down when we found it," Evans said.

Thornhill turned the box round. The corners were reinforced with scraps of what looked like tin tacked into the wood.

"Was the lid still on?"

"It had come adrift, but only just."

Thornhill lifted the lid off. Inside were half a dozen bones, a scrap

25

of yellowed newspaper and a small metallic object. The bones were so small they might have come from a chicken or a cat. Was that a femur? Another looked like a humerus with a ball-and-socket joint.

Cyril George uncapped a fountain pen and made a note. The nib scratched on the paper. It was very quiet: the thick stone walls insulated the room from the sounds of the outside world.

The bones had yellowed with age and the marrow had gone. Thornhill touched the possible femur with his fingertip. Its surface felt rough and dry. There was nothing intrinsically disturbing about the bone, which he found disturbing in itself. Time had drained away its significance. All that was left was a decaying piece of animal matter, a sign of mortality, tangible evidence of an episode which must have brought suffering to at least one individual, probably more. And it affected him no more than the portion of rib in a lamb chop. Thornhill wondered whether his job had worn away something important inside him, its absence making him a little less than human. It was an old worry and he barely noticed it.

"Where exactly were they found?" he said.

"In a heap of rubbish. Old cesspit, I reckon. We were clearing out part of a yard behind the Rose in Hand."

"The what?"

"This whole place is the Rose in Hand." Evans jerked his thumb towards the window, towards the reflection of the office in the dark, cracked glass. "Used to be an inn."

"Did you look around the box?"

"To see if anything had fallen out? I had a quick dekko. There was nothing obvious. We were lucky to find what we did."

Lucky? The word danced in Thornhill's mind. "How do you mean?"

"The rats got the rest, look."

"Could they be cat bones? A small dog?"

Evans shrugged. "Anything's possible. But I've seen the bones of babies before."

"Because of your father's job?"

"Aye." Evans' dark eyes stared calmly at Thornhill. "And I saw kiddies' bones during the war as well – in Burma."

George made a show of consulting his wristwatch. "I hate to hurry you chaps, but time's getting on."

Thornhill ignored the interruption. He picked up the scrap of newspaper. It was brittle with age. As he touched it, a few flecks broke away from the main piece. The fragment was roughly triangular. He laid it on the palm of his hand. Each of the three sides was about two inches long. The print was small and blurred.

AT THE BULL HOTEL will be offered for sale on January 15th, the entire household effects of the late Jas Gwynne of High Street, Lydmouth. Together with . . .

He turned the paper over.

. . . and the Reverend Mr Brown proposed a vote of thanks to Mr Chad, the Acting Superintendent of the Band of Hope Sunday School. He himself would bring up the sum collected to four guineas (cheers), which would be remitted to the Church Missionary Society without delay . . .

Thornhill put down the piece of newspaper and picked up what he assumed to be the brooch. He could make out the shape of a knot: on closer examination, it looked like an ornate clove hitch. He turned the brooch over and found the remains of a catch on the back. There was a hallmark, too. A scratch ran through the mark, revealing the glint of the metal beneath the black tarnish. Someone, probably one of the workman who had found it, had wanted to find out if the brooch was made of silver.

"Well?" George said testily. "What do you think?"

Thornhill put the brooch gently back in the box. "It's hard to know at this juncture, sir." He looked at Evans. "Do you think all these things were originally inside the box? Or could they have been thrown away at different times?"

Evans shrugged his heavy shoulders. "The lid was off the box, but only just. The base was still resting on it. On the other hand, it's hard to know how much it had been disturbed before we came along."

"What would you say if you had to come down one side or the other?"

"More likely than not they all came together, all in the box. There was a bit of china nearer the top – must have been a hundred and fifty years old."

Thornhill nodded. "I'd better have a look at where you found it."

"Can't it wait till the morning?" George said.

Yes, Thornhill thought, it almost certainly could. But the decision had nothing to do with George.

"I'd prefer to have a look tonight, sir. You never know."

George screwed up his mouth. "You'll need a torch. It's as black as pitch out there."

"I've got a torch in the car."

"Still, there's no need for me to stay, is there?"

"No, sir."

"I'll push off then. Evans will lock up after you."

Thornhill watched as George got up. "I shall have to take away the box and its contents. I'll leave you a receipt, of course."

"By all means."

"And where can I find you in case I need to get in touch with you this evening?"

George stuffed the file into his already bulging briefcase. "Why should you want to do that?"

"I probably shan't," Thornhill said.

George stared across the room at him. The building contractor's eyes were a very pale and cloudy blue. "As you like." He scribbled something on a business card and passed the card to Thornhill. "That's my home phone number. You've finished in here, I take it?"

Thornhill nodded.

"Good. Then if you take away your bones, I can at least lock up the office. Then all Evans need do is lock the gate to the road."

"Do you have a night watchman?" Thornhill asked automatically.

"Yes – but he spends most of his time on the other side of the site. There's an old warehouse – that's where we keep anything worth stealing. Evans will introduce you if you want."

Thornhill wrote a receipt. George drummed his fingers against the surface of his desk. Evans stood by the door, his weight evenly balanced on his two legs and his face expressionless. It was impossible to tell whether he minded George's habit of treating him like a well-trained dog. Thornhill gave George the receipt and picked up the box.

Suddenly Evans cocked his head. "Someone's banging out there. On the gate. I think."

"It may be Doctor Bayswater," Thornhill said. "I asked him to meet me here."

"A doctor? For that?" George grinned, revealing a mouth crowded with jagged yellow teeth. "Bit late for a doctor, isn't it?"

"The wicket's on the latch," Evans said. "I'd better let him in."

"Come on." George herded Thornhill out of the room. "You can talk to him in the yard."

It had started to rain again. Evans was standing with the doctor just inside the gate. Bayswater was hunched under a big umbrella and carrying a black bag. George muttered something which might have been a greeting as he slipped through the wicket gate to the street beyond.

"What have you got, then?" Bayswater said. He was a stooping man in late middle age. "Bones, they told me. Personally, I don't see why they couldn't have waited until the morning."

"Is there somewhere we can go with a light?" Thornhill said to Evans.

The man nodded. "The passage outside the site office is the only place. Unless you want to come over to the warehouse."

"The nearer the better," said Bayswater. "I hope this isn't going to take long. I've got calls to make."

Evans took them inside. Thornhill put the box on the floor under the single bulb that dangled from the ceiling. He lifted off the lid. Bayswater crouched beside the box, the skirts of his raincoat trailing on the dusty floor. He was hatless, and in the unflattering overhead light his grey hair looked like a wire brush. He poked at the bones and then picked up the curved one which Thornhill had tentatively identified as femur. He tossed it back into the box and it rattled against the others.

"Might be human. Might not. God knows, eh? You'll need to ask a pathologist if you want chapter and verse on them. You know that as well as I do."

Bayswater picked up the scrap of newspaper. He held it a few inches away from his eyes and studied both sides. Thornhill noticed he wasn't wearing glasses: he wondered whether the omission were due to vanity or forgetfulness. Bayswater let the piece of paper flutter back to the box.

"Does that go with the bones?"

"It might do," Thornhill said.

"Looks like a bit from one of the local rags – they still have auctions at the Bull Hotel." He got to his feet, grunting with discomfort as if his knees were giving him pain. "That should help you date it anyway. If I were you, I'd go and see Charlotte Wemyss-Brown. Kill two birds with one stone."

"Who's she?"

"Her grandfather founded the *Gazette*. The family still owns it. Besides, she knows a lot about local history. And that's what you want – a historian, not a policeman or a doctor."

Bayswater picked up his black bag.

"Thank you for coming out," Thornhill said.

"Next time you might like to consider whether calling me out is necessary or not." Bayswater stamped down the corridor towards the doorway. His voice, which was as beautifully modulated as a BBC announcer's, rose higher and higher in volume. "Use your intelligence, my dear fellow. If those bones are human, and it's a big if, the odds are they belong to someone's by-blow and they've probably been underground since Queen Victoria's Golden Jubilee."

In the yard, he put up his umbrella and, without saying goodbye, went through the wicket gate into the road. Thornhill watched him go. In the yard it was dark enough to conceal his face, for which he was glad. Evans stood to one side, saying nothing.

Thornhill took a deep breath and the anger receded a little. "I'll just get a torch from the car."

"No need," Evans said, "I've got one here."

The two men cut through the ruined barn and emerged into the smaller yard at the back. The torch beam zigzagged across the slippery cobbles and slid across gleaming puddles. When Evans raised the torch, the light caught on silver tendrils of mist which twisted in the breeze. It was darker here than it had been nearer the main road. Thornhill shivered and looked up at the dark grey sky.

Evans led the way towards the remains of the little outbuilding. The torch picked out the pile of rubbish in the wheelbarrow which was still outside the doorway. When they were inside, Evans handed Thornhill the torch.

"We found it down there, look," he said. "Near the back wall."

Thornhill made a pretence of examining the place. He soon realised there was little to see except rain and rubbish. He picked up a half-brick, felt something cold and slimy on its underside and let it fall to the ground. He crouched down and gingerly examined the spot that Evans had pointed out. Besides earth and stones, he found pieces of broken glass, dead leaves, the yellowing root of a nettle and a fragment of Willow Pattern china.

"We'll have another look in daylight," he said. He handed the torch back to Evans. "Thanks for your help."

As they left the outbuilding, the torch beam picked out the gates on the far side of the yard.

"Is there another entrance?" Thornhill asked.

"There's a lane at the back," Evans said. "When there were stables, they used to take the horses out to pasture that way."

A moment later, they reached the front yard. Evans collected his bag and they went outside on to the road.

"I'm going up to the High Street now." Thornhill said as Evans was locking up. "Can I give you a lift?"

Evans looked at him. "Thanks."

"Where do you want to go?" Thornhill asked driving up to the centre of the town.

"The library. If it's not out of your way."

Neither of them said anything else until they had reached the High Street. Thornhill stopped outside the building which housed the town's museum and library. He kept the engine running.

"By the way – just for the record – who was with you when you found the bones?"

"Frank Thomas. Emrys Hughes." Evans yanked his door handle; the door swung open, letting in a blast of icy air. "Charlie Meague."

Evans got out of the car. "Thanks for the lift." He shut the door and walked unhurriedly through the rain up the steps to the library.

Thornhill kneaded his gloved fingers together in an attempt to squeeze the cold out of them. The rain slid diagonally down the windscreen from left to right. Cars, a bus and two lorries swished past.

Charlie Meague again, he thought. In his job, Thornhill had long ago learned to respect the power of coincidence. Williamson was right, at least in this: Lydmouth was a small world.

Several people came in and out of the library. Almost everyone was in a hurry because of the weather. There was one exception – a man in a billowing raincoat. He was hatless and had a nautical beard which in profile gave him a resemblance to the head of King George V on prewar coins.

The man sauntered down the steps from the library and glanced about him. He raised his face and sniffed the air as though it brought him a bracing sea breeze rather than the foggy vapours of a cold November evening. Thornhill watched him crossing the road and strolling into the pillared entrance of the Bull Hotel.

None of the passers-by gave the Austin or Thornhill a second glance. From a purely professional viewpoint, this was, if anything, an advantage, but it also made him feel anonymous and insignificant. It reminded him yet again that he was a stranger here.

In his previous job, he had been based in an area he had known since boyhood. He had not been sentimentally attached to the Fens, but they had a stark simplicity which he had appreciated – not at the time, but since the move to Lydmouth. In the Fens of north Cambridgeshire, the flatness, the huge fields, the ruler-straight dykes, the scarcity of trees – everything made concealment difficult. Here, in this land of trees, rivers, hills and unexpected valleys, it was the reverse. He looked at the people who flowed along the pavements, their faces dark and closed. Most of them were swathed against the winter cold and he felt that they were hugging secrets to themselves.

Thornhill glanced over his shoulder at the box on the back seat. There was another secret – and one which in all probability would remain a secret for ever. He had gone to Templefields as a matter of routine, mainly to avoid giving Williamson further grounds for criticism. But the contents of the box had caught his imagination and he wished that they hadn't. A handful of bones, perhaps from a baby. A scrap of newspaper, probably from the last century. The silver brooch that might or might not have something to do with the other items. Weren't knots in jewellery often designed to be given and received as tokens of true love?

31

There was something pathetic about the cluster of grubby objects. "Someone's by-blow," Dr Bayswater had said with an implicit sneer attached to the verdict: silly girls shouldn't get themselves pregnant, and if they did, they had to cope with the consequences.

Suddenly the pity of it became unbearable. Part of the pity was for Thornhill himself and part of it was for whatever had happened at the Rose in Hand all those years before.

He raised his hands, balled them into fists and hammered them against the steering wheel.

5

When the phone rang, Charlotte left the room to answer it. Jill heard the voice of her hostess in the distance, but could not distinguish the words.

Philip sidled back to the trolley where the drinks were.

"Top up your glass?"

Jill smiled and shook her head.

With his back to her, Philip poured himself some gin. He turned back to Jill and raised his glass.

"Cheers."

She smiled dutifully at him, raised her glass and took an unwanted sip of sherry.

"So what are you going to do if you're not going to be Bystander?" he asked. "Carry on as before?"

"I don't think so. In fact I know so. I've resigned."

"With nothing to go to?"

"I feel like a change, that's all. Perhaps I'll freelance for a while."

"Rather you than me."

Charlotte came back into the room; Jill knew from her face that something had pleased her.

"Do you know an Inspector Thornhill, Philip?"

"He's a new chap. CID, isn't he? I haven't met him yet."

"He wants to come and interview me." Charlotte announced. "It seems that they've found some old bones at Templefields. He's on his way."

Philip glanced at the clock as he sat down. "Bit late, isn't it? We'll be having dinner soon. Couldn't it wait till the morning?"

"Actually it was my suggestion." Charlotte sat down and picked up her sherry. "He was quite happy to leave it till the morning." She sipped her drink and peered over the rim of her glass at her husband. Her eyes were bright and shrewd. "But I thought it would be something for the *Gazette*. If there's anything worth having, one wouldn't like the *Post* to get it first."

Philip shrugged. "You've got a point, I suppose. But on Jill's first evening . . ."

"But I'd be interested—" Jill began.

Charlotte overrode her. "Jill knows what it's like, darling. I'm sure she won't mind a bit. I've had a word with Susan and asked her to put dinner back twenty minutes. Nothing's going to spoil."

Philip shrugged. "You know best in that department."

"Besides, it sounds as if I was right. I said this would happen, you know. That dreadful man George – bulldozing his way through that wonderful collection of old buildings. Heaven knows what he's going to destroy."

"I told you Charlotte's got a bit of a bee in her bonnet about local history," Philip said. "She did a couple of articles for the *Gazette*."

"Most people don't even realise why it's called Templefields," Charlotte explained to Jill. "It was originally owned by the Knights Templar. There's said to be medieval masonry in some of the cellars though I must admit I've never seen any myself. It may go back even further. The Romans were at Lydmouth, you know."

"I didn't know you wrote for the *Gazette*," Jill said.

"Not as a journalist, dear. I'm the secretary of our little local history society. I was writing in that capacity."

Charlotte, Jill remembered, had read history at Oxford just before the war.

"I'll get a pad," Philip said. "I'm sure Thornhill won't mind."

Glass in hand, he got up and left the room. Charlotte's face acquired a knowing expression. The silence lengthened.

"Poor old boy," Charlotte said at last, bending towards Jill and speaking in a hushed voice. "We lost our senior reporter on the *Gazette* last week. Heart attack, I'm afraid. Philip's had to plug the gap. He's been working very hard, poor lamb."

The doorbell rang.

The two women heard Philip's footsteps cross the hall, the door opening and the sound of men's voices. The sitting-room door opened. Philip, still with his glass in his hand, ushered in a slim, dark-haired man.

"This is Inspector Thornhill, dear," Philip said. "Inspector, this is my wife, Mrs Wemyss-Brown, and this is Miss Francis, a friend of ours from London."

"It's very kind of you to see me at such short notice," Thornhill said to Charlotte. "Especially at this time of day."

"Not at all, Inspector. It's never too late to help the police, after all."

"Would you like a drink?" Philip asked.

"Thank you, but no."

"Do sit down," said Charlotte graciously. She indicated the chair beside hers. "Now – how can we help you?"

34

Thornhill sat down. He took his time answering. He was dressed in a tweed jacket and flannel trousers. The elbows of the jacket had been neatly patched with leather. Jill envisaged an adoring wife, industriously devoting one evening a week after supper to the family's mending. She thought Thornhill might have seemed quite handsome if his expression had not been so supercilious; he looked, she decided, like a grammar-school master whose absolute control over the boys in his charge had gone to his head.

At that moment, he glanced up: his eyes met hers. Quickly, she looked away. She took a sip of her drink. All this – her assessment of him and the meeting of their eyes – had taken no more than a couple of seconds.

Thornhill turned to Charlotte. "As I said on the phone, Mrs Wemyss-Brown, some bones have been found in Templefields. There were a couple of other things found with them. We wondered whether you might be able to help us identify them."

"I shall be delighted to give you all the help I can, Inspector. By the by, is there any reason why you'd prefer us not to treat this as a news story? It's not top secret or anything, is it?"

"No – the workmen who found the bones must have spread the story by now."

Philip put down his drink. He sat up, took a shorthand pad from his jacket pocket and uncapped his fountain pen. For an instant, Jill glimpsed the Philip she had known all those years ago. Deep inside the plump and prosperous citizen there still lurked a cub reporter eager for glory.

"This afternoon, four of Mr George's workmen were clearing out what appears to have been an old cesspit at the back of the former Rose in Hand inn." Thornhill cleared his throat: to Jill he sounded absurdly formal, as though he were in court. "They disturbed a box. Either inside it or near it were a few small bones. Luckily the foreman, Ted Evans, used to help his father who was the sexton at St John's. He thought the bones might well belong to a baby. Dr Bayswater thinks he may be right."

For Jill, his words were like an incision reopening a wound. There was no escape from what had happened. Even this provincial policeman was in the conspiracy to remind her.

"Why just a few bones?" she said, desperate to distract herself.

He looked at her, and his face was cold and bleak. "Rats, Miss Francis. That's the most likely explanation."

The thought of it made her feel ill. He shrugged, brushing aside her interruption.

"I should emphasise that all the indications are that the bones are very old," he went on. "The workmen also found a small silver

35

brooch and a little bit of newspaper. I wondered if you could help me identify the newspaper, and also perhaps give me an idea of the history of the Rose in Hand."

"A pleasure, Inspector," purred Charlotte.

He was already taking two envelopes from an inside pocket. "I'm afraid the piece of newspaper is rather fragile." He opened one of the envelopes and shook out the yellowed triangle of newspaper with surprising gentleness into the palm of his hand. "Perhaps we might put it on something."

Philip got up to fetch a book. Jill noticed he'd already covered nearly a page of his pad with neat shorthand hieroglyphics. Thornhill took the book with a muttered word of thanks and transferred the piece of newspaper on to it. He passed it to Charlotte, who examined it for a moment.

"Well, judging by the advertisement it's obviously a local paper, as I am sure you realised. James Gwynne – now let me see – probably the grandfather, or perhaps the great uncle, of John Gwynne." She looked at Philip whose head was still bent over his pad. "They were before your time – they used to keep the draper's shop at the bottom of Lyd Street. They moved to Cardiff just before the war."

"Do you think it's from the *Gazette*?" Thornhill asked.

"It certainly looks like our typeface and layout. I suppose it might be the *Post* – but I doubt it. They've not been going for more than fifty years, and this looks older." She looked up. "May I turn it over?"

Thornhill nodded. "But please be careful."

Charlotte slid the scrap of newspaper off the book, turned it over and replaced it. "Now I think that Sunday School was closed down before the war – the First War, I mean. Before my time, of course, but I remember hearing my aunts talking about it. There was some problem with the last superintendent. It was all rather hushed up."

Jill thought briefly of some of the possibilities: embezzling the collection, perhaps, interfering with choirboys or displaying Romish tendencies – or even fathering unwanted babies on members of the congregation.

"What about the Rose in Hand? Can you tell me anything about that?"

"Well, of course, parts of the cellars may go back to the Middle Ages. The Knights Templar owned the—"

"I was thinking of more recent history. Perhaps the last hundred years."

"How obtuse of me," Charlotte said with unconvincing humility. "You must be assuming that the newspaper and the bones belong to roughly the same period."

"It seems the most likely possibility at present."

36

"The place used to be a coaching inn. Quite a substantial establishment, I believe. But the coming of the railways put an end to all that. And they built the Railway Hotel, of course, which must have been a lot more convenient for travellers. Also, they opened a coal pit to the east of Templefields in the 1850s and I think that helped change its character."

Philip looked up. "My wife means that no one lived there who could afford to live elsewhere. Which is more or less the case today."

Thornhill nodded. "So – sixty or seventy years ago, Templefields would probably have been a working-class area? A bit of a slum, perhaps?"

"Oh, yes," Charlotte agreed. "I know the Rose in Hand had rather a bad reputation in my grandfather's day. It attracted a lot of undesirable people. Indeed, as I'm sure you know, the area itself still does."

Jill thought that "attract" was not the word she herself would have chosen. She said, "May I have a look at it, please?"

Charlotte glanced at Thornhill, who nodded. Jill leant forward and Charlotte passed her the book on which the triangle of newspaper lay.

"Assuming that does come from the *Gazette*," Thornhill went on, "would you be able to find it in your files? Then we could date at least the newspaper, if not the bones."

"My husband will get one of our people to go through the backfile first thing tomorrow morning," Charlotte said. "Did you say you found something else?"

Thornhill opened the second envelope and shook a tarnished brooch on to the palm of his hand. He passed it to Charlotte.

"No need to worry about fingerprints, I suppose," she said with a smile.

Jill handed the book back to Thornhill. He took it from her without meeting her eyes. She disliked men who would not look her in the face.

Charlotte passed the brooch to Jill, who turned it over in her hands. The hallmark on the back looked perfectly clear. With a little cleaning and a magnifying glass, it should be legible. She thought she could make out an anchor, which meant the piece had been assayed in Birmingham; but the inspector would be able to find out that sort of thing himself. He must be sick of members of the public offering him help he didn't need.

She turned the brooch over again. Her throat tightened. A true love's knot. There was no knot that couldn't be undone – or if you couldn't undo it, you could cut it or burn it or simply let it rot. She put the brooch on the arm of Philip's chair, turned towards the fire and pretended to warm her hands. The manoeuvre prevented the others from seeing her face.

"Ah, well." Charlotte was saying. "No doubt the obvious explanation is also the correct one. Some poor unfortunate servant girl. A stillborn child – we must hope it was stillborn, in any case. Desperate to conceal her shame. Of course, in those days the line between right and wrong was very clearly drawn. If people do these things, then they must expect to have to pay the price."

Jill stared at the flames. What do you mean – *do these things*? she wanted to say. Fornicate? You stupid woman, you don't really believe that the wages of sin should be death? And what about the man, for God's sake? What price did he have to pay?

"And mark you, there was a lot to be said for making it quite clear where people stood. None of this shilly-shallying we get today. Making excuses. Some things you can't excuse and that's the end of it."

"Yes," Thornhill said. He busied himself with returning the brooch and the piece of newspaper to their envelopes. "You've been very kind."

"And what happens now, Inspector?" Charlotte asked.

"I'm not sure. I shall have to talk about this with the super-intendent."

"Mr Williamson?"

Thornhill nodded. "In case we do take this further, is there anyone else you would advise me to talk to about the history of the Rose in Hand? It's not that long ago, is it? There must be records and so on.'

"You need to have a word with John Harcutt. He probably knows more about nineteenth-century Lydmouth than anyone else."

Thornhill put the envelopes in his pocket and took out a notebook. "Harcutt? Could you give me his address please?"

"He lives in Edge Hill, Inspector. It's that big white house on the main road – opposite the church. Chandos Lodge."

Thornhill stood up. "You've been very helpful."

He said goodbye. Philip got up to show him out. As the door closed behind the two men, Charlotte reached for her cigarette case.

"Seemed quite pleasant, I thought," she murmured.

"I thought he looked a bit like a schoolmaster."

"I suppose these days you need a certain amount of education to become a detective inspector. Quite a good-looking man, too. I wonder if he's married."

They heard the thud of the front door closing.

"Someone sewed those patches on his jacket."

38

"Yes, dear, but that might have been his mother, or a sister or something."

"I still think he's married," Jill said. "He looks that sort of man."

6

Victoria Road sloped gently up to the park and the cemetery. It was considered to be one of the better residential addresses in Lydmouth. It was also one of the more expensive. Edith Thornhill had cajoled her husband into renting a house at the lower, cheaper end of the road. It was semidetached and late-Victorian. Thornhill would have preferred to buy, but that would have to wait until they had saved enough money for the deposit.

He parked the Austin immediately outside the house. The landing light filled with a dim yellow radiance the uncurtained windows of the front bedroom he shared with Edith. He let himself into the hall. Three empty tea chests and a smell of polish greeted him. The wireless was on behind the half-open door of the kitchen. He didn't call out for fear of waking the children.

As he hung up his coat and hat, he caught sight of his face, tired and serious-looking, in the mirror by the pegs. He wished he could hang up his job and everything that went with it at the same time as his hat and coat. These days he seemed to carry his working life around with him wherever he went and whatever he did: it was like a weight on his shoulders which as the months and years passed grew steadily heavier. His shoulders twitched; a second later he realised that he was trying to shrug the weight away.

He walked down the hall and pushed open the kitchen door. They called it the kitchen, though in fact they used it as a living room and did their cooking in the scullery at the back; the kitchen was the warmest room in the house because it contained the boiler which heated the hot water. Edith was sitting in the armchair darning one of the children's socks. A man was saying something about the National Debt on the radio, but Thornhill didn't think she was listening to him.

She looked up and smiled. "Hello, Richard."

He bent down and kissed her cheek. "Sorry I'm late. Are the kids asleep?"

"Well, they're upstairs. Come and get warm while I fetch your supper."

The scrubbed deal table was laid for one person; Edith must have

40

eaten with the children. The man talking about the National Debt had a voice whose cultivated arrogance reminded Thornhill of Dr Bayswater's. He reached out a hand and switched off the radio. In the silence, he heard the clatter of a pan in the scullery.

The inactivity irked him. He slipped upstairs to say goodnight to the children. At present, and at their own request, they were sharing a room, perhaps to help them cope with the novelty of their surroundings. For once they were both asleep. Thornhill felt obscurely cheated. It was much colder upstairs, and both children had burrowed deep under their bedclothes. All he could see of them were two patches of hair.

He went back downstairs. Edith was sitting in the chair again with a couple of socks on her lap and his baked beans and toast were waiting on the table. She assumed that the police canteen provided him with a proper hot meal in the middle of the day: usually she was right.

"Did you have a good day?"

No, he wanted to say, it was awful. He said, "Not too bad, thanks. And you?"

Talking in a low, placid voice, she took him step by step through her day. She was an orderly woman who liked to describe things chronologically. Thornhill finished his baked beans and helped himself to an apple and a slice of Cheddar cheese. While he ate, he watched Edith. She was almost as tall as he was, with the sort of light-brown hair which had once been fair. She wore no jewellery except the thin gold wedding band. Suddenly, he wanted to go to bed with her. Not in an hour's time – but now. And it didn't have to be bed, either. The table would do. Or the floor. Anywhere.

He cut himself another slice of cheese with a hand that trembled slightly. She was telling him what David's teacher had said about his reading. This was followed by an account of Elizabeth's attempt to run away to their old house in Cambridgeshire while they were walking back home from school. Still talking, Edith went into the scullery to make some tea.

"What kept you so late?" she called through the open door.

He pushed back his chair and followed her into the scullery. Lust made him clumsy and he banged his arm against the corner of the cooker. The water had boiled while he was eating. Edith had her back to him and was spooning tea into the pot. He stared hungrily at the shapeliness of her waist.

"Some workmen found some bones at that building site near the station," he said. "They may have belonged to a baby. They're probably about sixty years old."

"The poor thing." She brought the kettle back to the boil and started to fill the teapot. "Was it in a graveyard?"

"No. A cesspit."

"Oh, dear. But I suppose it might have been a natural death. An illness or something."

"Perhaps."

"Talking of illnesses, I thought Elizabeth was looking a little peaky this evening. I took her temperature, but it was normal."

Thornhill put his hand on her right hip. He sensed – or imagined he did – the warmth of her body and the softness of her flesh through the thick tweed of her skirt. The crudeness of his reactions shocked him: touching her had the effect of doubling his urgency.

"David must come into contact with lots of germs at school," she went on, stirring the tea vigorously. "I know he hasn't been ill himself but do you think it's possible that germs can leapfrog on to someone else? He might have passed it on to her without having had it himself."

Thornhill put his other hand on her left hip. It was hard to breathe normally and his mouth was dry. He stroked his hands down her thighs and moved his body against hers.

"Oh, darling, don't. I'm sorry but there's such a lot to do before bedtime."

"Yes, of course."

He stepped backwards. The scullery was unbearably hot. Edith put the teapot on the tray and covered it with the cosy. She saw him watching her and smiled, as if to reassure him that she wasn't annoyed. He smiled back. Behind the mask, anger and shame churned silently inside him, blending with what was left of the lust.

"Let me." Thornhill picked up the tray and waited for her to precede him out of the room.

"Thank you, darling," she said.

7

Charlie Meague waited until midnight.

He had never needed much sleep, even as a child. During the war, he had developed the ability to catnap just as Winston Churchill was said to do. He waited in bed because it was the warmest place to be.

Though he didn't sleep, he let his mind lose its focus. Thoughts and images paraded themselves before him. A memory kept recurring: the box he had found this afternoon – not its contents, but the box itself. What haunted him was its familiarity. It was as if he had dug it up before, which was impossible. Somewhere another memory twitched and stirred in its hiding place. There must, he thought vaguely, be a good reason why that memory was so well hidden.

His mother's snoring changed its rhythm, distracting him. She was lying only a few inches away on the other side of the thin partition wall. He heard every cough and wheeze and sniff. She had had bronchitis in winter for as long as he could remember. It must be like trying to breathe through treacle.

The old woman had had a bad day. One of her ladies had given her the push, and her cough was bad again; he had come back home to find her blue-faced and gasping for air. He'd tried, with some success, to take her mind off her sorrows by buying her three port and lemons at the King's Head. He would have preferred to drink at the Bathurst Arms himself, but it was much farther away; besides, all things considered, it was probably safer to keep away from the Bathurst.

In the pub, Charlie had enjoyed watching Ma Halleran queening it behind the bar and listening to her reliving her nocturnal adventure. Her account of her burglary became more dramatic with every retelling. The woman was a barefaced liar. She needed locking up.

"The bitch," his mother had murmured between coughs and genteel sips, and for once she didn't mean Ma Halleran. "The bitch. All the years I worked there, and she didn't even give me the chance to explain."

Charlie had been tempted to point out that even if the bitch in question had given his mother the chance to explain, there was nothing she could have usefully produced in her defence. She had

43

been trying to steal that silver box, that was all there was to be said about it. His mother was lucky that Mrs Wemyss-Bitch hadn't gone to the police. He just hoped that the old battle-axe wouldn't tell the other people his mother worked for.

In any case, it had been such a stupid thing to do. As so often when he thought about his mother, Charlie Meague was torn between exasperation and affection. At the age of six, he had realised that he was cleverer than her. He had never seen any reason to revise this conclusion. If the silly cow had thought about it, she would have known that sooner or later the theft would have been discovered. And of course they would suspect her of having done it. It was always easier to suspect the cleaning woman than a friend. Besides, in this case, Mrs Wemyss-Brown would have told herself that the crooked streak obviously ran in the family. In Lydmouth, people had long memories. Like son, like mother, they'd say to themselves: bad blood will out. What irritated Charlie most of all was the reason why his mother had done it. Though he had said nothing to her, she knew that he needed money: she had stolen the box for him.

The house cooled around him. At least it was no longer raining. He had left the curtains undrawn and through the window there were stars. There might even be a frost tonight.

If his mother had been capable of putting two and two together, she would have guessed what he planned to do by the questions he had asked her. Perhaps she had guessed, but preferred not to admit it even to herself. It was better that she shouldn't know.

The church clock struck the three-quarters. He was tempted not to wait any longer. But he had decided to go at midnight, so midnight was the time he would go. Carn had taught him the value of planning, if nothing else. If you made a plan you followed it through. You didn't improvise unless you had to, because that's when things tended to go wrong. By midnight, most people would be likely to be asleep.

Charlie reached out a hand for the tobacco tin beside the bed. He rolled himself a cigarette in the dark. A moment later, he struck a match. The tiny bedroom briefly filled with light. He lit the cigarette and leant on one elbow to smoke it.

On the other side of the partition wall, his mother coughed; her bed creaked and the phlegm bubbled in her throat.

It was only a matter of time before Carn traced him to Lydmouth. Charlie didn't want to think about that. Instead, he thought of that bastard Evans and how he had acted over the box and its contents. Look at the way he'd been when they found that brooch. Charlie sucked furiously. He would have to be careful with Evans. He needed the job. After all, it gave him a reason to be in Lydmouth, and it gave him some money too.

Charlie shut his eyes and remembered how Evans had flattened the rat with the back of his shovel. There had been a surprising amount of blood. It had made the flagstones greasy, but the evening rain might have washed it away.

The cigarette burned lower. Charlie tried to empty his mind of everything. In the past, he had found that this was the best way: to give himself a little peace before he went into action. But the memory of the wooden box forced its way back into the emptiness. In the end it was easier to let it stay. He had seen that box somewhere else. Or one very like it.

The clock on St John's tower began to strike midnight.

Part Two

Thursday

1

"You did what?" Superintendent Williamson enquired, dangerously calm. "Why didn't you clear it with me first?"

"I tried to, sir," Thornhill said, trying not to sound aggrieved, "but you'd left."

"You should have phoned me at home."

"I tried that too. There was no answer."

"Then you should have waited."

Thornhill was still standing because he hadn't been asked to sit down. He stared at the blotter on the superintendent's desk. There was a lifelike doodle of a cat in one corner.

Williamson grunted and reached for his pipe. His weathered, blunt-featured face ought to have belonged to a farmer. "I'd have thought even in the depths of the Fens someone might have mentioned that the press needs careful handling."

"Yes, sir, but I thought that this wasn't exactly a controversial issue. Dr Bayswater seemed to feel that—"

"There's people in this town who believe that Bayswater's as mad as a hatter. But that's not the point. The point is, any CID officer who talks with the press has to clear it with me first. No ifs, no buts, no exceptions. Understood?"

"Yes, sir."

Williamson slowly filled his pipe. He went on in a quieter voice "We'll have to pull out all the stops on this one, you realise."

"I don't follow."

"Because the Wemyss-Browns are going to splash the story in the *Gazette*. It may go further afield. God knows where it will end. Even the nationals might get interested."

"I'm sorry, but I don't see why that should matter."

"Two reasons." The superintendent leaned across the desk and raised a finger. "One, because it means we'll have to waste resources following it up. For God's sake, we're tight enough stretched as it is. Now, thanks to you, we'll have to go off on this wild-goose chase. It's a job for an archaeologist, if you ask me, not a police officer." He raised another finger. "Two, because publicity's a good friend and a

49

bad enemy. If you're not careful, you could make us a laughing stock. Even worse, they'd accuse us of wasting ratepayers' money."

"So what do you want me to do?"

"Get those bones off to the lab, have them identified. Go and see old Harcutt. At least he's not a blabbermouth unlike some I could mention. If you'd have come to me, I'd've put you on to him right away. And then you can waste an hour or two writing up a nice neat little report. I want a copy on my desk by the end of the day – sooner, if you've got any sense. And if the press want to talk to you, refer them to me. All right?"

Thornhill didn't reply because he guessed his resentment would show if he did. He had known that Williamson had a reputation for being brusque before he had applied for the job at Lydmouth. But this wasn't brusqueness: it was the verbal equivalent of beating an underling over the head with a piece of lead piping. He counted silently to five in an effort to get his breathing under control.

Williamson pointed his finger at him. "And why haven't you got yourself a poppy yet?"

Before Thornhill could answer, the phone on the desk began to ring. The superintendent scooped up the receiver.

"Williamson." He listened for a moment. "He's on his way," he said at last. He slammed the receiver back on to the rest and looked up at Thornhill. "I'm afraid your historical studies will have to wait. There's been another break-in. Masterman's. You know it? That little jeweller's in Lyd Street. And this time there's been some violence."

2

Lyd Street was a winding thoroughfare which led down to the river –
to the place where for centuries there had been a harbour where the
barges used to load and unload before the coming of the railways.
Masterman's shop was halfway down the hill on the left-hand side
with a patrol car standing at the kerb.

Thornhill parked the Austin behind it. Two women with shopping
baskets were peering through the window, engaged in an animated
conversation which stopped abruptly when he got out of his car. With
averted heads, the women walked up the hill.

He gave himself a moment to examine the front of the shop. First
impressions were always important because you saw things with a
clarity uncompromised by subsequent knowledge. Masterman's was
a small, single-fronted establishment. The woodwork had been
painted a dingy green before the war – certainly before the last war
and possibly before the previous one as well. The detachable bars
were still padlocked across the window. The display had not been
restocked since the night. All that could be seen were two alarm
clocks and a few pieces of china, some of them labelled 'A Present
from Lydmouth', set against a sunbleached green velvet backcloth.
There were darker marks on the velvet where the sun had had less
opportunity to do its work; here must usually stand the more valuable
items which went in and out of the window every day. With a little
imagination, you might infer that trade was sluggish, almost static,
and that the shopkeeper was set in his ways.

There were two doors: on the right of the window, the shop door
which was still shuttered and on the left the door to the private
accommodation. Thornhill rang the bell on the left. A moment later
there were heavy footsteps on a flight of stairs inside. The door
opened to reveal a uniformed constable with a spotty face. He was so
large that he filled the doorway like a barrier. His boots gleamed like
a guardsman's.

"I'm sorry, sir," he began, "Mr Masterman is not . . ."

"I'm Detective Inspector Thornhill." He felt the anger inside him
straining to get out. "Is Sergeant Kirby here yet?"

The man swallowed. "I'm sorry, sir. I didn't realise that—"

"All right," Thornhill said. He felt guilty because for a few damning seconds he had wanted to treat this boy as Williamson had treated him. "This is my first week in Lydmouth. What's your name?"

The constable stood back to allow Thornhill into the narrow hall. "Porter, sir," he said miserably.

"Sergeant Kirby?"

"He's upstairs with Mr Masterman. The doctor's here too."

A strip of streaky brown linoleum ran down the hall. On the right there was the door to the shop, and at the end of the hall was another door which presumably led outside at the back. The place smelled of drains and old, tired vegetables. Two monochrome engravings in dark wood frames hung on the walls. Thornhill glanced at them as he passed. They appeared to depict the respective martyrdoms of St Sebastian and St Peter. He went up the stairs with the constable plodding behind him. The handrail was dusty.

Before he reached the head of the stairs, one of the doors at the top opened. Bayswater appeared.

"Ten to one there's nothing that a good night's rest won't sort out," he said to the room behind him, "but I suppose you'd better get up to the hospital and have an X-ray. I'll call an ambulance. Soon we won't need doctors at all, you know. Just technicians." He saw Thornhill coming up the stairs and his lips twisted. "Ah, the new boy. How are you getting on with your bones, Inspector?"

"Good morning, Doctor. Is it all right if I talk to Mr Masterman now?"

"Talk away, my dear man. But don't let *him* talk too much."

Bayswater waved his hand in a vaguely benedictory gesture and clattered down the stairs; his mood had mysteriously improved since the evening before. Thornhill and Porter stood aside to let him pass. A few seconds later, the front door slammed. One of the other doors on the landing was slightly open. Thornhill caught a movement in the room beyond. Someone had been watching them through the crack.

He went into the room the doctor had just left. It was furnished as a sitting room, with two windows overlooking the street. Porter clumped after him and, at a nod from Thornhill, shut the door.

Detective Sergeant Kirby was standing close to the old man's chair, which had been pulled up to the coal fire blazing in the grate of the tiled fireplace. Kirby was a sturdy man in his late twenties; he had well-greased yellow hair and regular features. He took a step towards Thornhill. His eyes were wary.

"This is Inspector Thornhill," he said to the person hunched in the chair. He looked at Thornhill. "And this is Mr Masterman, sir."

The old man wore a shabby dressing gown over a jersey and trousers. His thin nose was large in relation to the rest of his face, which gave him the appearance of a young bird, and his hands were clasped round a mug of warm milk.

"How are you feeling, sir?" Thornhill asked.

Masterman said nothing but his body quivered. The milk slopped, almost reaching the brim of the cup. Kirby took the cup from his hand and put it on the table beside him. The old man glanced at Thornhill and then quickly looked away. It was possible, Thornhill knew, even probable, that he would never recover fully from the events of last night: that they would leave a lasting legacy of apprehension and timidity which would exist quite independently from any physical effects.

"I imagine you've already told Sergeant Kirby what's happened, sir?"

Kirby nodded. Masterman didn't move.

"Then I'll ask him to tell me and you can let me know if he gets something wrong or leaves something out. All right?"

Kirby already had his notebook in his hand. He flicked back a couple of pages. Thornhill glanced round the room. It was much as he had expected. The books had been swept off the bookshelves; the drawers had been taken out of the bureau and turned upside down to deposit their contents on to the floor. He glimpsed old letters, cheque stubs, pencils, rusty nibs and paperclips. On either side of the fireplace were recessed cupboards, the open doors revealing bare shelves within. At the foot of one of them lay a heap of china – cups, saucers, plates and jugs.

Kirby cleared his throat. "Mr Masterman hasn't slept well since his wife died last year. Last night he was lying upstairs in his bed with the light off and he thought he heard a noise downstairs at the back. That was at about half past twelve. He wasn't sure – his hearing, he says, isn't what it was and he might have imagined it. But he took the poker and he came down to have a look. The only telephone's downstairs in the shop, by the way. He didn't switch on the light. He came down the stairs as quietly as possible to this floor. He listened. He couldn't hear anything. He went down the next flight of stairs, down to the hall."

"Still without turning on the light?"

"I don't need the light," Masterman said in a dry, thin voice. "I've lived in this house fifty years come next summer. I know my way round blindfold. Saves electricity, look. I'm not made of money, you know. Fifty years and I never had nothing like this happen before."

Kirby coughed gently. "The intruder was waiting at the foot of the stairs. He hit Mr Masterman over the head. When Mr Masterman woke up, he found himself in his own cellar."

"It was cold," the old man interrupted. "It went right to my bones."

"Mr Masterman had been tied up with his own clothesline. His attacker had also wrapped him in an eiderdown which he'd taken from Mr Masterman's bed."

"Just as well he did. Otherwise the cold would have killed me. And that would have been murder, wouldn't it? He would have hung."

"Was Mr Masterman gagged?"

Kirby shook his head. "No need. The shop next door is empty and the people who live on the other side are away. Besides, it's a good solid cellar. You could have a dance band down there without anyone noticing."

"I might have starved to death," the old man said. "Worse than a bloody savage, he was. I'm surprised the shock didn't kill me."

"When Mr Masterman regained consciousness, he worked out where he was. He got up the steps to the cellar door, then waited for eight o'clock. There's a woman who comes in to cook his breakfast every day. Mrs Crisp – she's still here. As soon as he heard her in the hall, he started banging on the door."

"In my day a burglar would have thought twice about attacking an old man." The voice sank lower and slipped into a whining monotone. "I'll be seventy next year. I blame the war. No one has any standards. It's the war that did it. And then the bloody Socialists. Something for nothing – that's all they want."

"Do we know what's taken yet?" Thornhill glanced round the room. "The man seems to have had enough time to do a thorough job."

"The great booby." Masterman cackled disconcertingly. The false teeth moved independently of his jaws, giving the impression that his mouth was inhabited by a small alien organism. "I fooled him. I fooled him proper, I did."

"How do you mean?"

The old man sat up in his chair; his triumph had given him a shot of energy. "He was looking in the wrong place, wasn't he? Thought himself so clever."

"What Mr Masterman means," Sergeant Kirby said, "is that the safe is actually in the cellar. That's where he keeps anything worth stealing. He used to have a strongbox up here." Kirby waved towards the nearer of the two windows. "In the window seat there. Nothing fancy – just an iron-bound box with a lock. But Mr Masterman bought a proper safe a few years back, and he was advised to have it installed in the cellar. It's actually cemented into the masonry."

"And he didn't even know." Masterman's eyes sparkled. "It's at floor level. I've got an old chest in front of it."

"So do you know if anything's actually missing?"

"Canteen of silver cutlery." Masterman said promptly. "Beautiful workmanship. A couple of rings that belonged to the wife. They were kept in the window seat."

Suddenly exhausted, he rested his head against the back of his chair. His eyes closed. Thornhill crossed the room and lifted the window seat. The iron box was Victorian, if not earlier. It was solid enough. There was no sign that the two locks had been tampered with.

"Keys?" Thornhill said.

"The thief took Mr Masterman's set from his bedroom. They included the two for the strongbox."

"What happened to them?"

"He left them in the back door when he went."

"Thoughtful of him.. Was there a key for the safe on the ring?"

"Combination lock," Masterman said. "No expense spared."

"What else is gone?" Thornhill asked.

"There may be one or two ornaments," Kirby said. "It's early days. No one's really sure what might have been taken."

There was a knock at the door. At a nod from Thornhill, Porter opened it. A grey-haired woman in a sagging apron stood outside. She looked furtive, but Thornhill knew that the proximity of the police often had that effect on people.

"Mrs Crisp," Kirby said to Thornhill in an undertone.

"I just wanted to find out about his dinner," she said. "Will you be wanting your chop, Mr Masterman?"

"'Course I will," the old man said without opening his eyes. "I need building up, don't I?"

Thornhill and Kirby left Porter with Mr Masterman while they examined the rest of the building. On this floor, besides the sitting room, there was a small kitchen and a bathroom, and on the floor above two bedrooms. One bedroom was used solely for storage and the other was Mr Masterman's; his wife's brushes were still arrayed on the dressing table and her slippers stood beside his at the foot of the bed. The furnishings were old and uncared for. The only decorations were devotional engravings similar to those in the hall.

"Does Masterman have anyone to come in and help him with the shop?" Thornhill asked as he and Kirby were going downstairs to the hall.

"Not since his wife died. Too mean, if you ask me."

Kirby used Masterman's keys to unlock the side door from the hall into the shop. The shop was in much the same state as the rooms upstairs: everything had been thoroughly and messily searched. Behind the counter there was a door leading to a back room which Masterman used as a workshop.

Kirby nodded towards the grimy window above the workbench. "That's the way he came in."

The window provided a view of a small yard. Thornhill examined the frame from the inside. There were four vertical iron bars, two of which had been wrenched away at the bottom. The lower halves of the bars were pitted with rust.

"The wood's rotten," Kirby said. "In some places it's as soft as a sponge."

There was little to be learned from the workroom itself besides the fact that it had been searched as thoroughly as everywhere else. The two men went back through the shop, down the hall and out through the back door. The yard contained a dustbin, a coal bunker and a disused privy housing a large black bicycle. A gate set in the brick wall opened into an alleyway running parallel to Lyd Street. The gate was secured by a bolt at the top as well as by a lock.

Thornhill went into the alley and shut the gate behind him. There were two or three inches between the lintel and the top of the gate – quite enough for him to get his hand through and reach the bolt. He went back into the yard.

"So where did Masterman hide the key for the gate?"

Kirby grinned, and for the first time Thornhill saw him as a person rather than simply the detective sergeant that fate had allocated him.

"He told me it's always on his key chain with the others." Kirby dangled the bunch of keys from his fingers. "But the cleaning woman says there's a spare, and it's kept down here. See – just above the lintel – there's a little ledge below where the bricks start. Handy for deliveries, she says. If he's busy with a customer, he doesn't want to have to deal with that sort of thing. So they leave the goods in that little shed with the bike in it. Especially since his wife died. But Mrs Crisp says they used to do it long before that."

"Local knowledge?"

"Looks like it, sir."

"But rather incomplete local knowledge."

Kirby nodded. "Think it's the same one who did the pub?"

"It's early days." Thornhill looked round above the level of the walls, trying to get his bearings. "That's east, isn't it? So Templefields is over there."

"Two or three hundred yards away if you go by the alleys. Nearly twice as much if you go by road."

Thornhill strolled over to the window again. He knew that Kirby was waiting for him to say more. He looked at the frame. The marks of the crowbar were quite obvious in the wood. Everything would have to be measured and tabulated. It sometimes depressed him how much effort went into trying to cope with these small and rather inefficient robberies. They kept on coming at you from all sides. Whether you solved individual crimes or not, the frustration remained because your efforts could do nothing to stem the flow of equally futile cases.

"Kirby, I want you here for the next few hours. Get the fingerprinting done. Have them photograph that window, especially the mark of the crowbar. Try to find out what damage has been done and what's missing. You know the drill. Talk to the woman, talk to Masterman. See if he's got any enemies, anyone who might have a grudge against him. Find out exactly when he had the safe installed and who knew about it."

Kirby looked surprised. Thornhill knew that his predecessor in the job had had the reputation for being reluctant to delegate, whereas he himself tended to go too far in the other direction.

"Right. I'll leave you to it." Thornhill led the way back into the house. "I'll be back in an hour or two."

He opened the front door and stepped on to the pavement. After he'd shut the door behind him, he stood outside the shop, looking up and down the hill, from the High Street to the river. For an instant he pushed this dreary little case to the back of his mind.

So this was Lydmouth on a bleak November morning. Nostalgia swept over him. He wished he were back in the Fens.

At ten fifteen they had ten minutes to themselves. A few of the men brought tea in Thermos flasks, some had sandwiches, and most of them took the opportunity to have a smoke.

During the morning, they had been clearing rubble from one end of the old warehouse and they took their break there. It was a dry day with the clouds gradually retreating eastwards and allowing sunlight to filter through, but the wind was so cold that no one wanted to hang around in the open air. Puffs of smoke rose from a score of pipes and cigarettes into the shadowy roof space.

Charlie Meague was leaning against a wall and rolling himself a cigarette when Cyril George came into the warehouse. No one said anything but everyone knew the boss was here. Some men reacted by talking a little louder than normal.

George beckoned Ted Evans over to him. "I've just had the police on the phone." He made no effort to lower his voice. "They say we still can't do anything with the building where you found those bloody bones. They may want to have another look."

"So you want me to keep the men on this side today?"

"We haven't got much choice, have we?"

"There's enough to do here. No one will be idle."

"Just as well. I don't employ skivers."

George marched out of the warehouse. With him went the tension that his presence brought. Evans sipped his tea. Someone cracked a joke, but the laughter was muted.

Cigarette in mouth, Charlie Meague sauntered outside. No one challenged him. If his departure were noticed, it would be assumed that he was looking for a private corner to answer a call of nature. He walked quickly across the warehouse's yard and through a small side gate that led to a cobbled alley running between the warehouse and the Rose in Hand. Soon he turned left into a lane running parallel to the main road. No one was in sight. A moment later, he reached the back gates of the yard where they had found the bones.

The gates were locked and a row of spikes ran along the top of them. But when he was a boy, Charlie had got in easily enough by climbing up in the angle between the left-hand gate and the crumbling brick pillar beside it. It was even easier now that he was taller.

He reached the top of the wall, swung his legs over and slithered down the other side. He took a last drag from the cigarette and ground it into the cobbles with his heel.

An old door had been laid across the opening that led into the outhouse where the privy was. Someone had daubed KEEP OUT in red paint across it. Charlie approached cautiously. The building seemed to be much as he'd left it, except that the box was no longer there. He could see the remains of the rat on the floor. He averted his eyes. Something had feasted off it during the night.

It was a shame that the box had gone, though he hadn't really expected it to be there: he guessed that Goody-Goody Evans would have given it to George, along with the contents. Probably the police had it now. But there was just a chance that he might be able to find something else. The police hadn't searched the place properly yet. It must have been dark by the time they had arrived last night. In any case it had been pissing with rain and there had been no reason why they should have thought there was any need for urgency.

Perhaps, Charlie thought, perhaps there was nothing to find, here or in the box. But sometimes you had to back your hunches. That had been another of Carn's little sayings. Genghis Carn was full of little sayings: *If you don't ask, you don't get.*

Charlie shivered. He had the sense that something had touched him – his mind, not his body; when they were children they used to say that there was a ghost walking over your grave. He glanced over his shoulder. The yard was still empty. He'd half expected to see Carn standing there with his hands in his pockets and the know-it-all smile on his pasty face.

A ghost walking over your grave.

For an instant the elusive memory tried to nudge its way to the surface. Something to do with the box? But the memory slipped away, down into the depths. Charlie shivered again. But why not, it was a cold day, wasn't it? He was too tired, that was the trouble; when you were tired, you started imagining things.

He stepped over the door into the privy and crouched beside the place where he'd found the box. He picked up a brick, moved part of a rotting plank and scooped aside a pile of dead leaves. Nothing but more rubbish. Talk about needles and haystacks.

He stood up. Evans was a bastard about time-keeping, as about so much else. He turned to leave and found himself looking at Evans himself. He was standing outside in the yard with one hand resting on the door that said KEEP OUT.

"Having trouble with your reading?"

59

Charlie's heart scarcely missed a beat. He knew it wasn't worth antagonising Evans any more. The best thing would be to give him a version of the truth. "I wondered if there might be something else here – something we missed."

"Another silver brooch?"

"Maybe. Worth a try."

There was no flicker of sympathy in Evans's eyes. Maybe Evans had already been here on the same errand. Charlie moved towards him and Evans stepped back to give him room. He even tried the effect of a smile as he climbed over the door, but Evans just stared at him, turned and walked towards the ruined barn; he hadn't needed to scramble over the gates as Charlie had.

"Has Mr George got the box the bones were in?" Charlie asked, falling into step beside him.

"Why?"

"I didn't look at it properly yesterday. I just wondered if there was anything else in it."

"Come on, Meague," Evans said. "Be your age. As far as I'm concerned, you've had your last chance. This is real life – you're not a bloody child any more. If there's a next time, you'll be out on your ear."

4

Edge Hill lay on the road north, the road for Ross and Hereford, Worcester and Birmingham. On Thornhill's prewar Ordnance Survey map, it was marked as a separate village about two miles to the north of the centre of Lydmouth. Nowadays, however, the village was linked to the town by ribbon development stretching along both sides of the road, mainly semidetached, pebble-dashed houses built in the nineteen thirties.

The wide, straight road encouraged drivers to go too fast. Thornhill would have missed the village altogether if he had not glimpsed the church. He was almost too late to stop. He braked and pulled over to the left without signalling, a manoeuvre which earned him a volley from the horn of the lorry thundering along on his tail.

The church was at the apex of a triangular green with a war memorial. Thornhill identified Chandos Lodge without any difficulty. It stood at one end of the side of the triangle which was furthest away from the church, separated from the green by the main road. The house was L-shaped and clad with stucco, with the main façade at right angles to the green. It was certainly large – the number of bedrooms might well run to double figures – but in calling it white, Mrs Wemyss-Brown had erred on the charitable side. The white had long since given place to a variety of other colours: greys, browns, greens and even blacks.

Thornhill locked the Austin and walked across the grass. The wind had blown back many of the clouds exposing a blue sky, and the sun was out. It was astonishing how a little sunshine could make a man feel more cheerful. He allowed a few drops of optimism to seep into his mind: with time, all things were possible: Williamson might mellow with further acquaintance or – perhaps more plausibly – be incapacitated by illness and forced to retire; Edith would revert to her old self; he would have more time to spend with her and the children.

He had to wait to cross the road because of the traffic. Although Chandos Lodge stood within its own garden, the house itself was surprisingly close to the road; when it was built, in the high noon of railway prosperity, no doubt the noise of traffic had not been a consideration.

There were two entrances from the road: wrought-iron gates, one leaf of which was propped open, led to a short carriage drive to the front door; and further down the road in the Lydmouth direction there was a pair of wooden gates with the roof of what looked like a coach house behind it.

Thornhill crossed the road and walked carefully up the drive, skirting the occasional pile of dog turds. Once, it had been covered with gravel, but now its surface was scarred with ruts and potholes and dotted with tussocks of bright grass and puddles gleaming with the brilliant blue of the sky.

The nearer he got to it, the worse the house appeared. Some houses were beautiful, even in decay, but Chandos Lodge had been ugly from the start. Now, in what might be politely described as the evening of its life, it was becoming steadily uglier. Some of the tall, ground-floor windows had been boarded up. Those huge expanses of glass hinted at enormous rooms behind, and the place must be the devil to heat. The large garden had become a wilderness of long, lank grass and overgrown shrubs and trees.

Before driving to Edge Hill, Thornhill had tried to telephone Major Harcutt from the police station. Harcutt proved not to be on the phone. Thornhill assumed that this was because he was old-fashioned; but Chandos Lodge suggested that the reason might be that he couldn't afford it.

A dog was barking inside the house. The barks became more frenzied as he went up the three steps leading to the front door which was recessed between a pair of squat pillars. There was a bell pull of the kind designed to communicate by means of wires with invisible servants. He tugged it. but heard nothing, and the pull itself felt suspiciously slack. There was no knocker, so he rapped briskly on the door with his knuckles. These attempts to announce his presence were, he felt, mere formalities whose ostensible purpose was irrelevant: the dog's barking must have been audible on the green.

Without any warning, the front door swung open. An old man, hunched over a stick, stared at Thornhill. He wore corduroy trousers, leather slippers and a baggy tweed jacket over what looked like several jerseys. There was a poppy in the lapel of the jacket. The dog, a border collie with a mad gleam in its yellow eyes, barked continuously and strained towards Thornhill. The old man had what Thornhill hoped was a firm grip on its collar.

"Yes? What is it?"

"Good morning, sir. I'm looking for Major Harcutt."

"You've found him."

"I'm Detective Inspector Thornhill." His promotion was still recent enough for the rank to give him a thrill of pride. "I wonder if you could spare me a few moments?"

"Those bones, eh?"

"As a matter of fact, yes. How did you know?"

The old man didn't answer. He was younger than Thornhill had at first thought – in his late sixties, perhaps. Small blue eyes peered out of a face hatched with broken veins. He shuffled back from the doorway, leaving Thornhill to come into the house, shut the door behind him and follow his host.

The hall stretched the height of the house. A dark-stained pine staircase rose into the gloom. As Thornhill breathed out, his breath condensed in the still air. Major Harcutt looped the dog's lead around the newel post at the bottom of the stairs. On the floor beside the post was the bottom half of a tarnished silver soup tureen filled with water, with a khaki blanket in a heap next to it.

"Sit," Harcutt snapped.

The dog stared at him.

The major smacked the dog's nose. "Sit, miss! Sit, I say!"

The dog slowly lowered its hind legs until it was almost, but not quite, sitting on the blanket. Its baleful eyes swung back to Thornhill.

"Good dog. Good Milly."

The major set off down a passage on the left of the hall. Thornhill kept his overcoat on because Harcutt had made no move to take it. As he trudged across the tiled floor after his host, he felt sand or grit beneath his shoes.

"Can't beat a dog, eh? She's my daughter's, actually. Know where you are with dogs."

Harcutt turned right under an archway. The tiles gave way to linoleum. He opened a door and, again without a backward glance, went into the room beyond. Thornhill found himself on the threshold of a square, low-ceilinged room which was a little less cold than the hall. A high-backed sofa had been drawn close to the fireplace. With a shock, Thornhill realised that Major Harcutt had company.

As he came into the room, the heads of two women turned towards the doorway. Two pairs of eyes stared at him over the back of the sofa.

"Ah – Inspector Thornhill," said Mrs Wemyss-Brown; she was wearing a hat and what any well-trained CID officer would have recognised as a mink coat. "We were only just in time."

The other woman said nothing. She looked gravely at Thornhill.

"Good morning, Mrs Wemyss-Brown." He struggled to remember the other woman's name; the brief lapse of memory flustered him.

"And – and Miss Francis. I hope I haven't called at a bad moment. I could always come back another day. I tried to telephone ahead but—"

"But, of course, Major Harcutt isn't on the phone," Mrs Wemyss-Brown interposed smoothly. "That's why we're here." She flashed a smile at Harcutt who by now was standing over the gas fire and trying to warm his hands. "Having set the police on to you, Jack, it seemed the least we could do was to let you know."

"That's all right," Harcutt said ambiguously; he smoothed his moustache and stared at the floor.

Thornhill turned his hat between his hands. Jill Francis was still looking at him. Not staring – she wasn't that sort of woman – but he knew her attention was on him; no doubt she was wondering whether he always acted so gauchely.

"Well," he said to no one in particular. "If you're sure it wouldn't be inconvenient?"

"Not at all, Inspector." Mrs Wemyss-Brown beamed at him, taking his words to herself. She stood up amid creaks and rustles. "We must be getting back. We were on the verge of leaving when you arrived."

Jill Francis followed suit. Last night, Thornhill hadn't realised what lovely eyes she had. Still, they didn't make up for the fact that she was so remote and arrogant. Not that it mattered. Neither her personality nor her appearance had anything to do with him.

The two women moved towards the doorway. Harcutt detached himself from the gas fire and followed them.

"Goodbye, Inspector," Mrs Wemyss-Brown said, inclining her head towards him. The coat came down to her thick calves. Her perfume swept over him.

He mumbled goodbye. His attention was on Jill Francis, who gave him what he thought was a very cold, small smile, the bare minimum that civility required. She said nothing to him, nor did he to her.

He heard Mrs Wemyss-Brown talking to Major Harcutt as the three of them walked down the hall: "You must come and have a bite of lunch with us, Jack. It's been ages since we had you at Troy House."

The major muttered something indistinguishable in reply. The dog gave an experimental yap.

Harcutt yelled, "Sit down, miss!"

Thornhill stuffed his hands deep into the pockets of his overcoat and wandered towards the window which overlooked a cobbled yard and part of a high stone wall. An archway in the wall gave a view of the garden, a sunlit wilderness. He would have liked to throw open the window and let in the pale winter sunlight and the fresh, cold air.

He walked up and down, partly to keep himself warm, and partly to get an idea of the major from his belongings. The room smelt like a spit-and-sawdust bar in a pub – of tobacco, stale alcohol and unwashed bodies. It seemed smaller than it was because it was crowded with furniture – a large dining table covered with papers, chairs, a large bureau which was probably eighteenth century, two sofas and several tall, glass-fronted bookcases. Apart from the gas fire, there appeared to be no form of heating. It was possible that Harcutt slept in here as well: there was a nest of grubby blankets and eiderdowns on the other sofa. Horsehair was oozing out of the armchair closest to the fire. One wall was brown with damp and the plaster near the ceiling was beginning to lift off. The tiled surround in front of the fireplace was littered with ash and cigarette ends. There were dog hairs everywhere.

Perhaps this had once been the housekeeper's room. That would explain why the furniture looked so out of scale – Harcutt would have brought in pieces from the main reception rooms. Thornhill glanced at the bureau. It was closed, but on top of it was a tray of poppies and a collecting tin. There was a difference, he told himself to salve his conscience, between active eavesdropping or prying on the one hand and merely being observant on the other.

A Second Empire clock, its hands at ten to seven, gathered dust on the mantelpiece. Beside it, in a battered silver frame, was a photograph showing a much younger, pipe-smoking Harcutt with his left arm round a stout woman and his right arm round a little girl with a pigtail dangling across her chest. They were standing like a row of dolls along the wooden railing of a verandah with the light behind them and their faces in shadow. All three of them were smiling. but there was something curiously rigid about their pose. Though the photograph was obviously a snapshot, and not a very good one at that, it had a formal quality.

There was movement in the hall and Thornhill turned quickly towards the door as Harcutt bustled into the room. He had a sense of purpose about him which had not been there before.

"Phew. Thought she'd never go." Harcutt moved towards the bureau which stood against the wall to the right of the fireplace. "Later than I thought." He glanced at his watch, as if to verify this. "Care for a drink? I usually have a spot of something before lunch myself."

"Not for me, thank you, sir."

"Oh, yes, of course. Mustn't corrupt the constabulary." The major's surliness had vanished. He rubbed his hands together. "I find it helps the digestion. Gives one an appetite."

With sudden urgency, he opened the flap of the bureau, revealing a mass of old newspapers, files and letters. He reached behind the pile

65

and brought out a bottle and a glass. The glass already contained half an inch of whisky. Thornhill turned away and pretended to study the photograph on the mantelpiece. He heard the chink of glass against glass and the gurgle of liquid spurting from the bottle.

"Ah, that's better." Harcutt came to stand by the fire. "Do sit down, my dear fellow. I'd keep your coat on if I were you."

Thornhill sat on the sofa, in the place where Jill Francis had been sitting. Harcutt turned up the gas and the fire hissed as the flames rose higher. That was one advantage of being so near the road, Thornhill thought: the gas company must have extended the gas main to Edge Hill when the semidetached houses had crept along the fields from Lydmouth.

"We've got a problem with the central heating," Harcutt went on. "Something to do with the boiler, I understand. The engineers seem to take an age to sort it out. Costs an arm and a leg too. It's all the same these days. They don't care what sort of a job they do, they just want your money. And the more the better."

He swallowed another mouthful of whisky and wiped his moustache with the back of his hand.

"It's not like the army, you know. In the old days, I'd just get on the phone and someone would have been round in a jiffy. When I was in Egypt, I remember old ..."

With the skill born of long practice, Thornhill gently slipped an interruption into the flow of words: "I understand you know a lot about Victorian Lydmouth, sir."

"Yes." The major blinked, needing a few seconds to adjust to the change of subject. He took another sip of whisky. "Yes, Charlotte told me you want to pick my brains about those bones." His pale, red-rimmed eyes glanced down at Thornhill and back to the glass in his hand; the action was natural enough, but the speed with which it was accomplished gave it a furtive air. "I asked her where they'd been found, and when she said the Rose in Hand I said to myself, 'Ah, I know what that means.'"

"Indeed? What does it mean?"

"Sounds remarkably like the apprentice work of Amelia Rushwick."

Thornhill took out his notebook. "I'm afraid you'll have to make allowances for my ignorance, sir."

"Eh? Not a local man, are you? Where do you come from?"

"Cambridgeshire. But my wife has local connections."

"Very glad to hear it. I'm all for people staying where they belong. Roots, you know, whatever people say, they're important. Yes, well – be that as it may. Where was I?"

"Amelia Rushwick, sir."

"Let me see. Give me a moment to get my thoughts straight."

The major swallowed some more neat whisky. He shook a cigarette out of the packet on the mantelpiece and lit it with a spill. He sat down in the armchair closest to the fire.

Thornhill wondered how soon he could decently get away. It was unlikely that this old soak was going to be able to tell him anything useful. But the signs were that Harcutt would spin out the interview as long as possible, just for the company. No wonder Mrs Wemyss-Brown hadn't invited him to Troy House recently.

"Did you know that the Rose in Hand was quite a prosperous place once upon a time?"

Thornhill nodded.

"Went downhill in the nineteenth century. By the 1880s it had a very bad reputation indeed, and that's when the Rushwicks leased it. Can't tell you the dates offhand – I'll check them if you want – but I think their tenancy began in about 1884 and lasted until 1891. In those days the site was owned by the Ruispidge Estate. Of course, that doesn't mean the Rushwicks didn't sublet it. Under the counter, as it were. Difficult to keep track of things when you're trying to pin down that class of person, I find – don't leave many records, you see. Where was I? Yes, the Rose. It had a bit of a reputation. Haunt of vice, you know the sort of thing. Now, the Rushwicks' eldest daughter was called Amelia. Amelia Rushwick: name mean anything to you?"

"No, sir."

Major Harcutt looked around. He lowered his voice and leant forward: "Sex mad."

He leant back to watch the effect of his words on his visitor. Thornhill merely looked expectantly at him. Harcutt swallowed twice and smoothed his moustache.

"She was born in 1870," he went on, speaking more rapidly than before. "Grew up in Lydmouth, must have lived with her parents at the Rose in Hand. Then she went off to London in the late eighties – almost certainly with a man. Once she got there, she found her own level soon enough. Afterwards, when she was arrested, her parents claimed they'd thrown her out of the Rose. But they would, wouldn't they? If you ask me it was a case of the pot calling the kettle black."

Harcutt fell silent. He dabbed at his lips, looking first at the empty glass and then at the bureau where the bottle stood beside the tray of poppies.

"Anyway," he went on, "there were only two things Amelia could do and she did them both. She became a part-time barmaid and part-time prostitute. More the latter than the former, I'll be bound. Saw women like that when I was in the army sometimes. All ages, all sorts and conditions, too – colonel's lady or Judy O'Grady – natural tarts."

He sucked in his cheeks and turned the glass round in his hands. His watery eyes stared into the past and seemed to find it fascinating.

"What happened next?" Thornhill asked.

"She met this man Ferrano. Half-Italian. Sold ice cream. I shouldn't wonder. Anyway you know what these wops are like. Amelia fell in love with him, or so she claimed. Then Ferrano said he was going back to Italy. And Amelia said she wanted to go too. Trouble was, she had twins by a previous liaison. She had them fostered most of the time, but that cost money. They were about three years old. Ferrano said they couldn't come back to Italy, oh, no. He put his foot down. Didn't want someone else's little bastards in tow. Got plenty of his own, no doubt." The major's Adam's apple bobbed up and down. "So she smothered them. Poor little beggars."

"She smothered her own children?"

"Yes – that's what I'm telling you. Just to be with this Italian fancy man of hers. Makes your blood run cold, doesn't it?"

Harcutt struggled to his feet, scattering cigarette ash on the carpet. His face was much redder than it had been before. Supporting himself with one hand first on the mantelpiece and then on the wall, he made his way towards the bureau.

"Sure you won't join me?"

"No, thank you, sir."

Harcutt sat down heavily on the chair in front of the bureau. With great deliberation he refilled his glass and took another sip. "You could understand a foreigner doing that sort of thing but not a British girl. She told everyone she'd packed them off to another foster home. But the landlady got suspicious. They were behind with the rent. There'd been words. Anyway the landlady complained to the police, and they finally dug up the garden. And there were the children. Still in their nightgowns."

"This must have made quite a stir at the time. Do you know of an account of the case I could look up?"

"Any amount of them." Harcutt picked up the bottle and studied the label. "You know the *Notable British Trials* series? It's in there. I'll find you the reference before you go."

Thornhill felt sorry for Amelia, sorrier for her children. He wondered whether Ferrano had pulled the strings. And talking of strings: "What happened to her?"

"Oh, she was hanged, of course. Last thing she said on the scaffold was that Ferrano had nothing to do with it. Ferrano was a witness for the prosecution, would you believe. Even so, there she was, ready to meet her Maker, and she was still so besotted with the man that she wanted to do her best by him. Extraordinary, isn't it?"

"It is extraordinary."

Thornhill scribbled in his notebook. Major Harcutt cleared his throat so vigorously that the phlegm rattled in his chest. Absently he uncorked the bottle and refreshed his glass. His method of imparting information had been idiosyncratic, but he'd provided plenty of material. Presumably, too, he would not have had time to look up the case because Mrs Wemyss-Brown had only just told him about the bones found at the Rose in Hand.

"You've got an impressive memory, sir."

"Eh? Oh, I looked into the case a few months ago for my book. Did I tell you I'm writing a book? The history of Lydmouth in the nineteenth century. Fascinating. Let me see if I can get you the reference."

Harcutt put down his glass, opened a drawer and pulled out a file. He flicked through its contents, grunting impatiently as he failed to find what he wanted.

Thornhill thought about the nature of Amelia Rushwick's relationship with Ferrano. If Harcutt's version of the facts was accurate, she must have loved him with an intensity that most people only read about – either that or she had been mad. How had Ferrano felt about being the object of such overwhelming devotion? Thornhill wondered whether the twins had felt pain and whether death was in fact preferable to life for children in their situation in the slums of Victorian London. Superintendent Williamson was going to be very unhappy about the CID wasting their time on a possible victim of a Victorian murderer.

"Here we are, Inspector. *Notable British Trials*, volume 49, edited by Harry Hodge and published in London. They've got a copy in the library in town. Not on the open shelves, of course. You have to ask for it."

Thornhill took down the details. He shut his notebook and stood up. "This has been very useful, sir. I don't think I need take up any more of your time."

"It might not have been Amelia's baby," Harcutt went on, the muscles in his cheeks making chewing motions as he spoke. "Mustn't jump to conclusions. In those days there were an awful lot of unmarried mothers in the working classes. Barely better than animals, some of them. I imagine a lot of them disposed of their young in what we would consider a rather unorthodox way."

"Yes, sir." Thornhill put the notebook in his overcoat and picked up his hat from the sofa.

"The Rose in Hand is just the place you'd expect them to do it, too. Lot of people coming and going. Sort of place where I imagine you didn't ask too many questions. Still, it is tempting to think of it as Amelia's. There's a certain neatness to it."

"Quite."

"Might be a footnote for my book in this. Tell me, was anything else found with – ah – the bones? Something that might help identify where they came from? Or when, of course. If you could pin it down to the late eighties, for example, you'd strengthen the theory."

Thornhill took his first tentative step towards the door. "I should have made clear from the start that we're not even absolutely sure that they *are* human bones. We should have a laboratory report within a day or two. But Dr Bayswater thinks it very possible that they are."

"Ah, Bayswater." The major sniffed. "He's my doctor."

"The site had been rather disturbed. Rats had got in. After all, it was originally a privy." Thornhill watched the major's face and saw the skin puckering horizontally along the forehead. He wondered whether the old man were wincing. He thought probably not. "We only have a few bones. We also found a scrap of newspaper and a brooch."

"Victorian?"

"Mrs Wemyss-Brown believes the newspaper comes from the *Gazette*, probably in the late nineteenth century. We're following up that line."

"What sort of brooch?"

"It's in the form of a true love's knot."

Harcutt grunted. He put one hand on the bureau and levered himself to his feet. He peered at the mantelpiece. Thornhill guessed he was looking for his cigarettes.

"I suppose you can check the hallmark on the silver," the major went on. "I mean, if they go together, the bones can't be earlier than the date of the brooch."

As he was speaking, he took a step towards the mantelpiece. His jacket snagged on the wooden arm of the chair causing him to stumble forward and lose his balance. The glass flew from his hand and smashed on the tiles in front of the fireplace. He flung out his right arm towards the top of the bureau in a desperate attempt to save himself. Instead, his fingers closed on the tray with the poppies. The tray tipped. The poppies sprayed into the air and pattered on to the carpet. Meanwhile, the major fell against the side of the sofa which caught his thigh halfway between waist and knee. He would have toppled forward had Thornhill not put out an arm to save him.

"Steady, sir."

Harcutt looked shrivelled and insubstantial, but his body was heavy and solid. Thornhill helped him to the chair by the fire. The old man, breathing heavily, stared glumly at the gleaming dark stains among the ash, the fragments of glass and the cigarette ends in front of the fireplace. His colour had heightened and he was trembling.

"Bloody hell. Waste of good whisky."

"Is there anyone I can fetch, sir? Your daughter?"

Harcutt shook his head. "She doesn't live here now. Pass me a cigarette, would you, there's a good fellow." His voice came in little jerks and spasms. "See that cupboard on the right of the sideboard. Find another glass in there."

Once Harcutt's cigarette was safely alight, Thornhill crossed the room and opened the cupboard in the sideboard. Rank after rank of ornate glasses stretched away into the darkness, enough for a twelve-course dinner party in the last century, with each course accompanied by a different wine. On the shelf below was more tarnished silver. Thornhill took out a water tumbler. It was larger than the whisky glass had been, but he doubted if Harcutt would mind.

"It needs a wash, sir."

"Eh?"

"I need to wash the glass," Thornhill said more loudly. "It's filthy."

"All right, I can hear. There's a bog in the hall. Second door on the left."

Thornhill left the room. In the hall, the dog looked at him and began to growl deep in her throat. The growls increased in volume as Thornhill drew nearer. He went into the lavatory and washed the glass in a basin brown with grime. The only towel was much the same colour as the basin so he dried the glass on his handkerchief. Though the window was several inches open, the room smelt badly. He glanced into the lavatory bowl and looked quickly away.

He pulled the chain and went back to Harcutt. The old man's eyes were full of tears, but he watched attentively as Thornhill poured two fingers of Scotch into the glass.

"Good man," Harcutt wheezed as he took the glass.

"Are you all right?" Thornhill hesitated, fighting the temptation not to get involved any further than he already was. "Would you like me to fetch a doctor?"

Harcutt swallowed a third of the whisky. "I'm perfectly all right. Fit as a fiddle, really. Such a lot of fuss about nothing. Don't mean to seem ungrateful, but I'm fine."

Thornhill shrugged. He knelt down on the hearth rug and began to pick up the fragments of glass one by one and put them in a pile on the hearth.

"Oh, don't bother with that. There's a woman who comes in with my evening meal. She'll see to it."

When Thornhill had finished with the glass, he turned his attention to the scattered poppies. Harcutt watched him, but said nothing.

"If you don't mind, sir, I'll buy one of these while I'm here."

"I noticed you weren't wearing one." Harcutt ground out the remains of his cigarette into the ashtray. "In my opinion, people are getting deplorably slack about Remembrance Day. It was very different in the twenties, you know."

"I'm sure it was." Thornhill put the tray back on the bureau and fed a handful of coppers into the slot in the tin. He chose a poppy and pushed its wire stem into the buttonhole of his overcoat.

"People used to care about the dead. Wanted to pay the debt they owed them. I knew a lot of good fellows who died so we could be sitting here at our ease." Harcutt nodded in agreement with himself, apparently oblivious of the fact that Thornhill was neither sitting nor at his ease, and raised his glass. "Here's to them."

While the major was talking, Thornhill had crossed the room to the door.

"Thank you for your help," he said. "No, don't bother to get up. I'll see myself out."

Harcutt, who had made only a half-hearted attempt to rise, subsided into his chair. "Anything I can do, my dear fellow, just say." His voice was slightly slurred. "Give you chapter and verse on the Rushwick case. Just let me know. Always at the constabulary's service, eh?"

5

Charlotte was proving to be an impressive driver, armed with both mechanical and psychological skills. It was rarely difficult to park in the High Street, she told Jill, except on market days. Usually you could pick and choose. But on that morning it so happened that there was only a single space in the line of parked cars immediately outside the Bull Hotel. It was not a large space, and a baker's delivery van was trying to get into it.

Charlotte would have none of that. Sounding her horn, she overtook the van and pulled in beside the car parked immediately in front. She began to reverse the Rover into the space just as the van was trying, much less skilfully, to enter it in a forward direction.

The van driver put his hand on his horn and kept it there. He also braked, which was a tactical error. Charlotte simply continued to reverse and soon the Rover filled over half the space. In this case, possession was over fifty per cent of the law.

The baker's van reversed jerkily into the path of an oncoming bus. The bus stopped. Its horn blared. The van driver rolled down his window. Jill could see his lips moving and the anger in his eyes, and she could just hear his voice through the closed windows of the Rover.

"Bloody women! You shouldn't be allowed on the road. Think you own the place, do you?"

Charlotte appeared not to hear, just as she had appeared unaware of the van from the start; she had conducted the entire series of manoeuvres automatically while her conscious mind was engaged in discussing hemlines.

"Personally I always think that Balenciaga is a safer guide," she said.

The bus driver leant out of his window and swore at the man in the van.

"But anyway it's quite absurd, the way they assume that everyone's legs are the same length." Charlotte's eyes darted to Jill's slim legs and back to her own, more substantial pair. "It's just the same with waists. Or, for that matter, busts."

"For Christ's sake," the van driver shouted, rather plaintively.

"People don't show any respect these days, do they?" Charlotte remarked, suddenly revealing that she had been aware of the entire incident. "It's extraordinary how attitudes have changed since the war."

Before she could stop herself, Jill said, "I imagine the baker thinks it extraordinary how some attitudes haven't changed."

"Yes, I know." Charlotte smiled, coping magnificently both with the baker and with Jill's implied criticism. "People can be so naïve. After all, it's simply a matter of economics."

Jill smiled back, refusing to become embroiled in an argument conducted on a ground of Charlotte's choosing. By the time the two women got out of the car, both the van and the bus had moved on.

Charlotte stood on the pavement and settled her skintight gloves over her fingers; her rings bulged against the leather like arthritic swellings. "We could go to the Gardenia, I suppose."

"Wherever you like."

Charlotte's expression was shrewder than Jill found entirely comfortable. "But I think perhaps the Bull. The coffee isn't as good, but the seats are much more comfortable. And one rarely meets people in there. People one knows, that is."

The Bull Hotel was a large white building, rather older than its eighteenth-century façade suggested. Charlotte led the way into a dark hall smelling of boiled vegetables. Jill didn't know whether to feel relieved or annoyed or both; Charlotte had clearly divined that her guest was not in the mood for the sort of company they were likely to meet in the Gardenia.

An elderly man wearing a faded striped waistcoat dozed behind the reception desk. Directly above him was the dusty head, set slightly askew, of a glassy-eyed stag, flanked by cases containing stuffed fish. "Good morning, Quale," Charlotte said as she passed him, and the man jerked awake.

Beside the desk was a notice board, on which most of the posters were already concerned, in one way or another, with the approach of Christmas. Jill glimpsed advertisements for the Conservative Party's Christmas Dance, the Lydmouth Amateur Dramatic Society's production of *Cinderella* and a carol service at St John's. The thought of Christmas made her lips tighten and her eyes water as if she had bitten a lemon. As she knew from experience, Christmas was the worst time of the year to be lonely. And this year, the loneliness would be different because there would be nothing to look forward to in the New Year.

Charlotte swung right into the hotel lounge, a large and lofty room with three tall windows overlooking the street. In the centre was a mahogany dining table covered with rows of newspapers and magazines. The rest of the room was furnished with low tables surrounded by clusters of armchairs and sofas in faded chintz covers. There was a marble chimneypiece against one wall which supported an enormous mirror, its murky glass dotted with brown spots. A log fire burned in the grate. It was a room made for a large number of people, and they had it to themselves.

"Ah," Charlotte said. "This is more like it."

She led Jill to the table nearest the fire. Their reflections, slightly distorted, swam towards them in the mirror. Jill automatically assessed her own appearance. Why was it, she wondered, that old mirrors so often conveyed a sense of depth and mystery and half-hidden possibilities?

They put their coats and hats on the sofa. The armchairs needed recovering but they were certainly comfortable. Jill was glad to get the weight off her feet, which was absurd because she had walked only the few yards from the car. At the hospital they had told her she should have plenty of rest. In any case, perhaps sadness was physically tiring.

A sad-faced waitress in a black dress and a white apron slouched into the room to take their order. Charlotte interrogated her about the type and freshness of the biscuits.

"Not that I particularly want any," she said when the waitress had gone. "But it's the principle of the thing. If someone isn't willing to make a fuss, then standards always start to slip. Don't you agree?"

To avoid answering, Jill diverted the conversation: "Talking of slipping standards – Major Harcutt seemed a rather sad example."

"Poor old Jack," Charlotte said. "He used to be so dashing as a young man. He's a bit of a hero, you know – he got some sort of medal in the Great War. I remember my mother saying that all the young girls were in love with him."

"Was he regular army?"

"Yes, he came out in the thirties. It was when his elder brother died. I suppose he felt he had to take over the business – the Harcutts used to be coal merchants – quite substantial ones, too. But Jack couldn't make a go of it. Between ourselves, I suspect he's not much of a businessman. He sold up just before the last war and went back to the army for the duration."

"Strange house – I shouldn't like to live there myself."

"The Harcutts bought it just before the First War. The boys' mother was a terrible snob, and I imagine she thought it would improve their standing in the county. Not that they had any in the first place. Silly woman. It's a terrible white elephant."

Jill remembered the overgrown garden, the boarded-up windows and the smell of poverty. "It must need a great deal of maintenance."

"What it needs and what it gets are two different things. Not much money in the bank, I fancy. I doubt if Jack really cares any more. He's not really been the same since his wife died. Cancer, poor thing. It happened very suddenly."

The waitress arrived with their tray. Before pouring the coffee, Charlotte examined the cups to make quite sure they were clean. After her first sip, she sighed.

"I just don't know what they put in it. Philip claims they've got a great big saucepan in the kitchen. And they empty out all the half-used coffee pots into it, he says, and just reheat it as needed. Of course, sometimes they must add some more water and some fresh coffee, but not enough to affect the overall taste."

"I've tasted worse." As Jill spoke, the aftertaste reached her palate and she detected a curious compound flavour that reminded her of chicory, and of things she had never actually tasted, such as engine oil, burnt rubber and tar. "Though I must say I can't remember when."

Charlotte helped herself to a biscuit. "I wonder what the policeman made of Jack Harcutt. He really does know a great deal about Lydmouth's history. But I'm not at all sure he was at his best this morning." She leaned a little closer to Jill and lowered her voice to a powerful whisper. "Did you smell his breath, dear?"

"No."

Charlotte nodded. "Well, I did. Enough said, I think. One must be charitable. I suspect the poor man's terribly lonely. There's a daughter, but I don't think they're close. Mark you . . ." Charlotte broke off; she looked up and then quickly back to the fire.

Jill had her back to the door, but she heard footsteps, deliberate and masculine, coming into the room, the creak of springs as the newcomer sat down and the rustle of newspaper. She glanced at the mirror, but from this angle it gave her an uninformative view of the ceiling.

"Yes," Charlotte went on, "Jack was quite a different man before his wife died. Much jollier." She looked at Jill. "Of course the loss of a loved one can have a terrible effect on people, can't it?"

"Yes. So they say."

There was a moment's silence. Jill felt a bubble of panic rising inside her. It was as if Charlotte were hunting her, and she wouldn't stop until she had found what she wanted: the dark and painful place inside Jill.

The waitress drifted into the room. Jill heard the murmur of voices as the man behind her ordered coffee.

"Don't mind my asking, dear, but are you feeling all right? Philip was saying last night that he thought you looked a little peaky. I must say, I think he's right. When we saw you in London, you—"

"I had a bad cold a few weeks ago. I don't think I've quite thrown it off."

"We shall have to feed you up, and make sure you have lots of rest and country air. Philip's really most concerned." There was the tiniest hesitation. "And so, of course, am I."

There was a barb concealed in the sympathy. Jill knew that Charlotte had never quite forgiven her for having been the object of Philip's affections when they were both young reporters. Worse still, perhaps, was the fact that Jill had been happy to give him friendship, but not love; Charlotte might interpret this as a reflection on her choice of husband.

Charlotte had never directly admitted that she knew about this episode. Jill had never referred to Philip's two proposals, and Philip himself was far too tactful to have mentioned them without prompting. Yet the knowledge hung between the three of them, an unacknowledged cloud. Charlotte had always gone out of her way to encourage the friendship. In her more cynical moments, Jill wondered whether she wanted to keep an eye on how her husband behaved with his old flame. Better the devil you know, Charlotte might be thinking; knowledge was strength, because forewarned was forearmed.

As the waitress was leaving the lounge, Charlotte told her to bring their bill; time was getting on and she was anxious not to be late for lunch – partly because she enjoyed her food and partly, as she herself admitted, because it would never do to offend Susan, and Susan was a stickler for punctuality.

As Jill was adjusting the set of her hat in the mirror, she saw the man who had come in after them. He was sitting in a corner, screened by the *Daily Mail*, but she sensed that he was watching them – perhaps herself rather than Charlotte. She told herself not to be so egotistical. Besides, she disliked intensely the impartial attention that strange men paid her for all the wrong reasons; and she found even more disturbing the suspicion that she might feel worthless and bereft if their eyes drifted over her without registering her presence as a woman. At present she felt enough of a failure as it was.

The two women moved towards the door and the man lowered the newspaper. His eyes met Jill's. In an instant, she took in the details of his appearance: small, wearing a baggy brown pin-striped suit, with a waxy complexion and a nautical beard. He recognised her, just as she recognised him: it was the man from the train, the man who had been reading about the month of the dead, the man whom she had found, for no reason at all, so terrifying that she had to run away from him.

He smiled slightly and nodded his head in an ambiguous way which might have been taken as a bow. Perfectly properly, he was acknowledging the fact that they had met before without trying to presume on so slight an acquaintance. Jill nodded back and hurried to the door.

Once they were out in the hall. Charlotte murmured, "Who was that? Do you know him?"

"He was in my compartment in the train coming down. He closed the window for me."

"They get all sorts at the Bull these days. I wonder if he's staying here." Charlotte beckoned the waitress who was hovering in the hall. "Is that man in there a guest?"

"Yes, ma'am. He's Mr James. I think he's a commercial traveller or something."

The waitress studied the ground as she spoke; her hands were clasped together in front of her. Jill realised with a rush of distaste that the woman was scared of Charlotte – and perhaps scared of her, too.

They went outside into a sunlit winter day. Charlotte looked up at the sky and smiled.

"I wonder what Susan has for lunch for us." She glanced assessingly at Jill. "I'm afraid Philip won't be back – he's got too much to do at the *Gazette* since our senior reporter died. Still, that will mean we can have a nice old gossip."

6

Mrs Margaret Meague coughed and brought up thick, green phlegm, which she spat into her crumpled handkerchief. She was fully dressed and wearing a coat and a hat; she had drawn the armchair up to the kitchen range and taken the further precaution of draping two blankets over her. Still she was cold. And she could not stop coughing, either, or gasping for breath; there was not enough air in the world.

It was always like this in winter. That was when the pains in her chest came back and the coughing and the wheezing started again.

She would have to talk to Charlie when he came home. Charlie would know what to do. Charlie was clever. It wasn't his fault that he had been unlucky. He had problems, of course, but he'd sort them out. Thank God he was in work because now that the fat cow at Troy House had given her the push, she would need to take the money he wanted to give her. He was a good boy.

A good boy, a good boy, every good boy deserves favour: who said that? The teacher at school? The one who liked to hammer your knuckles with the ruler until she saw blood? Margaret Meague shivered and drew the blankets more tightly round her. Every good boy deserves favour. What had goodness to do with it?

Oh, God – she thought she was running a fever. Why was it so hard to breathe? It was only November. But things were already very bad. It was going to be a bad winter.

7

Holding Elizabeth by the hand, Edith Thornhill came slowly down the steps from the library. She noticed two well-dressed ladies getting into a dark blue Rover on the other side of the road. The younger woman was wearing a hat and a coat which must have come from London if not Paris. Edith barely noticed the stab of envy, automatically repressed.

She and Elizabeth had walked to the High Street from Victoria Road. On their way they'd called at the baker's and the butcher's and left orders at both shops. They had bought aspirin from the chemist's and opened an account at the baker's. Edith had spent nearly fifteen minutes hesitating over a rack of ties in Butter's, the men's outfitters. Christmas was beginning to loom, a menacing blank near the bottom of the kitchen calendar, and she hadn't the faintest idea what to buy as a present for Richard. Not that they could really afford to buy each other more than token presents, despite the rise in income which his promotion to inspector had brought: the rent of the new house and the move from Cambridgeshire had cost far more than they had expected.

Now Edith was tired and Elizabeth was fretful. It was only half-a-mile home, but Edith thought they would catch a bus and blow the expense. Besides, if they caught the bus, she wouldn't have to hurry past the window of Madame Ghislaine's which was the one halfway decent dress shop in Lydmouth.

They joined the queue at the bus stop. Elizabeth whined and demanded to be picked up. It was simpler to let her have her way. Edith Thornhill stood there with the child's arms wrapped tightly around her neck, watching the Rover pulling away from the Bull Hotel and purring down the High Street. No doubt the two ladies would soon be eating a proper lunch, cooked and served by someone else, who would also do the washing-up. No cheese on toast for them.

Elizabeth's arms tightened even more.

"Do let go, darling. I've got to breathe, you know."

"I want Daddy," Elizabeth muttered.

8

Thornhill and Kirby carried their glasses into the dining room of the Bathurst Arms. They had the room to themselves, apart from a couple of farmers arguing quietly over a newspaper in one corner and a man who looked like a solicitor's clerk wolfing liver and bacon near the door.

He let Kirby choose where they sat – a table in the bow window. The Bathurst Arms was a small hotel at the bottom of Lyd Street and the window had a view of the river. Birds were flying low over the water, and beyond the river the wooded hills rose to the blue horizon.

They could have eaten in the canteen at headquarters, but Thornhill had preferred to go somewhere neutral, even though it was more expensive. Going back to headquarters meant running the risk of seeing Superintendent Williamson. Second, he wanted to hear how Kirby had got on with the Masterman case and there would be fewer interruptions here than there would be in the canteen. Third, it was time to try to find out what kind of a man Brian Kirby was and Thornhill was more likely to be successful if the attempt took place on territory where their difference in rank was not reinforced by their surroundings.

He took a second mouthful of beer. It was lighter than he was used to in the Fens and had a tang he wasn't sure he liked. But they had come to the Bathurst Arms on Kirby's suggestion, so some sort of compliment was called for.

"Not bad. Nice balance."

"Rather better than the food," Kirby said. "Whatever you do, don't have the Brown Windsor soup or the Spotted Dick. And I'd advise against the steak and kidney. By the way it tastes, you'd expect it to get up and neigh."

A waitress took their order. She looked barely old enough to have left school. Kirby ordered bangers and mash, with apple pie to follow.

"I'll have that as well." Thornhill waited until they were alone. "How long have you been down here?"

"Three and a half years. Quite long enough."

"Miss the bright lights?"

Kirby shrugged. "It's not just that. Sometimes I feel they're living in another century down here. They're all related and they all know each other." His voice slipped without warning into the local accent. "He's my aunt's second cousin, look. My sister used to sit beside him at Sunday School." His voice reverted to normal. "Still, there are compensations."

They talked about London for a few minutes. Kirby had been born in Camden Town, and he'd done his two-year probationary period at the Paddington Green station. Halfway through an anecdote about a station sergeant whom Thornhill could claim to know by reputation, Kirby stopped and rearranged his features into a smile that was the next best thing to a simper.

A woman had come in with a loaded tray and was making her way towards their table. It was not the waitress, but someone rather more striking. The farmers and the clerk were watching her as well.

Standing unnecessarily close to Kirby, the woman bent over the table and put down their plates, one by one. Her skirt was stretched tight over her buttocks, her artificial strawberry blonde hair dazzled and her perfume was pungently unsubtle. She leant across Kirby to straighten his fork. One of her breasts almost, but not quite, touched his arm. Thornhill wondered whether the woman might be one of the local compensations which Kirby had mentioned.

"Got everything you want, Mr Kirby?" she enquired.

"No, Gloria. You know I haven't."

"Now don't be naughty." She grinned at him. "Whatever will your friend think?"

She tucked the tray under her arm and strolled out of the room. It was possible, Thornhill thought, that her rump was naturally designed to sway so vigorously both from side to side and up and down as she walked, but almost certainly nature had received every encouragement from art. He looked away, ashamed of his desire.

"She expects a bit of chitchat, sir," Kirby said with a hint of apology in his voice. "She's the landlady as well as the cook, by the way. She's very good at keeping us informed. Professionally, as it were."

Was he protesting too much? On the whole, Thornhill believed him. If there were anything improper in the relationship, Kirby would hardly have brought him here to witness it. Unless, of course, Kirby couldn't bear to keep away, or unless he was the sort of man who enjoyed the risk of seeing how far he could go.

Thornhill nodded towards the door that Gloria had used. "I'm surprised the dining room isn't busier."

Kirby's smile had a trace of smugness which wasn't altogether appealing. "Oh, she doesn't come out for everyone, sir. Just for the favoured few."

"I see. Is the girl her daughter?"

"Young Jane? She's a stepdaughter. Gloria used to be barmaid here, they say, but then she married the boss. Now she *is* the boss."

Kirby forked half a sausage laden with potato into his mouth. For a while, they ate in silence. The potato was on the lumpy side and the sausages tasted of bread.

Thornhill drank some more beer. "How did you get on with Masterman?"

"We got him into an ambulance. That was the main achievement of the morning. Besides that, not much is new. Whoever turned the place over wore gloves – but these days they all do. There were no other contact traces we could find."

"Inside knowledge?"

"I tried that line, but I didn't get anywhere. The Mastermans have been around for donkey's years. Hundreds of people must have been in that sitting room, and probably dozens of them knew that Masterman kept his valuables in the window seat."

"When did he get his new safe?"

"Eighteen months ago."

"Why?"

"We had a rash of break-ins round then. That's when his wife died, too. He collected on the life insurance."

Thornhill pushed his plate aside. He stared out of the window at the wooded hills: there must be all sorts of animals up there – deer, badgers, foxes, you name it. In the spring they could take the children up there and let them loose.

A match rasped as Kirby lit a cigarette. Thornhill abandoned both the view and the future. It was time to get back to work.

"What do you reckon then?" he said. "Local talent?"

Kirby scratched his head. "I don't know. Whoever did this at least had local information, plus some ability to plan. There again, he could have treated old Masterman a lot worse than he did. That eiderdown showed a bit of kindness, or at least a bit of forethought." He took a shred of tobacco from his lower lip, examined it and deposited it on the ashtray. "We've a few home-grown villains who could have done the job. But the eiderdown seems wrong." Kirby looked up, his eyes wary again. "I'm just thinking aloud, sir. Don't take any notice."

"No, I'm interested. I want a list of the possibles. We'd better start checking them this afternoon, if only to rule them out. Tell me, did Charlie Meague's mother ever work for Masterman?"

Kirby frowned. "I don't know. I can find out if you want. But breaking and entering – that's not Meague's cup of tea, is it? And why Masterman's?"

"Why not?"

"A tinpot jeweller in his own back yard? If all they say is true, Meague's used to bigger things."

"People change. More to the point, perhaps, he might be desperate."

"But you don't really think Charlie Meague's behind it? And the King's Head job, too? Mrs Halleran just wants us to nick him because she hates his mum. Mr Williamson said—"

"I don't think anything," Thornhill said, more emphatically than he'd intended. "I'm just trying to keep an open mind."

Kirby's face went blank – it was as though the emotions had been wiped away by a sponge. Thornhill was irritated with himself. He'd allowed his antagonism to Williamson to spill over to Kirby, which was both unfair and a tactical mistake.

"Don't misunderstand me. Ten to one Meague's got nothing to do with it." Thornhill hesitated. "But according to Mr Williamson, Jimmy Carn might be heading our way."

"The bloke they call Genghis? What's he got to do with Lydmouth?" The wariness in Kirby's face evaporated, and Thornhill mentally awarded him a good mark for the speed of his reaction. "I haven't seen anything about it in the *Police Gazette*."

"I understand it's nothing definite. But there's a chance that Charlie Meague used to work for Carn."

Kirby's forehead wrinkled. "What's the timing? Carn gets out of prison. At roughly the same time, Charlie Meague comes home to Mum. A few weeks later, there's a rumour that Carn might be coming down to Lydmouth."

"Meanwhile, Charlie gets a labouring job at Templefields."

"He's getting his hands dirty? That's a surprise."

"He was one of the men who found those bones yesterday afternoon."

Kirby leaned back in his chair and picked his teeth with a matchstick. "He could be trying to go straight. Anything's possible."

"What do they say about him in the canteen?"

"They think Charlie's as bent as a corkscrew, and always will be. But so far he's been clever enough not to get caught. Apart from his little youthful indiscretion."

"So what's he doing down here?"

Kirby dropped the match in the ashtray, picked up his glass and swallowed the last of his beer. "Either he wanted to spend more time with dear old Mumsie or he was too scared to stay in the Smoke."

"Or both."

"How about this, sir? Meague owes Carn money, which he hasn't got. Carn comes out of prison. Meague comes down here to lie low. Carn comes after him."

"Sheer speculation," Thornhill said. "But it's very tempting. Then you'd have some sort of a motive for the break-ins, too." He nodded towards Kirby's empty glass. "Want the other half?"

Thornhill took their glasses into the bar. A small crowd of men was waiting to be served. He found himself humming as he stood there, idly reading the list of darts fixtures pinned to the wall, and he recognised the tune as one he and Edith had danced to when they were courting. He felt more cheerful than he had for several days. The change of mood wasn't due to the food and drink he had consumed, which lay heavily in his stomach, but to the conversation with Kirby. He didn't yet know if he liked the man, let alone trusted him – it was too early to tell. But at least they could discuss a case like colleagues.

A man who had just been served pushed his way back to his seat. The crowd broke up and reformed. Thornhill smelled a familiar perfume.

"Yes, dear?" Gloria said, leaning the upper half of her body across the bar counter towards him. "What can I get you?"

His cheerfulness vanished. Suddenly his mouth was dry and he had to swallow. She made him feel like a sweaty little schoolboy desperate to relieve a need he hardly understood. He forced himself to look away from the straining blouse poised so invitingly near to him. Lust was a cuckoo among emotions: it tried to elbow all the others out of its way.

It wasn't his turn to be served. He was about to point this out but, when he opened his mouth to do so, his nerve deserted him. The rational part of him pointed out that Gloria was giving him preferential treatment not because she liked him but because she knew or at least guessed that he was a police officer. He didn't like her, he told himself firmly, and he didn't want her to like him.

"Same again?" she said, smiling as though there were a shared secret between them.

"Yes, please. Best bitter, I think it was."

He put the glasses on the counter and pretended to be absorbed in finding his money. He was aware of her looking at him as she drew the first pint and aware too that he desperately wanted to look at her.

"Enjoy your lunch?"

"Yes, thanks."

"We do a special on Saturday. A lovely roast and two veg. Mr Kirby used to come in with his old boss sometimes."

So Gloria knew who he was. Thornhill felt disappointed – and immediately angry with himself for the disappointment. She put the glasses on the bar and he held out a ten-shilling note.

"I can put it on the slate if you want."

"No, thanks." Thornhill took a deep breath. "I like to pay as I go."

9

Seen in silhouette at dusk, the roofs, chimneys and gables of the Rose in Hand resembled an enormous crouching animal, a magnified insect. As he passed the inn on his way home after work, Charlie Meague averted his eyes. He turned right towards Minching Lane and put the Rose behind him.

His route took him through a cluster of small factories, garages and workshops; next there were terraces of tiny cottages built of red brick, several pubs and two chapels, one with boarded-up windows. Soon he came to an older part of the Templefields where there were fewer people.

Before the war, this network of cobbled lanes and stone-flagged courts had been teeming with life. But it had not been much of a life, Charlie reminded himself, because he automatically distrusted the way memory made a paradise out of the past. Here you'd see children with rickets, with lice running through their hair. Most of the men had been out of work and they gambled for pennies on street corners, with one of their children acting as a lookout for the copper. The women were squat, muscular and almost always angry; they were more formidable than their men. On Friday and Saturday nights, there were fights – big ones involving dozens of men whose desperation was fuelled by alcohol, and the fights had often ended with blood on the cobbles and sometimes a body or two as well.

Among the poor there were gradations, just as there were among the rich. Charlie's mother had taught him that the people who lived in Minching Lane could look down, metaphorically as well as literally, on those who lived, whole families to a single room, in these decaying courts. They were rough. They were dirty. They were vulgar. The mothers weren't married to the fathers.

It was true that Charlie didn't have a father. Mr Meague had gone to look for work in 1929, probably to Birmingham, and he'd never come back – much to his wife's relief. Still, at least Charlie had known who his father was, and he'd had the reassuring knowledge during childhood that his parents had been married – and in chapel, too; he'd seen their marriage certificate which proved it. Moreover, although the Meagues had been poor, Mrs Meague was rarely short of work as a cleaner; in those days, she'd been a strong, vigorous woman who tackled the work given her if not with enthusiasm then at least with a grim determination.

Charlie entered a narrow, winding alley which led steeply uphill to Minching Lane. Halfway along, he paused and listened. He could hear nothing but the occasional car or lorry in the distance. It was strange to feel so alone in the middle of Lydmouth. Since the war, most of the inhabitants had moved out, either to Nissen huts in the former army camp on the outskirts of town or to the new housing estates. This part of Templefields was a ghost of its old self; it had reached the end of one part of its life and had yet to begin the next.

He turned right into a small yard. Tall, narrow buildings reared up in front of him and to either side. He knew from experience that the alley he had turned off magnified sound. If anyone came along it, he would hear the footsteps – unless, perhaps, the person was trying to be quiet.

Immediately to his left was a doorway. Charlie ducked under a low lintel and went down three steps into a semibasement. The room smelt of damp stones and soot. He struck a match. The floor was littered with broken glass, old newspapers and cigarette ends. Teenagers had used the place in the summer, but it was too cold for them now.

Charlie moved across the room to the fireplace. The iron range it had once contained had been ripped out. The opening itself was large and very old. He stood inside it and looked upwards, but he could not see the sky. Stretching to his full height, he felt the lip of a ledge at the back of the chimney. His fingers touched hessian.

The sack was still there. It wasn't worth getting it down. If he tried to sell the contents, he would have to do it outside Lydmouth, preferably in a city large enough to guarantee anonymity. He went back to the alley and continued on his way to Minching Lane.

The proceeds from all this danger and effort had been disappointingly meagre. A bottle of whisky, a few packets of cigarettes, a few cheap trinkets: he doubted that he could get more than twenty pounds for the lot, even if he found the right buyers. He dared not drink the spirits or smoke the cigarettes in public. Even taking them home would be asking for trouble.

Beside, twenty pounds was a drop in the ocean. Carn claimed that Charlie owed him nearly nine hundred, and Carn, for all his soft-spoken ways and his bookish tastes, was not a man to let debts slide.

Charlie wasn't afraid just for himself. If that were the case, he could emigrate – he could even make sure the police discovered that he was behind the two robberies, and so be transferred to the relative security of prison. But it wasn't that easy.

"Always concentrate on the family," Carn had said to Charlie in the days of their partnership before he had gone to prison. "It's much more sensible. Psychology, see? That's how you make a man really do his best. After all, if you take it out on *him*, you've written off all hope of that money for ever. You can get a lot of leverage with a child, you know."

A child?

At that moment, just as Charlie emerged into Minching Lane, the revelation came at last – and from a completely unexpected direction. One memory, of Carn's dry, overprecise voice laying down his rules of conduct, acted as a bait to draw another from the shadows.

Charlie remembered Tony as a child, poor kid, and how sometimes they met in the summerhouse. That was where he had seen a box like the one they had found at the Rose in Hand: in the summerhouse.

The shock of remembering was immediately overlaid by different, stronger emotions. His mother's house was just beyond the King's Head. Its single ground-floor window was dark, and that was all wrong for this time of day, at this time of year. Panic gripped him and he broke into a run.

The door was unlocked. Charlie pushed it open gently, as though there were a possibility that it might hit something breakable.

"And there's another thing," Carn used to say, "you've got to look at the wider picture. It really doesn't do to get a reputation for being soft. Gives people quite the wrong idea. If you let Tom get away with murder, then Dick and Harry will want to, too."

The door opened straight into the kitchen which was also the living room. The first thing that struck Charlie was the chill in the air. He switched on the light and kicked the door shut with his foot. He was sweating and his heart was trying to leap into his mouth.

His mother was sitting in the armchair by the range. She was shrouded with blankets. Her head was resting on one shoulder, as if the neck could no longer take the weight. Wisps of grey hair twitched in the draught from the door.

The guilt and the anger rushed over him. She was dead. That bastard Carn had found her.

Then she moved her head. "Charlie," she croaked.

"Mam? What's wrong?"

He crossed the room and took her hands. They were very cold. He felt her forehead which was burning hot. She looked at him with dull, puzzled eyes in a blue, bloated face.

"Just one of my turns," she wheezed. "You'll have to get your own tea."

"You let the fire go out, you silly woman. Why ever did you do that?"

He touched the side of the kettle and found that it was as cold as the room. She couldn't have had a warm drink since the tea she'd made before he went to work. He ran upstairs and fetched more blankets from his mother's bed.

Quickly, he riddled the grate and laid a fire. Luckily there was plenty of kindling because he'd chopped a batch the previous evening. He threw it on the fire with a reckless abandon. Yellow flames licked up the dry wood but they gave off very little heat.

"There's bread and dripping in the larder," his mother mumbled. "You'll need to buy some milk for your tea."

"You need a doctor," he said, still speaking loudly and angrily. "I'll phone from the pub."

"But you have your tea first."

"Just shut up, will you?"

"No need for a doctor. Anyway, it will cost."

"Not any longer," Charlie said.

"I don't like Dr Bayswater," his mother whined. "He's got a cold heart."

10

When Jane unbolted the door, the usual four men were waiting outside. They pushed past her and filed into the public bar of the Bathurst Arms.

There was a fifth man outside tonight: a little chap with a beard. He was carrying a book under his arm, and he wasn't in such a hurry as the regulars. He smiled at her and went into the lounge bar.

She served him first because lounge prices were higher than the ones in the public bar. It was one of her stepmother's rules, accepted as fair and reasonable by all her regular customers, that the lounge took precedence over the public. Jane suspected that most of them would have accepted it if her stepmother had said the moon was made of green cheese.

The man laid a pound note on the counter. "A large whisky, my dear."

While she was filling the glass, her stepmother came into the serving area. By the smell of her, Jane thought, she'd emptied an entire bottle of perfume over herself.

"Evening, Gloria," chorused the regulars, leaning as one man across the counter to get a better view of her.

Gloria began to take their orders. The same counter, divided in the middle by a wooden partition, served both bars.

Jane put down the whisky. "Soda, sir? Water?"

"Soda, please."

She was surprised to see that the man was looking at her, not at her stepmother. She passed him the siphon and made to take the pound note. The man put his hand on it. Startled, Jane looked up at his face and saw that he was smiling.

"I wonder if you can help me – I'm looking for a friend of mine. A man named Charlie Meague."

"Who?"

"Charlie Meague."

Suddenly her stepmother was standing beside her. "It's all right, Jane," she said grimly. "Sort them out over there. I'll deal with this gentleman."

11

Major Harcutt thought of himself, with some justification, as a man of iron routine. After supper, he would sit and work for a couple of hours; sometimes he listened to the radio or read a biography, but such indulgences were exceptional. He thought of these hours as his writing time. He had always worked best after dinner.

It was in fact some time since he had actually written any of his book. He had finished the introduction several years before and revised it twice since then. He had also mapped out the framework of the chapters. But, given the complexity of the subject, the wealth of material available and the constant stream of new discoveries, he found it necessary to devote most of his time to research.

On the evening after Inspector Thornhill's visit, he tried to follow the same routine, but with only partial success. He was not used to these interruptions – first Charlotte Wemyss-Brown and that friend of hers, and then the policeman. It had upset the whole day. He had planned to take the poppies round the village, and later to have a word with old John Veale, the secretary of the Edge Hill branch of the British Legion, about the arrangements for the Remembrance Day Parade on Sunday; but with all the excitement there simply hadn't been time.

It had been disturbing, too, to hear of the dead baby. Well, that was hardly surprising. But no historian, Harcutt told himself, could be entirely remote from his material. He had been pleased by the way he had handled the interview: the way the facts had come when he called them, marshalled in the right order. All in all, he flattered himself that he'd acquitted himself rather well. He imagined the young policeman sitting down and writing his report: 'Thanks to Major Harcutt's expert services, we can tentatively identify . . .'

It was all over now. All gone. He wondered whether they would give the bones a Christian burial.

Because of the excitement, Harcutt found it difficult to settle to his work. He had an extra drink after dinner to settle his nerves. Usually he took the dog out for her last run at ten o'clock and afterwards he would have his nightcap before going to bed. Tonight, however, he decided to take her out nearly twenty minutes before his usual time. Milly was badgering him, nuzzling his leg with her nose. The truth was, the major was restless, and his restlessness had communicated itself to the dog.

Swaying slightly, he stood by the door of the room and dressed himself in his overcoat, scarf, gloves and hat. When he opened the door, Milly slipped into the hall and pattered towards the front door. Harcutt let her outside. It was another clear, cold evening which might well bring a frost with it. The major slipped on his rubber overshoes, took his stick and walked carefully down the drive. The collie, a black shadow, zigzagged in front of him. The ruts and the puddles made the ground underfoot rather treacherous, but Major Harcutt was used to negotiating these obstacles. He had almost reached the gates before he realised that he'd left Milly's lead in the hall.

The dog was waiting patiently at the kerb.

"Good girl," the major muttered. "Daddy's pleased with you."

He'd put her on the lead when crossing the road since she was a puppy. But come to think of it, there was really no need. Milly was a well-trained animal – he'd seen to that.

"Sit," he said sternly.

Obediently she lowered her rump to the pavement. The major came towards her and laid his hand on her collar. Even at night, there was a certain amount of traffic, but at this moment the road was clear. The two of them walked across. He let go of Milly's collar and the dog loped away, her paws silent on the grass, in the direction of the church. It was very dark, apart from scattered lights in the houses fronting the green.

Today was an anticlockwise day. Harcutt marched round the green twice every day, after breakfast and after supper, and each day was either an anticlockwise day or a clockwise day.

This evening he walked quickly, keeping his ears and eyes alert for the sound of other people or other dogs. There had been one or two rather nasty incidents on the green in the past. He could not deny that, when provoked, Milly had a bit of a temper. On one occasion she'd nearly torn the ear off that nasty little mongrel belonging to the Veales who lived in the cottage nearest the church. There was also the question of dog messes. Complaints had been made to the parish council. Major Harcutt had been led to understand that several people were strongly in favour of putting up a notice on the subject.

As he was passing the Veales' cottage, their dog barked while Milly was doing her business on the grass, and the front-room curtains twitched. Milly barked back, and Harcutt had to drag her away. They completed the circuit without any other problems.

On their return, they had to wait to cross the road because several cars came along, travelling at speed in the Lydmouth direction. As they waited, Harcutt realised that there was a man standing between the gateposts of his drive. He strained to see who it was, but failed. The dog saw the man too, and wanted to investigate.

Frowning, the major crossed the road, his hand gripping Milly's collar. There was enough light to see that the man was wearing an army greatcoat. A bicycle with a basket attached to its handlebars was leaning against one of the gateposts. It did not occur to Harcutt that there might be any reason to be frightened. He had a stick and a dog, there was plenty of traffic passing and in any case he had never been a physical coward.

"Yes," he said. "What is it?"

"It's Major Harcutt, isn't it?" The voice was local, though the accent had been eroded by other influences. "I was just passing. Thought I'd look in."

"Do I know you?"

Milly growled and Harcutt tightened his grip on the dog's collar. She'd bitten people before, including the baker and the vicar, and he'd heard rumours that some people wanted her to be put down.

"You used to employ me. Remember?"

"I've employed a lot of people in my time, young man. I really can't be expected to remember every single one. Now if you'll excuse me . . ."

"No, I mean here." The man waved towards the dark block of the house. "I didn't work in one of the yards, look. I worked in your garden. Before the war, it was."

"Really?" Harcutt bent down and said to the dog: "Be quiet, miss."

"My mam helped out with the cleaning. And I was the gardener's boy."

The dog growled, but the major said nothing. Two lorries went by on the road behind him.

"It was the summer of 1938 I started. I left about a year later. Remember?"

"I most certainly do." The major's breathing had become rapid and laboured. His fingers tightened round the stick.

Charlie Meague came a step closer. He was several inches taller and Harcutt automatically took a step backwards; the dog strained to attack the visitor.

"You still interested in history, then?" Meague asked.

"Now listen to me. I don't think that's anything to do with you. It's very late and I really can't stand here talking any longer. I'll bid you goodnight."

He started up the drive, dragging the growling, reluctant dog after him.

Meague raised his voice a little so it would be audible over the engine of a passing car. "Because I thought you'd like to know I'm working on that building site at Templefields, and we found some old bones yesterday. And some other stuff. Did you hear about that?"

The major stopped.

"Thought you might like to find out what was there." Now the voice had a silky, insinuating quality. "For your book, that is. You still writing the book, are you? But if you don't want to know, well – that's up to you. I'll be off then."

The major turned back in time to see the man throw his leg over the bicycle and pedal away. As Harcutt turned, his foot slipped into a rut and he almost fell. His arms flailed as he fought to regain his balance and he lost his grip on Milly's collar.

The dog ran barking to the end of the drive and chased after the departing cyclist. A car passed, sounding its horn.

"Come here, miss. Come here!"

Harcutt broke into a stumbling run. He blundered out of the drive and on to the pavement. Meague had already cycled across the road. The red light on the back of his bicycle was moving steadily along the green; for an instant it seemed to Harcutt that Meague for some mysterious reason of his own must be tracing the route that he and Milly had taken a few minutes earlier.

The throb of another engine had been growing steadily louder for the last few seconds. As the major reached the pavement, a pair of headlights dazzled him. Only yards away was a lorry, pushing before it a cushion of air; something was rattling and flapping above the roar of the engine. The dog was not on the pavement. She was running across the road.

"Milly!"

The noise grew louder, the light became even more blinding, and the rush of oncoming air battered him. Major Harcutt ran into the road after his dog.

Part Three

Friday

1

"Brings back a few memories, eh?" Philip said as he ushered Jill towards the room where the press briefing was to take place.

"Extraordinary. It makes me feel eighteen again. I'm not sure I like it."

Philip grinned at her. "Tricky things, memories. I try and avoid them myself."

Jill had forgotten the smell of a police station. Like most people, she rarely had occasion to go into one. But once, in the years she had spent learning her trade on the *Paulstock Observer*, she had been familiar with the insides of both police stations and magistrates' courts; they had been part of her professional habitat.

The years had passed and she had changed, but the smell remained the same – and it was the smell which unlocked the memories. Lydmouth police headquarters, like other police stations in the past, was a masculine place, and it smelled of polish, sweat and tobacco. Underneath the odour of institutional authority were other, lesser smells – sour and almost feral, which reminded her of enclosed places in a zoo.

"Williamson loves to see his name in print," Philip had told her as they were driving to police headquarters. "Of course, what he'd really like is a roomful of reporters from the nationals, but beggars can't be choosers."

Philip had invited her on the grounds that a provincial press conference might amuse her. She found the assumption that she needed amusing rather disturbing. In the car, he had tactfully mentioned that the occasion was something of a novelty for him as well – usually the *Gazette*'s senior reporter would have covered the meeting. His tact was even more disturbing.

The briefing was held in what was rather grandly called the Conference Room, which was on the ground floor and at the front of the building. There were five other journalists present, ranging in age from a seventeen-year-old boy waiting to do his National Service, to an elderly man named Mr Fuggle – 'pronounced with a long "u", as in "bugle", if you please'. They treated Philip with the deference befitting a man who was not only the editor of the most influential newspaper in the area, but also married to its owner. Before the briefing began, there were murmured condolences about the *Gazette*'s senior reporter: the man himself seemed less regretted than the inconvenience that his heart attack had caused the Wemyss-Browns.

Superintendent Williamson came into the room as St John's clock was striking nine thirty. Thornhill followed, carrying a bundle of files. On being introduced to Jill, Williamson examined her with interest, his pipe poking out of the corner of his mouth at the ceiling.

"Pleasure to have you with us, Miss Francis." The pipe dipped towards her. "I hope you won't find anything too – ah – shocking."

Thornhill nodded coolly at her and smiled at Philip. If he didn't want to be friendly, Jill thought, that was his affair. He'd nicked his jaw while shaving that morning.

Once the introductions were over, Jill said very little. She sat beside Philip and kept her head down. She knew that her very presence would have an inhibiting effect on the meeting: she was the only woman present, as well as the only stranger – unless, of course, they counted their new inspector as a stranger.

"This is Inspector Richard Thornhill," Superintendent Williamson announced before he launched into the briefing itself. "He replaces our late-lamented Mr Raeburn, who, you'll be glad to hear, sends you all his best regards." He rapped his pipe vigorously on the ashtray before him. "Now let's get down to business."

He began with the burglaries at the King's Head and at Masterman's the jeweller's. He made much of the thoroughness of the police investigation so far and hinted strongly that the police knew who was responsible for them. He urged the gentlemen of the press to emphasise to their readers the importance of locking up properly at night and of depositing their valuables, where possible, in the bank.

As Williamson was talking, Philip wrote in shorthand, the hieroglyphics flowing smoothly and rapidly from the tip of his pencil. Jill glanced at the pad. He saw the direction of her gaze, grinned and added another sentence in shorthand for her benefit: "He hasn't the faintest idea who did it."

Mr Fuggle, who claimed that his hearing was not what it had been, twice asked the superintendent to repeat himself.

"Does it on purpose," Philip wrote. "Fuggle loathes Williamson."

Williamson had a sense of theatre, and he saved what he felt was the best until last. The atmosphere in the room changed when at last he moved on to the bones which had been found in Templefields. It would be inaccurate to say that the reporters showed any trace of excitement – they had their dignity to consider – but Jill sensed that their interest had sharpened, as hers would have done in their place. The discovery was a little out of the ordinary. The unusual was newsworthy.

"As you've probably heard, four workmen found some bones and one or two other items in a disused cesspit the day before yesterday. The cesspit was under one of the outbuildings belonging to what used to be the Rose in Hand public house." Williamson's voice droned like a cruising aircraft. "We've had the bones tested, of course, and I can now confirm that they definitely are human." He paused for dramatic effect. "They belonged to a baby."

Hunched over the scarred table, the reporters scribbled on their pads. Jill thought their concentration had suddenly acquired a greedy quality. The story was meat and drink to them. They were feeding off a dead baby.

Her fingernails dug into the palms of her hands. She wanted to scream at these stupid men. Although she had known in advance that the briefing would cover the bones from the Rose in Hand, she had been wrong to assume that foreknowledge would rob the story of its power to disturb her.

"I remember the Rose in Hand," Mr Fuggle said dreamily. "There used to be fights there when I was a lad. Loose women, too, I shouldn't wonder."

Jill noticed that the index finger of Thornhill's left hand was tapping on the file in front of him on the table. He darted a glance towards her.

"In the circumstances, we've found it very difficult to date the bones with any degree of accuracy," Williamson continued. "But the external evidence suggests they go back to the 1890s. We think the cesspit went out of use around the turn of the century."

"These bones," said Mr Fuggle. "Did someone say something about a box?"

"I was coming to that. We think the bones were originally in a home-made wooden box, though it's hard to be sure because the site had been disturbed."

"What was that?"

Superintendent Williamson raised his voice: "Been disturbed."

"By what?"

"God knows – some sort of animal probably."

Mr Fuggle clicked his tongue against the roof of his mouth, revealing the gleaming dentures within. "Any flesh left?"

"No. Just a few bits of bone. Nothing very impressive, I'm afraid – like something the dog digs up in the garden. Now, as well as the box we found two other items which may be associated with the bones. One was a silver brooch in the form of a clove hitch. According to the hallmark, it was made in 1882 in Birmingham. The other item was a fragment of newspaper." Williamson nodded at Philip. "Mr and Mrs Wemyss-Brown have very kindly identified this for us. It comes from the *Gazette*."

"To be honest," Philip said, "one of our copy boys did all the hard work. He spent most of yesterday ploughing through the backfile."

"Be that as it may," Williamson said, "the fragment of newspaper has been identified as belonging to the issue dated the eleventh of November, 1888."

"What was that?" Mr Fuggle asked.

"The eleventh of November, 1888," Williamson bellowed.

Mr Fuggle beamed round the table. "Remembrance Day." He fingered the poppy in his buttonhole. "Except, of course, they didn't have Remembrance Day then, did they?"

Williamson scowled at him. "Thank you, Mr Fuggle."

A man in his twenties held up his pencil. "Superintendent, are the police treating this as a crime?"

"To be frank, at the beginning we weren't quite sure how to treat it. But the weight of evidence suggests that if there was a crime, it belongs so far in the past that it's nothing to do with us. It's a job for the historian. Which brings me to my next point. Now, what I'm going to tell you isn't fact or even official opinion: it's merely personal speculation albeit based on informed knowledge. Have any of you heard of Amelia Rushwick?"

No one had, though Mr Fuggle, once the name had been repeated to him twice, thought that it rang a bell.

"She was a celebrated Victorian murderess who happened to grow up in Lydmouth. Her parents kept the Rose in Hand." Williamson paused, deliberately building up the suspense once again. "She was born in about 1870, I understand, and moved to London in the late eighties. She made her living" – another pause, during which his eyes flicked towards Jill – "as a lady of the night. In 1895, she was put on trial for murdering her own twin children so that she could run off with her fancy man – some Italian, I gather. The jury found her guilty and she was hanged." Williamson leant back in his chair. "In those days they had a pretty clear notion of what was right and what was wrong."

Jill watched Thornhill's finger tapping the time away. His head moved slightly in what might have been a shake of disagreement.

"The point is, gentlemen, here we have a woman, no better than she should be, who we know had a habit of getting rid of her

102

unwanted children. Now we find bones belonging to a baby in the place where she grew up. The evidence seems to suggest, and I won't put it more strongly than that, that the baby was put in that cesspit around the time Amelia Rushwick was living at the Rose in Hand."

"Yes, but can you prove it?" asked the young reporter.

"Of course we can't prove it." Williamson said. "But there's no real reason why we should try, is there? Given the facts we've got, I don't think anyone will seriously suggest that this could be something worth wasting more police time on. Not to mention more ratepayers' money."

"Victorian murder case," the young man muttered. "Crime of passion? Human tragedy?"

"Tragedy?" Mr Fuggle said with sudden asperity. "That's a big claim for a few scraps of bone. The woman got what she deserved, and anyway, for all we know the baby at the Rose in Hand was stillborn."

Williamson produced the rest of the information he had about Amelia Rushwick, including the reference to *Notable British Trials*.

"Most impressive, Superintendent," Mr Fuggle murmured. "Where did you get all this from? Or are *Notable British Trials* your usual bedtime reading?"

Williamson looked disconcerted as though reluctant to allow that anyone else had had a hand in amassing the information. "Inspector Thornhill here interviewed an old gentleman called Major Harcutt. Some of you may know him."

"Harcutt," said Mr Fuggle, "and Son."

"Eh?"

"They used to be coal merchants before the war. Big firm."

"Yes, well. I understand that this Harcutt, Major Harcutt, is something of an authority on Victorian Lydmouth."

"What was that?" Mr Fuggle asked, patting his jacket pockets.

"I said, he's something of an authority on Victorian Lydmouth."

"Is, did you say?" said Mr Fuggle. "Or was? Ah, here it is." He drew out a battered cigarette case.

Williamson frowned. "What do you mean?"

"You haven't heard?"

Mr Fuggle selected a cigarette, tapped it on the case and put it in his mouth. There was a further delay as he tried to get his lighter to work. Two of his colleagues offered him a match.

"As far as I'm aware, Major Harcutt is alive and well," the superintendent said, allowing a note of sarcasm to creep into his voice.

Fuggle allowed himself a short burst of coughing before speaking.

"It's only that there was some sort of an accident last night at Edge Hill. I heard them talking about it in the office just before I came here. A lorry, I think they said." He coughed again. "Dear me, this weather does terrible things to the chest. Yes, a lorry knocked someone down, I understand. I think the name was Harcutt. It was certainly Major somebody."

"Thank you, Mr Fuggle. I expect my colleagues in Traffic can bring me up-to-date on this."

Soon afterwards, the press briefing ended. As the reporters filed out of the Conference Room, Jill glanced at her watch: it was almost ten thirty. She hoped Philip wouldn't linger. He and Williamson were chatting by the window, which was streaked with rain. Outside in the High Street, drably dressed shoppers scurried from one shelter to another under a grey sky.

"And how's Bunty?" Philip was asking Williamson, his face alive with sympathy. Philip had the knack of sounding concerned about other people's personal problems.

The only other person still in the room was Inspector Thornhill who was sitting at the table annotating a file and taking care to avoid meeting anyone's eyes. Jill pretended an intense interest in the portrait of a Victorian chief constable which hung above the chimneypiece. She was close enough to hear Thornhill's breathing. Suddenly it struck her as ridiculous and humiliating that she should have to pretend to do anything just to avoid talking to a man.

On impulse, she turned away from her contemplation of the portrait and said: "What will happen now?"

His head jerked up, and she saw the surprise in his eyes.

"I mean, what happens in these cases? Who decides to close the investigation? And are the bones formally buried?"

"I'm not really sure. This is the first time I've been involved in something like this. I imagine Mr Williamson will discuss it with the chief constable."

"The brooch makes it odd, doesn't it?" She was finding it hard to say what she meant this morning.

"Yes, that occurred to me." he said, and for an instant his face lost its closed and cautious expression. "It makes it hard to write off Amelia Rushwick simply as a monster."

She blinked, unwilling to accept that he had followed her line of thought so closely. "If the baby and the brooch were hers, it's as if by burying them together she's burying the relationship too."

He nodded. "Yes – the brooch must have had a cash value. Yet she threw it away as if she couldn't bear to keep it."

Williamson glanced over his shoulder. "Ah. Sounds as if we have an amateur trick cyclist on the force." Smiling broadly, he turned back to Philip. "They're everywhere. you know. We don't have original sin these days – we don't even have crime. All we have are unfortunate members of society whose mothers didn't cuddle them enough when they were babies. That's why they cosh old ladies and nick their handbags. Simple, isn't it? You wonder why no one ever noticed it before."

With jovial efficiency, Superintendent Williamson herded them out of the Conference Room. Jill glanced back as she and Philip were walking down the steps from the front door. In the reception hall, Williamson was saying something in a rapid undertone to Thornhill, who had his back to the doorway. Williamson's face had lost its appearance of good humour.

In the High Street, she and Philip waited at the kerb to cross the road; the Rover was parked on the other side.

Philip threw the car keys into the air and caught them. "What did you think of Williamson?"

"Formidable."

"He's a useful friend," Philip said, "and a very bad enemy."

2

The Royal Air Force Hospital was in Chepstow Road on the outskirts of town. Shortly before eleven o'clock Dr Bayswater drove past the guardhouse and up the approach road at precisely three times the maximum speed laid down by the RAF's mandatory signs. In front of the main entrance a permanently grounded Spitfire pointed its nose in the general direction of Birmingham. Beside it stood a pole, at the top of which a bedraggled RAF flag snapped and cracked in the wind. The hospital was a long, low, brick building which had developed wings in unexpected places during the twelve years of its life. By arrangement with the Regional Hospital Board, civilian patients were treated there as well as service personnel.

A dwindling practice had its advantages: among them was the fact that it afforded Bayswater more leisure. By half past ten, he had seen all the patients waiting in his surgery. Since then he had taken care of his house calls – three in number that morning, and as usual conducted with speed as his priority rather than any desire to develop an unwanted reputation for having a good bedside manner. His last visit had been to a house in Chepstow Road itself, so it had not taken him long to reach the hospital.

He left the Wolseley in the area of the car park reserved for consultants. He had little time for medical men in the services, partly on the grounds that they typically gave themselves airs because they wore uniforms to which they were only nominally entitled. In Bayswater's view, they had a foot in two camps and belonged in neither: he expected them to be poor doctors and poor servicemen. He marched through the swing doors into the hospital. The man on reception duty looked up.

"Where have they put that Meague woman?"

The clerk consulted his notes. "Ward Eight, Doctor. And we've got another of your patients here. A Major Harcutt."

"Who? Oh – I know. What's wrong with him?"

"I believe he was involved in some sort of road accident. He's in Ward Eleven."

Bayswater grunted, a sound that might have been meant to express gratitude or disapproval or irritation. He set off along the corridor to the right of the reception desk. The hospital was characterised by long, straight corridors with large, metal-framed windows which made them hot in summer and freezing in winter.

Ward Eight was reserved for women. Bayswater poked his head into the sister's office. He liked the look of her: she was a slim, pretty woman whose head was dwarfed by the absurd square headdress they made her wear.

"Good morning. Dr Bayswater, isn't it?"

"You've got Mrs Meague here, I believe. How is she this morning?"

"Poorly, I'm afraid. We're treating it as acute bronchopneumonia, but the antibiotics haven't had time to take effect. She's there." The sister nodded through the window of her office which looked out into the communal section of the ward – a long, high-ceilinged room with twenty beds. Margaret Meague was in the nearest bed, the top of which was shrouded in an oxygen tent.

Accompanied by the sister, Bayswater approached the bed. Mrs Meague was lying on her back, apparently asleep. Her breathing was like a dog's panting after exercise and her skin was still badly cyanosed despite the steady flow of oxygen.

Bayswater glanced at the notes at the foot of the bed. Her temperature had been 102 degrees earlier in the morning. They were giving her Aureomycin, but he knew as well as the sister that there was a significant chance that the antibiotics had come too late to help.

"She was worried about her son during the night," the sister said. "Apparently she tried to get up and cook him his tea. Actually got out of bed and collapsed on the floor."

"Silly woman. I'll look in again this evening or perhaps tomorrow."

Dr Bayswater set off for Ward Eleven. He was in sight of the doors leading to the ward when a voice from behind hailed him.

"Dr Bayswater, are you going to see Jack Harcutt?"

Bayswater turned. Charlotte Wemyss-Brown was advancing down the corridor towards him. Too much fat, he thought, and the fur coat made her look like a grizzly bear.

"How is he?" she asked.

"How should I know? I haven't seen him yet."

"Now, now." Charlotte waved her finger at him. "You mustn't be tetchy with me."

"I only heard he was here when I got to the hospital this morning."

"Philip heard about it at the police station. Some sort of road accident, I understand. I phoned the hospital, but they didn't seem to know anything. It's so hard to find anyone who understands plain

English these days, don't you find? One has to be on the spot if one wants to get any information or anything done."

Dr Bayswater was not the sort of man who habitually opens doors for ladies. But Charlotte paused at the entrance to the ward, fixed him with her eyes and simply waited. Before he knew what he was doing, he pulled open a leaf of the doors and stood back against the wall.

A nurse poked her head out of the sister's office beside the doors. She was a heavy-built woman with red hair and glasses. "I'm sorry but it isn't visiting hours now. If you'd like to come back this afternoon . . ."

"You're obviously new here, dear," Charlotte said kindly. "This is Dr Bayswater who has come to see one of his patients – Major Harcutt. Where's Sister?"

"She'll be back in a moment. She—"

"I'm Mrs Wemyss-Brown, and the major's a very old friend. The major needs me to make certain arrangements on his behalf."

"I see." The colour rose in the nurse's cheeks, but she was not foolish enough to apologise. "In that case, would you wait while I fetch his notes." She slipped back into the office.

Charlotte hissed in Bayswater's ear: "Gone to make sure you really are his GP."

Bayswater ignored her. He began to saunter down the corridor.

The nurse returned with a brown Manila envelope. "This way, please."

"What exactly is wrong with him?" Charlotte asked.

"He's sprained his left ankle. Apart from that, there's a certain amount of bruising. He's really very lucky it was no worse. Of course, for a man of that age the shock itself isn't easy to cope with."

"Twaddle," Bayswater said absently, as if most of his attention was elsewhere. "Depends on the man and depends on the nature of the shock."

The nurse's colour deepened still more. She stopped by one of the doors and peered through the small window set in it at eye level. "He's awake." She pushed open the door and twisted her features into a toothy smile. "You've got some visitors, Major."

Harcutt was lying on his back in the high hospital bed and smoking a cigarette. He had the room to himself. One of the many things Bayswater disliked about Lydmouth RAF Hospital was its habit of forcing civilians to conform to the hierarchical absurdities of service life. Anyone whom the hospital authorities deemed to be an officer, active or retired, had a far better chance of a bed in one of the smaller wards than most other patients. Harcutt had been staring at the ceiling, but his eyes slid towards the door as it opened.

"Charlotte," he said. For a second, his mouth worked, as though he were chewing something. "I want to go home."

"So you shall, Jack."

"I have to sort out the poppies. Everyone's depending on me."

"I'm sure we'll manage somehow. Now, Dr Bayswater's come to look at you. Isn't that kind?"

Harcutt stubbed out the cigarette in the ashtray. "There's no reason why I shouldn't discharge myself, is there?"

"It's up to you," Bayswater said. "No one can stop you making a bloody fool of yourself if you want to."

"But there's nothing really wrong with me. Just a few bruises."

"You needed a wheelchair this morning," the red-haired nurse said. "You had to be helped in and out of bed."

Bayswater waved her aside. "Let's see this ankle of yours."

"Would you like me out of your way?" Charlotte asked, meaning the question to be rhetorical.

"Yes," Bayswater said.

Charlotte compromised by standing just outside the door while Bayswater skimmed through Harcutt's notes and examined the injured ankle. She could see what was happening and hear everything that was said because the door wasn't closed; her foot was in the way.

"Let's have a look at the bruises now," Bayswater ordered.

Harcutt unbuttoned his pyjama jacket. Charlotte caught a glimpse of his scraggy chest with the blue and purple smudges of the bruises, the points of the collarbones pricking against the pale skin and a mat of dirty grey hair below the neck. How very different from Philip's pink and well-fleshed body. Of course, Harcutt was in his sixties, to all intents and purposes an old man. She forced herself to look away. There was something dreadfully unpleasant about old bodies.

"All right. Do yourself up." Bayswater handed the notes to the nurse. "What happened, exactly?"

"I was walking Milly." Harcutt shut his eyes and the eyelids fluttered. "That's the dog. Let me get this straight. We'd gone round the green. You know the green at Edge Hill? Went back across the road. For once, Milly wasn't on the lead. Well-trained dog."

There was a long pause. Harcutt had finished buttoning up his pyjama jacket, so Charlotte judged that the professional part of the consultation was over. She slipped back into the room.

"And then what?" Bayswater prompted.

The major shook his head wearily. "Milly must have heard something on the green. Anyway, she ran across the road. You know what dogs are like when they're chasing something. Talk about single-minded . . . Anyway, there was a lorry. Travelling ridiculously fast. It's against the law, of course, but the police don't give a damn."

He groped for his cigarettes. Charlotte came forward with a match. His hand was trembling so much that she had to steady it with hers.

"I tried to stop her. Christ, I tried. She went under the front offside wheel. And the lorry nearly got me too. Just jumped back in time. Not as young as I was. Came a cropper. And Milly – it didn't seem possible, somehow. Still doesn't."

"Your dog's dead, then?"

"Of course she's bloody dead. That's what I'm telling you. Anyway, she wasn't my dog. She was Tony's."

"Who's he?"

Charlotte coughed. "She, actually. Antonia's the major's daughter. I imagine she must have been one of your patients at one time."

"Then you imagine wrong."

"Of course she hasn't lived in Lydmouth for ages, has she, Jack? Not since before the war." Charlotte smiled sweetly at Bayswater. "Perhaps you simply don't remember."

"Nothing wrong with my memory, thank you." Bayswater looked at Harcutt. "They'll probably want to keep you in for a few days. Best place for you to be."

"I want to go home," said the major obstinately.

"Use your common sense. You live in that big place on the main road, don't you? Have you got anyone living in?"

Harcutt shook his head.

"I thought not. The state you're in, you'll need someone around for a few days, if not weeks. And when I say days I mean all twenty-four hours' worth. Can you afford a nurse?"

Harcutt brushed ash from the sheet and said nothing.

Bayswater sighed. "Well, if you're determined to discharge yourself, get your daughter to come and stay. That's the best thing. At least you won't have to pay her."

"I don't want her to come," Harcutt said pettishly. "Besides, she won't be able to. She's got a job."

"But, Jack," Charlotte said. "This is an emergency. Family comes first where a woman's concerned – you know that. Anyway, you'll need to let her know what's happened. Where does she work?"

"School near Newport. Dampier Hall."

"The place for handicapped girls? I know. I'm sure they'd—"

"I don't want her disturbed. I can manage perfectly well by myself."

"Aren't you being just a little bit unreasonable, Jack?"

Harcutt's face darkened. He twisted round to stub out his cigarette and knocked the ashtray to the floor.

"Whoopsy," the nurse said brightly. "I'll get a dustpan and brush."

No one spoke. She left the room.

"Look here, Harcutt. If you want to make a fool of yourself that's up to you. But you're better off here, believe me. Good day to you."

"Now don't worry, Jack," Charlotte said. "I'm sure we can sort something out. I'll be back."

She followed Bayswater down the corridor, passing the red-haired nurse who was hurrying back with the dustpan and brush. "Try to keep him calm," Charlotte advised the nurse as she passed. "I won't be a moment."

Bayswater was already through the first set of swing doors. He was walking quickly and Charlotte had to hurry to catch him up.

"I think the kindest thing to do," she said breathlessly, "is to contact Antonia ourselves. Don't you agree?"

"Nothing to do with me."

"Oh, but it is. Major Harcutt's one of your patients, after all."

"That doesn't mean I'm responsible for all the lunacies he's capable of."

"But you agree that he needs someone looking after him?"

"Of course I do. I thought I'd made that perfectly clear."

"Thank you so much for your help," Charlotte said. "Goodbye."

She walked thoughtfully back to Harcutt's room where the red-haired nurse was on her knees, sweeping up the contents of the ashtray. Harcutt was making a strange grunting noise and his face was screwed up. For an instant, Charlotte hovered in the doorway, wondering what was happening and whether it would be embarrassing and not the kind of thing she would care to witness. Neither of them saw her.

"What is it, Major?" the nurse asked.

"Nothing. I've got a bit of ash in my eye."

3

All morning, rain-laden squalls gusted out of the grey sky. By midday, the damp had seeped through Charlie Meague's jacket and his cap was as wet as a sponge.

Together with Evans, Emrys Hughes and Frank Thomas, he had spent the morning stripping the roof from the back of the Rose in Hand. The slates were in relatively good condition. Cyril George was not a man to buy new materials when old ones would do.

The four of them joined the other men drifting towards the warehouse for their sandwiches. To the east, there was a strip of duck-green sky between the horizon and the mass of grey clouds above with smudges of mauve moving slowly across the green. Charlie quickened his pace and caught up with Evans just as they were going into the warehouse.

"My mum's up the RAF Hospital."

Evans glanced at him but did not stop. "Why?"

"They reckon it might be pneumonia."

"Sorry to hear that."

They went into the warehouse. Evans sat down on a packing case and opened his bag. He had a Thermos flask, sandwiches wrapped in greaseproof paper and an apple. Charlie waited, looming over him.

"Not much fun for anyone," Evans went on. "It's the time of year. Terrible month for germs, November."

"The visiting hours are between two and four this afternoon."

Evans looked up, a sandwich halfway to his mouth. "So that's what's on your mind."

"I've got a bike. I could be there in ten or fifteen minutes. I don't think I'd stay long. I'll work late."

"How do I know that this isn't some cock-and-bull story?"

"You could check with the hospital. Or with Dr Bayswater."

"Why should I want to do that? It's not *my* mother."

Charlie pulled out his tobacco and began to roll a cigarette with hands that trembled a little. "Look, I'll make it up. You won't lose by it. Nor will Mr George."

"That's not the point, is it? The point is, I can't be sure you're not taking me for a ride. Do they have different visiting hours on different days?"

Charlie shrugged. "Between seven and eight tomorrow evening."

"Well – there you are – no problem, is there? How long is she going to be in there?"

"I don't know."

"If you want to take time off for visiting her during the working day, Meague, you get yourself a letter from Bayswater or from the hospital. It's like the Boy Scouts say: be prepared."

Charlie licked the edge of the cigarette paper and gummed it down. He put the cigarette in his mouth and lit it. The desperation inside him came to the boil.

Evans put down his sandwich, unscrewed the cap of his Thermos and poured himself a cup of tea. "Is there anything else?"

"You're a little shit," Charlie said in a conversational tone. "But I expect you already knew that."

Evans's head snapped up. There was a sudden silence throughout the warehouse. Though neither Evans nor Charlie had been speaking loudly, the other men knew that something was happening – something that might break the monotony of work. Neither Evans nor Charlie was popular. From the audience's point of view, a fight between them would be an unalloyed pleasure.

There was a noise in the yard – footsteps on the asphalt.

Both Evans and Charlie glanced towards the doorway. Two men were standing there. The smaller, older one looked like some sort of clerk – a surveyor perhaps. The younger was a broad-shouldered young man with fair hair. His overcoat was open, and he had his hands in his pockets and his hat on the back of his head. Charlie hadn't seen either of them before, but the younger man's smile, smug and superior, gave him a clue about the men's identity before anyone spoke.

Had someone seen him last night? Had Harcutt talked? Or was Harcutt dead?

"Mr Evans," said the older man. "Good morning. Sorry to break in while you're eating."

Evans stood up. "What can we do for you?"

"I understand you have a Mr Meague working here. I'd like a word with him."

Charlie's adrenaline was already running high: he was keyed up for violence; he even wanted it, because the strain of not knowing – about his mother as well as about Harcutt – was becoming unendurable. For an instant, everyone was absolutely still. Charlie's eyes darted to and fro and the possibilities surged through his mind.

113

He'd have to go through the doorway and the two busies were there. And Evans could be relied on to do his little bit from the rear. Don't be stupid, he told himself: that's just what the bastards want. They'd give him a bloody nose, stuff him in a cell and throw away the key.

He raised his hand in a half-salute. "What do you want?"

"Just a chat," the man said. "If Mr Evans can spare you."

"I can do that all right," Evans said, glancing at Charlie. "No problem. Off you go."

The elder of the two policemen cocked his head and looked at Charlie with bright eyes. "Let's go for a walk, eh?"

The three of them moved towards the lane. Charlie was conscious of Evans and the rest of the bumpkins staring after him.

"I'm Inspector Thornhill. This is Sergeant Kirby."

"Pleased to meet you." Charlie paused to let the sarcasm sink in. "I'm sure."

Thornhill made no reply. He led the way into the lane and turned in the direction of the back gates to the Rose in Hand.

Charlie said. "Where are we going? I don't have to come with you, do I? Not unless—"

Kirby stopped abruptly, and laid his hand on Charlie's arm. "Unless what?"

"It doesn't matter."

Thornhill sauntered a few steps up the lane; he appeared not to have heard. "Is that the Rose in Hand over there?" he asked, looking back.

Kirby released Charlie, who nodded at Thornhill.

"I thought it was. Still getting my bearings around here. You were one of the men who found the bones, weren't you?"

"Me and three others." Charlie felt dismay creeping over him. "Why?"

"They've caused quite a stir. You'll get your name in the *Gazette*, I shouldn't wonder."

"That won't do me much good."

"Nothing else was there, I suppose? Besides the newspaper and the brooch. Nothing that could have belonged with the box?"

"I don't know. Ask Evans."

Thornhill nodded, his face serious and calm. "Yes, good idea."

Charlie flicked his cigarette butt away. He was beginning to relax. The buggers were fishing – didn't know what they were looking for. *As long as Harcutt hadn't talked*. The three of them walked on, passing the rear gates to the Rose in Hand. The lane began to move uphill towards Minching Lane. This was the route Charlie usually took to walk home.

"You and your mother use the King's Head a good deal," Thornhill said; it was not a question. "Very convenient for you. Practically next door."

Charlie grunted. So that was it: Ma Halleran had been stirring it. "You must know Mrs Halleran very well."

"What do you think?"

Thornhill sighed. "What I think is neither here nor there. It's what I can prove that counts."

They walked on in a silence that grew a little more awkward with every step. Thornhill was in front of Charlie and Kirby was a pace behind. By now they were within a stone's throw of the derelict building where Charlie had hidden the proceeds of his burglaries. He wanted to hurry past the entrance to the courtyard. Instead he made himself slow down.

"How long has your mother been a cleaner?" Kirby asked.

Hair prickled on the back of Charlie's neck. "As long as I can remember."

"Your dad walked out on you when you were a kid, didn't he? Maybe that's when she started."

"Maybe."

Kirby quickened his step and came alongside Charlie. "Worked for Mrs Halleran once, didn't she? A few years back, during the war."

"What are you trying to say?"

"I like to get the full picture. Surprising what you pick up sometimes. She used to work for Mr Masterman, too?"

"Who?"

"Come on, Charlie. You know Masterman. Chap who's got a jeweller's on Lyd Street. Got turned over the other night. Someone hit him over the head."

"Oh, yeah. *That* Masterman."

"Bit of a coincidence," Kirby went on. "I wonder who else your mother has worked for. Must ask her some time."

"You do that."

The idea of it worried Charlie enormously. His mother would go to pieces if they started to question her, especially in her present condition. The bastards wouldn't wait: they wouldn't give a damn that she was ill. The first name they'd dig up would be Mrs Wemyss-Brown's, and that would lead to the business with the silver box.

Thornhill came out into Minching Lane and stopped. "Seen your friend Carn lately?"

"Who?"

"Your friend Jimmy Carn," Thornhill said. "Or maybe you called him Genghis."

"He's no friend of mine."

"You don't know him?"

"I didn't say that. I know a lot of people. I said he wasn't a friend of mine."

"So you do know him?"

"I might have bumped into him."

"You might indeed," Thornhill agreed. "After all, you shared a flat in Pimlico with him for three months."

Charlie shrugged, acknowledged partial defeat. "I didn't see much of him. It was a business arrangement."

"It certainly was. Carn sublet that flat to at least nine different people. Simultaneously. And he took a nonreturnable deposit from each of them."

"Nothing to do with me, was it?"

"Maybe not. Carn's out of prison now." Thornhill stared up at Charlie. "But you know that, don't you?"

"Why should I?"

"News gets around. Carn's a nasty man to cross. But I dare say you know that, too."

Thornhill started walking again in the direction of the Meagues' house and the King's Head. He no longer seemed so meek and mild.

"Where are we going?" Charlie asked.

Sergeant Kirby fell into step beside him. "Thought we'd pay a call on your old mum. See if she can remember who she's worked for over the years."

"You're out of luck."

"Why's that, Charlie?"

"She's in hospital, that's why. Pneumonia."

"We still might have to see her. Which ward's she in? Who's her GP? How long's she been ill for?"

Charlie reluctantly told him.

"I don't think we need keep you any longer," said Thornhill. He added, with that unnerving politeness of his, "Thank you for your help, Mr Meague."

Charlie, breathing heavily as though he had been running, watched the two policemen strolling down Minching Lane. They glanced at the Meagues' house as they passed. A moment later, they turned off in the direction of the town centre.

It could have been worse. They obviously suspected he might have done the burglaries; they even suspected why; but they couldn't prove a thing, even if they talked to his mother, unless they found a trace of him at Masterman's or the King's Head, or unless they found the stolen goods and were able to connect them with him. So far they had found neither, otherwise they would have arrested him.

He was safe, so long as he kept his head and did nothing stupid. The big relief was that Harcutt hadn't talked: he hadn't told the police of

Charlie's conversation with him the previous evening. But *why* hadn't Harcutt talked?

He came to a decision. The police had given him a few minutes' grace, so he might as well make good use of them. A moment later he was in the hallway of the King's Head.

On either side were doors to the bars; in front of him was the telephone. He could hear Ma Halleran's voice raised in argument – probably with her son Mike who was weak in the upper storey, a circumstance his mother found infuriating. Charlie found a couple of pennies and fumbled through the telephone directory until he found the number of the RAF Hospital.

"Major Harcutt?" said a refined and adenoidal voice at the hospital switchboard. "One moment – yes, he's in Ward Eleven. I can put you through to the ward, if you'd like."

A door opened; Ma Halleran came into the hall and stood there, arms akimbo, staring at Charlie.

"Hello?" said the switchboard operator. "Hello, caller? Hello?"

Charlie put down the phone.

"What are you doing here?" Mrs Halleran asked. "I thought you had a job to go to."

He smiled at her. "How many cases of Scotch did you say you lost the other night? Three was it? Is that what you told the police?"

Smiling to himself, he slipped out of the pub and walked back to the Rose in Hand. He was feeling more cheerful. Harcutt was alive. And he hadn't told the police about meeting him. So maybe there was still hope.

At the warehouse, the men were still having their dinner. But he knew at once by the silence that something had happened, or was about to happen. He saw Evans standing just inside the doorway. Beside him was the burly figure of Cyril George.

"I want a word with you," George said to Charlie. "Outside."

Charlie backed into the yard. George, hands in pockets, came after him, followed by Evans.

"You're sacked," George said. "Come and get your cards and your money."

"Why?"

"I don't like troublemakers."

George set off across the yard without a backward glance.

"Come on, Charlie," Evans said, smiling and rubbing his big, capable hands together. "Don't want to keep the man waiting, do we?"

4

Sometimes Antonia Harcutt had lunch in the dining hall, but more usually she brought sandwiches and ate them at her desk. Her desk was in the outer office – more of a glorified corridor, really – which guarded the approach to the warden's study. Miss Plimfield always had lunch with the staff and the girls. The advantage of eating in the office was that it allowed Antonia to do crossword puzzles while she ate; and, of course, her reference books were at hand if she happened to need them.

The phone rang while Antonia was eating her second Spam sandwich and wondering whether there were five or six Great Lakes in Canada. The ringing startled her, for it was unusual to have a telephone call at this time. As she seized the handset, a piece of meat slipped from the sandwich and fell on her lap.

"Good morning, that is, good afternoon," she mumbled. "The Dampier Hall School for Handicapped Girls."

"Good afternoon." The voice was female and accustomed to command. "Could I speak to Antonia Harcutt?"

"Oh, yes, that's me." Antonia realised that she should have said 'I', not 'me', but then she would have sounded pretentiously pedantic, so really one couldn't win.

"Good. This is Charlotte Wemyss-Brown."

The name was familiar, but Antonia couldn't place it. The failure brought her to the edge of panic. "I'm afraid I . . ."

"You remember. We were at school together." There was, Antonia thought, a hint of impatience in the voice. "You were a few years younger than me. I was Charlotte Wemyss then, of course."

"Oh, *yes*." To her great relief, Antonia's memory began to work again. "You were head girl, weren't you?"

There was a chuckle at the other end of the line. "For my sins."

All the prefects had worn purple badges on their navy-blue tunics, but only the head girl had a canary yellow sash as well. Charlotte Wemyss had inspired more fear in Antonia than most of the teachers. Charlotte had been a buxom girl with an implacable sense of what was

118

due to her authority. Hadn't she won an exhibition to Oxford just before the war? And her father had owned the *Gazette*.

"You lived at Troy House, didn't you?"

"Still do. Listen, I'm afraid I've got some bad news. Your father's had an accident."

Antonia stared with round, fascinated eyes at the moist pink triangle of meat which lay on the tweed of her skirt. *He's dead, he's dead, he's dead.*

"Nothing to worry about, thankfully. Bruising, sprained ankle, that sort of thing."

She swallowed. "What happened?"

"He was nearly knocked down by a lorry last night. Just managed to jump clear in time. But I'm afraid Milly wasn't so lucky."

"The *dog's* dead?"

"I'm so sorry, dear. I understand she was yours."

"Milly wasn't mine."

"Oh." After the briefest of hesitations. Charlotte made a sound like a muted whinny and plunged on: "He's in the RAF Hospital for a night or two. But he hopes to get out tomorrow. So when can you come?"

"What?"

"He's desperate to get home, poor man, and really he's in no state to manage by himself yet. I gather that – ah – professional help is out of the question. Besides. I think he's feeling very fragile. You're the only person he can call on."

"Are you sure he wants me? Did he say—"

"Of course he wants you. He *needs* you."

"But we're far too busy here. It's the middle of term." Antonia hesitated, aware that her voice was sounding breathless. "I wouldn't be able to get the time off."

"Oh, I don't think that would be a problem," Charlotte said, as implacable now as she had been as a girl. "It's a family emergency, after all. And it's not as if you're a businessman running a company or something." A laugh set the telephone's earpiece vibrating. "Don't worry, Antonia, let me have a word with the warden. I'm sure Miss Plimfield will understand.

"You know her?"

"I've met her once or twice at Red Cross meetings. Is she there?"

"No, she's having lunch." Antonia picked up the piece of Spam and laid it on her plate. "But anyway, it's quite out of the question."

5

"In Lydmouth," Williamson said, waving his fork for emphasis, "there's no such thing as a coincidence. Or rather, it's *all* coincidence. Everyone knows everyone else. Pass the sauce."

Thornhill pushed the bottle across the table. "But the fact that Mrs Meague once worked for them is still a common factor between Mrs Halleran and Mr Masterman."

"Doesn't mean it's significant." Williamson picked up the sauce and added, to Thornhill's surprise, "Thank you."

"Also, we know that Meague may need money, if there's any truth in this Carn business. And finally, Charlie Meague's up to something, I'm sure. He was *relieved* when we went."

Williamson upended the bottle of brown sauce over his mixed grill and hammered the palm of his hand on to the base. "As if he was expecting you to ask him about something else?"

"Yes. Or as if he wasn't sure what we knew or what we could prove. And by the end he seemed almost pleasantly surprised."

With a soft, squelching noise, a dollop of sauce shot out of the bottle and landed on Williamson's lamb chop. "Could be something or nothing. He's the type who'd act guilty anyway, who probably *is* guilty of something or other."

For a moment they ate in silence with the clatter of the police canteen around them. So far, the meal had been an unexpectedly amicable affair. Williamson, mellowed by the food, ate quickly and efficiently as though against the clock. He finished in first place by at least a dozen mouthfuls. He sat back, wiped his mouth surreptitiously on the back of his hand and started to assemble his smoking equipment.

"Do a damn good mixed grill here," he said. "About the only thing they can do. You know that woman?"

"Which one?"

"The one at the briefing, of course. Little Miss What's-her-name."

"Jill Francis. She's staying with the Wemyss-Browns – I met her the evening before last."

"Good-looker. Wemyss-Brown told me she is a journalist from London. Might be the start of national interest in that Rushwick business." The superintendent's eyes gleamed. "Could need careful handling. Leave her to me, all right?"

"Yes, sir. But I don't think she was working."

"Journalists are always working. If you hear anything about her, I'd like to know. Try and sound out Wemyss-Brown if you see him." Williamson scowled, his memory drifting back to the press briefing. "That bastard Fuggle."

"Is he always like that?" Thornhill said, with real sympathy.

"Sometimes he's worse. That reminds me. Young Porter had a word with Harcutt about the accident this morning. On the surface it seems quite straightforward. But I had a look at the report from the local constable at Edge Hill. There was a witness. A Mrs Veale, some sort of neighbour. No love lost between her and Harcutt. The interesting thing is, she says she saw someone talking to him just before he was knocked down."

"Who?"

Williamson shrugged. "How do I know? Lorry driver didn't see anyone. Harcutt didn't mention it to Porter either. But Mrs Veale reckons they were having some sort of quarrel. She says the dog was barking its head off. Then the man rode off on a bike and the dog chased across the road after him."

"So that's what caused the accident?"

"If Mrs Veale can be believed."

"Where was the man going? Towards Edge Hill church?"

"There's a lane goes off by the church. You can get back to town that way. So what's Harcutt up to?"

Thornhill pushed his plate away and frowned. He watched Williamson who was fiddling with the poppy in his buttonhole. The poppy reminded Thornhill of his interview with Harcutt and reminded him how the old man had knocked the tray of poppies to the floor. That in turn reminded him of another niggle. Thornhill had registered it in passing during his visit to Chandos Lodge the previous day – an unexplained piece of knowledge, tiny and perhaps not mysterious at all. It certainly wasn't substantial enough to share, least of all with a man like Williamson.

"There's no obvious sense to it," Thornhill murmured. "Unless Porter didn't give him the opportunity to mention the man on the bike."

"He says he specifically asked Harcutt whether he'd seen anyone just before the accident. Apparently there may be some question about insurance – the lorry skidded into a wall."

"I suppose he could just be covering up a quarrel or something – it's not necessarily suspicious. Maybe Harcutt found the whole thing embarrassing. Maybe he simply forgot."

"Then why don't you jog his memory?" Williamson said.

6

Miss Plimfield and Charlotte Wemyss-Brown arranged it between them; Antonia had nothing to do with it. Antonia thought that the two older women enjoyed showing how kind and helpful they were. The fact that their kindness and their help were a form of bullying escaped them entirely.

"You must stay as long as he needs you," Miss Plimfield announced after she had talked to Charlotte. "After all, who better than a daughter to look after a father?"

"But the work – who'll do it?" Antonia asked, wondering whether Miss Plimfield were trying to get rid of her.

"Don't worry about that. We'll cope. No one's indispensable." Miss Plimfield gave a trill of laughter and added without conviction, "Even me."

Antonia knew from experience that no one else would do the work in her absence. When she had been forced to take ten days off with flu the previous year, she had returned to find her filing system reduced to chaos, her appointments diary missing and herself held directly to blame for Miss Plimfield's inability to organise herself and the school.

"Mrs Wemyss-Brown will collect you at three thirty, Antonia. You've plenty of time to pack a suitcase. Off you go."

With the exception of Miss Plimfield, the staff slept on the top floor in what had been the servants' bedrooms when Dampier Hall was a private house. Antonia had a small, north-facing room with a sloping ceiling and a dormer window overlooking the kitchen garden. She lifted her suitcase down from the top of the wardrobe and packed, swiftly and efficiently.

The rooms of her colleagues were full of personal touches – pictures, photographs, ornaments, books, bedspreads and rugs – but Antonia kept hers as bare as she could. Sometimes she would sit on her bed and look slowly round the room, relishing its secure impersonality; a stranger could have learned nothing about her from her surroundings. The room was like a layer of insulation guarding her privacy. At one time she had been attracted to the idea of becoming a nun. but in the end she had decided that her inability to believe in God would present an insuperable obstacle.

She was ready before three o'clock, which gave her time to set her desk in order and leave a note for Miss Plimfield. By a quarter past three Antonia had settled down to wait among the clutter of wheelchairs in the hall. Charlotte might be early. It would never do to keep her waiting.

Just before three thirty, she heard an engine outside. She picked up her case and opened the heavy front door. A navy-blue car rolled to a halt. A slim, elegant woman got out. Puzzled, Antonia stared at her, trying to fit what she saw with her memory of Charlotte Wemyss.

"Hello, are you Antonia Harcutt?"

Antonia nodded; she put down her case on the step as though preparing herself for battle.

"My name's Jill Francis. I'm a friend of Charlotte's. She asked me to collect you."

Antonia held out her hand. She felt hot and she knew that an ugly, dark-red blush would be spreading like a guilty stain over her face. She was aware that Jill was saying something and had to ask her to repeat it.

"Your father discharged himself from hospital just after lunch, which took everyone by surprise. He took a taxi back to Chandos Lodge. Luckily the hospital phoned his GP and he phoned Charlotte."

The implications rushed over Antonia – first and foremost, that she would see her father in an hour or two.

Jill explained that they had tried to phone Dampier Hall but hadn't been able to get through; it must have been while Antonia was packing. In the end Charlotte had decided to go to Chandos Lodge while Jill fetched Antonia.

"I understand the house is in a bit of a mess," Jill said. "Charlotte thought she'd see if she could do something before you came."

"It's awfully kind of you. I'm afraid I'm causing a lot of trouble."

"Not at all. It's a lovely drive down from Lydmouth." Jill put the suitcase in the back of the car. "Shall we go?"

Antonia lingered. "Is he – is he all right?"

"Your father? I haven't actually seen him since the accident, but Charlotte said he just seemed a bit bruised and shaken. But he must feel all right if he's discharged himself."

Antonia gave an awkward little laugh. "Couldn't wait to get back to his home comforts."

They got into the car. Jill started the engine and glanced at Antonia.

"I'm sorry about your dog."

"There's no need. My father gave it to me. but I couldn't keep a pet here, even if I'd wanted. It's always been his dog really."

Soon they were driving down to Newport. Jill asked about the school and what had led her towards teaching the disabled.

"Oh I don't teach. I'm only a secretary. It was just an accident, really, I did a secretarial course, and when I'd finished I started applying for jobs." The awkward laugh slipped out again. "This was the first one I was offered."

"How long ago was that?"

"Nearly five years."

"So they seem to like you."

"Not many secretaries will take a residential job for the salary the school pays."

For a few miles they drove in silence. Antonia sat straight-backed in the front passenger seat, gripping the strap of her handbag with both hands. Jill wasn't wearing a wedding ring, she noticed, which was surprising because Antonia thought that men would find her attractive.

After Newport they took the road north.

"Look at the trees," Jill said. "Don't they look wonderful in the autumn? I don't know how anyone can bear to live in London."

"Is that where you live?"

Jill nodded. "I'm a journalist. Do you know Charlotte's husband, Philip? We used to work on the same paper."

"It sounds very glamorous."

"It's not all it's cracked up to be."

The journey to Lydmouth was shorter than Antonia had expected. As they drew closer, Antonia's hands tightened round the strap of the handbag. It had been nearly two years since she had seen her father. He had turned up at the school just before Christmas and it had been hideously embarrassing.

During one of the lulls in the conversation, Antonia wished, not for the first time in her life, that a lorry would come roaring round one of the bends ahead on the wrong side of the road. She wouldn't have time to realise what was happening. In an instant she would be dead, just like Milly, and she would never have to go to Lydmouth again. Why should the dog have all the luck?

They had reached the outskirts of Lydmouth already. The town looked shabby, and everything seemed to have shrunk since Antonia had last lived here before the war. They drove through the town centre and out to Edge Hill. Instead of turning into the drive of

125

Chandos Lodge, Jill parked the car on the green. Antonia got out and stared at the rusting gates and the discoloured and decaying house at the end of the drive.

"It looks like a ruin," she said. "What's happened to it?"

Jill glanced at her. "Old age, I think. These old places need a lot of looking after. When were you here last?"

"A few years ago. It was summer then. Somehow it didn't seem so bad."

They crossed the road and walked up the drive. The door was unlocked. In the hall it was colder than it had been outside. Antonia noticed the dog's blanket and the tarnished soup tureen at the foot of the stairs. The place looked and smelled filthy. She felt deeply ashamed that someone like Jill, someone so neat, clean and organised, should see the house in this condition.

"It's disgusting." she muttered. "I'm sorry."

"Don't be sorry," Jill said, her voice suddenly sharp. "It's not your fault."

Antonia shrugged. "It feels like it."

She led the way down the corridor to what, in the old days, had been the housekeeper's room. The door was ajar and a woman was talking inside about the importance of getting another dog. Antonia glanced at Jill who smiled encouragingly at her. She pushed open the door.

"Antonia! There you are." Charlotte Wemyss-Brown bustled across the room and, before Antonia realised what was happening, planted a kiss on her cheek. "Come and tell your father what a naughty boy he's been, causing all this worry."

She herded Antonia towards the fireplace. Her father sat in his armchair in front of the gas fire. Since she had last seen him, his face had grown redder and more ravaged. What shocked her most of all was the fact that he hadn't shaved. His cheeks were speckled with sharp white bristles. The effect was sinister: it made him a little less than human.

"Hello, Tony." he said, lifting his head as if expecting a kiss.

"Hello." Antonia added, because she thought it might seem strange to the other women if she did not: "How are you?"

"Bloody awful. Aches and pains all over the shop." He reached for his glass. "But I'm hungry. What's for supper?"

Charlotte plunged into the silence which followed this question. "We haven't discussed the food question, Jack. Leave it to us. First we'd better sort out the bedding, I think. We'll be back in a moment."

She led Jill and Antonia out of the room and shut the door. "I think we'd better make up a bed for your father in there. The less he has to

126

move the better, and it'll be warmer for him. What about you? He thought you'd probably want to sleep in your old bedroom."

"No, I don't." Antonia hesitated, then went on in a rush: "It's a long way from here. Besides, the last time I looked inside, most of the furniture had gone."

"So where do you suggest?"

"There's a little room at the top of the stairs. Perhaps there."

"I brought you some sheets. I'm not sure there are any clean ones here."

"Thank you. You're very kind. I'm sorry to be so much trouble." To her dismay, Antonia felt her eyes filling with tears. "I'm sorry everything's in such a mess."

Jill patted her arm. Automatically, Antonia jerked away as though stung. She stared at Jill, her mouth working.

"I'm sorry," she said again.

"Don't be silly," Jill said.

"There's a Mrs Thing from the village who comes in five mornings a week," Charlotte announced in what was evidently a diplomatic attempt to provide a distraction. "But I don't think she does a very good job."

The next half-hour had a dreamlike quality. Everything was familiar, yet nothing was the same. The house and its contents seemed hardly to have changed since 1939 except to grow older, shabbier and dirtier.

First, the three women swept and dusted the little room at the top of the stairs.

"I'd keep away from the corner by the fireplace if I were you," Charlotte said. "There's a hole in the floorboards."

They made up the narrow bed with Charlotte's sheets and with blankets they found neatly folded in the linen cupboard – slightly damp but otherwise undamaged; their condition, Antonia thought, was a tribute to the efficiency of their former housekeeper who had left in 1938. Leaving Antonia to look for pillows, Charlotte and Jill went downstairs to make a hot-water bottle.

While the others were downstairs, Antonia slipped across the landing and opened the door of the room which had been hers as a child. It was cold and damp because there was a hole in the window as if someone had thrown a stone through it. The bed had lost its mattress and the frame with its bare springs looked like an instrument of torture. The chest of drawers had gone. Someone had taken all the books from the shelves and stripped the pictures from the walls. A heap of soot filled the hearth and on top of the pile, half-buried in the soot, was a spiky ball of feather and bone which had once been a sparrow.

She opened the built-in cupboard on the right of the fireplace. It was empty, apart from two wooden hangers on the rail. Inside her was an absence of feeling which in its way was more terrible than pain.

As she turned to go, she caught sight of something pale in the far corner of the cupboard. She bent down. It was a naked doll with a china face. Memory obligingly supplied her name and provenance: Alexandra, a present from Aunt Maud on Antonia's eighth birthday.

There were footsteps on the stairs. Quickly Antonia shut the cupboard door. Charlotte appeared, breathing heavily and cradling a stone hot-water bottle wrapped in a towel.

"Was this your room?"

"Yes."

"I see what you mean about the furniture. Do you know, I've kept my old bedroom almost exactly as it was? Philip says I make nostalgia into an art form."

Antonia nodded unsmilingly. "Shall we go downstairs? Let's have some tea."

"Jill's put another kettle on." As they were going down the stairs, Charlotte murmured, "I looked in on your father on my way up. He was just staring at the fire. He's feeling very sorry for himself, I'm afraid."

"Because of Milly?"

"Partly. But I think it's more than that. The accident's made him realise how frail he's getting. It's shaken him very badly." Charlotte hesitated. "He's also worried about money."

"He could sell this place.'

"That might be easier said than done. Of course some of the contents might be quite valuable. It could be worth having a valuation done."

They went into the kitchen, a large room which was dank in winter and cool even in summer. Jill was washing up.

"I found some cups and saucers," she said, smiling at Antonia. "I hope you don't mind. I'm making myself at home."

"Of course I don't mind. Anyway, it's not my home."

The sink and the draining board were piled with dirty pans and crockery. A kettle steamed on the blackened top of the gas cooker. In the centre of the room was a large deal table sprinkled with crumbs and mouse droppings; there was also a basket – so clean and new that it could belong only to Charlotte – containing a bottle of milk and a loaf of bread.

"Mrs Thing – the charwoman, whoever she is – sometimes brings him a meal to heat up. Apart from that, he fends for himself." Charlotte sniffed. "Or fails to fend, as the case may be. I expect you'll want to think about the future, dear. He can't go on as he is."

Antonia said nothing. She opened the larder door. The tiled floor was awash with empty bottles. On the shelves were more crumbs and several tins of baked beans.

"Have you thought about coming back home?" Charlotte said. "It could be the simplest solution."

Startled, Antonia spun round to face Charlotte. "But that's impossible. My job—"

"Perhaps we could find you another job. Something local. It's just a thought."

"Shall I make the tea now?" Jill asked.

Whether by accident or design, this caused a diversion while they looked for the tea caddy. While Jill made the tea. Antonia cut the bread and Charlotte laid the tray.

"We can do without a milk jug and a sugar bowl, can't we?" she said as she lifted the milk out of her basket. "By the way, Antonia, the hospital gave your father some tablets in case he had trouble sleeping." She held up a small brown bottle. "I wondered if you'd like to take charge of them. As head nurse."

Antonia reluctantly took the bottle and stuffed it in the pocket of her skirt. Jill picked up the tray and the three of them left the kitchen with Charlotte in the lead.

"Here's a nice cup of tea, Jack," she announced as she opened the sitting-room door. "And some of Susan's home-made bread." Her voice sharpened and hardened. "Where's he gone?"

"I'm here." Harcutt's disembodied voice snapped. "Trying pick up these bloody poppies."

The three women hurried into the room. He was on his hands and knees between the sofa and the gas fire. The hearth rug was covered with poppies.

"Thought I'd count them." he muttered. "Seem to be more than usual. They fell out of my hands."

Charlotte helped him up and persuaded him back to his chair. Antonia started to pick up the poppies.

"It's a hell of a worry," Harcutt said. "I haven't taken them round the village yet. And the tins need collecting from the shop and the pub. It'll be Sunday before we know what's hit us."

"Don't worry, Jack." Charlotte patted his arm. "We'll sort it out."

He shook off her hand. "But we need to sort it out *now*. Tony, will you do them?"

Antonia, still on her knees, looked at him. First Charlotte, now her father: they were all at it – pushing her back to the past, intent on destroying everything she had made for herself. They were herding her into a trap. She wanted to scream but she knew it would change nothing.

The Adam's apple jerked in his scrawny neck. "Please."

Jill put down the tray on the table behind the sofa. "Is there a lot of work involved? I'll help, if you want."

7

It was years since Gloria had been in Minching Lane: she thought of it as enemy territory.

Time was short. She had given her husband his tea and left him with the *Gazette*. Harold was incurious by nature, like most men, so long as his creature comforts were not disturbed. And the older he got the more his creature comforts involved dozing in front of the fire with a full belly and the newspaper on his lap. These days he left the running of the Bathurst Arms almost entirely to her.

Gloria hurried along the uneven pavement, wishing she hadn't worn high heels. She had always disliked and feared Templefields; even the paving stones and the cobbles were hostile. The wind was behind her and blowing in powerful, uneven gusts which increased her unsteadiness. She had covered her hair with a dark headscarf and the big raincoat concealed her figure. The shoes were the only touch of vanity she had allowed herself. A girl had her pride.

If she hurried, she should just be able to get back for opening time, and there would be no need for Harold to know she had been out. Her mind ran busily into the future, laying plans to meet contingencies.

She passed the King's Head. The Meagues' house was only a few yards away, but there was no light in the windows. Nevertheless she knocked on the door. It wasn't dark yet, not quite; in any case they might be at the back of the house. She waited, pressing her hand into her side where there was a stitch. Charlie and his mother should both be at home. It was too late for work and too early for the pub. *Please come.* She knocked again. The wind chilled her legs.

She stepped back and looked up, trying to see if there was smoke coming from the chimney. Behind her a door opened.

"You're wasting your time."

There was a chink of milk bottles. Gloria turned. Mrs Halleran was standing in the lighted doorway at the side of the King's Head.

"Where are they?"

"She's in hospital. Pneumonia, they say. God knows where *he* is."

131

In her eagerness Gloria moved forward into the oblong of light streaming from the doorway. "But he's still in Lydmouth?"

"He was at dinner time." A greedy expression settled over Mrs Halleran's doughy face. "Hello – it's Gloria, isn't it? Gloria Simms that was."

"Yes."

"This is a surprise. Don't often see you in this part of town. Not nowadays."

Gloria hesitated. "I was looking for Charlie. If you see him, could you tell him?"

"All right." Mrs Halleran raised her bushy eyebrows. "Any particular reason shall I say? Or is it just for old times' sake?"

Gloria was already clacking along Minching Lane, regretting she had come, regretting above all that she had talked to Mrs Halleran. "Just tell him I called, all right?"

8

"Thank you for coming," Antonia said as she opened the front door. "I'm sorry if I've . . ."

"Don't worry, dear." Charlotte drew on her gloves. "It's always distressing when a parent is ill."

As the door opened, the wind rushed into the house. The branches of the trees lining the drive rustled and trembled, giving off a continuous moaning roar. Jill glanced down at Antonia who stood, small and slight, with her knees slightly bent as though she needed to brace herself in order to cope with the wind and these strange women on her doorstep. It made a welcome change, Jill thought, to feel sorry for someone other than oneself.

"I'll see you tomorrow then," Antonia said suddenly to Jill. "If that's all right."

"Of course it is. At about eleven."

"I do wish I could come and help," Charlotte said. "But I *promised* I'd help at St John's. Anyway, I hope you both have a good night." She leaned a little closer to Antonia. "Don't think me interfering. but I'd try to keep him away from the whisky if you can. Especially if he has one of those tablets."

"Yes," Antonia said. "I'll try."

"Go back in the warm, dear. Goodbye."

Antonia closed the door. Jill and Charlotte picked their way down the drive. Dusk was falling, and they had to watch their step. Neither of them spoke until they were nearing the gates.

"Strange little thing, isn't she?" Charlotte murmured. "Thanks for all you've done. She seemed to take to you, I thought. But all this can't be much fun for you on your holiday."

"That's all right," Jill said. There was a bang to their right, somewhere in the depths of the overgrown garden. "What was that?"

Both women stopped. There was a gap in the trees at this point and they peered across what had once been a lawn to a high stone wall with more trees growing along it.

"Sounded like a door banging," Charlotte said.

"Is that some sort of shed over there?"

"Yes, I think it is."

From the same direction came the tinkle of breaking glass.

"It might be the wind," Jill said.

"Either that or someone's over there. We'd better go and see." Charlotte swung her handbag in the direction of a faintly shimmering ribbon of grey which lay diagonally across the grass. "That's a path, I think, so we needn't get our feet wet."

Jill almost laughed: both the casual, unthinking courage and the concern to avoid wet feet were typical of Charlotte. She herself was aware of a strong reluctance to investigate, a reluctance that grew even more pronounced as they left the drive. The path was paved and the stones were slippery after the rain.

"No point in telling the Harcutts," Charlotte muttered. "It would only delay things."

With every step they took, the light seemed to fade from the sky. They continued until they had almost reached the belt of trees. Charlotte laid her hand on the sleeve of Jill's coat.

"Look – there's the shed. In fact I think it's some sort of summerhouse."

It was about thirty yards away from them, its outlines blurring into the trees around it. Above the roof, the branches swayed to and fro like dervishes in the dusk. In front of it was a little verandah with a door in the centre flanked by a pair of windows.

There was another bang, louder than the first. Even Charlotte gasped. The wind had snatched the door and thrown it with surprising force against the wall.

"At least it's only the door," Jill said, relieved that nature, not man, was responsible for the disturbance. "That's probably how the window got—"

Charlotte clutched her arm, forcing her to be quiet. Standing in the doorway was the figure of a man. If they could see him, Jill realised with a shock of fear, he must be able to see them. He broke into a run – away from them, mercifully, following the line of the wall.

"Stop!" Charlotte called. "Do you hear me? Come here at once!"

The man ran on, of course, a dark shadow against the gathering darkness. He disappeared through an archway near the back of the house. Jill realised that she was trembling.

Charlotte snorted. "Someone was up to no good. Just as well we came along."

She strode towards the summerhouse and cautiously mounted the three steps to the verandah. Jill followed. The window to the right of the door was broken. Charlotte opened her handbag and took out a small torch. The beam danced around the verandah and the little room behind it.

"Nothing worth stealing, you'd think."

"Perhaps the man didn't know that."

"Odd, though. Would you like a look?"

Jill took the torch from Charlotte and peered into the interior of the summerhouse. The air was dry and almost warm in comparison with the chill of the wind outside. A broad shelf ran the full length of the back wall: it was covered with a jumble of rotting seed trays, empty flowerpots and rusting tools. Two deck chairs had been propped against the wall to the left next to a wheelbarrow without a wheel. Everything was covered with dust.

Charlotte sniffed. "Of course for all we know he *did* take something."

Jill remembered the running figure. "In that case it must have been something pretty small."

She held the torch while Charlotte refastened the door. They walked back across the lawn. The windows on this side of the house were in darkness.

"Should we tell the Harcutts?" Jill said, just before they reached the drive.

"Oh, lord. If we do, they'll get into a panic." Charlotte stopped abruptly. "What's *that*?"

"What?"

Jill listened. Footsteps were coming up the drive. As intrepid as ever, Charlotte plunged forward and switched on the torch.

"Good evening," said Inspector Thornhill.

9

Already, by Charlie's second visit, the hospital had acquired a familiarity which made it no longer intimidating. In a sense he felt privileged because, owing to the seriousness of his mother's condition, he had been given permission to visit her outside normal visiting hours. Her illness gave him a vicarious self-importance.

He left his bicycle in the rack provided for visitors and went into the reception area. The clerk on duty ticked off his name on a list.

"How's Mr Harcutt, by the way?" he said casually. "Ward Eleven."

"Major Harcutt?" There was a faint emphasis on the rank, as well as a sudden coolness in the voice. "He went home just after lunch."

"Oh. He's OK, now?"

"I really couldn't say." The coolness became frosty. "I understand he discharged himself."

In Ward Eight, the curtains were drawn around his mother's bed. The presence of so many women and the absence of other men made Charlie feel out of place; he feared that all the women were staring at him, which in these circumstances was not an agreeable sensation.

The nurse said to him in an undertone, "She's very poorly, I'm afraid, and she gets tired very quickly. I'll just give you five minutes."

Margaret Meague was propped up against a heap of pillows inside the oxygen tent. "All this dust," she gasped, "all this dust. I'll never get it done in time."

"You don't have to do it, dear," the nurse said. "Here's your son Charlie to see you."

Another patient called for the nurse; she slipped through the gap in the curtains, leaving Charlie alone with his mother. A woman was sobbing softly in the neighbouring bed.

"Charlie?"

"Yes, it's me." He couldn't think what to say. He wished the other woman would stop crying.

"Did you get your tea?"

"Yes."

In and out went her laboured breathing, and each word she

136

managed to say was a triumph of will over infirmity. The other women had flowers and cards and chocolates on their bedside tables; she had none. He wished he had brought her something.

"You'll be better soon," he said.

"You're a good boy."

"Ma – you remember the Harcutts at Edge Hill?"

The fingers picked at the blanket. He noticed with surprise that the hands were very clean and that the nails had been trimmed. She began to cough. Her eyes bulged. Seconds became minutes. He thought that she had not registered the question, that she would never stop coughing again.

There was a lull. She wrenched the words out of herself: "Old bastard give you the sack."

"That's him."

"Said money was missing."

"Bloody lie, too. You remember Tony?"

"Miss Tony." She coughed again, shaking her head from side to side on the pillow as though trying to shake the illness away. Then, for a few seconds she was quiet. She said softly, "It's in their faces. You can always tell."

"Tell what?"

"When they've got a bun in the oven."

The coughing began again. This time it was much more violent, and she brought up green phlegm. The nurse came rushing back; with her came the sister who told him to wait for her outside. Bewildered, Charlie glanced at his mother and went.

A few minutes later the sister came to join him in the corridor where he was smoking a cigarette.

"She's not at all well, Mr Meague," she said. "Her lungs can't cope and her heart's suffering. Do you understand what I'm saying?"

The smoke was making his eyes water. He had never allowed himself to think that his mother might be dying. She had come to hospital so that they could make her better: that was the point of hospitals. He frowned at the sister.

"Can't you do something?"

"We're doing everything we can. But sometimes that's not enough."

He looked down at her – the top of her head was on a level with his shoulder – and realised that he had no idea what to say or do. The situation lay outside his experience.

"You're not on the phone, are you? Is one of your neighbours?"

He told her to phone Mrs Halleran at the King's Head.

"If we don't ring you, and I hope we won't have to, why don't you ring us in the morning? See what sort of night your mother's had."

He nodded. There was a window opposite him and he stared at their reflections in the black glass.

"Go on." She gave him a gentle push. "There's nothing you can do here."

10

The door of the public bar opened and Gloria looked up, without hope, because hope hadn't survived the previous disappointments. But this time there he was – Charlie Meague in the flesh, taller and broader than he was in memory, perhaps less graceful, but still Charlie.

She murmured to Jane: "Why don't you make us a cup of tea? I'll serve this one."

Charlie glanced round the room, meeting the stares of the regulars. Gloria did a quick calculation. As far as she knew there was no one here tonight who would recognise him. Unfortunately it wouldn't be easy to talk: there were three men leaning on the bar, flies round the honey pot, and Harold was listening to the radio in the back room.

Charlie moved towards her. In the old days he had been a wonderful dancer. He looked tired.

"Evening, stranger." she said smoothly, for she had rehearsed her opening lines several times. "Haven't seen you for a while."

"Long time, no see. Large whisky and a pint of best."

The other men at the bar had stopped talking and were assessing Charlie as a possible rival for Gloria's favours. At any other time their behaviour would have amused, even flattered her. Now it was merely inconvenient.

She gave him his drinks and he held out a ten-shilling note to her. Their fingers touched as she took the money. She moistened her lips with the tip of her tongue.

"How's old what's-his-name?" he asked as she opened the till. "Harold, is it?"

"Fine, thanks."

She gave him his change. One of the other customers wanted serving, and wanted to be flirted with. Out of the corner of her eye she watched Charlie settling at the table by the window. He pulled the *Gazette* out of the pocket of his overcoat and began to read.

After a decent interval, she began to go round the room collecting glasses, emptying ashtrays and wiping the tables. He was reading the article about the Templefields bones. He looked up with apparent reluctance when she reached his table. His lack of interest in her as a woman surprised and piqued her.

"Got your name in the paper. I see," she said. "Fame at last."

He nodded. His face was sullen and despondent, she thought. Where had all the laughter gone?

"You've been down here for weeks," she went on softly in a voice that made the words an accusation. Quickly she changed the subject: "What's wrong with your ma?"

"Pneumonia. They think she's dying."

"Oh, Christ, Charlie. I'm sorry."

He finished the rest of his beer. "I'll have the same again."

Her concern spilled over and turned to anger. "I thought you did your drinking in the King's Head now."

"I'm drinking here because Ma Halleran said you wanted to see me."

"It's not for my sake, don't think that. But there's something I thought you might like to know. I was trying to do you a favour. Should have known better, shouldn't I?"

She emptied his ashtray into the waste bucket and moved away. To her pleasure he followed her up to the bar.

He put the two empty glasses down on the counter. "The same again."

For a moment there was no one in earshot. She leant across the counter.

"There was a man in here last night. He was asking after you."

Charlie's face stiffened. "What was he like?"

"Little chap with a beard. Sat at the table where you're sitting, reading a book, a proper book. Jane – that's Harold's girl – she served him. He had a large Scotch."

"What did you say?"

"Said I didn't know you, of course. Charlie, he wasn't a copper, was he?"

He shook his head. Another customer came up to the bar. Gloria turned away with Charlie's glasses. After she had served him, he went back to his table. She didn't know whether to be glad or sorry – glad he was staying or sorry that he wanted to drink rather than talk to her.

Jane came back with a cup of tea and the news that her father couldn't find his cheque book. Knowing that this was the sort of problem that deeply disturbed Harold, Gloria went to help him find it.

When she returned, she looked in the direction of the window. Charlie was still at his table. But he wasn't alone. He was talking to the little man with a beard.

140

11

Edith Thornhill sat by the boiler darning yet another sock. Her husband had finished his supper and was apparently engrossed in the *Gazette*. He had spoken hardly a dozen words to her since he had come home.

Richard was hugging to himself his problems with his new job, and she felt guilty about this because she had been far more enthusiastic about the move to Lydmouth than he had. She also felt guilty because she knew that he wanted to make love to her but she wouldn't let him; she felt angry with herself for feeling guilty – she had as much right to say no as he had to say yes – but the guilt was too deep-seated and irrational to respond to reasoning. She never questioned her love for him, but she did wonder why he had to treat sex with such mechanical urgency, as if he were a famine victim consuming a loaf of bread. He was in general a considerate man, which made his lack of consideration in this respect particularly shocking.

She picked up another sock from the seemingly bottomless supply in the mending basket. She was also worried about the children, and Richard's apparent lack of concern for them increased the animosity she felt towards him. David had a haunted look in his face and had wept on the way to school this morning: something was wrong there, and he wouldn't tell her what it was; like father, like son. Elizabeth's cough was getting worse: could it be turning to whooping cough?

She felt torn in all directions, as though her family threatened to dismember her emotionally. Hadn't she a right to her own life, if only for half an hour a day? She was a bondservant to her husband and her children and her house: she cooked, cleaned, washed, mended and penny-pinched; she gave them love and they gave her dirty socks, usually in need of darning.

She laid aside the current sock with a sigh. In the distance, she heard Elizabeth beginning to cough. Her eyes itched with tiredness and a yawn slipped out. She sensed that Richard was looking at her.

"There's an article about the Templefields bones in here."

"Oh, yes." She made an effort, since any conversation with him was better than this awful silence. "The case you're working on? The dead baby?"

"Yes, it's by the editor, man called Philip Wemyss-Brown." Still looking at her, he dropped the paper on to the table, stood up and stretched. "Tired?"

She nodded. "I haven't been sleeping well." Elizabeth's cough had kept her awake for the last two nights, that and the other worries.

"We could have an early night."

"It's only half past eight."

"So?" His eyes were very bright.

"I – I really should finish this mending."

"Damn the mending." He got up and stood behind her chair. His hands slid down and cupped her breasts. His breath was warm on her neck.

"Richard, I'm tired. I'm sorry."

His hands sprang away from her as if her body had given him an electric shock. "You're always bloody tired."

"I'm sorry, but there it is."

He picked up the newspaper. "I'm going out."

"Where? Why?"

"I might as well do something useful. It's work."

He stalked out of the kitchen. His outrage had a comical aspect to it, but there was nothing comical about Edith's feelings. She heard him in the hall and guessed he was putting on his coat.

She got up and went to the door. She didn't know what she was going to do – whether she would shout at him or plead with him or submit to him. In the event there was no need to make up her mind: as she opened the door to the hall, Elizabeth started to cry as well as cough.

Richard was by the front door. He had his hat on the back of his head and hadn't bothered to button his overcoat. She thought, inappropriately, how handsome he looked.

"Don't wait up," he said, not looking at her. "I don't know when I'll be back." He opened the door.

"Damn you," she said, quietly, in case the children were listening, and headed for the stairs.

12

Dinner dragged its way through three courses, followed by cheese and fruit. Afterwards, Philip washed up, a cigarette between his lips and a glass of brandy conveniently to hand on the windowsill, while Jill dried and Charlotte put away and made the coffee. Susan's working day came to an end once she had helped to cook dinner; only on special occasions did she also help serve and clear away.

"You're not a special occasion," Philip had told Jill on her first evening. "You count as family, I'm afraid."

"In a manner of speaking," Charlotte had added.

On balance, Jill thought, she was neither one thing nor the other.

This evening, both Philip and Charlotte were in a cheerful mood – Philip because he had sold his story about the Victorian murderess and the Templefields bones to one of the nationals, the *Daily Express*, and Charlotte because she had spent the day rearranging the Harcutts' lives; Good Works agreed with her.

"I phoned Madge this evening," Charlotte announced as she spooned coffee into the jug; she added for Jill's benefit, "She's the headmistress of the High School. We've had a wonderful stroke of luck. Their assistant secretary is leaving at the end of term. She's going to have a baby."

"You're plotting," Philip said.

"Well, it would be perfect for Antonia, wouldn't it? If she got the job, she could live at home and look after her father. I explained the situation to Madge, and between ourselves I think it's as good as settled. The school has a policy of favouring applications from Old Girls."

The telephone started to ring in the hall. Charlotte went to answer it.

Ash fell from the end of Philip's cigarette into the soapy water. "What did Thornhill want with Harcutt?"

"He didn't say," Jill said.

"I wonder if the police have found out something else, something they needed to check with him. Maybe I should give him a ring tomorrow. Did he say he'd tell the Harcutts about the man you saw?"

"Yes. And he's going to get the local bobby to keep an eye on the place." Jill began to polish a plate. "He thought it was probably someone having a look round on the off chance – someone who thought the major was in hospital and who didn't know Antonia was back."

"But they'd have seen the lights and our car in the drive."

"No, the Harcutts live at the back of the house. And he wouldn't have seen the car because I parked on the green. The drive's in a terrible state."

Charlotte bustled back into the kitchen. "It's for you."

Philip turned, reaching for a towel. "Who is it?"

"No, for Jill." Charlotte's face was alert with curiosity. "Someone called Oliver Yateley. *Very* charming."

Very slowly and very carefully, Jill put down the plate on the table.

"I didn't know anyone knew you were down here," Charlotte said.

"Nor did I," Jill replied.

"The name sounds faintly familiar. Perhaps we met him when we were up in London?"

"I don't think so."

Jill went into the hall. The handset was waiting for her, lying like a menacing black slug beside the cradle. This was one eventuality for which she was entirely unprepared. She had thought that she would be safe in Lydmouth.

She picked up the handset. For a second she listened to the electric near-silence of the open line. Somewhere on the other end of this piece of wire was Oliver, breathing and biding his time. She could break the connection and cast him back to the limbo of memory; but that wouldn't work because he would telephone again and again until he reached her. Oliver was persistent if nothing else as she knew to her cost.

"Oliver."

"Jill – thank God. I've been phoning everyone I could think of."

"Where did you get the number?"

"The address book in your desk. Listen, darling, I—"

"You've been to my flat?"

"Of course I have. What else could I do?"

"I want to have the keys back. Or do I have to change the locks?"

There was a silence. She imagined him spending the evening, perhaps several evenings, working doggedly through the address book – "Is Jill with you, by any chance? No? So sorry to bother you" – until at last he reached the Wemyss-Browns near the bottom of the alphabet. It was humiliating to think that his pursuit of her had been so public. She missed something he was saying and had to ask him to repeat it.

"I found the roses in your wastepaper basket."

"What do you expect? A dozen red roses aren't going to make me change my mind."

"Darling, you haven't been well. I need to see you, to talk to you properly. And what's this I hear about you resigning? You're in no state to make decisions at present. What do you think you're going to live on?"

"It's nothing to do with you, Oliver. Will you just stop pestering me?"

She put down the phone, closed her eyes and leant against the wall. It's over, she said to herself, and nothing matters any more. She was dry-eyed, which pleased her; she was too angry to cry.

She went back to the kitchen. The door was an inch ajar. She could hear Charlotte's voice inside.

"Helping Antonia could be a blessing in disguise. It'll take Jill's mind off things."

13

With his head down and his hands deep in his pockets, Richard Thornhill walked into the wind. Without making a conscious decision, he headed towards the centre of the town. He drove himself hard, feeling that exhaustion was desirable because it led eventually to oblivion.

A lorry rolled by and for an instant he thought how easy it would be to step in front of it, like Harcutt's dog: the driver wouldn't have a chance of stopping. That would show them all. Bloody women. To make matters worse, he was aware, though for most of the time he managed to suppress the knowledge, that he was making a fool of himself.

At this hour, the High Street was almost deserted, even on Friday night. The idea of going up to his office slipped into his mind, only to be summarily dismissed. He hadn't come out on a filthy evening merely to plough through a few more of his predecessor's files. He deserved to enjoy himself for once, didn't he? A pint of beer, or perhaps two, was a far better idea.

The Bull Hotel was the nearest place. But Thornhill walked past it. His heart beating a little faster, he turned into Lyd Street. He walked quickly down the hill, warmed by the exercise and by a sense of guilty excitement. On the way, he passed on the left the dark windows of Masterman's the jeweller's.

At the bottom of the hill, near the river, was the Bathurst Arms. There was no harm in it, for God's sake, Thornhill told himself angrily as he opened the outer door. Laughter, cigarette smoke and the smell of beer washed over him. He went into the lounge bar.

The room wasn't crowded, though there was a decent sprinkling of drinkers. Gloria wasn't in evidence. He realised from his disappointment how much he had counted on seeing her. The plain young girl, Gloria's stepdaughter, took his order; there was no sign of recognition on her dull, pinched face. He glanced beyond her, into the public bar, where a noisy game of darts was in progress.

He paid for his drink and took it to a table near the fire. The beer tasted sour, and it sat heavily on his stomach. He drank quickly, tried to concentrate on the *Gazette* and told himself that this was the life, that he should do this more often.

Bravado dictated that he should have at least one more pint. He carried his glass to the bar. A few seconds before he got there, a tall man staggered across the public bar and slammed four glasses, two pints and two shorts, on to the bar top.

"Same again, my love," he bellowed to the barmaid.

While she was serving him, he began to roll a cigarette. Thornhill glanced at him and quickly looked away: it was Charlie Meague, and he was well on the way to becoming as drunk as a lord. The situation was one which made Thornhill automatically wary. Alcohol could remove many inhibitions, including the one about not hitting policemen. He changed his position to get a better view of the public bar: he was curious to see whom Meague was drinking with.

A small, bearded man was sitting near the window with a book open on the table in front of him. Thornhill's attention sharpened. He'd seen that man before – coming out of the library on the evening they had found the bones and going into the Bull Hotel. The thin, pasty face stirred other memories. Genghis Carn might be looking for Charlie Meague. If you took the beard away from that face, it would look not unlike the description of Carn in the *Police Gazette*.

Meague swore. He was making heavy weather of rolling his cigarette and had spilled tobacco into a pool of beer on the counter.

"If you'd wiped that up, my girl." he complained to the sad barmaid, "I could have used that tobacco. It's a bloody waste. What are you going to do about it?"

There was a roar from the men around the dartboard. Several people were in the process of leaving the lounge bar. Thornhill heard the clack of high heels in the private corridor behind the bar and he smelled perfume. He looked up eagerly. Gloria came in.

"Charlie," she said, "haven't you had enough?"

"No." With unexpected speed, Charlie's hand shot out and seized Gloria's arm. He lowered his voice until it wasn't much above a whisper. "I haven't had enough of you, either."

"Let go of my arm."

He obeyed. "You should have married me, girl."

"Don't be stupid. You're making a fool of yourself. And of me."

She hadn't seen Thornhill; she and Charlie were concentrating too hard on each other. Though their voices were quiet, their faces were intent and angry. The two of them might have been alone. The barmaid had turned away and was refilling the smaller glasses with whisky; the tips of her ears were red. Gloria was wearing a pink dress that outlined her waist and hips and made her look like a tart. Thornhill no longer wanted to see her, let alone talk to her.

Thornhill put his glass on the counter – gently to avoid disturbing the two people and whatever form of intimacy held them together. He grabbed his coat and hat and joined the tail end of the group leaving the bar.

Outside, the wind came roaring up the river and blew the hat off his head. Someone laughed. He bent down, picked it up and crammed it on his head. He felt foolish, unsatisfied and sad: he disgusted himself. Why did desire have to make a mockery of love? He walked slowly up the hill. It was time to go home. There was nowhere else to go.

Part Four

Saturday

1

The following morning, Charlotte drove Jill to Chandos Lodge. She pulled up beside the green, opposite the Harcutts' gates, leaving the engine running and the wipers squeaking to and fro.

"Sure you can get back all right?" she asked as Jill was opening the door.

Jill nodded at the bus stop. "I just wait there till a bus comes."

"I feel terribly guilty about this. But they do like St John's to look its best on Remembrance Sunday, and that means they need all the able bodies they can find. It's like a three-line whip in parliament."

"Don't worry, I'll manage."

"You won't forget to mention the job, will you? The sooner Antonia applies for it the better."

Jill said she wouldn't forget and closed the door. Charlotte gave her a regal wave and the Rover pulled away. Jill put up her umbrella and walked up the drive of Chandos Lodge. The front door opened before she got there.

"I saw you coming from my window," Antonia said, her sallow skin flushing unbecomingly. "Shall we go out straightaway?"

"Whenever you like."

"I'll just get my coat." She drew back to let Jill into the hall. Her eyes were red-rimmed and her mouth half-open; she looked like a tired rabbit. "Horrible weather. Makes me think of funerals, for some reason."

"They say November used to be called the month of the dead." Jill glimpsed a flood of morbid and unanswerable questions welling up in her own mind. How, for example, do you grieve for the nameless, for the unknown soldiers, for people who never had a name in the first place, who were hardly even people? She forced herself to concentrate on the present, not the past, and on the living rather than the dead. "How's your father today?"

"Physically he's much better, but morale's a bit low."

"Has he seen yesterday's *Gazette*? There's an article about the bones at Templefields. I brought him a copy."

For an instant, Antonia's lips twisted as though she had detected an unpleasant taste in her mouth. But she nodded briskly. "Thanks, he'll like that."

"He's mentioned as an expert on Victorian Lydmouth."

There was a cough from the stairs, the sort designed to draw attention. A small woman wearing a pinafore was standing on the half-landing, her head alertly cocked in an attitude suggesting that she had been monitoring their conversation; she was carrying a dustpan and brush and her hair was swathed in a turban. Here, Jill thought, was the cleaner Charlotte had referred to as Mrs Thing: she did not usually come in at weekends, but Charlotte had arranged for her to do an extra three hours this morning.

"Do you want me to do the kitchen now" – there was a barely perceptible pause to mark the absence of the 'Miss' which might have been tacked on to the question before the war – "Antonia?"

"Yes, please, Mrs Forbes. We'll go out with the poppies in a moment."

"Bit late, isn't it? Everyone I know's got theirs by now."

"Yes, but it'll stop my father worrying about it. Could you keep an ear open for him while I'm out?"

Mrs Forbes pursed her thin lips. "I'll have to go at twelve, come what may. Got to cook our Terry's dinner."

"Well, not to worry if we're not back. I expect he'd be able to cope."

Mrs Forbes stood there, waiting, imperceptibly menacing and saying nothing; and in her silence she conveyed a question or perhaps a demand.

Antonia's shoulders twitched. "Oh, sorry. I almost forgot. I'd better give you your money before we go."

Mrs Forbes advanced down the stairs like a victorious army. "I usually have a cup of tea and a fag about now. All right?"

Antonia took a step backwards. "Oh, yes, of course."

Mrs Forbes walked, head back, splay-footed, the mistress of all she surveyed, down the hall, past the door of the major's room and into the kitchen. Antonia said she would fetch her coat, but first she took Jill to see her father.

"I hope you don't mind," she whispered.

The room was tidier than Jill had seen it. The major was sitting at his bureau, apparently examining a row of medals which he thrust into a drawer as they entered.

"Jolly good of you to help with the poppies." he said. "Hell of a responsibility for one person, you know."

Jill gave him the *Gazette* folded open at the Templefields article. "Charlotte thought you might like that."

He held out a trembling hand for the newspaper and glanced at the first paragraph of the article. "Something for the files, eh? Very decent of you to think of me. Mark you, I'm beginning to think I'll never get that book finished. Sometimes I wonder if it's all worth it."

"I'll just get my hat and coat," Antonia said, declining to try to boost her father's morale – perhaps, Jill thought, because she had tried and failed too often before.

After the door had closed behind her, Harcutt leant forward. "Good of you and Charlotte to take my girl under your wing. Needs taking out of herself, you know."

Jill smiled and wondered how to change the subject.

"Shy, you see. Of course, if she came back home, she'd soon fit in again. This is where she belongs, eh? There are school friends and so forth. People like Charlotte and yourself."

"But I wasn't at school with her," Jill pointed out. "I'm just visiting Lydmouth."

"No – well, that's as maybe. Still, you see my point?"

The door opened and there was Antonia on the threshold, saving Jill from having to answer him. The only point she could see was that he hoped his daughter would come home for good because he was desperate for company.

Antonia picked up the tray of poppies, Jill took the collecting tin and the two women left the house. It was still raining, though not so heavily. Edge Hill, Antonia explained as they trudged down the drive, consisted of the houses near and around the green, together with a new council estate behind the church. She spoke haltingly as though her attention were elsewhere.

"Are you all right?" Jill asked. "Do you feel up to this?"

"I'm fine. It's just that I didn't sleep very well. Strange bed, I suppose." Antonia frowned. "*Everything* seems strange."

"Perhaps you should take something to help you sleep. Ask Dr Bayswater for some tablets."

"Perhaps."

Since it was Saturday morning, and raining, they found many people at home; but, as Mrs Forbes had foretold, most of them already had poppies. One or two of them recognised Antonia but far fewer than Jill had expected.

"They all know my father," Antonia said. "But I haven't lived here since 1939." After a pause, she added, "And of course I was very different then."

As they worked their way round the village, the two women carried on a conversation which ebbed and flowed between the houses they called at. They spent five minutes telling each other how awful the weather was.

"Sometimes," Antonia said, "I think I'd like to go back to Africa. All that sun and blue skies."

"When were you out there?"

"During the war, and just afterwards. My aunt used to live in South Africa, and I stayed with her."

"Did your father send you away because of the war?"

"Partly, I suppose." Antonia glanced at Jill with murky brown eyes, opaque and mysterious. "He was in the army, of course. But in fact I think he was glad of the excuse. After my mother died, he must have found it rather hard to cope with me."

"Where did you live?"

"Johannesburg. Aunt Maud was a nurse at a hospital there. But then she died, and I had to come back to England."

They were working their way along a row of cottages facing north across the green. Antonia opened the gate of the last cottage, the one nearest the church. Immediately a small white dog scampered down the side of the house, barking furiously.

Antonia retreated, putting the gate between herself and the dog. The front door opened and a tiny woman wearing a white apron appeared on the step. She screamed at the dog, which retreated in its turn.

"I've already got a poppy," the woman called to them. "You're just wasting your time."

Antonia nodded and began to move away.

"Wait a minute. It's Antonia, isn't it? The major's girl?"

"Yes," Antonia said.

"Maggie Forbes said you were back. Remember me? Mrs Veale? Haven't seen you for years. Come here, so I can have a proper look at you."

The dog watched them with baleful eyes as they opened the gate and came up the path. The rain pattered down on their umbrellas.

"I won't ask you in, if you don't mind," Mrs Veale told them. "I've just cleaned the floor. You haven't grown much, have you?"

"Nor have you," Antonia said, showing more spirit than Jill had credited her with.

"Come back to look after your dad?"

"Just for a few days."

"I thought you might be back for good. What with his accident and Mrs Forbes leaving."

Antonia said nothing. She stared at Mrs Veale, and her stillness was unnaturally rigid.

"Hasn't Maggie told you yet?" The old voice was as sharp as a

154

knife. "Her Ernie's coming out of the Merchant Navy after Christmas, and she wants to spend more time at home. And you won't find it easy to get someone else, not for that house. Still, it won't make much odds to you, will it?" The eyes dropped down to Antonia's hands, searching for corroboration in the absence of a ring. "Not married, are you?"

"No."

"So it's not as if you've got a husband to look after." The small, bright blue eyes examined Antonia's face. "Don't leave it too long, mind. Or you may find it's too late. I married my John when I was sixteen."

"Perhaps I don't want to get married, Mrs Veale."

"Of course you do. Every woman does, whatever they say."

"We must be getting on."

Mrs Veale hadn't finished. "Wish I could say I was sorry about your dog, but I can't."

"She wasn't my dog."

"When all's said and done, she was a nasty bit of work. Look at our Freddy's ear. See? The right one – it's all ragged. It was your Milly did that. *And* she was always doing her business on the grass where the children play, either that or on the paths."

"I'm sorry to hear that," Antonia said. "Now we really mustn't keep you any longer, Mrs Veale."

"And I don't know why your dad won't tell the truth about the accident. Milly was chasing someone, you know, someone on a bike. That's how it happened. And whoever it was had just been talking to your dad by your gates."

"How could you tell?" Jill asked. "It must have been dark."

"I could see well enough. There's streetlights, aren't there, and there were cars passing. Anyway, he cycled quite close, he did. I was standing by the gate, trying to see where Milly was. Didn't want to let Freddy off the lead while that dog was on the loose. If you ask me, that dog of yours wasn't just nasty. It was wrong in the head."

"We must be going," Antonia said. "Goodbye."

She and Jill heard the door closing as they were going down the path. The dog took the sound as a signal to advance on them again.

Jill shut the gate in his face. "Now I know why I prefer cats." She glanced at Antonia and saw that there were drops of water on her face – not rain, but tears. "What's wrong? That old beast upset you? I thought you handled her very well."

"Sorry." Antonia sniffed; her nose was pink. "She was like that when I was a kid. Always looking for your weak spots."

Jill wondered which of Antonia's weak spots Mrs Veale had found. Aloud, she said, "Best not to pay her any attention."

Antonia blew her nose. The two women walked towards the church. A moment later, as they were nearing the council houses, Antonia said, "Can I ask you something personal?"

"Of course."

"Do *you* want to get married?"

"No."

"Why does everyone think one does? It's not the same for men."

"I suppose it's because some people haven't got used to the idea that women can have lives outside their families."

"It's none of their business." Antonia frowned, her dark eyebrows becoming one. "I'd hate not having a job."

"That reminds me," Jill said. "Charlotte gave me a message for you. Apparently there's a vacancy coming up for a secretary at your old school."

"Oh, I see." Antonia's voice was harsh, and there were spots of colour in her cheeks. "You're all in it, aren't you?"

"In what?"

"I won't come back to that bloody house. You tell Charlotte that. I'm never going to live in Lydmouth again."

2

Major Harcutt heard the distant thud which signified the closing of the front door. Mrs Forbes liked to make sure that one noticed her comings and goings. He levered himself out of his armchair and, using the back of the sofa as a support, limped slowly to the bureau. He had planned to wait until the evening for the first drink of the day, but this was such a splendid opportunity that it was a shame to waste it.

The key was in his pocket. He unlocked the bureau and pulled the bottle and the glass from behind the stack of books. As he was uncorking the bottle, he heard a tap on the window.

Startled, he looked round. A man in a flat cap was standing outside: he had his hands on either side of his face and he was peering through the glass. The major knew at once that it must be the Meague fellow, though he hadn't seen the man in a good light since he, Meague, was a boy.

Harcutt shook his head, as though hoping to shake away what he had seen. The man pointed to himself and then in the general direction of the back door. His message was unmistakable: "Let me in."

"Go away!" the major snarled.

The face vanished. Harcutt poured himself a couple of inches of whisky and drank it in two mouthfuls. He put the bottle and glass back in their hiding place and relocked the bureau.

As he was moving back to his chair, he heard footsteps in the corridor. The door opened and Meague swaggered into the room.

"What are you doing here?" Harcutt demanded, clinging to the back of the sofa.

"Just come to see how you are." The voice was soft, almost pleading.

"Who said you could come in?"

"Wasn't that what you said just then? When I tapped on the glass?" Charlie Meague smiled, a flash of white teeth in a dark, unshaven face. "Anyway, the back door was open."

"I don't want you here. Go away or I shall call the police."

"How?" Meague asked, moving closer. "You still haven't got a phone in this place." His eyes flicked round the room. "Not what it was before the war, is it? You've let things go to seed."

Harcutt knew that the one thing he mustn't do was mention Tony. It was a nightmare. He longed for rescue, but he prayed that the man would be gone by the time she got back. His fingers tightened on the back of the sofa until shafts of pain shot up his forearms.

Meague sauntered to the fireplace and picked up the photograph of Harcutt with his dead wife and living daughter. He stared at it for a few seconds, put it down and turned his attention to the Second Empire clock. "Mind you," he said, hefting the clock in his hand, "you've still got some valuable stuff here, haven't you? I've got contacts in the antique trade, you know. I could get you a fair price for something like this."

"When I tell the police, you'll—"

"*Shut up, you old fool*," Charlie Meague shouted. Then he smiled, and when he next spoke his voice was as gentle and insinuating as before. "You're not going to tell the police. You daren't. You haven't told them about seeing me the other night. I know why. You know why. Ah," he looked down at the seat of the sofa where the *Gazette* was lying open at the Templefields article, "you've seen the paper, too. Interesting, isn't it?"

Harcutt felt the sweat breaking out on his forehead and trickling down his spine.

Meague tossed the clock a few inches into the air and caught it. "I had a look in the shed the other day."

"It was you they saw?"

"Mrs Windbag and her friend? Yes. The box is gone."

"What box?"

"Let's make it a thousand, shall we? Nice round sum."

"Don't be ridiculous." To his shame, Harcutt discovered that he was shaking with rage and fear. There was a buzzing in his head.

"I'll make it pounds, not guineas, for old times' sake."

"I don't have that sort of money. And even if I did—"

"You can do it, easy." Charlie Meague tossed the clock into the air once more and caught it. "If you want, I'll even help you raise it. Act as your agent, eh? All above board. I'll charge you a commission."

"Go away."

Still holding the clock, Meague slowly advanced round the sofa. The closer he came, the larger and stronger and more malevolent he seemed. Harcutt realised it was possible that this man was going to hurt him, even kill him. People would wait years to get their own back. Revenge, they said, was a dish best eaten cold.

Charlie Meague waggled his finger at the major. "I know what's on your mind: you're wondering where it will all end, aren't you? Well, you needn't worry. I'm a reasonable man. One thousand pounds, that's all I ask. OK? I won't be back."

"You must have gone off your head," Harcutt said, and humiliatingly his voice emerged as a whisper.

"Not me, chum. I leave that sort of thing to you."

Charlie Meague turned and paced back to the fireplace. He walked slowly and deliberately, as if he had every right to be where he was. He tossed the clock into the air again, high above the tiled hearth. This time he didn't bother to catch it.

3

The phone rang just as Thornhill was about to go out to lunch with Sergeant Kirby.

"Thornhill," said Superintendent Williamson. "Hoped I'd catch you. What happened with Harcutt last night?"

On the other end of the line, there were raised voices, perhaps from the wireless. Williamson was at home.

"He denied talking to anyone before the dog was killed," Thornhill said. "He claimed Mrs Veale was a short-sighted, senile old woman out to make trouble."

"And he could be right. Alternatively he was so drunk he can't remember."

From the background chatter at the other end of the line there emerged a louder, clearer voice: "Ray! It's on the table. It's getting cold."

"But the odds are it doesn't matter," Williamson said. "Let it ride."

"Yes, sir." Thornhill had already reached the same conclusion. "There's something else: we've found Carn."

"What's he up to, then?"

"Not sure. I saw him having a drink in the Bathurst Arms with Charlie Meague last night. He's grown a beard, by the way. Meague was very drunk."

"Do we know where he's staying?"

"Sergeant Kirby got a positive identification at the Bull Hotel. He's been staying there since Wednesday."

"Not short of a bob or two if he's at the Bull. Assuming he deigns to pay his bill. What name's he using?"

"Mr James."

"Go and frighten him, will you? Do it first thing after lunch. I want him off my patch."

"Apparently he's gone to Gloucester for the day, to look at the cathedral."

"Bloody hell. Well, see him this evening instead."

4

On the dark, polished wood of the chest, the poppies looked like spots of blood. Jill brought out a second handful of flowers from the other pocket of her raincoat and let them trickle on to the chest.

"What on earth have you been doing?" Philip asked as he shut the front door. "Embezzling from the Earl Haig Fund? Don't tell me you've betrayed your sacred trust?"

Jill smiled at him. "I paid good money for these. Nearly a pound in assorted change."

"But why so many? Isn't it a little ostentatious? Most people make do with one or two."

Charlotte came into the hall of Troy House, her eyebrows arching in surprise at the sight of the poppies.

"We only sold about six," Jill explained. "So I thought I'd better make a bulk purchase just before we got back to Chandos Lodge."

"How's Jack?" Charlotte asked. There was something in her voice that suggested that she did not care for Philip to exchange badinage – especially, perhaps, with Jill.

"Rather glum," Jill said. "A lot of unsold poppies would have made him even more depressed. Anyway. it's all in a good cause."

Philip hung up her raincoat. He smelled of beer and exuded cheerfulness. "Like a drink before lunch?"

Apart from the soup, the food was cold. While they ate, Charlotte questioned Jill about Chandos Lodge and its inhabitants.

"Did you mention the job?"

"Yes." Jill hesitated. "She's not too keen, actually."

"Whyever not? It's made for her."

"I don't think she likes the idea of living at home."

"Can't blame her," Philip said. "I wouldn't want to live with Jack Harcutt in that barn of a house either."

"But it's her duty, Philip," Charlotte said firmly. "He's her father. Blood's thicker than water."

"You can't make her if she doesn't want to."

Charlotte dabbed her lips with her napkin. "It's not a matter of making her. We need to persuade her to understand what's *right*."

She abandoned the subject for the time being and turned back to Jill. "We thought we might make a little excursion this afternoon. I mentioned you were here to Chrissie Newton. She was at St John's this morning. She said, why didn't we all come to tea, and before we actually have tea, Giles could show us the house. Sir Anthony's away."

"Giles is the agent for the Ruispidge Estate." Philip explained to Jill. "They're nice people. They—"

"Of course they're nice people. Philip," Charlotte said. "They're our friends."

"And the house is interesting, too," he went on. "You like these old places, don't you?"

"It sounds lovely," Jill said, wishing a polite refusal were possible. She suspected that Philip and Charlotte were plotting behind her back to keep her cheerfully occupied.

The telephone began to ring. They heard Susan crossing the hall to answer it.

"Of course the house isn't what it was before the war," Charlotte said. "Such a shame, the way these old places are going downhill, just because of the *punitive* levels of taxation. I simply can't understand why the government doesn't realise—"

The door opened a few inches and Susan put her head into the room.

"It's for you, dear," she said to Jill.

Jill put down her napkin. Everything, it seemed to her, was happening at about two-thirds its normal speed. She knew who the caller must be. She knew, too, that Philip and Charlotte were looking at her and trying not to make their concern and curiosity obvious. There was even time to look out of the window and see the leafless branches of an ash tree outlined against the grey sky, and time to tell herself once again that November was a depressing month which was no doubt making everything worse.

She went out of the dining room, closing the door behind her. Susan gave her a smile which Jill thought contained an element of complicity and padded away on her slippered feet. Jill picked up the handset, praying for a miracle, and said hello in a voice which wasn't much louder than a whisper.

"Jill. How are you?"

"Oliver," she said wearily, "I don't want to talk to you. I thought I'd made that clear last night."

"Well, I want to talk to you. You can't just walk out on everything and everyone like this."

"You mean I can't just walk out on you, don't you? Well, I can. I have. And there's nothing you can do about it."

"Look. You've had a lot to cope with lately. Perhaps I haven't been as sensitive as I should have been. But can't we just sit down together and talk about this like two rational adults?"

"This has got nothing to do with being rational. I'm going to put the phone down."

"If you put the phone down, I'll be standing on your doorstep in about five minutes."

Suddenly Jill felt cold. "What do you mean?"

"What I say. I'm at the Bull Hotel. I've got your address."

"You can't just force your way in like that."

"I warn you – I mean it. I've got to see you."

"I don't want you here."

"Then the simplest thing to do would be for you to come here. Come and have dinner with me, Jill. Please."

5

For lunch Antonia heated a tin of soup. Afterwards her father went to sleep in front of the fire. He snored and snuffled in his armchair with his legs apart and his flies unbuttoned. The remains of the clock, which he had somehow managed to drop while she was out with Jill, lay on the hearth, but she could not be bothered to clear them up now. Even one more moment in her father's company would be one too many. She could not bear to stay with him, though there was no heating in any of the other rooms. She carried Friday's *Gazette* upstairs with her, took off her shoes and climbed into bed.

Despite her tiredness, she was too tense to sleep. She made the effort to read the article about the Rose in Hand, partly to discover whether her father had in fact contributed anything of value to it, partly because the subject held a morbid fascination for her, and partly to keep her mind off the monstrous suspicion that everyone was conspiring to get her back to Chandos Lodge to be her father's nurse-housekeeper.

A few words caught her eyes. With a jerk, she sat up in bed. But it's quite ridiculous, she thought; people just don't *do* that sort of thing. She draped the eiderdown round her shoulders and read the article more carefully. Her mouth was dry and her heart was beating louder and faster than was comfortable. She read the descriptions of the box and the brooch for the third time. If only there were photographs, she thought. The possibilities oppressed her. She had thought that nothing could make her life worse than it already was, and now she knew she had been wrong.

Certainty, Antonia told herself, is always better than uncertainty. She got out of bed and, still with the eiderdown draped like a mantle across her shoulders, crossed the landing and went into the large, chilly bedroom which had been her mother's. Even on grey days it was full of light because of the huge bay window overlooking the lawn and the summerhouse. Antonia hated the room. She sat down at the dressing table and stared at her reflection in the dusty mirror.

"How could you do this to me?" she asked her mother across the years. "Can you hear me? I hate you."

164

She opened the drawers one by one and spilled their contents on to the floor. She found decaying underwear, yellowing letters tied with ribbon, a photograph of her father, much younger and in uniform, perfume bottles, face powder, brushes, tweezers, scissors, spiders, silk scarves and long gloves for evening wear. But she did not find what she was looking for.

She searched the rest of the room, but cursorily. It was at the dressing table that her mother would sit before dinner, brushing her hair and making the final adjustments to her appearance.

"I think I'll wear the pearls," she'd say. "Tony, be a darling and do them up for me, will you?"

Antonia stood up. The eiderdown fell from her shoulders. She felt uncomfortably hot. She went to the window and looked down at the summerhouse. It had been an even worse mistake to come back to Chandos Lodge than she had expected. If she had known what was in store, she told herself, she would have killed herself rather than come back. As she said the words silently to herself, she knew she was lying: she wouldn't have killed herself, because when she had tried before she had discovered that she was too much of a coward; she couldn't even manage her own death.

An idea occurred to her. One of the two wardrobes had a drawer beneath the hanging section. She knelt before it, grasped the handles and pulled. Nothing happened. She tugged again, throwing her weight backwards; each jerk was accompanied by a harsh, grunted word and each word was an obscenity.

With the seventh word, the drawer shot out. Still on her knees, Antonia pawed through the contents – framed prints, more letters, books and, at the bottom, a photograph album with thick black pages and a maroon binding. She lifted it out and opened it. On the flyleaf her mother's flowing handwriting confronted her:

Our Kashmir Album
Srinagar 1932

She turned the pages desperately. The images blurred – grey snowcapped mountains, a grey houseboat on a grey lake, people drinking tea, her father in shorts, her mother with a broad-brimmed hat, its shadow turning her face into a blank, black mask. Near the end of the album, Antonia found what she was looking for, what she feared to find, in a studio photograph of her parents. She saw on her mother's dress a brooch in the shape of a true love knot.

6

At six o'clock on Saturday evening, the Rover slid to a halt outside the pillared porch of the Bull Hotel. Philip was capable of flashes of unshakable obstinacy and, despite Jill's protests and Charlotte's tacit opposition, he had insisted on driving her from Troy House.

"Looks rather busy, doesn't it?" he said. "There's a Masonic dinner this evening, I think. Shall I come in for a moment?"

"Philip, I'm quite capable of going into a hotel on my own."

"Sorry. Look, give me a ring when you'd like a lift back. Unless you'd rather I waited?"

"No. I'll get a taxi."

Jill got out of the car and shut the door before Philip could think of any more well-meaning suggestions. Since Oliver's telephone call, it seemed to her that she had spent most of her time and energy fending off questions from Philip and Charlotte.

"There's someone I have to see staying at the Bull Hotel. You won't think me rude if I go, will you? I shan't be long."

"A friend?" Charlotte had asked.

Jill had ducked the question by saying that the meeting was to do with her leaving her job, which was true, though misleading. She could distinguish the thread of concern entangled with Philip and Charlotte's curiosity; but all she wanted, now as then, was to be left alone.

She waved at Philip, who was staring anxiously at her through the car window, and walked quickly into the hotel. The big building hummed with movement and noise, readying itself for the evening's dissipations; artificial light gave a kindly gloss to the peeling paintwork and the grubby wallpaper, and the place was filled with an illusion of prosperity whose reality had probably departed long before the war.

Behind the desk was the elderly man who had been on duty when Jill and Charlotte had come for coffee on Thursday. This time he wasn't dozing; he looked like a relatively alert tortoise in a striped waistcoat.

"Good evening, madam," he said as she approached the desk.

"I've come to see Mr Yateley. My name's Francis."

"Ah, yes. Mr Yateley mentioned you would call. He's in the lounge." The watery eyes examined her with the weary prurience of an old man; desire had died leaving behind a handful of lechery's rituals now shorn of their purpose. "Perhaps you would like me to . . . ?"

"That's all right, I know the way."

Jill walked past the desk. There was an unpleasant familiarity about the situation – she had met Oliver at so many hotels. She was conscious that the man at the reception desk was following her with his eyes.

She hesitated in the doorway of the lounge. The room looked very different from her memory of it. The curtains were drawn across the tall windows and the log fire cast a welcoming glow over the battered furniture and the faded fabrics. At least a dozen people were already there, most of them in groups around the tables, some with glasses in front of them. For an instant, all the conversations stopped, and it seemed to Jill that everyone was looking at her. Was her nose red, or was one of her stockings laddered? Damn them all, she thought, what right had they to stare at her?

As swiftly as blinking, everything changed. No one was staring at her. These were ordinary people engaged in ordinary activities. There was one exception and that was Oliver: he was hurrying across the room towards her, his hands spread wide. Before she could move away, he placed his hands on her arms and bent to kiss her. At the last moment she turned her head and the kiss landed on her cheek. She noted that he had very recently shaved, presumably in her honour.

"Come and sit down and I'll get you a drink." He glanced round the room. "Or perhaps it would be better if we went upstairs."

They had gone upstairs together in all those other hotels, but Jill was determined that they would not go upstairs in this one. "I'd rather stay here." She seized the initiative and moved towards the table near the fireplace, the table where she and Charlotte had sat. Oddly enough, the thought of Charlotte was a comfort at this moment: it was impossible to imagine Charlotte ever being involved in such a shabby and complicated business as this. She would have been able to cope with Oliver because it had never occurred to her that men were anything other than overlarge small boys in long trousers.

Jill avoided the sofa and sat down in one of the armchairs. Oliver waved one of the waitresses over.

"What would you like?"

"I don't want a drink, thanks." The waitress hovered by their table. Oliver looked up.

"I'll have a dry martini." He turned back to Jill. "I'm so glad you've come."

He sat down on the sofa. He had already changed for dinner and Jill speculated uncharitably about his motives: was it because he was hoping to persuade her to dine with him or was it merely that he thought, with some justification, that he looked rather good-looking in a dinner jacket? It had taken her a long time to realise that Oliver was vain, and an even longer time to think of his vanity as anything other than an endearing weakness.

For a moment. Oliver studied her in silence. He was a tall man with a strong-featured face and broad shoulders. He wasn't good-looking, but as he advanced into middle age, his face grew increasingly distinguished.

"You're looking peaky," he said abruptly. There was more than a hint of his native Yorkshire in his voice, which was often a sign of emotion in him, though Jill would not put it past him to simulate it. "How are you – physically, I mean? Are you back to – ah – normal?"

Jill wanted to say that she wasn't normal, that she would never feel normal again and that part of her didn't even want to feel normal. Instead she said, "I'm all right."

"These things happen. In a way it's a blessing it ended as it did."

"It wasn't an 'it'."

He appeared not to have heard her. "Best to put it behind us, eh? Make a fresh start."

"Us?"

"Yes. Nothing's changed." He looked accusingly at her. "I haven't changed."

"I know. That's the trouble." Jill felt tears filling her eyes and turned her face towards the fire. She couldn't even ask him the one question to which she wanted an answer: "Why me?"

7

On the way out of police headquarters, there was a mirror in which all officers were supposed to check their appearance before they left the building. Thornhill glanced into it as he came downstairs and saw to his irritation that at some stage during the afternoon he had lost the poppy from his lapel. He supposed he would have to buy himself another. Otherwise Williamson would be sure to hear of this dereliction of duty from one of his spies.

The High Street was quiet at this time of evening. Haloes of mist clung to the lamps. Thornhill walked along the pavement towards the Bull Hotel. He had allowed Kirby to go off duty an hour early – for his own sake rather than Kirby's. The sergeant was taking a girl to the pictures this evening and had spent the afternoon in a state of poorly suppressed excitement which Thornhill had found cumulatively irritating. The irritation had approached snapping point when he glimpsed a packet of condoms in an open drawer of Kirby's desk. It was wiser to send the man home, thereby salvaging a little dignity if nothing else.

Thornhill went into the hotel. An elderly man behind the reception desk glanced incuriously at him and returned to his newspaper. There was a tray of poppies and a collecting tin on the desk. The sight of them reminded Thornhill of Harcutt's tray and tin and once more the tiny discrepancy stirred like a fish in the murky depths of his mind.

"Police," Thornhill said, laying his warrant card on the desk.

The old man sat up with a jerk and straightened his striped waistcoat. "Sorry. Didn't recognise your face." He glanced at the card. "And what can I do for you, Inspector?"

"I'd like to have a word with one of your guests. I believe his name is James."

"I thought that might be it. Mr James isn't back yet. As I told your Mr Kirby, he went to Gloucester for the day."

"Any idea when he'll be back?"

"No." The voice was regretful. "If only I'd known you was interested. Always glad to help the police."

Thornhill shrugged. "While I'm here, I might as well see the register."

The old man pushed a heavy leatherbound volume across the desk.

"Thank you, Mr—"

"Quale."

Thornhill opened the book and flicked forward through the pages until he reached the last few entries. Only two guests had registered in November. One was Genghis Carn, modestly concealing his identity under the surname of James: he had given himself an address in Shepherd's Bush.

Thornhill took out his notebook and made a note of the details, as he did so, he noticed the other entry which had today's date. The name was Oliver Yateley and the address was in Dolphin Square, London SW1. Both the name and the address nudged Thornhill's memory. Dolphin Square, he remembered from his days in London, was somewhere in Belgravia near the river: a huge block of service flats favoured by the wealthy.

"You're not very busy at present."

"It's the time of year. Nothing much happens in November."

Thornhill took out his purse, fed a couple of pennies into the tin and selected a poppy. He looked up at the clock on the wall: technically he was off duty. "I'll have a drink while I'm here. Let me know if Mr James comes in before I go. Discreetly. Where's the bar?"

"Down there – just beyond the lounge."

As Thornhill was passing the open door of the lounge, there was a chorus of masculine laughter from the room. Automatically he glanced in the direction of the noise. Cyril George, the building contractor in charge of the Rose in Hand site, was sitting at a table near the fire with two other men, one of whom was telling a joke involving a vicar and an Irish burglar.

Thornhill's attention was drawn by the couple sitting on the other side of the fireplace – a prosperous-looking man in a dinner jacket and a dark-haired woman who was staring into the fire. With an unpleasant jolt he recognised the woman as Jill Francis, identifying her with absolute certainty although he could not see most of her face; that in itself was disturbing. Terrified that she might turn round and see him gawping at her, he hurried along the hall and went down the steps into the cocktail bar. He wished he hadn't seen her.

8

"When are you coming back to London?" Oliver asked, putting down his glass.

"I don't know." Reluctantly, Jill looked away from the fire and stared at him. She found it hard to understand how she could have loved this man. It wasn't altogether his fault. At present there was a coldness inside her that precluded love.

"Come back to town with me," he murmured. "Tonight. I've got the car – we could be in Dolphin Square by ten o'clock."

"Oliver, why can't you understand? I'm not coming to your flat ever again. I don't even want to see you again."

"But you must." He stared at her, his face filling not with pain but with incomprehension. "I couldn't bear it without you."

"You'll have to. Anyway, don't my feelings count? And what about Virginia?"

"Virginia's got nothing to do with this," he said angrily.

"She's got everything to do with it. She's your wife, remember." Jill took a deep breath. "And she's the mother of your children."

"Oh, for Christ's sake. That didn't seem to bother you before."

"It does now."

There was a burst of laughter from the businessmen at the neighbouring table.

"We've been through all this," Oliver said with exaggerated patience. "I've got a job to do, Jill. It's an important job, and to do it properly I need to have Virginia in the background. I don't like it any more than you do. But it's the way the world works."

"It's the way you work."

"It doesn't mean I don't love you." He swallowed. "Jill, I *need* you."

"If you want to be a hypocrite, that's your affair. But I don't have to be one as well. Not any more."

"Don't be so bloody naïve," he snapped, his face flushing. He picked up his martini and swallowed the rest of it. "I'm sorry, darling. I know you're under a lot of strain."

Jill stood up, holding her handbag like a shield. "I don't think you know the first thing about me." She was aware that the businessmen had stopped talking. "I'm going now. Goodbye."

She turned and walked towards the door. Oliver scrambled up and followed her.

"You can't do this to me," he said in a whisper, his face flushing. "I love you."

"It's too late." She reached the hall. The lascivious old man at the desk was watching them.

"Marry me," Oliver said.

"It's too late for that too." She stopped so sharply that he almost bumped into her. "If you don't leave me alone, I shall ask that man to call the police."

9

In the cocktail bar, the tables had glass tops and the chairs and the bar stools were made of chrome with leather seats – perhaps the result of a half-hearted attempt to modernise the hotel. There was a sprinkling of customers. Thornhill ordered a dry sherry. When the drink came, it was inordinately expensive.

As he turned away from the bar, he was surprised to hear someone calling his name. Fuggle, the elderly journalist who had baited Superintendent Williamson at the press briefing the previous day, was sitting at a corner table with a thickset man in tweeds. Fuggle waved Thornhill over, pointing at an empty chair beside his.

"Won't you join us? Do you know Giles Newton?"

Newton smiled and offered his hand. He was a man in his fifties, with a square face and a crop of thick, curly grey hair.

"We've been talking about that Rose in Hand business," Fuggle said, when Thornhill had sat down. "You should have a word with this gentleman, Inspector. He knows all about the place."

"Really?"

Newton smiled. "That's a slight exaggeration." He had the sort of accent which Thornhill associated with an expensive and unfairly privileged education. "I work for the Ruispidge Estate, you see, and the Estate used to own the site."

"Still owns the rest of Templefields," put in Fuggle, his eyes gleaming. "And indeed a good deal of other property in Lydmouth, including this very hotel. Which is of course why we're here."

Thornhill's confusion must have been obvious in his face, for Fuggle smiled gleefully and Newton rushed to explain.

"We've been discussing the Conservative Party's Christmas dance, Mr Thornhill. Fuggle's on the committee. I represent the Estate. By tradition it's held at the Bull Hotel."

"Shall we be seeing you and your good lady at the dance?" Fuggle enquired.

"I doubt it," Thornhill said, wondering how the reporter had discovered that he was married.

Fuggle glanced at the clock behind the bar. "Oh, dear me, is that the time? I really must fly. You'll excuse me, gentlemen?"

In the space of a few seconds, he had finished his drink, slipped on his overcoat and left the room.

Newton smiled at Thornhill. "Mrs Fuggle is said to be something of a tartar. Let me get you another drink. Same again?"

He beckoned the barman who scurried across to their table. Thornhill reflected sourly that when he tried to summon waiters or barmen with that casual assurance they generally pretended not to see him – unless they knew what he did for a living.

"Sad business, really," Newton said a moment later, after ordering the drinks.

"I beg your pardon?" Thornhill's mind had wandered off to Jill Francis: he was speculating about the reason for her being at the Bull without either of the Wemyss-Browns.

"The bones at the Rose in Hand. Do you feel pretty sure that Victorian murderess was responsible?"

"Amelia Rushwick? It seems the most likely solution. What happened to the Rose in Hand after her parents' tenancy ended?"

"That's what Fuggle was asking me." Newton began to fill a pipe. "I looked up the records yesterday after I'd seen the article in the *Gazette*. The Rushwicks left in 1891. Then there was someone called John Farndale. He was there for three years. After that, the place was taken by a Mr and Mrs Jones who ran it as a temperance hotel. They lasted less than eighteen months and had to be evicted for unpaid rent. Then the Rose more or less gave up the ghost."

The barman brought their drinks over.

"Cheers," Thornhill said, sipping his sherry. "How do you mean, 'gave up the ghost'?"

"Simply that it was no longer a paying proposition. The Estate couldn't find a tenant for the pub, or not the sort they wanted. Reading between the lines, the whole of Templefields was going downhill – a bit of an albatross – so they decided to let it rot. They did the minimum of maintenance and split up the pub and outbuildings – leased them out for whatever they could get, commercial or residential. That was the situation when they took me on."

"When was that?"

"In 1937. By that time the pub was empty, practically derelict. I remember we tried to let the yards separately. Major Harcutt was quite interested at one stage – you know he had a coal merchant's business in those days?"

Thornhill nodded. His attention was distracted by movement near the door. The man he had seen with Jill Francis came into the room and perched on one of the bar stools.

"Of course Harcutt's interest may have been historical rather than commercial," Newton went on. "He sold up a few months afterwards."

The man ordered a dry martini in a carrying voice which, unlike his face, had a familiar quality.

"Has the Estate any plans for the rest of Templefields?" Thornhill asked.

"Not really." Newton grinned, and his face looked ten years younger. "Not unless the council make us an offer we can't refuse. Tell me, how are you liking Lydmouth?"

"It's early days."

"Takes a while to settle in, doesn't it? I found that. It's still a very close-knit community. After a while they begin to accept you. But unless you're actually born here, they'll still call you a foreigner until the day you die."

"In some ways it seems a very old-fashioned place."

"To look at it," Newton said, "you'd think the clock stopped in about 1923 and everything will always be the same. But it's changing. Most people don't realise how much or how fast."

They talked for another ten minutes. Thornhill offered to buy the next round but Newton glanced at the clock behind the bar and declined.

"I'd better go. Wouldn't do to be late for dinner, though my wife's not in the same league as Mrs Fuggle."

Thornhill left as well. To his surprise, he found himself wishing that the conversation with Newton could have lasted longer. On his way out, he noticed Jill Francis's friend ordering another dry martini. In the hall, he paused to have a word with Quale: Carn still hadn't returned. Thornhill said he would call back later in the evening and Quale's eyes gleamed with excitement.

He went outside. It had started to rain again. He lingered in the shelter of the porch to button his coat. Talking to Newton seemed to have cleared his head. It was time to go home to Edith and the children, wave an olive branch and have some supper. He had been behaving like a sulky schoolboy.

He walked quickly back to headquarters and collected his car. The sherry had given him an appetite. He drove up to the High Street and turned right. The rain was growing heavier by the minute, the drops of water bouncing off the roadway and thrumming on the roof of the car.

After fifty yards, he stopped at a zebra crossing: two girls teetered across on their high heels, moving at suicidal speed. He glanced idly through the car's nearside window and saw a woman sheltering from the rain in the doorway of a men's outfitters, her pale face clearly visible in the light from a streetlamp. He recognised her and on impulse rolled down the nearside window.

"Miss Francis, can I give you a lift?" Suddenly he realised that she might not be able to see who it was. "It's Richard Thornhill."

She hesitated. For a moment, he thought she would refuse. Then she walked quickly across the pavement. He opened the door from the inside. She climbed into the car.

"You're going back to Troy House?"

"Yes."

"Caught in the rain? Not a night for walking."

"No."

He let out the clutch and the car moved off.

"It's kind of you to give me a lift," she said in a rush.

"Not at all."

The conversation languished. Thornhill felt mildly aggrieved – after all, he was doing the woman a good turn. Perhaps she reserved her conversation for the favoured few, like the well-heeled gentleman – Yateley? – in the lounge of the Bull Hotel. He drove automatically, his attention focused on his passenger. At one point he glanced at her as they were passing a streetlamp: there was enough light to see that she was staring through the windscreen; she might have been alone.

Thornhill pulled up outside Troy House, leaving the engine running. She fumbled for the door handle and couldn't find it. Probably she expected him to get out, walk round the car in the pouring rain and open the door from the outside; but he wasn't in the mood for courtly gestures. Muttering an apology, he leant across her and opened the door. For the first time he saw her face clearly.

"You've been crying," he said before he could stop himself. He sat up sharply, chilly with embarrassment. "Sorry."

"Don't be. You're quite right." She gave a shaky laugh. "It's ridiculous, isn't it?"

After a few seconds had passed, he said, "Do you want a handkerchief? I've got a clean one."

"Thank you. I forgot to take one. So silly of me."

He gave her the handkerchief and looked away while she blew her nose and wiped her eyes.

"I'll have it washed and give it back to you," she said. "Thank you again. Good night."

"Good night."

She got out of the car. Thornhill watched her walking up the path to the front door of Troy House. He felt puzzled and also a little flattered that she'd deigned to take not only a lift but a handkerchief from him. She opened the door, half turned to give him a wave and disappeared into the house. A moment later, he drove away.

10

Dr Bayswater stared down at Mrs Meague. Her eyes were closed and she was gasping for air.

"When did it happen?"

"She took a turn for the worse around tea time," the sister murmured.

"Does the son know?"

"Unfortunately not. He was in at lunch time and she seemed much better then. We've phoned the pub near their house and left a message."

"He'd better hurry," Bayswater said, "or it may be too late."

The sister was called away. Bayswater grunted angrily and sat down on the chair beside the bed. The old woman's red, work-roughened hand was lying on the blanket. The fingers twitched. The lips were moving. He bent nearer to her.

"Charlie."

"He's coming," Bayswater said gruffly.

"Charlie."

Gingerly, he touched her hand. Her fingers wrapped themselves around his.

"Charlie," she said again. "Poor Miss Tony. But it wasn't you, was it?"

Bayswater said nothing.

The thin body twitched under the blankets. The head moved a fraction on the pillow and the weak fingers gripped Bayswater's a little more tightly. "It wasn't you, Charlie, was it?"

"No," Dr Bayswater said firmly. "It wasn't."

The fingers relaxed their grip a little, but they tightened again in a moment when the breathing grew even more laboured. Since he had last seen Mrs Meague, her face had become bluer and more swollen. She disliked him, he thought, and was probably afraid of him.

Dr Bayswater sat beside the bed. There was a crick in his neck and he wanted to empty his bladder and have a smoke. He watched the clock on the wall of sister's office. He was still sitting there when she came back fifteen minutes later.

"She doesn't know you're there," the sister said, surprised to see him.

"I know." Dr Bayswater scowled at her. "I'm not a bloody fool."

11

Charlie swaggered through the public bar as if he owned it and leant against the counter. Gloria was serving a customer in the lounge bar; neither her husband Harold nor her stepdaughter was in sight, which suited Charlie very well.

While he waited he examined the back of her, taking his time and dwelling on the curves and hollows with a relish which was both nostalgic and anticipatory. Then and now, she was beautiful and desirable; but freshness had given way to a gorgeous ripeness. He guessed from the way she held herself that she was conscious of his eyes. At last she finished and sauntered across to him.

"How's your mum?" she asked as she was pulling his pint.

"She's better. Saw her dinner time – I reckon she's turned the corner."

"That's good."

"So I'll have a Scotch with that. I'm celebrating, aren't I?"

Avoiding his eyes, Gloria put down the pint glass on the counter and turned away to fetch his whisky. He thought she was angry with him. It was crazy – she kept a pub and she didn't like a man drinking. But when she came back with the whisky, she leant on the counter, her head close to his and her perfume strong in his nostrils. He smiled, delighted by his own power: she couldn't keep away from him.

"There's a copper in the other bar," she said quietly.

His pleasure vanished. He lowered his voice to match hers: "Working, is he?"

"I don't know. He's a detective sergeant, name of Kirby. Comes in here for his dinner sometimes. He's with a girl, but that doesn't mean anything."

"Not that it matters, of course. I've done nothing wrong."

Charlie was aware that Gloria's eyes were anxious; her concern irritated him because it implied that he was vulnerable. He wanted admiration, not help. He heard a door opening behind him and sensed that her attention had switched away from him. His irritation

180

increased: it seemed that any passing customer took precedence over him.

"There's your friend again," Gloria said coldly. "I expect you'd like to buy him a drink. It's usually that way round, isn't it?"

Charlie turned. Genghis Carn was standing a couple of feet away from him. He smiled impartially at the space between Gloria and Charlie.

"How kind. A pint of best please and a large Scotch."

Gloria's lips tightened into a bright red line. She shrugged and picked up a clean pint mug.

"And how's Mrs Meague today?" Carn enquired.

"Better, they say," Charlie said shortly.

"Glad to hear that. Takes a man's mind off his work when there's sickness in the family – in my experience, anyway."

Gloria banged the mug down on the counter. A little of the beer slopped over the rim. Carn thanked her and lifted the mug to his lips. "Here's to you."

Automatically Charlie drank. Gloria brought the whisky. While Charlie was paying for both sets of drinks, Carn wandered across the bar to a table in the corner furthest away from the dartboard. Charlie followed him, and they sat down with their backs to the wall.

"Gloria says there's a copper in the other bar," Charlie muttered. "A detective sergeant – I don't know whether he's on duty or not."

"And why should that concern me?"

"Listen, Jimmy, I didn't mean—"

"When's your mother coming out of hospital?"

Charlie hesitated, rubbing the stubble on his jaw. "I don't know. It could be some time yet."

"I imagine she'll be in a delicate state of health for some time. You must be careful not to let anything upset her."

Charlie drank in silence.

"Rather an attractive young woman," Carn went on, flicking his eyes towards the bar and then back to Charlie's face. "If you like that sort of thing. Known her long?"

"Since we were kids."

The silence lengthened between them. Charlie began to roll a cigarette to give himself something to do. His fingers were clumsier than usual.

Carn picked up the matchbox beside Charlie's tobacco tin and took out a fresh match. He broke it in two, ensuring that the wood splintered into a long, diagonal fracture. Breathing heavily, he used half of the match as a toothpick. He deposited a pale shred of meat on the side of the ashtray.

"She's the landlady?" he asked.

"Husband manages the pub for the brewery. Well, it's his name over the door, but I reckon she runs it."

"Responsible job. Shouldn't care for it myself, the licensed trade. So many things can go wrong, can't they?" There was a pause while Carn dug out another scrap of his supper and placed it next to the first. "And, let's face it, when a man's had a few drinks, he doesn't always behave very rationally."

Charlie's fingers were damp with sweat and the cigarette paper clung to them unexpectedly. Tobacco cascaded on to the table. "Why don't you just say it straight out?" he said. "What do you want?"

"I want what's mine."

"You'll have it, Jimmy. I promise. I've got it all arranged, I—"

"I was going to tell you last night," Carn cut in, his voice soft and nasal, "but you were too drunk to remember your own name. I can't wait, you see – I want it now."

12

Antonia made their supper with bad grace – undercooked boiled eggs and burned toast. She refilled her father's glass twice during the meal.

"You're a good girl, Tony," he said after the second time, sounding surprised.

Had he forgotten everything, she wondered? Or was he able to pretend to himself that none of it had happened? She could not understand how anyone, least of all her father, could be so stupid. She kept her head down as she chewed the charred toast. She knew he was looking at her.

"Tony? I want to go to the service tomorrow. You'll come too, won't you? Hate to ask, but the thing is, I may need a bit of help."

Still chewing, she nodded. She did not want to speak to him.

"Well, that's all right then. Knew you would. I won't be able to march with the chaps beforehand, of course. If we had a wheelchair, you could push me. But there it is, eh? So you'll phone for a taxi, then? First thing in the morning."

His voice trailed away. She had forgotten his graceless way of demanding and receiving favours as though they were his of right. It had always made giving him anything a difficult and unpleasant process. Thank God for small mercies: none of the busybodies had thought to provide them with a wheelchair. The local Legion headquarters was at least a quarter-mile from the church: she would have had to push his dead weight uphill, and it would probably have been raining.

After the meal, he smoked a cigarette and stared at the hissing flames of the gas fire while she cleared away. She washed up in the kitchen, which felt like a haven because he wasn't there. The meal had done little to warm her – she felt cold, physically and emotionally.

When she had been a child and her mother was still alive, Antonia had been convinced that there must be more to her father than met the eye. She had made up stories about him – little fantasies, designed with love and crafted with care, the sole purpose of which had been to permit him to reveal his love for her. "Love", of course, in those days, had been a word with many shades of meaning, all of them innocent. In the hypothetical case of her father, love had manifested itself in many, deeply gratifying ways, such as sensitivity towards her feelings, appreciation of her latent qualities and admiration for her achievements (which were, as even she had been forced to admit, as yet unachieved).

The trouble with life, Antonia thought as she dumped the crockery into the sink, was not that dreams didn't come true, but that they came true in such unexpected and bloody awful ways. She chipped an egg cup and, with a gratifying sensation of wickedness, tossed it into the dustbin outside the back door where it joined the remains of the clock her father had broken earlier in the day.

Leaving the plates to drain, she went quietly back to the living room. Her father was slumped in his chair with his eyelids closed and the air whispering and rustling through his nostrils. She stared at him, cataloguing the features of his ugliness to feed her hatred.

It was, she thought, as good an opportunity as she was likely to get. After all, he slept in this room and since the accident he had only left it to use the lavatory down the hall. "Father," she said quietly. She could not bring herself to call him Daddy. "Father?" she repeated, this time more loudly.

He didn't stir in his chair and the rhythm of his breathing continued undisturbed.

She raised her voice almost to a shout: "Father!"

Nothing happened. Antonia glanced round the room and decided to move in a clockwise direction, reserving the bureau until last. She worked her way steadily round the walls. She opened drawers, peered into cupboards, rifled through the piles of papers, opened files and sorted through files of ancient accounts.

One of the sideboard cupboards was devoted to the affairs of the local branch of the British Legion which took up so much space that the door would no longer close. There were many letters from all over the world, including a bundle from Aunt Maud in South Africa during the war; Antonia glanced at one or two of these and found references to herself: 'Antonia is enjoying the typing course more than the shorthand. She's too busy to write but sends her love . . .'

While she worked, she listened continuously to the breathing that struggled along her father's congested airways and kept him alive. Oh, yes, she thought, now that one had seen the possibility, it all fitted together and it all made sense: it was all of a piece with his sly and ruthless devotion to his own interests. At the fireplace, she paused to look at the photograph of her parents and herself. She picked up the frame and studied her mother's face.

How could you leave me, you bitch? This is all your fault.

The longer Antonia searched, the more frantic and fevered she became. Finally she came to the bureau which she had saved until last as a child saves the most desirable morsel on the plate until the end. Her father's medals were lying on the blotter beside the tray containing the rest of the poppies. She went through the contents of the drawers and she rummaged through the pigeon holes. She found the whisky bottle and the spare whisky bottle and two used glasses. She found her father's wallet, his cheque book and his will, which, she was interested to discover, left everything to her mother, 'my beloved wife'.

At last Antonia was forced to admit defeat, though in a sense it was a kind of victory since it was a confirmation of what she had suspected; at least she was no longer deceived. She stared at the little row of medals which her father had taken out in preparation for the Armistice service. He had laid them in a neat row across the cream blotter, their ribbons precisely parallel and the metal newly burnished. Most of them, she knew, were campaign medals or war medals – the sort of decorations which so many men had, which signified nothing apart from the fact that they had been in uniform at a particular time and in a particular place.

The decoration in the centre of the line, however, belonged in a different category. The ribbon was white watered silk with a purple stripe down the centre. From it depended a silver cross on each arm of which was an imperial crown, and in the middle was the imperial cipher GRI. Her father had won the Military Cross in 1917 for an act of valour under enemy fire. He had told Antonia when she was a girl that it had involved shooting a lot of damned Huns in a trench. He referred to the decoration in an offhand manner, but Antonia suspected that its award was perhaps the one unequivocally satisfactory achievement of his entire life.

She lifted the blotter and with a flick of a wrist sent the medals cascading in a chinking, brightly coloured stream to the bottom of the wastepaper basket.

For an instant the breathing stopped. Harcutt stirred in his chair. "What was that?"

"Nothing, Father."

185

13

Mr Quale stared at Thornhill with moist eyes and ran a forefinger round the substantial gap between his collar and his wrinkled neck.

"You're in luck, Inspector. He came back on the 7.29. He's having his dinner." Quale pursed his lips and nodded knowingly. "Lamb cutlets, I fancy. I understand he's partial to a bit of lamb."

"I'll go and have a word with him," Thornhill said, shying away from Quale's evident enjoyment of his role as the policeman's friend. "Is he alone?"

"Oh, yes, Mr Thornhill. I made sure of that. I took the liberty of having a word with Mr Forbin, our head waiter. Only too glad to oblige."

And his face made it only too obvious that such obligations had to be discharged in hard cash. Thornhill put a half-crown on the desk.

"Thank you, Mr Quale."

"Thank *you*, sir." The gratitude was faintly tinged with sarcasm, which implied that half-a-crown had been too little. "The door opposite the lounge."

Neither Mr Quale nor Mr Forbin had needed to exercise much ingenuity to keep Genghis Carn away from the other diners. The dining room was as large as the lounge, and despite the fact that it was Saturday night, most of the tables were empty. Carn was sitting by himself near the huge sideboard which dominated one wall.

The head waiter hurried over to Thornhill as he hesitated in the doorway. Forbin was a small, slovenly man of a similar age to Mr Quale. He swerved to make an apparently unnecessary diversion round a table. Thornhill guessed that the man wanted to angle his approach to the doorway so Mr Quale was in his line of vision, and that a signal must have passed between the two men.

"Mr Thornhill," said the head waiter, beaming; his waistcoat strained across his potbelly and had lost one of its buttons. "I hope we shall have the honour of seeing you here for pleasure, as well as for business. This way, sir."

Thornhill followed Forbin's swaying coat tails across the room to Carn's table. He thought it probable that Carn had caught a glimpse of them in the big mirror above the sideboard. One of the diners glanced up at Thornhill as he passed. It was the man who had been with Jill Francis in the lounge and who had later come into the bar for a dry martini. His face was flushed and he was working his way through a bottle of Burgundy.

Forbin drew up beside Carn's table. "A visitor for you, sir," he announced.

Carn looked up from his book. He dropped his spoon into his spotted dick and pushed the bowl away.

With a flourish, Forbin pulled back a chair. Thornhill sat down and declined the head waiter's offer to bring him some refreshment. Carn's pale, protuberant blue eyes stared at Inspector Thornhill, while one hand rested on the open pages of the book as if marking the place. At close quarters, the pallor of his complexion made him seem a little less than human.

"Mr James Carn?" Thornhill said quietly, once Forbin had reluctantly withdrawn.

The head nodded.

"I understand you registered here as Mr James."

"Who might you be?"

"My name's Thornhill." He slid his warrant card across the table.

Carn took his time examining it. "There's no law against changing your name. Not that I have, of course."

"Did I say there was, Mr Carn?" Thornhill paused. "What are you doing in Lydmouth?"

"It's a free country, Inspector. Can't a man have a little holiday?"

"I thought you'd just had a long holiday with free board and lodging."

Carn laid down his spoon. "I've paid my debt to society. That episode's neither here nor there."

"Charlie Meague is in Lydmouth, isn't he?"

"Who?"

"Don't come the innocent. Rather an odd coincidence, I'd have thought. Perhaps you plan to combine business and pleasure?"

Carn shrugged. He picked up his spoon and took a small mouthful of his pudding.

"We'd like you to take your holiday somewhere else, Mr Carn."

"And why should your wishes influence me, Mr Thornhill?"

"Two reasons. First, I'll have a word with the manager, and I doubt if he'll want your custom once he's heard what I've got to say. And that goes for any other hotel or lodging house in this town. Second, we're going to be keeping an eye on you – and on Charlie Meague."

"That sounds like harassment to me, Inspector. Perhaps I should have a word with my solicitor."

"You can do whatever you want as long as it's within the law and as long as you're out of Lydmouth by tomorrow."

Carn's eyes dropped back to his book. "Is there anything else?"

Thornhill pushed back his chair and stood up. "I'm going to see the manager now."

The manager was thirty-five going on fifty, a portly fellow with a vague expression and an RAF handlebar moustache. He greeted Thornhill's news with a mixture of fascination and horror.

"Don't worry, old man, he'll have his bill with his coffee. Bloody cheek, eh? I say, do you think he'll try and do a flit?"

"I don't think he's that stupid," Thornhill said. "But let us know if he does."

When he had finished with the manager, Thornhill walked slowly down the hall to the front door. There was nothing to prevent him going home now, but he felt restless. Nor was there much to draw him home: the children were asleep and he and Edith were still wary of each other after the previous evening.

As he was passing the door of the dining room, he glanced inside. Carn was no longer at his table. Coming towards the door was the tall man he had seen with Jill Francis. The man's foot caught in the edge of the threadbare carpet running down the hall. He stumbled and would have fallen if Thornhill had not put out an arm.

"Terribly sorry," he said loudly, clinging to Thornhill's arm. "It's a damned deathtrap, that carpet."

"Are you all right?"

The man straightened up and leant against the wall. "Not particularly," he said in that voice which was so irritatingly familiar. "Still, I would have been even less all right if you hadn't caught me. In my book, that deserves a drink. Come and have a brandy."

Thornhill would usually have declined an invitation to help a drunk get drunker, even when the drinking was to be done at the drunk's expense. But he allowed the man to take his arm and propel him across the hall and into the lounge. His motives were mixed. Although he didn't particularly want to go home, there was nothing else he wanted to do. He had a professional excuse for staying in that his continued presence at the hotel might encourage Carn to believe that the police were serious. He was curious, too, about this man who didn't belong in Lydmouth any more than he did. But the real reason, which Thornhill made himself admit as his host waved him towards an armchair, was that he wanted to discover the nature of the man's connection with Jill Francis.

"My name's Oliver Yateley, by the way. Coffee and brandy?"

"That's very kind of you. I'm Richard Thornhill."

Yateley blinked at him as if he'd forgotten why he'd asked him for coffee and brandy. He struggled forward in his chair and held out his hand. "How do you do? I should warn you, go easy on the coffee. You could probably strip paint with it." A waitress came to take their order. "Large brandies, mind," he told her, articulating each syllable with precision. "No point in your having two journeys where one will do." He turned back to Thornhill. "You're not staying here, are you?"

"No."

"So you live in Lydmouth?" Yateley frowned. "Don't take it personally, old chap, but I couldn't stand *living* here. I'd be dead from the neck upwards within a week."

"I've only just moved here, so I'm not a good judge."

"I mean, look at this place." Yateley waved his arm around the lounge. "It's so damned dreary."

The waitress brought them their coffee and brandy.

Thornhill poured the coffee while Yateley went through the complicated procedure of finding his cigar case. He offered it to Thornhill who refused.

"Still," he said between puffs as he tried to get his cigar drawing properly. "It can only get better, even in Lydmouth. Just wait till the next election. Yes, there'll better times coming. You mark my words."

There'll be better times coming – the phrase jogged Thornhill's memory. "I've heard you on the radio, haven't I? Talking about politics?"

Yateley frowned slightly and then nodded. Smoke billowed round his face giving him the appearance of a pantomime demon. On the whole he did not seem displeased to be recognised.

"I thought there was something familiar about your voice."

"The wireless – yes – goes with the job. Nowadays, if you're in politics, you can't just sit on your backside between elections. You have to reach out to your voters. Next thing we know it'll be television. It's a harsh mistress, politics, believe you me. I sometimes think I've had to sacrifice everything to it." He leaned closer to Thornhill and sucked deeply on the cigar. His cheeks were pink and his eyes gleamed; he displayed all the symptoms of a man approaching the confidential stage of a maudlin evening. "And I mean everything." He hesitated, but only for a second. "For example, if I hadn't gone into parliament, I'd have made a fortune by now. And then there's the effect it has on one's personal relationships."

Yateley flung out an arm and picked up his brandy, jogging Thornhill's coffee cup as he did so. He appeared not to notice the spillage and swallowed the contents of his glass.

Thornhill knew almost immediately that something was wrong. Yateley put down the glass and had another suck of his cigar. But his eyes were pleading as they gazed at Thornhill, and he swallowed three times in quick succession. Nature, Thornhill guessed with a hint of malicious pleasure, was exacting its price for overindulgence.

Yateley struggled to his feet. "You'll have to – um – excuse me a moment."

He dropped the cigar in the general direction of the ashtray, but his aim was poor and it fell on to the table instead. He blundered across the room, pushed his way through a knot of men who had congregated in the doorway and stumbled out of sight. Thornhill picked up the cigar and stubbed it out.

Somewhere in the hall, a man started shouting. The words were indistinguishable, but the outrage was obvious. Another man replied; the voice was Yateley's.

Suppressing his reluctance to get involved, Thornhill got up and joined the group of men in the doorway. Yateley was leaning against the wall near the dining-room door and muttering angrily. Facing him was the building contractor, Cyril George. There was a dark stain on George's trousers and pieces of glass on the carpet.

"I expect an apology," George was saying, and he jabbed his forefinger repeatedly into Yateley's chest to emphasise his words. "Barging around like a storm trooper – who do you think you are?"

George was very nearly as drunk as Yateley, but far more aggressive. He was with friends, one on either side of him, both with flushed faces, whose very presence no doubt encouraged him to take umbrage. They were all big men, plump and prosperous in their dinner jackets. The three of them had probably come down from the Masonic dinner upstairs.

"Well?" George said. "I want an apology, sir. I want some more brandy. And I don't want to see your face in this hotel again."

Yateley licked his lips which were very pale; he swallowed and said in a strangled voice, "Why don't you bugger off?"

Thornhill slipped into the hall. Forbin was standing in the dining-room doorway and Quale was watching the encounter from his desk; neither man was likely to intervene. George took a step closer to Yateley. Thornhill put a restraining hand on the building contractor's right arm.

"Let go of me," George snapped, showing his jagged yellow teeth. Then his cloudy, bloodshot eyes widened as he recognised Thornhill. "Sergeant, you can bloody well make yourself useful for once. This man's causing a public nuisance. I want him off the premises. Can't you arrest him?"

"I'll deal with this," Thornhill said.

190

"A night in the cells would do him the world of good. Look at him. Drunk as a lord."

"I'd like you gentlemen to move along now."

No one moved.

"Listen, Sergeant," George said. "Do I have to spell this out? Superintendent Williamson is a personal friend of mine. In fact, he's upstairs at this very moment."

Thornhill had met this sort of pressure many times in his career and once or twice he had buckled under the strain. He said in a tight, controlled voice, "Then I suggest you go back and join him, sir."

He stepped forward and took Yateley's arm. Taken by surprise, Yateley followed docilely when Thornhill began to tow him down the hall.

"Mr Quale," Thornhill said. "May I have this gentleman's room key?"

Quale passed the key across the desk. His face was alive with interest and he was smiling, revealing a set of gleaming false teeth.

Thornhill urged Yateley towards the stairs. His attention strained towards the men behind him. You could hear their voices murmuring, but they hadn't moved. He thought it would be all right. He hated situations when there was a threat of physical violence and he doubted his own ability to control them. There was also the small matter of how Williamson would react to the incident.

Yateley grasped the banisters and Thornhill urged him upstairs. When they reached the top of the stairs, he and Yateley zigzagged arm and arm down the landing, twice colliding with pieces of furniture, to Room 15. Thornhill propped him up against the wall while he unlocked the door.

"Lavatory," Yateley said. "Oh, Christ."

Thornhill guided him to the bathroom on the opposite side of the corridor. Thornhill saw him collapse on his knees in front of the bowl. Oliver Yateley coughed once and moaned softly. He rested his arms on the porcelain rim of the lavatory, exposing the heavy gold links on his shirt cuffs. As Yateley began to vomit, Thornhill closed the bathroom door.

He was tempted to walk away. All the signs were that Yateley's life was in a mess. If Cyril George made good his threat of telling Williamson, then the mess would envelop Thornhill too, whatever he did now.

On the other side of the bathroom door, the retching continued. Thornhill crossed the landing and stood in the doorway of Room 15. The sagging brass bedstead, the shapeless armchair and the faded curtains were all familiar: he had seen them before in a dozen bedrooms in provincial hotels past their prime. The air smelled of leather and cigar smoke. He advanced a yard or two into the room. In front of him was the dressing table and on it was a leatherbound writing case. It was closed, but the zip had not been fastened; the corner of a photograph protruded from the top.

The bathroom was silent. Thornhill took the print between finger and thumb and gently eased it halfway out of the writing case. He found himself looking at Jill Francis. She was wrapped in a fur coat and smiling at the camera, or rather at the person, probably Yateley, behind the camera. The photograph had been taken in a street which Thornhill knew at once was not English. A second later, he registered the fact that the signs on the shops were in French. It occurred to him, belatedly, that Yateley and Jill might well be husband and wife. He was almost certain that there had been a wedding band on the third finger of Yateley's left hand.

Thornhill hurriedly pushed the photograph back into the case. Near it, beside a pair of silver-backed brushes, was a small pile of letters. The one on the top was addressed to Oliver Yateley, Esq., MP at the address in Dolphin Square.

The lavatory flushed. He moved away from the dressing table and pretended to examine a picture on the wall near the door – a painfully inept oil painting of bluebells and sheep in a forest glade. The sound of running water came from the bathroom. A moment later, the door opened and Yateley emerged, his face ashen. He crossed the landing and came into the bedroom.

"I thought you might have gone," he said, slurring the words more than before. "Thanks." He sat down on the bed and put his head in his hands. "Made a bit of a fool of myself."

"Is there anything I can get you?"

"I could drink a gallon of coffee. On second thoughts I'd better make it tea. Do you think one could find some aspirin in this place?"

Thornhill went downstairs to find out. Encouraged by a second half-crown, Quale promised to arrange a pot of tea and some aspirin.

"The gentleman had a drop too much, eh?" he said. "It does happen."

"Have you seen Mr James?"

"He went upstairs half-an-hour ago." One of Quale's eyelids drooped in a wink. "With his bill. I understand Mr James is leaving us in the morning."

Thornhill nodded and turned towards the stairs.

"Mr George left about five minutes ago," Quale said casually. "Him and Mr Williamson left together."

"Thanks," Thornhill said over his shoulder as he went upstairs.

Almost certainly, Quale had seen and overheard the entire altercation, and he was shrewd enough to understand the implications.

In Room 15, Yateley was still sitting on the edge of the bed with his head in his hands. But he must have got up while he was alone, because the writing case was open on the dressing table, and beside him on the bed was the photograph of Jill Francis.

Thornhill shut the door. "They'll be sending up some tea in a moment."

Yateley raised his head. There were tear tracks on his cheeks, which embarrassed Thornhill.

"You'd rather be by yourself, I expect," Thornhill said. "Take some aspirin and get some sleep. Best thing to do."

"For God's sake," Yateley said, "please don't go."

"I'll have to go soon."

"Yes but not now. Have a drink – there's a hip flask in my bag. Or have a cigar or something. But stay with me for a little."

Thornhill shrugged and sat down in the armchair beside the fireplace.

"Sorry," Yateley said. "Can't remember your name."

Thornhill told him.

"That man downstairs called you sergeant."

"I'm a detective inspector in the Lydmouth CID."

Yateley blinked, assimilating the information. "You got children, Thornhill?"

"Two. A boy and a girl."

"I've got three. Not that I see much of them. They're up in Yorkshire most of the time, and I'm in town. They cost me an arm and a leg, and his mother makes the boy call me 'Sir'." He pulled a handkerchief from his sleeve and blew his nose loudly. "I've made a fool of myself tonight, in more ways than one. I'd rather that it didn't get about."

"I hope it won't. As far as I'm concerned, there's no reason why it should." Thornhill glanced at the photograph on the bed. "Is that Mrs Yateley?"

"No." Yateley shook his heavy head from side to side. "That's the trouble." He was very drunk, and the urge to confide was still strong. "Funny creatures, women. She was going to have a baby, you know. Absolutely impractical. Sheer bloody lunacy, for her as much as me. She's got a job, you see – career woman. Hasn't got a penny apart from what she earns. And it wasn't as if I was in a position to help." He stared angrily at Thornhill, as if daring him to criticise, as though it were his fault. "Damn it," Yateley snapped. "What does it matter? She wanted a child, and that was that. Nothing else counted. Then she had a miscarriage which, if only she'd see it, was a real stroke of luck. By the way she acted, you'd have thought her mother had died or something. Or me. But it was only a miscarriage, for God's sake. It wasn't even a person. Just a bit of waste matter her body rejected."

Thornhill sat without moving in the armchair. His hands were cold. He felt oppressed by all the suffering in the world. and his inability to do anything about it. He, too, felt guilty. The silence between the two men stretched into something long and uncomfortable.

"I say," Yateley said. "You do understand this is completely confidential?"

"Yes, sir," Thornhill said, taking refuge in formality. "I understand."

14

By the time Dr Bayswater left the hospital, it was almost half past eleven. He drove up Chepstow Road into the town. Instead of going home, he turned towards Templefields. A moment later, the Wolseley drew up in Minching Lane. He got out of the car and knocked on the door of the Meagues' little house, whose windows were in darkness. He waited a few seconds and then tried again, this time hammering on the door. There was a scrape as a door opened further down the street.

"What's all the racket? Some people are trying to get to sleep."

Dr Bayswater turned. He saw Mrs Halleran standing in the lighted doorway leading to the private quarters at the King's Head. She was still dressed, though her hair was in curlers, and she had armed herself with a poker.

"I'm looking for Charlie Meague."

"Oh – sorry, doctor. Didn't realise it was you." The woman's tone was unctuous and gloating. "Have you been up the hospital? They rang me twice this evening. I told them to try the Bathurst Arms."

"He wasn't there, either."

"She's been taken worse, has she?"

Bayswater nodded and turned to go. "I'll drop by in the morning," he said. "If you see Meague, tell him to get in touch with me or the hospital, will you? Good night."

He got back into the car. He was just about to close the door when he heard Mrs Halleran shuffling across the wet pavement in her slippers.

"Is she dead, doctor? Is she dead?"

15

Before she went to bed Antonia shook two barbiturates into the palm of her hand. She had given two to her father an hour earlier. She stared at the tablets for a moment, debating the pros and cons. Eventually she made up her mind and slipped them into the pocket of her cardigan.

Her father, still dressed, was asleep in his chair in front of the fire. He had the whisky bottle and a glass on the table beside him. It was the new bottle, the one which she'd found hidden in the bureau when she was searching the room; he must have got up to fetch it while she was washing up in the kitchen. He had managed to spill the remaining poppies and they lay all over the hearth rug. She did not bother to pick them up.

With a sense of relief she left the room, closing the door behind her. The wind was very loud tonight. For the third time that evening, she checked that all the outside doors were locked and bolted. Collecting a glass and a hot-water bottle from the kitchen, she went upstairs where she got ready for bed as quickly as she could. She kept on her vest, and wore bedsocks and a dressing gown over her nightdress. Her chilblains itched furiously. After a while, she stopped shivering.

The wind moaned and rustled through the trees in the garden. The house filled with a host of tiny creaks and patterings. Rain tapped on the windowpane like a distant typist. Somewhere, Antonia thought, there was a baby crying.

Part Five

Remembrance Sunday

1

Charlie Meague counted the strokes of the church clock across the green. The wind gusting through the trees made it difficult to hear, which was why he made the number not twelve but thirteen. He was relieved that the waiting was over. In the last few hours, his head had been full of pictures he did not want to see. Carn liked knives and razors, and the fact that he had the manners of an old maid just made it worse. Charlie had seen his handiwork in London. On one occasion, Carn had got carried away with the pretty daughter of a former colleague and the business had gone beyond mutilation.

With the empty kitbag over his shoulder, Charlie slipped out of the summerhouse and walked diagonally across the lawn. It was no longer raining but the wind had grown steadily stronger throughout the evening. He slipped through the archway to the yard between the back of the house and the outbuildings. A strip of light streamed across the cobbles from the window of the room which Harcutt used. Although the curtains had been drawn across the window, there was a triangular gap near the bottom where they failed to meet. Charlie crouched and peered inside. By shifting his position, he could see most of the room.

A standard lamp was burning behind the sofa. Major Harcutt was in the armchair beside the sofa, his legs stretched out towards the fireplace. His hands were folded across his stomach and his eyes were closed. Charlie noted the bottle and the glass on the table beside the chair. Harcutt's face was turned away from the window. The old boozer was dead to the world.

Charlie moved cautiously through the yard, past the back door until he came to the casement window of the scullery. Before the war the window had been loose in its frame. One of the maids had told him how, after a night out, she could open the catch with the blade of a knife. He knew that it was still possible to do this because he had taken the trouble to check. The catch slid up and he pulled the window open. He slipped off his boots and, knotting the laces together, slung them round his neck. He hauled himself up on to the sill and dropped lightly down to the tiled floor of the scullery.

The old fool was asking for trouble, living alone in this ill-guarded house; he had made it almost too easy. Charlie hadn't wanted to get the money from Harcutt this way – making the old man give it to him would have been far better. But Carn had given him no choice. Bloody faces passed through Charlie's mind: his mother's and Gloria's, their eyes full of reproach and their mouths open as they screamed.

Still, Charlie told himself, it could have been much worse. No one was going to get slashed. He knew the house, and he had seen enough on his previous visit to know that apart from the decay following neglect very little had changed since before the war. Best of all, if Harcutt suspected who was responsible for the burglary, he wouldn't dare tell anyone of his suspicions.

Using his torch as little as possible. Charlie padded through the kitchen and along the hall. He paused outside Harcutt's door. There were no sounds from within. He continued along the hall until he came to the foot of the stairs. Method is everything, Carn used to say: make a plan and stick to it.

Charlie worked his way round the reception rooms overlooking the front and side of the house. First there was the dining room where the sideboard yielded a canteen of silver. Next came the big drawing room which was disappointing because it had been stripped of its pictures and ornaments; some of the furniture looked valuable, but Charlie regretfully realised it would be impossible for him to remove it without a van and another pair of hands. It occurred to him that there was no reason why he should not have his cake and eat it too: he could eventually persuade Harcutt to let him sell the heavy stuff, just as he had originally planned. Why stop at a thousand pounds? By one means or another he could bleed Harcutt white.

There was also a study which now seemed to be used mainly as a repository for empty whisky bottles. Charlie ran through the drawers of the big partner's desk and struck lucky: in the centre drawer was an unlocked tin box containing two heavy gold hunters, a pair of jade earrings and three rings – two set with opals and one with diamonds.

Leaving the kitbag in the hall, he went slowly up the stairs. Every other tread creaked, but he didn't think the old man would hear him. At the top of the stairs he hesitated, wondering which bedroom would have been Mrs Harcutt's. If there were valuables up here, that was where they would most likely be. As a boy he had never had reason to come upstairs.

He tried a door at random and found himself looking at a small, cold room with a heap of soot in the fireplace. There was a bare bedstead but no other furniture. He opened a built-in cupboard and flicked the torch beam inside. A small, white face loomed out of the darkness. For an instant he thought it was alive. He almost dropped the torch and ran. It was only a doll, he realised, and he shivered.

Even so, he left the room more quickly than he'd entered. Instead of continuing in his methodical circuit round the landing, he went across to the door at the head of the stair which was the furthest away from the door of the room he'd just been into. There was no calculation in this, only a powerful feeling that he didn't want to be close to that pale baby face on the cupboard floor.

He opened the door. This room was warmer. He ran the torch across the floor. The beam caught the corner of a suitcase. He raised the beam to waist height and found first a chest of drawers and then a bed.

He received his second shock. There was a long, human shape under the eiderdown on the bed.

Charlie snapped off the torch. He stood there, listening, every nerve straining to gather information. His own breathing, his heartbeat and the wind outside threatened to drown out all other noises. He held his breath. From the other side of the room came the sound of breathing, soft, slow and steady.

He backed through the doorway. He didn't know who was in that bed and he didn't want to know. There was enough in the kitbag, surely, to keep Carn satisfied for the time being. As he fled, Charlie's mind filled with a jumble of speeding thoughts. Images of bloody faces pushed their way back into his head. He wondered whether his mother would survive the shock and whether he would want Gloria if her face were carved up like something in a butcher's shop. Carn had a taste for symmetry which he expressed with red stripes and flaps of skin. When the blood had drained away, what would be left? Charlie glimpsed a bloodless baby face on the cupboard floor and heard the slow, steady breathing from the bed.

He padded down the stairs, pausing to listen after each creak and squeal from the old wood; he was terrified of waking whoever was in the little room. It had been a mistake to come to this house, a mistake to go to ground in Lydmouth. It was always a mistake to go back. When you started remembering, there was no stopping and eventually the past could swallow you up. And today, he thought, was Remembrance Sunday.

2

Antonia lay in the darkness and prayed for the world to end.

She had prayed for the world to end many times before in this house, but the world had continued. She concentrated on her breathing, for it was important to keep it regular and slow; deep sleep was sometimes a refuge.

The beast retreated, taking its hot, masculine smell away with it. She heard its soft footfalls on the stairs and the squeaks it made. She would have liked to scream and scream but there was no one to hear except the beast. She had thought that she was safe now, but of course there could never be any safety; there would always be a beast waiting. Her emotions bubbled inside her, and each bubble burst with a silent scream. She lay there, waiting and listening. The sounds diminished in volume. Eventually, even the creaking stopped. She could hear only the wind in the trees and her own breathing. The hot-water bottles were cold.

Tonight she had been lucky. The beast had apparently shown mercy. But she remembered from before that you could never be sure that it was not a terrible trick, that the beast would not return. The beast might still be lurking in the darkness, waiting for the right moment.

Antonia sat up in bed. She swung her legs down to the floor. The cold air chilled the skin of her legs. She found her slippers and padded across to the doorway. She flicked down the light switch. The room filled with harsh, blinding light.

Nothing happened. The beast did not pounce. For the first time, Antonia entertained the possibility that she had imagined, or even dreamt the whole thing. But her bedroom door was definitely ajar. She was sure that she'd shut it before getting into bed or as sure as she could be. Perhaps the catch had failed to engage fully and the wind had blown the door open. Or perhaps the beast had left the door ajar as a sign that he would return.

Whimpering softly, Antonia dragged a chair across the room and rammed it against the door. She pulled the dressing table to join the chair. She tugged the heavy bedstead out from the wall and pushed it so its head was resting against the chest of drawers. She was as safe as she could make herself though that would never be safe enough. She looked in the mirror of the dressing table and saw a white face with huge dark eyes.

Leaving the light on, she got back into bed. The two sleeping tablets were on the bedside table. She swallowed them with the help of water. She lay down, and waited.

For a long time, everything remained the same. Her muscles were still tight and her mind would not rest. The tablets weren't strong enough, or perhaps the hospital had given her father placebos. She wanted to go to the lavatory but she did not dare leave the safety of her room. She had thought that the past was safely locked away, but now the beast had reappeared and unlocked it.

At last, the drug began to take hold. At first she thought she was imagining it. The effect came in waves, ebbing and flowing. Gradually a pleasant sense of helplessness slid over her. The barbiturates made her feel as if she were in a lift going down and down into the bowels of the earth. There was nothing she could do, even if she'd wanted, other than sink into the welcoming darkness. The tablets blunted all emotions – joy, sorrow, anger and despair. Death must be like this, she thought, when everything has its true value, which is nothing.

She felt very peaceful. She was puzzled, too. The beast had come to her tonight. But how could that be possible? The beast was dead.

3

On Sunday, breakfast at the Bull Hotel was a subdued affair. The solitary waitress moved to and fro between the tables as though there were an invisible yoke across her shoulders. Carn sat at one table, Yateley at another.

As Carn was contemplating the grey interior of a boiled egg, the manager came into the dining room. He smoothed both wings of his RAF moustache and advanced, hesitantly and by a circuitous route, towards Carn's table.

Yateley waylaid him. "Could you have my bill made up? I want to leave immediately after breakfast."

"Yes, of course, sir." The manager added mechanically, "I hope you have enjoyed your stay."

Yateley did not reply. The manager edged closer to Carn's table. Carn looked up from his book, and their eyes met in the big mirror.

"I've had them bring your bags down. Mr James," the manager said hurriedly, looking down at the carpet. "They're in reception."

Carn stared up at him. "I'll collect them later. Around lunch time, perhaps."

"But I understood from Inspector Thornhill—"

"Do you know," Carn interrupted, "if you dropped this egg, it would bounce?"

"Yes, indeed," the manager said. "An amusing thought, eh?"

"But I'm not laughing, am I? See if they can do me one with the white hard and the yolk runny. All right?"

4

Edith heard her husband whistling as he came downstairs. He opened the kitchen door and the children squirmed with anticipation. The parent who rarely put in an appearance had an unfair advantage over the one who was always there.

Richard Thornhill was smiling as he came into the room. He dropped a kiss on Edith's hair, and she smelt Palmolive shaving cream. He sat down opposite her and began to eat his egg. He was wearing his best suit because they were all going to St John's for the Remembrance Day service.

While they were eating, the children fired questions at their father. They wanted to know how they would spend the rest of the day after lunch. Thornhill promised them a drive in the car.

"We could go and have a look at the Forest," he said, his eyes meeting Edith's. "If we're lucky we might get a bit of sun and the kids can run around. The leaves should be worth looking at."

Something had happened, Edith knew, something that had relaxed the tension between them. The strain was still there, but it had slackened.

Richard finished his egg and took a slice of toast. David and Elizabeth squabbled over who should pass him the marmalade. He looked across the table at Edith.

"I met a Member of Parliament last night," he said.

"The Lydmouth one?"

He shook his head. "Chap called Yateley, Oliver Yateley. He was staying at the Bull. I think he's on the radio, sometimes."

"I know. He's got a nice voice. Touch of Yorkshire in it."

"Which party?"

"Labour, I think. He's only a backbencher. He was on the wireless the other night, in fact. They were talking about the abolition of capital punishment."

Richard grunted. "What does he know about it? He's probably never met a murderer in his life."

Edith frowned at him: she felt that the children were too young to hear this sort of conversation. "What was he doing at the Bull? And how did you come to meet him?"

"He was visiting a friend. Then he had a little too much to drink and one of Lydmouth's worthies decided he needed teaching a lesson. I happened to be passing and I had to sort them out."

"An MP? You'd think he'd be more careful about that sort of thing – if only as a matter of self-preservation."

"I suppose an MP can be as stupid as anyone else when he's had a few drinks. It was all rather petty."

At that moment, the telephone began to ring, shattering the fragile truce. David, who was old enough to be aware of the implications, screwed up his face. Edith pushed back her chair and stood up.

"I'll answer it," she said abruptly.

She went out of the kitchen, closing the door behind her. The telephone was in what they called the dining room, though at present it lacked a dining table. She picked up the handset and recited their still unfamiliar number into the receiver.

"Mrs Thornhill? It's headquarters, Sergeant Fowles speaking. Could I have a word with Mr Thornhill, please?"

"I'll fetch him."

She put the phone down. Anger surged through her, surprising her with its violence. Yet again the job was going to take Richard away from them. Yet again the children would spend all day whining for their father. Yet again she and the children would sit down for their Sunday lunch and pretend they were a complete family. Before their marriage, Richard had told her that it wasn't much fun being a policeman's wife. At the time she hadn't believed him.

He was already in the hall. As he passed her, he murmured, "I'm sorry."

"It's not enough," she said.

5

The police car turned into Victoria Road and pulled up outside the Thornhills' house. Thornhill, who had been waiting at the window, gave David and Elizabeth a hug apiece and dropped them on to the sofa. "Goodbye," he called down the hall. Edith was washing up. There was no answer.

He was already wearing his overcoat. Picking up his hat and umbrella, he went out to the car. Kirby was in front with the uniformed driver. Thornhill got into the back seat. The radio chattered quietly.

"Morning, sir," Kirby said. "Rum business, isn't it?"

Thornhill waved at the two pale faces at the bottom of the sitting-room window; their features were blurred because their breath had misted up the glass. The driver let out the clutch and the car moved smoothly away.

"Any further news?" Thornhill said.

Kirby shook his head. "Not really. There wasn't a WPC available, so the wife of the local constable has gone in to sit with Miss Harcutt. Oh, and Mr Williamson says he'll be along after church."

"Does Dr Bayswater know?"

"Yes, sir. He'll join us there as soon as he can."

Thornhill settled into his seat. Kirby's keenness exasperated him. So did the man's fresh, rested face. The sergeant was due to be on duty today in any case.

"Sir? I saw Carn and Charlie Meague last night."

"Where?"

"They were drinking in the Bathurst Arms. I don't think they saw me. We were in the lounge, you see, me and the girl, having a drink after the pictures, and they were in the public. I just caught a glimpse of them when I went to the gents."

"What were they doing?"

"Just talking. Judging by their faces, it was business rather than pleasure."

"What time was this?"

"About nine thirty."

"I had a word with Carn last night – before you saw him – while he was having his dinner. He should be leaving Lydmouth today."

They were nearly at Edge Hill. Two hundred yards before the green, they passed a knot of men gossiping and smoking outside the hut which served as the local headquarters of the British Legion. One or two were in uniform, but most wore dark civilian clothes. Thornhill had a confused impression of flat caps and bowlers, poppies and medals. One man had shouldered his umbrella like a rifle.

The car turned into the drive of Chandos Lodge. The local constable had had the sense to get the gates open. He was waiting for them at the front door, a thin man with a worried face, probably on the verge of retirement; he had forgotten to do up one of his tunic buttons. Kirby introduced him as Lincoln.

"I tried not to touch anything, sir. But it's very hard to know what's been taken. The place is in a terrible state, but then it usually is. My wife knows Maggie Forbes, she helps out with the cleaning, and she says—"

"Where's Miss Harcutt?" Thornhill interrupted.

"She's in the kitchen with the wife. I didn't know where to put her. Her dad's room is the only one with a fire. The wife made her some tea."

Kirby and Lincoln followed Thornhill into the hall. It was very cold.

"I opened the doors and windows," Lincoln said. "There was a terrible smell of gas when I first got here."

"Who called you?" Thornhill asked.

"Miss Harcutt, sir." He shook his head. "Near out of her mind, she was. Ran across the green to our house – she just had an overcoat over her night things and wellingtons on her feet."

They reached Harcutt's room. Lincoln opened the door and stood aside to allow Thornhill to precede him. The room still smelled faintly of gas. There were other smells too, of alcohol and incontinence and old age. Thornhill walked slowly towards the fireplace, taking care not to brush against anything.

Major Harcutt was slumped in the armchair in front of the fireplace. His eyes were closed and his mouth was open. There was a damp patch on his trousers. Apart from the colour of his skin, he looked as he had in life.

His face was bright pink. Thornhill had expected that. Coal gas contained up to ten per cent carbon monoxide, which fastened on to haemoglobin, the red pigment of the blood, and prevented it from combining with oxygen. There would have been plenty of time during the long winter night for Harcutt to absorb a fatal dose. Alcohol had probably helped to immobilise him: there was still half an inch of whisky in the glass and the bottle on the table was a third full.

Thornhill touched one of the veined hands. It was cold. Harcutt wasn't officially dead until the doctor said he was. But the life had already left this mass of flesh and bone and the inexorable processes of decay were at work. None of the policemen needed to be told that.

For a moment, Thornhill stood still. His eyes darted about the room. The faded carpet between Harcutt's chair and the bureau was dotted with poppies. The sash window was wide open at the top and the curtains moved gently in the wind. He noted the bottle of sleeping tablets on the mantelpiece.

"Who turned off the gas?" he asked Lincoln.

"Wasn't me, sir. First thing I checked when I got here."

"What exactly did Miss Harcutt tell you?"

"Not a lot. And she weren't making much sense, either. It's the shock, look. Kept muttering about gas. She must have smelled it when she came downstairs, come in here and turned it off."

Thornhill could see too many possibilities for comfort. He looked at Kirby. "I want the full treatment. Get on to headquarters. We'll also need to keep out the sightseers." He turned back to Lincoln. "How many men would you need to seal off the grounds?"

"One for the front, one for the back gates and maybe a third man to keep an eye on the back wall. You can climb over in places."

Thornhill turned back to Kirby. "Got that? Three uniformed men. Lincoln, you'd better take me along to the kitchen."

Mrs Lincoln looked up when her husband ushered Thornhill into the kitchen. Her relief was obvious. She and Antonia Harcutt were sitting at the kitchen table. There was a pot of tea between them. Antonia sat with her hands on her lap, staring straight in front of her. She was still wearing her overcoat over her dressing gown and wellington boots on her feet.

"I'm Inspector Thornhill. We met on Friday afternoon, if you remember. I came to ask your father something."

Antonia's eyes did not move.

"Won't even drink her tea," Mrs Lincoln said in a loud, chiding whisper. "She's like my brother's youngest was after the bomb hit their house. Their doctor said, the best thing—"

"Thank you, Mrs Lincoln."

The flow of words stopped. Thornhill drew up a chair and sat down. He glanced behind him at Lincoln and gestured with his eyes. The constable understood and left the room.

"Antonia, I need to know what happened."

She licked her lips. A line of dried dribble ran down from one corner of her mouth.

Mrs Lincoln leant forward, her round face lined with concern. "Perhaps there's someone she'd like with her. Is there, my love?"

Thornhill gave Mrs Lincoln a nod. "Of course. Antonia, can we arrange for someone to come and be with you? A friend perhaps, or a relation?"

She looked at him with blank, dead eyes.

He persevered: "What about Mrs Wemyss-Brown? She's an old school friend, isn't she?"

At last there was a flicker of emotion in Antonia's face. "No – not Charlotte. I don't want her."

"Surely there's someone we can fetch?"

Antonia frowned. "Do you think Jill Francis would come?"

6

It was the hammering that wrenched Charlie Meague out of deep sleep. At first he thought it was the blood pounding in his head, and with each thump his headache stabbed a little deeper.

The banging continued relentlessly. He rose a little further from the depths of sleep. Now he knew that the banging came from outside him. Someone was using a hammer and nails.

Hammer and nails. The words brought to mind the box in the cesspit at the Rose in Hand. Now there was a question: why hadn't the lid been nailed to the box? Answer: so that the rats and the damp and the cats could get in there more quickly and hasten the work of corruption.

Oh, Christ, someone was at the door. Suddenly, Charlie was fully awake and his memories of the night flooded into his mind. His first thought was that the police had come for him. It was against reason, but fear had its own logic. He scrambled out of bed. Apart from his boots, he was fully dressed. He stood to one side of the window, pushed the edge of the curtain up an inch and stared through the crack at the street. At the kerb was parked a Wolseley, its maroon paintwork caked with grime. The sight of the car gave birth to another fear which grew rapidly and elbowed the first out of the way.

Charlie stumbled down the stairs. His head and his heart thumped painfully in time with each other. On his way home last night he had swallowed nearly half a bottle of the whisky he had stolen from the King's Head. He padded across the floor and unbolted the front door.

Bayswater pushed past him and came into the house.

"What is it, Doc?"

"Your mother took a turn for the worse yesterday evening."

"How's she feeling now?"

"There's no easy way to put this."

Charlie swayed. "What are you saying?"

"She's dead."

"No. No – she was fine, yesterday. I saw her myself."

Bayswater frowned at him. "I'm sorry, but there you are. The

211

hospital did everything they could." His eyes roved round the cold, damp room. "She wasn't a well woman. No resistance left."

Charlie sat down on the arm of his mother's chair. "When did it happen?"

"Late yesterday evening. I tried to get hold of you, but you weren't in."

Charlie said nothing. He felt the cold of the flagstones seeping through the thick wool of his socks. He noticed that there wasn't any kindling – he would have to chop some before he could light the fire. Bayswater's eyebrows were grey and bushy and some of the hairs hung down in front of his eyes. Charlie wondered whether his mother had any money ferreted away. It would all be his now. He hoped she had ironed his shirt before going into hospital.

"There are things you'll have to do, and decisions you'll have to make," Bayswater said. "You'll have to register the death and get in touch with an undertaker. Did your mother have insurance?"

Charlie shrugged.

"I expect you can find out. You can talk to the clergyman, too, assuming she went to church or chapel. He'll help. That's what they're paid to do."

"It doesn't make sense. I told you – she was all right when I saw her yesterday."

"She wasn't all right. Some people go up a little before they go down. It's the way it happens. Maybe she made an effort because you were there."

Charlie said nothing. He stared at the ashes of the fire.

After a while, Bayswater said, "Well, I must be going. Take my advice, keep busy. Come and see me if you need anything."

Charlie nodded slowly. Bayswater let himself out of the house. Charlie listened. He heard the Wolseley's engine starting and the car drawing away.

"The silly cow," Charlie said aloud.

His voice frightened him: it sounded strange and unnatural in the emptiness of the house. Silence was safer. He stayed where he was on the arm of the chair. Time drifted on, carrying him with it. He didn't feel unhappy, merely numb. Also, he wished his head would stop hurting so much.

There were two taps on the door. Charlie got up. Ma Halleran, he thought – she'd know. The hospital must have tried to phone her the previous evening. And now the old bitch was coming to gloat and ferret. *Piss off, you bleeding vulture.* He opened the door.

Jimmy Carn smiled up at him. "Hello, Charlie. How's tricks?"

7

There should have been thirty-three men outside the hut, but there were only thirty-two. They stood chatting, waiting until it was time to form up. It would take them less than ten minutes to march to the war memorial on the green; after the wreath-laying ceremony, they would march on to church where the service was due to begin at ten thirty. Freddy, the Veales' dog, moved purposefully among their legs, sampling the wide range of smells.

Old John Veale, who had a bugle on a cord strung round his neck, lit another Woodbine; he'd left his right arm at Gallipoli, but had long since learned to cope without it.

"Did you see the police car?" he asked Terry Forbes who had only just arrived.

"No, Mr Veale. Where was it going?"

"Harcutt's place."

Terry grinned. "Indecent exposure, I shouldn't wonder. Either that or drunk and disorderly."

"Ah. You haven't heard, then?"

"I soon will." Terry was assembling the collapsible flagstaff that carried the Legion's standard. "If you don't tell me now, my mum will tell me after church."

"Must have been between half eight and nine," Veale went on, ignoring this. "The old woman said Antonia was running across the green – in her nightie, can you believe? She went into the Lincolns' house. Five minutes later, she came back out with Lincoln and his missus. And they all went back to Harcutt's place. Haven't been seen since." Veale, knowing that there was no longer any risk of losing his audience's attention, paused to remove a shred of tobacco from his lip. "Maybe twenty minutes later, along comes the police car. Plain-clothes men. You know what that means."

"Detectives?"

Veale nodded. "Something serious going on. You mark my words, young Terry."

Forbes raised the standard and settled the base of the staff into the sling he wore across his chest. "Seems odd without old Harcutt fussing around."

"A lot more restful, you mean. That man's too fond of playing bloody soldiers." Veale pulled out his watch. He raised his voice slightly: "Time's getting on. We'd better form up."

The men shuffled into three lines. Everyone was elaborately casual. Former officers stood side by side with former privates. There was no attempt to put the shortest on the left and the tallest on the right. Veale threw away his cigarette and stroked the bugle as though it were a live thing.

"By the left," he said quietly, almost apologetically. "Quick march."

The Edge Hill branch of the British Legion marched off towards the green. At their head was the standard bearer with his collapsible flagstaff. As they marched, something curious happened: they fell into step and their boots rang in time on the road; no one swung his arms high, but for a few moments they were no longer civilians. No one talked. Behind them were three small boys pretending to march, their demeanour hovering between mockery and respect. Behind the boys came Freddy the dog.

When the marchers reached the green, they swung left towards the war memorial. A moment later, Dr Bayswater's Wolseley turned into the drive of Chandos Lodge.

8

"This really won't do, old man," Carn said, scratching his neat little beard. "Are you ill or something?"

Charlie Meague stared at the floor. He'd gone back to his perch on the arm of his mother's chair. His head hurt. He stared up at his visitor who was wearing his brown suit underneath the unbuttoned raincoat. He noticed that Carn had bought himself a tweed cap. He wished the man would go away.

"So how did it go last night?" Carn asked for the second time.

Charlie shrugged.

"I'll tell you what we're going to do," Carn said slowly. "I'm going to go to Gloucester. There's a nice little hotel in Westgate Street – the White Boar. I booked a room yesterday. You can phone me there. OK?"

Carn paused, but Charlie still said nothing. Carn thrust his hands into the pockets of his raincoat and sighed.

"I want the money in cash within two days," he went on. "That's being generous to you, isn't it? If you can't manage cash – well – it's not ideal, but I'm prepared to stretch a point. Jewellery, for example. I'm broad-minded. But in that case, you have to get the stuff up to London, and I'll have to add on a percentage for the inconvenience. But it's up to you. I don't mind which way you do it."

Charlie stared at Carn's shoes which were brown and highly polished. There was a speck of mud on one of the toecaps. He heard and understood what Carn was saying, but the words lacked relevance; they were an irritant like the buzzing of a bluebottle in a room where you wanted silence. The buzzing varied in intensity and it was making his headache worse.

"If you don't do as I say," Carn went on softly, taking a gold cigarette case from his jacket pocket, "then we have to consider the alternative. It's really not very nice, Charlie. You wouldn't like it, and nor would I. Let me give you an idea. Take your dear old mum, for instance. A delightful lady, I have no doubt. But perhaps a trifle overweight in places? These old dears often are." He took out a cigarette and tapped it on the case. "Now when the dear old Bard of

Avon talked of a 'pound of flesh' sliced from a human body, he actually meant it literally, you know. It's perfectly possible. Imagine it, Charlie – like something from the butcher's. But in a case of this nature there'd be an interesting technical problem, wouldn't there? Because the flesh would have to be cut from a living body."

It wasn't the words, it was the buzzing. Charlie stood up. His mouth was closed, but he made a tiny, inarticulate sound.

Carn stopped talking and dropped his cigarette. He backed away, his pale eyes alert and his right hand digging into the pocket of his raincoat.

Charlie flung himself at Carn. The cigarette case fell to the floor with a clatter. The thought at the top of Charlie's mind was that he could not afford to let the man take his other hand out of his pocket. So he put his arms round Carn and squeezed.

Carn tried to drive his knee into Charlie's crotch. Charlie twisted his legs and covered the target just in time. Carn pulled his head back and smashed his forehead into Charlie's mouth. The pain was intense and the blood tasted salty. Charlie squeezed harder and pushed Carn towards the wall. In a struggle of this sort, Charlie had the advantage because he was taller, heavier and younger.

Carn tripped over the hearth rug and fell backwards, dragging Charlie down with him. Charlie did not let go because he knew that if he did, Carn would be able to get his hand out of his pocket.

Carn's head was resting on the stone hearth. His new cap had fallen into the pile of ashes that spilled from the grate; his breath was warm on Charlie's face and it smelled unpleasantly musty. Neither of them said anything. Charlie raised himself until he had one knee pinning down Carn's right arm and the other on Carn's chest. He looked into Carn's waxen face and Carn looked back.

There was a finality in all this, an absence of choice. Charlie seized Carn's head by its ears and banged it repeatedly and with all his strength against the hearthstone.

9

Sergeant Kirby paused in the open doorway of Harcutt's room. "I thought you were talking to Miss Harcutt, sir."

Thornhill looked up. He was crouching by the bureau and examining the contents of the wastepaper basket. He thought there had been a hint of criticism in Kirby's tone.

"She wants a friend to be with her. I'll wait till then."

"Do you want me to have a go?"

"If I'd wanted you to have a go, I'd have asked you."

"Just mentioning it, sir. Can't afford to waste time, I thought."

Thornhill stared at Kirby. "At present I'll make the decisions, Sergeant. All right? Come and have a look at this."

Kirby flushed and reluctantly came into the room, closing the door behind him. His eyes were hot and angry. Thornhill guessed that the younger man was keyed up by the excitement of robbery and sudden death, that he was hungry for drama and that above all he wanted to do something.

Thornhill pointed into the wastepaper basket. "What do you think of that?"

"They're his medals, aren't they?"

"Seems rather odd to throw them away."

"Might have been an accident." Kirby waved at the poppies on the carpet. "Maybe he tripped, or something, and knocked the medals and the poppies off the bureau."

"Maybe. It seems odd that the medals should fall so neatly into the wastepaper basket, though. That's the Military Cross, isn't it?"

Kirby nodded, his expression puzzled; he could not see the relevance of Harcutt's achievements. "Do you think he turned the gas on – and couldn't manage to light it? Or maybe he was so pissed that he thought he had."

Thornhill didn't answer. He got up and stretched. He was conscious that he did not want to look unnecessarily at the dead meat in the armchair. But why should a human corpse be more disturbing than a pig hanging in a butcher's shop? How terrible it would be if the fairy tales were true after all – if Harcutt were witnessing the humiliating treatment meted out to him after death. Thornhill moved to the fireplace and stared at the photograph of the little family.

"Or I suppose there could have been an interruption in the gas supply," Kirby went on. "Nothing to do with him."

"I wondered that. The mains inlet is in the scullery."

Kirby's head jerked up in surprise. "Do you mean . . ."

"At this stage I'm just keeping an eye on all the possibilities." Thornhill looked down at the poppies and remembered when he'd seen them on the floor here before. They reminded him that he'd never got round to asking Harcutt to explain how he had known that the brooch they found at Templefields was made of silver. It was too late to ask him now. In all probability the major had simply assumed or guessed that it was silver; either that or Jill Francis or Charlotte Wemyss-Brown had mentioned it to him after all.

"But if someone turned off the gas at the mains," Kirby said slowly, "and turned it on again, knowingly, I mean, that would amount to . . ."

There were footsteps outside. The door opened and Bayswater peered into the room. "Ha!" he said. "What have you got for me?"

PC Lincoln arrived. "I tried to make him wait, sir. He just wouldn't listen."

"That's all right, Lincoln."

Bayswater put down his bag and rubbed his hands together. With his head thrust forward, he moved towards Harcutt's body.

"And the lady's turned up, too," Lincoln went on. "Miss Francis."

"Damn," Thornhill said, and for an instant he felt dizzy. "Before you do anything else, Doctor, I wonder if you'd see Miss Harcutt. I want to know if she's well enough for me to talk to her."

Bayswater turned and raised his eyebrows. "Shock?"

Thornhill shrugged. "You tell me. I've arranged for her to have a friend with her. She's just arrived. Kirby, take Dr Bayswater along to the kitchen. I'll deal with Miss Francis."

He tried to keep his voice cool and succeeded in sounding bored and on the verge of yawning. He ushered the other men out of the room and shut the door behind them. He told Lincoln to stay on guard until Kirby returned.

Jill Francis was waiting at the foot of the stairs. She was wearing a long fur coat and hugging herself to keep the cold away. He had forgotten that she was so attractive – or rather, he'd tried so hard to forget in her absence that he'd almost succeeded. Her pale face with its blue eyes seemed to float in the gloom of the hall. He caught himself wondering what a woman like this could have seen in a great bear of a man like Yateley. It embarrassed him that he had seen her cry and that he knew about her lover and her lost baby. It seemed to him that the knowledge was a form of intimacy acquired in an underhand way. He also felt illogically irritated with her: she couldn't have chosen a worse moment to appear before him – he was in the middle of his first major case in Lydmouth and among colleagues he neither knew nor trusted. He wished she were a hundred miles away.

"I'm sorry to drag you out like this," he said stiffly.

"It doesn't matter." She took a step towards him. "How's Antonia?"

"It's been a great shock, naturally. The doctor's with her now. We'd better wait until he's finished. I'll take you in, and if he says it's OK, I'd like to try to ask her a few questions."

"Can I ask what's happened? The man on the phone just said her father had died suddenly."

"That's true as far as it goes." Thornhill hesitated. "Could I ask you to keep this confidential?"

"Of course."

"He seems to have died in his sleep. But we're not sure what caused it. There may have been a gas leak."

"And she found him? Poor kid."

"And there's another consideration. There appears to have been a burglary here last night. All in all, it's a very confused situation."

He ran out of things to say. Jill waited, apparently composed. He felt that she had no right to make him feel like this; it was an imposition. He wondered how on earth she could have wanted to have Yateley's child.

He cleared his throat and said, "I hope you hadn't got plans for this morning."

"Nothing important. I was going to church with the Wemyss-Browns. Incidentally, Mrs Wemyss-Brown said she would come along after the service. She thought Antonia would be glad of her support."

Her eyes met Thornhill's. For an instant, there was a shared hint of amusement. The moment was so brief and the hint so hard to pin down that immediately afterwards Thornhill thought he'd imagined the whole thing.

"She also said that Antonia was welcome to come and stay at Troy House," Jill went on. "She can't stay here, can she?"

"Probably not. By the way, there was something I wanted to check with you and Mrs Wemyss-Brown. Do you remember when you first came here to see Major Harcutt? On Thursday morning – I turned up while you and Mrs Wemyss-Brown were here."

Jill looked at him gravely. "I remember it very well."

"Mrs Wemyss-Brown said she wanted to warn Major Harcutt that I might be coming to see him. I expect she told him that some bones had been found at Templefields. Did either of you happen to mention the other things I showed you?"

"The bit of newspaper? The brooch?"

"That's it. Did you?"

"I don't think so. There really wasn't time. We'd only been there for a couple of minutes before you turned up."

"Neither of you told him that the brooch was silver, I suppose?"

"I told you – I don't think either of us mentioned the brooch at all. You can ask Charlotte, but I'm pretty sure she'll say the same. Why do you want to know?"

"I'm not sure. Just one of those little details."

There was another uncomfortable hiatus in the conversation – uncomfortable as far as Thornhill was concerned at least. Jill stared down the hall in the direction of the kitchen.

"You'll treat Antonia gently, won't you, Inspector?"

"Of course we shall." He felt, and sounded, indignant.

"Sorry," she said unexpectedly. "It's just that she's very vulnerable at the best of times."

The kitchen door opened and Bayswater came out. As he walked along the hall, he gave Jill a cool, assessing stare and then ignored her.

"You might as well talk to her," he said to Thornhill. "It might do her good to get it off her chest. I want to have a look at the body now."

"I'll arrange for Kirby to stay with you."

"Just to make sure I don't tamper with the evidence, eh? Well, I don't care what you do as long as you don't waste my time."

"The feeling's mutual," Thornhill said. "So I'll leave you to it."

10

What do you do with about a hundred and forty pounds of flesh and bone? There wasn't an easy answer.

Charlie sat in his mother's armchair and smoked one of Carn's cigarettes while he thought about the problem. The blood dried on his face. It hurt to smoke because his lips were sore and swollen. The world had contracted to this cold little room he had known all his life. Gradually he stopped shivering. He had never killed someone before, even in the war. It was a strange sensation. He didn't want to think about what made Carn *now* different from Carn *then*.

He briefly considered the possibility of going to the police. He imagined himself walking into the police station in the High Street. "I've just killed Genghis Carn. What are you going to do about it?" Everything would be sorted out for him, and there would be no more decisions.

The idea revolted him. They wouldn't believe him when he told them what Carn had threatened to do. If they didn't hang him for killing Carn, they would put him inside for most of his life. If the police got him, Charlie thought, he was finished; he might just as well have killed himself. So in that case, he had absolutely nothing to lose by trying to escape. Maybe he could go abroad. Maybe he could slip into another identity.

Charlie got up and knelt beside Carn's body. The little man was still lying on his back with his head on the hearthstone and his beard pointing towards the ceiling. From the front he looked undamaged – indeed, he might have been asleep. Charlie, obeying a reflex he had not known he possessed, had closed the dead man's eyes to stop them looking at him.

He went through Carn's pockets, beginning with those in the jacket and the raincoat. He emptied them methodically and put what he found on the seat of his mother's chair. The trouser pockets were more difficult. Charlie nerved himself to push his hands into the pockets at the side. He felt the hard thigh beneath the layers of clothing. The pockets were still warm with the heat of the living man.

Carn had been carrying a bunch of keys, a wallet, a letter from a woman named Sylvia, a grubby white handkerchief, a handful of small change, a box of matches, two penknives and a cut-throat razor. The wallet contained a driving licence, three stamps and a ten-shilling note. There was also the gold cigarette case which Carn had dropped on the floor.

Charlie sat back on his heels and absentmindedly took another of the dead man's cigarettes. So where was Carn's money? He had bought a round in the Bathurst Arms the previous evening, and he'd peeled off a fiver from a wad of notes. He couldn't have spent it between now and then. Nor was it likely that he'd left his cash with his luggage which was presumably still at the hotel; Carn was not a man to be parted from his money. Then Charlie remembered there was one pocket he had not examined.

He put the cigarette in the corner of his mouth and returned to his knees. It was a nasty job, but it had to be done. Squinting through the smoke, Charlie hooked his hands under Carn and gingerly rolled the body on to its front.

The money was in the back pocket of the trousers. Charlie stood up and counted it: there was nearly a hundred and fifty pounds in one-pound and five-pound notes. Charlie glanced involuntarily at his unwitting benefactor. From this angle, he could see the back of Carn's head. Apart from the blood, there was no obvious damage. Carn might just be unconscious. Charlie stretched out his hand and gingerly touched the back of the skull. To his horror, it gave at the slightest pressure; it felt like broken eggs in a sock. His stomach lurched and he hurriedly stood up. Carn was dead. There were no second chances.

Charlie tried to think out the implications of the situation as Carn would have done. The police were expecting Carn to leave Lydmouth this morning, so they might not be completely surprised if he simply disappeared. On the other hand, they knew of his connection with Charlie, and someone might have seen him in Minching Lane. So the coppers might come visiting just on the off-chance.

The first thing to do was to put the body where it wouldn't be too obvious. There was a disused well in the yard. That would be ideal.

Charlie went through the scullery and opened the back door. The well wasn't overlooked by the windows of other houses – it was in the angle between the scullery and the outside privy. The opening had been capped with a stone when the water main reached Templefields and the old iron pump had gone for scrap. The flagstone had not been cemented in. It did not look unusual because the yard was paved with a jumble of cobbles and flagstones. There was nothing to suggest it might cover a well.

He fetched the spade from the privy and used it to lever the stone away from the top of the well. It was clear from the amount of dried dirt that had accumulated between this stone and its neighbours that no one had moved it for years. He peered into the opening, down into the darkness at the bottom. The shaft was narrow, and it seemed to grow narrower as it got deeper; its walls were made of rough stone. He knew that the water was about fifteen feet down. When he was a boy, he and a friend had thrown a cat down there. The cat had howled as it fell, and they had listened to it thrashing about in the water.

There was a strong possibility that Carn might get jammed halfway down. Still, at least the body would be out of the way. Out of sight, out of mind. In Templefields the rats were everywhere. Maybe the rats would get Carn as they had the baby, and what the rats left uneaten would eventually be swallowed by water.

Charlie's natural optimism was beginning to return. It might be years before anyone realised there was a body down there. More likely than not, no one would ever find out, because time and the rats and the water would dispose of the evidence. Indeed, it occurred to him that there was no reason for him to run away. All he need do was put Carn down the well. He could fill the well with rubble at his leisure.

If anyone had seen him coming here, Charlie would simply say that Carn had called to say goodbye and left. They would find it very difficult to prove otherwise. They would need a search warrant to find Carn in the well, and why should they bother to look in the first place?

In a flash, the future seemed almost rosy: Carn was out of the way, but Charlie had Carn's money; old Harcutt, if properly handled, could prove a gold mine in the long term, and with no risk to Charlie; and then there was Gloria. Everything was possible, now Carn had gone.

"Hello! Anyone at home?"

The dream vanished. The voice had come from the house. But there was still a chance that its owner hadn't seen anything. With the spade in his hand, Charlie rushed through the scullery. The door to the street was open. He remembered he hadn't locked or bolted the door since he'd closed it after Carn came in.

On the threshold was Mrs Halleran, her eyes like glistening currants in her pale, doughy face. She wore a pinafore over her dress and a headscarf over her curlers. When she saw Charlie, she raised her bushy eyebrows at the spade and at his bloodstained face.

"I hope I'm not intruding," she said, her eyes darting round the room, "but I wondered if there was any news about your poor mother."

Mrs Halleran stopped talking, but she did not close her mouth.

Now it was too late. Her eyes had fixed on Carn's body near the fireplace.

There was a finality about this. too. and another absence of choice.

11

Antonia Harcutt lit another of her father's cigarettes. Her hands were steady, Jill noticed, but she held the cigarette awkwardly and kept glancing at it as though uncertain which end went where. Her self-control was frightening, Jill thought, because it had rigidity without strength: like china, if dropped on a hard surface, it would break.

Thornhill closed the kitchen door, shutting out Mrs Lincoln and the continuous murmur of her voice. He looked irritable and harassed.

"Do you mind if I ask you some questions now, Miss Harcutt?"

She stared at him and blinked. The smoke was making her eyes water. The skin around her eyes was puffy. "Yes, I feel better now. Sorry for making such a fool of myself – I'm not normally like this."

"I'm sure you're not," Thornhill said. "These aren't normal circumstances. I'll keep this as brief as I can and you must tell me if you'd like a break. What time did you go to bed?"

Antonia frowned and rubbed her eyes, "I'm not sure. Before midnight."

"And where was your father?"

"In there." Her head bobbed in the direction of Harcutt's room.

"And the fire was on?"

"I can't remember."

"It was a cold night."

"Yes, but I was in here for most of the time, clearing away. I only went in there to give him his tablets." She hesitated. "And say goodnight, of course."

"He had some whisky as well?"

She nodded.

"Were there poppies on the floor?"

"Yes. I think so. Everything's such a mess in this house. People seem to think it's my responsibility to clear it up."

"It must be very difficult for you. But don't worry about that – all I want is to discover what happened."

As he spoke, he smiled at Antonia. She did not smile back, but for an instant her face brightened. He pushed the ashtray closer to her

225

and bent his head over his notebook. His gentleness surprised Jill. She had expected him to be far more assertive. She noticed that he had made very few notes, and she guessed that he was using the notebook more as a means of punctuating the conversation than of recording it. He looked up, first at Jill and then at Antonia.

"How did your father seem when you said goodnight to him?"

"Much as usual. Not that I know him very well, really. I haven't lived at home since I was a child."

"Had he anything on his mind, do you know?"

"He was worried about money. And I think the accident made him realise how fragile he was." Antonia's eyes flickered, and Jill had a sense that she was nerving herself for an arduous undertaking. "He said as much to Jill and Charlotte."

Thornhill looked at Jill.

"That's correct," she said, wondering why she sounded so formal. "But of course I don't know how he was usually."

"I appreciate that." It seemed that formality was catching. "Miss Harcutt, can you take me through what happened this morning?"

Antonia stubbed out the cigarette. "I woke up late – I'd taken a couple of my father's tablets because I slept badly the previous night." She looked across the table. "That was your suggestion, wasn't it?" she said to Jill, and added in a rush, "And I was jolly glad I did." She turned back to Thornhill. "I knew there was something wrong as soon as I came out of my bedroom. I could smell gas. And when I came downstairs, I saw that things were missing from the dining room and the study." Her voice was picking up speed. "All the doors were open and they were closed last night when I went to bed. And I ran down the hall, and went into my father's room and then I saw him." Antonia reached for the cigarette packet. As she fumbled with the cigarettes, she sucked her lower lip. "He was such a funny colour," she said. "I've never seen anyone that colour before."

"The fire was unlit – and was the gas still on?"

"Yes – I heard it hissing." Antonia tried to light her cigarette. She failed, and Jill took the matchbox from her. Antonia went on, " I opened the window. That's what you're meant to do, isn't it?"

"You did absolutely right, Miss Harcutt," Thornhill said.

Jill struck a match and held it out for Antonia to light her cigarette. She saw dandruff at the roots of Antonia's hair. The sight disgusted her, but she knew her disgust was disproportionate and due to more than dandruff. She badly wanted all this to be over, not just for Antonia's sake, but for her own.

"I can't believe he's dead." Antonia massaged her forehead with her fingertips. "He *is* dead, isn't he? There's no possible doubt about it?"

"I'm afraid there isn't," Thornhill said. "May I ask you something else? Have you any idea who might have burgled the house?"

Antonia shook her head.

"This may seem a strange question, but can you tell me if a woman called Mrs Margaret Meague ever worked here? Or her son Charlie?"

Antonia licked her lips. She picked up the cigarette. She looked from Thornhill to Jill. But her face had lost its dazed expression. The muscles twitched beneath the blotchy skin.

"Oh, yes," Antonia said softly. "They both worked here before the war."

Then, at last, the tears began to roll down her cheeks.

12

In church, the congregation stood in an approximation of silence. Near the back a woman was crying softly. A man coughed. A child whispered urgently to his mother.

"Private George Andrews, the Gloucestershire Regiment," the vicar read out from the pulpit. "Able Seaman Frank Bannerman, RN Division, Lieutenant Philip Browne, Royal Artillery, Private Walter Evans, the South Wales Borderers..."

The vicar was an old man with a tired voice. He read slowly through the names of the twenty-seven men who constituted the parish's dead in two world wars. The last name on the list was Flight Sergeant Albert Veale, RAF.

When the vicar had finished. John Veale raised his bugle and filled the church with at least some of the notes of the Last Post. His playing wavered in pitch and volume. Even in his brief, two-handed prime, John Veale had never been much of a musician.

"It is important to remember," the vicar told them in his address, "because it is dangerous to forget."

13

"Belt and braces job, if you ask me," Dr Bayswater said. "Not that it signifies."

"What do you mean?" Thornhill said.

Bayswater took his time over lighting his pipe. The weather was cold, but dry, and Thornhill was glad of an excuse to be out of the house. The sky was clear and somewhere upwind and out of sight was a bonfire. It would have been a good day, Thornhill thought, for a walk in the Forest.

The two men were standing on the gravel outside the front door of Chandos Lodge. The doctor's Wolseley and the police car were parked side by side. A young constable was using the radio in the police car and keeping a wary eye on Thornhill.

"Don't quote me," Bayswater went on, "but I imagine the postmortem will suggest that the old boy slugged himself with whisky and barbiturates and then turned on the gas to finish off the job. There are worse ways to go."

"But why doesn't it signify?"

Bayswater appeared not to hear the question. "We know that Harcutt had a certain amount on his mind." He held up his hand like a teacher in front of a restive class and raised a finger for each point. "One, his wretched dog dies. Two, he suddenly realises he's getting old, that he needs help. Three, he hasn't got any money. Four, he's lonely. He was a fool in many ways, but you could argue that that was one of his more sensible choices."

"Then it's a shame he didn't leave a note," Thornhill said.

"But natural enough."

"It does help when people make their intentions clear."

"Either it simply didn't occur to him or he wanted his death to seem like an accident. Perfectly understandable."

"A note would have made things a little less confusing for those he left behind." Thornhill suspected that Bayswater was taking pleasure from being contrary. "Anyway, you still haven't explained why it doesn't signify."

"Eh?" Bayswater chewed the stem of his pipe. "Well, if there's nothing to show whether he intended to leave the gas unlit or whether it just happened by chance, and if it doesn't matter a hoot in any case, why not let it be accident? No point in upsetting people."

"Being diplomatic isn't the purpose of my job."

"It isn't the purpose of mine, either. But sometimes there's no harm in it. This world is bloody awful enough as it is. One doesn't have to make it worse."

Thornhill felt himself flushing. "Once you start bending the truth, there's a risk that you end up getting bent yourself."

Bayswater ignored this and concentrated on relighting his pipe. "Say it turns out to have been an accident," he continued as though Thornhill hadn't spoken, "and it probably will, then at least it'll serve some useful purpose."

"I'm afraid you've lost me."

"Because it would be yet another example of the folly of handing out barbiturates as though they were as harmless as humbugs. They're doing it all the time up at the hospital. Pill happy, those quacks in uniform. And they're not the only ones. They know damn well that the margin of safety with barbiturates is very narrow, but they won't act on it. It's easy to overdose. And giving barbiturates to a heavy drinker like old Harcutt is just asking for trouble. Alcohol enhances their effect."

Bayswater paused and glared triumphantly at Thornhill. He had the air of a man who has put an unanswerable case; its irrelevance seemed not to have occurred to him. Thornhill disliked the doctor's arrogance and found it interesting that he hadn't mentioned the third possibility – that Harcutt's death had been neither accident nor suicide.

Thornhill slipped in a question from an unexpected direction. "Was Antonia Harcutt ever pregnant?"

"What? What a thing to ask."

"I wouldn't ask if I didn't need to know. Was she?"

Bayswater hesitated. "There's the ethical question to be considered."

"We're talking about a man's death. I'm trying to establish what caused it."

"Well, even if I could tell you, I doubt if I would." Bayswater lowered his voice. "In any case, Antonia Harcutt hasn't lived in Lydmouth since before the war. She was just a child then."

"Yes, I know." Thornhill stared up at the façade of the house. He thought he saw movement behind one of the upstairs windows.

Bayswater peered at Thornhill. "You realise what you're implying?"

"An underage pregnancy."

Bayswater glanced at the house and said, choosing his words carefully, "The Harcutts weren't my patients – they were my father-in-law's. That means you'd be out of luck whatever happened. The poor old boy shouldn't have been allowed to practise in the last few years of his life. He was going senile. And it's no use asking to see the records. There aren't any records worth speaking of."

"But you knew the Harcutts before the war, didn't you? Socially, I mean."

"Yes – I knew a lot of people. I remember playing tennis here once or twice. The odd cocktail party. Harcutt used to entertain a good deal before his wife died."

Thornhill switched the direction of his questioning again. "Does the name Meague mean anything to you?"

"Of course it does," Bayswater snapped. "It's a local surname. There's a village on the other side of town where every other person is called Meague."

"I understand you've got a few Meagues on your list."

"One of them died of pneumonia last night."

"Oh, really?" Thornhill said. "That must be Charlie Meague's mother."

"Had to see him this morning, as a matter of fact. Why are you interested?"

"Lydmouth is much smaller than it seems, isn't it? Everyone seems to know everyone else."

"That's not an answer."

"According to Miss Harcutt, both the Meagues worked at Chandos Lodge before the war. Mrs Meague was a charwoman and Charlie worked as a gardener's boy. They both left rather suddenly in May 1939."

"Do you know what Mrs Meague said last night?" Bayswater asked. "Something about poor Miss Tony. And then she said, 'It wasn't you, Charlie, was it?'"

The two men looked at each other. *It wasn't you, Charlie, was it?* Thornhill guessed that Bayswater had seen the possible implications or at least some of them. The doctor relit his pipe for the third time.

"Listen, Thornhill. This rather changes things, doesn't it? I see what you're driving at – it's that Templefields business, eh?"

Thornhill had opened his mouth to reply when he heard the sound of a door opening behind him. He turned. The young constable was leaning out of the police car, his face shiny with excitement.

"It's headquarters, sir," he said, stumbling over the words in his haste to get them out. "They think it's a murder."

231

14

"The policemen seem to be getting very excited down there," Jill said. "I wonder if something's happened."

The remark wasn't the most tactful that Jill could have made, but she was feeling harassed. Antonia seemed to be in the process of developing a doglike devotion for her, the sort of schoolgirl crush that demanded a positively saintlike patience on the part of the adored. When Jill spoke, Antonia raised her head with a jerk and glanced towards the window.

"Are they?" she said hurriedly. "The police do a lot of rushing around, don't they?"

She appeared to lose interest in the policemen and directed her attention back to her clothes. She already had pulled most of them out of her suitcase and draped them over her bed. The effect reminded Jill of a stall at a Bring and Buy Sale.

Antonia stared doubtfully at her wardrobe and, with an air of quiet desperation, picked out a pale green cardigan. Jill noticed a maroon photograph album on the eiderdown underneath. Antonia laid the cardigan against a tweed skirt which was the colour of tinned peas.

"Do you think they go together? I've never been quite sure."

Jill cast a rapid eye over the rest of Antonia's wardrobe and decided that on this occasion tact and expediency should have priority over truth. "They look very nice."

Antonia began to undo her dressing gown. "Are you sure Charlotte won't mind having me to stay?"

"Of course not. Otherwise she wouldn't have asked you."

"I don't know." Antonia gave an unlovely wriggle. "People sometimes do things because they feel they ought to rather than because they want to. I thought it might be like that with her."

This was getting dangerously close to the truth. "Well, it isn't. After all, she knew you at school."

"Yes, but we weren't friends. She terrified me, in fact."

Jill smiled. "She must have liked you more than you realised."

She turned away, partly in the hope of ending this potentially awkward conversation and partly because she was curious about what was happening outside. Down in the drive. Bayswater was climbing into the Wolseley. There was a huddle of foreshortened policemen with Thornhill in their centre; he seemed to be giving instructions. As she watched, the group broke up. Thornhill opened the door of the police car and glanced up at the window of Antonia's bedroom. Jill drew back into the room, hoping that he had not seen her prying.

"I'll just go and wash my hands," Antonia said coyly. "I won't be a moment. You will stay, won't you?"

Jill said she would. Antonia scuttled out of the room, leaving the door open. Jill wandered across to the bed and picked up the heavy maroon volume.

Our Kashmir Album
Srinagar 1932.

She turned the black pages slowly. People were full of surprises – she would not have thought that Antonia was the type to enjoy the doubtful pleasures of nostalgia.

The past reached out clammy fingers, smelling of damp and must. There was something sad about these blurred snapshots and elaborate studio photographs. They recorded what was now a vanished culture, sahibs and memsahibs frolicking decorously in an alien land. There were no children on display – whatever had they done with the children? Everyone looked stiff and rather serious. None of the faces had a dark skin.

Jill paused at a photograph near the end of the album: it showed Harcutt in regimentals with a woman, presumably his wife, in a long evening dress; she was clasping his arm and looking up at him in a manner suggesting that she was only doing so because the photographer had asked her to. They were not a handsome couple, but they radiated the self-confidence of people who are content with their position in life, which they know on the best authority to be somewhere near the peak of creation.

It wasn't easy to equate the man in the photograph with the Major Harcutt whom Jill had briefly known. She looked at the woman, too, curious to discover whether there was any trace of Antonia in her, and wondering what sort of woman could have borne to marry a man like Major Harcutt. The putative Mrs Harcutt had dark hair and a plain, rather stern face. There was a strong suggestion of plumpness about her waist and hips. Her dress exercised a restraining influence on the flesh beneath.

"Not very interesting, are they?" Antonia said from the doorway. Her fingers fiddled with a button of her blouse. "Just a holiday in India."

"You don't mind my looking?"

Antonia reddened. "Of course not."

Jill began to close the book. As she did so, she noticed that Mrs Harcutt was wearing what looked like a silver brooch. It was pinned to the bosom of her dress, and it was in the shape of a true love's knot.

15

"By the left. Quick march."

The thirty-two men of the Edge Hill branch of the British Legion tramped along the north side of the green. As they turned on to the main road, a police car appeared at the gates of Chandos Lodge. It cut in front of the column, forcing the marching men to come to an unscheduled halt. The car drove off at high speed towards Lydmouth.

"By the left," Veale ordered, for the second time. "Who do they think they are? Quick march."

The men marched on towards their headquarters.

"Legion branch, halt."

The column shuffled to a standstill.

"Legion branch, dismiss."

The column turned to its right and, as it did so, dissolved into thirty-two men.

Terry Forbes began to fold up the flagstaff. "For a moment, I thought they were giving us a police escort," he said to John Veale.

"Stupid buggers," Veale said, drawing deep on his Woodbine. "Could have knocked us all down. No respect, have they? Not even the bloody police."

"There's gratitude, Mr Veale," Terry Forbes said.

16

Gloria had noticed before that there was a strange synchronisation about the laborious and prolonged bowel movements of her husband Harold and her stepdaughter Jane: it was like women in a nunnery having the curse at the same time.

There were two lavatories in the private quarters of the Bathurst Arms. Just before opening time on Sunday morning, she discovered that both of them were in use. This was irritating, because her own need was urgent. There was nothing for it but to go outside.

Gloria tucked the newspaper under her arm and opened the back door. The town was wrapped in its Sunday morning calm. Seagulls squealed over the river and somewhere a bell was ringing. She walked unsteadily on high heels across the cobbled yard to the lavatories reserved for customers. The door of the cubicle reserved for ladies opened directly into the yard. She went inside and bolted the door.

Christ, it was cold. The wooden seat was freezing and the draught swirled round her ankles. The only thing between her and the outside world was a door with a nine-inch gap between it and the concrete floor. Such gaps were essential, Gloria had discovered, to ensure that customers did not use the lavatories for purposes they were not designed for. She folded open the *News of the World*, and prepared to make the best of it.

She had hardly started when she heard footsteps in the yard. Someone had come through the wicket gate from the alley which led up to Lyd Street. Now Gloria came to think of it, it was strange that she had not heard the footsteps coming down the alley too. So maybe someone had been lurking in one of the outbuildings. The footsteps crossed the yard, hesitated and then walked slowly towards the door of the cubicle.

Oh my God, thought Gloria, that's all I need: a bloody pervert.

There was a silence. She guessed that the man would be bending down to peer under the door. Quickly she stood up and pulled down her dress.

"Gloria," Charlie said, his voice low and husky.

She snapped back the bolt and pulled open the door. "What the hell are you doing?"

"I wanted to see you."

He smiled at her, his teeth very white in his dark, unshaven face. Gloria, who was expert at assessing men's smiles, felt immediately wary. He had been in a fight – his lips were cut and swollen. He looked as if he'd slept in his clothes and hadn't washed for a week. He also made her feel dangerously warm inside.

"In ten minutes' time," she said, "you can come in the front door and buy yourself a drink. But I don't want you round here. What am I going to say if someone sees you?"

"Gloria – can you do me a favour?"

"I doubt it."

She began to walk towards the back door. He skipped in front of her. She stopped, feeling a not unpleasurable thrill of menace because he was much larger than she was. Despite herself, she found his urgency was exciting.

"Just hear me out," he said.

"Are you mad? Harold could look out of the window at any time."

"Bugger him. You weren't meant for Harold. You were meant for me."

She stared angrily up at him. "A girl can't wait for ever. You had your chance and you lost it. Now, will you get out of my way?"

He didn't move. "You and Harold have got a car, haven't you?"

"What if we have?"

"I want to borrow it."

"Don't be stupid. Harold would go crazy."

The muscles were working under Charlie's skin as though there was something trying to get out. "This is important."

"So is Harold's car."

"He doesn't have to know. All I need is the key. It's parked at the front – I can just drive off. *Please*."

Against her better judgement she said, "What's this all about?"

"I need to get away from Lydmouth. That's all. I won't damage the car, I promise. I'll go to Bristol, or somewhere, and leave the car in the station car park. I'll send you a wire so you know where it is. Or phone you."

In his urgency, he laid his hand on her arm to stop her from going into the house. She saw a rusty stain on the inside of the index finger and the thumb.

"What's that?"

He glanced at the hand. "I cut myself on a tin. Gloria, if you help me now, we've got it made. You and me." He let go of her arm and

237

took something from the inside pocket of his jacket. "Look at this." He opened his hand, and there in the palm was a roll of notes.

Gloria was a good judge of hard cash. He had at least a hundred pounds there, almost certainly considerably more.

"Where did you get that sort of money?"

"There's more where that came from," he said. "You can have anything you want. Cars, houses, holidays, furs." He dropped his voice and said huskily, "I'll treat you like a film star, I swear it."

Gloria's eyes slid away from the roll of banknotes and up to the blank windows of the Bathurst Arms.

"You'll get me the key, Gloria? And maybe a bit of food? I'm starving."

He loomed over her. He smelled sour. For the first time since his arrival, she was frightened. Part of her enjoyed that. Harold never made her feel scared. She smiled at Charlie.

"Of course I will," she said. "Wait there."

She ran past him. Everything was in slow motion. Her high heels made her awkward. She reached the back door, opened it and looked back. He was standing where she had left him.

"I'm sorry, Charlie, but I can't."

Still he did not move. "We're something special, Gloria. You know that. For old times' sake." His voice was very gentle and it seemed to come from a long way away.

"We were something special," she said harshly. "But that's all over."

She slammed the door, bolted it and leant against it. She was trembling. A moment later, she nerved herself to look out into the yard. It was empty. Her eyes felt hot and sticky. She needed to make sure her make-up was undamaged.

Upstairs someone pulled the chain of one of the lavatories. The first roar of water was almost immediately joined by a second. Harold and Jane even pulled the chain at the same time.

Harold was a kind man who left her alone for most of the time: and he had money in the bank.

Gloria began to climb the stairs. A girl had to look after herself. After all, no one else would.

17

"My dear," Charlotte Wemyss-Brown said, rising to the occasion like a trout to a fly, "you must think of Troy House as your home for as long as you like."

The telephone began to ring. At a glance from his wife, Philip went to answer it. Charlotte placed an arm under Antonia's elbow and steered her towards the stairs. Like many people, Charlotte laboured under the delusion that those who had suffered an emotional shock should be treated as invalids.

On the stairs, Antonia looked over her shoulder at Jill who was still standing in the hall. Antonia said nothing, but it was obvious from her face that she wanted Jill to come with them. Jill smiled at her and went into the drawing room.

She warmed her hands at the fire. She was ruefully aware that in one way Antonia had done her a service: the drama of Major Harcutt's death and Antonia's arrival at Troy House had entirely swamped Charlotte's curiosity about Jill's meeting with Oliver Yateley. Leaving Antonia to Charlotte was a little like leaving an early Christian to a hungry lion. But Jill desperately needed time to think. She was still struggling to work out the implications of what had happened at Chandos Lodge. She knew that she would have to talk to Antonia; she knew, too, that she would have to make up her mind what to do for the best. It would have been a difficult decision at the best of times, and it was even worse now.

The door opened and Philip burst into the room.

"My God," he said, striding towards the fireplace. "Jill, this is extraordinary. We've had a murder."

Jill's mind was still on the Harcutts. "What? Antonia's father?"

"No. This really is a murder." Philip's face became almost sly. "That was someone I know at police headquarters. Apparently, some London gangster has been found battered to death in a house in Minching Lane in Templefields. And you'll never guess who the police are looking for. It's actually someone we know, in a manner of speaking. Charlie Meague – he's the son of the charwoman that

Charlotte was telling you about. Do you remember? The one she had to sack."

"But—" Jill began, and stopped.

Philip changed course and headed for the drinks trolley. Jill had time to think that perhaps it was none of her business that Charlie Meague had once worked for Major Harcutt.

"I think I'll have a drink." Philip rubbed his hands together. "Can I get you one? And what were you going to say?"

"Nothing for me, thanks. Just that it seems a coincidence – two deaths in one day."

"Thank God for coincidences. Where would we be without them?" As he spoke, Philip poured himself a large whisky and added a squirt of soda. "Mind you, we won't be able to make the most of the Harcutt business, not in the *Gazette*. Charlotte and I have already had a chat about that."

"Because Charlotte knows the family?"

Philip sipped his whisky. "Partly." He grinned at Jill. "There's also the point that Charlotte thinks the *Gazette* should be above stories of raw human emotion – at least in the local news. She thinks our readers want to know the price of sheep and what Lady So-and-So said when she opened the church bazaar. And she may be right, too."

"What happens now?"

"It's anyone's guess. The only certainty is that Superintendent Williamson will call a press conference at some point. If not several."

There were heavy footsteps on the stairs. Philip gulped down half of his whisky. Neither of them spoke: it was not a guilty silence, but to Jill it smacked of collusion. Charlotte swept into the room, her face a little pinker than usual.

"All serene, darling?" Philip asked. "Would you like some sherry?"

Charlotte ignored him. "Antonia's in quite a state." she murmured to Jill. "Rather emotional and weepy. I wonder if we should get the doctor."

"Did you suggest that to her?" Jill said.

"Yes – she was really rather rude. Of course, one must make allowances. The poor child can't know what she's saying."

Charlotte sank into the armchair by the fire. Philip gave her a large glass of sherry.

"Shall I go up and have a word with her?" Jill asked. "Do you think it would help?"

"Oh – would you?" Charlotte took a cigarette from Philip's case. "She seemed to clam up on me. Then there's the question of lunch."

"The sooner the better, as far as I'm concerned," Philip said. "I'm starving. Church always has that effect on me."

"The trouble is, I don't know whether Antonia will want to join us or not. And whatever happens, we'll have to let Susan know. You know what she's like when her arrangements are upset. It's bad enough as it is, telling her there'll be four for lunch instead of three. So if you could find out if Antonia's coming down, that would be an enormous help."

As Jill left the room, she heard Philip say, "Darling, you'll never guess – we've had a proper murder."

Jill slowly climbed the stairs. She didn't want to have this conversation with Antonia – she didn't even like the girl – but there was no point in putting it off. She wondered parenthetically what on earth had happened to her life in the last few weeks: getting pregnant, losing the baby, leaving her job, breaking off with Oliver Yateley, and now this.

Antonia had been given the bedroom next to Jill's. She was sitting at the dressing table with her back to the door. Her eyes met Jill's in the mirror. She was smoking, and the little china dish on the dressing table already contained three butts. Jill closed the door.

"I wish I could go away," Antonia said slowly. "I hate Lydmouth. I never want to come here again in my life. Do you think they'd let me go back to Dampier Hall tomorrow?"

"I doubt it," Jill said. "I think the police will want you to stay here until they've sorted everything out."

Antonia's murky brown eyes flickered in the mirror. "What do you mean?"

"There'll have to be an inquest on your father, I imagine. And then there's the question of the burglary."

"Yes, I realise that. But it's not as if Newport is the other end of the earth, is it? Besides, there's my job to think about. They need me there."

Jill sat down on the bed. "You know that phone call?"

"What phone call?"

"As you and Charlotte were going upstairs. It was the police. Apparently someone's been killed in Templefields."

Antonia's shoulders rose and fell almost imperceptibly. She stared at herself in the mirror and rubbed her eyes.

"The victim was someone from London," Jill went on. "The police are looking for a local man. Charlie Meague."

Antonia's head snapped up. "Charlie? Don't be stupid. He wouldn't hurt a fly."

Jill chose her words with care: "They seem to think he's smashed a man's head in."

241

"It's not true. He's not like that at all. I used to know Charlie very well – when he worked for us. Just because he's poor, people think he's capable of anything."

"Charlie Meague was one of the men who found the bones at the Rose in Hand. Did you know that?"

Antonia did not reply.

"That's the thing about Lydmouth," Jill observed. "Everything's connected. Listen, I think you'd better tell me about the brooch."

Once again, Antonia's eyes met Jill's in the mirror. For a full moment, neither of them spoke. As the sixty seconds stretched towards eternity, Jill imagined the thoughts scurrying like terrified animals around Antonia's mind, looking for a way out that did not exist.

At last, Antonia said, "I don't know what you're talking about."

"You do. There was a brooch found with those baby's bones." Jill watched Antonia wincing. "The brooch was in the shape of a true love's knot. It was made of silver and it had a Victorian hallmark. I think we were meant to think that they belonged together, the brooch and the bones. That they were the sort of debris of an affair that went wrong. I think the hallmark and that piece of newspaper were designed to suggest a date for the bones. Nothing too crude or obvious. Just a hint, in case it was needed."

Jill stopped to give Antonia a chance to speak. Antonia was breathing heavily through her mouth. As Jill watched, she brushed a coil of ash from the dressing table to the carpet.

"I actually saw the brooch, you know," Jill went on. "Inspector Thornhill came round here on the evening they were found. He wanted Charlotte and Philip to help him identify the newspaper. And he showed us the brooch, too. He let us hold it. In one of those Kashmir photographs, your mother's wearing an identical brooch. But you already know that, don't you?"

Antonia rummaged in her handbag and took out a fresh cigarette. "You can't possibly be sure it's the same. There were probably thousands of brooches like it."

"It's a studio photograph, a professional job using a professional camera. You could blow up that brooch to life-size, or larger. Why was the photograph album in your room?"

Antonia lit the cigarette. She stared at the wavering flame on the match. The flame burnt down to her fingers. With a squawk of pain, she dropped it in her makeshift ashtray.

"Why shouldn't I look at photographs of my parents?"

"You hated your father, didn't you?"

Another silence filled the room. There was a distant clatter of plates from the dining room: Susan was laying the table for lunch.

"It's no crime to hate your father."

"No," Jill agreed. "Not if that's as far as it goes. Why did you hate him so much?"

Antonia had retreated into herself. Her head was wreathed with smoke. Her eyes were closed.

Jill took a deep breath. "Was it because of the baby?"

She watched Antonia's face in the mirror. Nothing happened. Smoke curled upwards from the cigarette in the bowl. Antonia swallowed. Two tears slipped out between her reddened eyelids and trickled down her cheeks. Jill got up from the bed and put her arm round Antonia's shoulders.

"Don't touch me!" Antonia jerked herself away.

Jill recoiled. She looked at Antonia in the mirror: her face was suffused with blood.

"You had a baby." Jill pitched her tone midway between a question and a statement. "And your father took it away from you."

Antonia's eyes opened into slits. "He said if people found out I'd go to prison." Her voice rose to a wail. "I was only fourteen – how could I know what to do? And he said it would be adopted and properly looked after. *He* would be adopted – it was a boy, I saw it."

"But surely people knew what was going on?"

"As soon as he found out I was going to have a baby, he sent me away – to Aunt Maud. I told you about her, his sister, the nurse. This was just before she emigrated to South Africa – she used to have a house in London. I went there. She looked after me. And as soon as the baby was born, my father took him away. It was just after the war started, in November. Everything was very confused. He said it was a private adoption. But I went through all his papers yesterday – there's no record of anything. He sacked Charlie and his mother, of course, while I was in London. He didn't say why, not to me, he didn't have to." Antonia's face seemed to crumple inwards. "All these years I believed him. I thought my son would be growing up. Each birthday I'd think, today he'll be so many years old. I thought of what he'd be doing, how tall he'd be, what he'd be wearing. I used to look at the children at school and try to work out what he'd be learning. But it was all a lie." She glanced angrily at Jill in the mirror. "But what do you know about it? Why should you care?"

Jill turned away so that Antonia could not see her face. After a moment she said, "Did Charlie Meague know what happened?"

"Charlie? He knew nothing at all. Can't you understand? Why do people have to be so stupid?"

Antonia covered her face with her hands and began to cry. The sobs wrenched her body. Jill reached out a hand towards her, but did not touch her. Suddenly she understood what Antonia had been

243

trying to say. Sadness rose like a tide inside her. She sat down on the bed. Her eyes filled with tears. The tears were not for Antonia, but for the lost babies.

A dull, rolling boom filled the house. Susan was beating the gong in the hall to announce that lunch was ready.

18

Kirby was the first inside the Bathurst Arms. He walked swiftly up to the crowded bar with Thornhill at his heels.

Gloria arched her back and smiled at the two policemen. Her actions and her appearance were impersonal, Thornhill thought, like a pornographic photograph: designed to appeal to every man.

"What can I get you, gentlemen?"

"This is business, Gloria," Kirby said, slicking back his greasy yellow hair. "Is there somewhere we can have a word?"

Gloria touched her cheek with a bright red fingernail. Her face was perfectly still, a flawless cosmetic mask. But the eyes were restless.

"You'd better come through." She opened the flap of the bar for them. "I won't be long," she said to her stepdaughter.

Jane glanced at Kirby and Thornhill. "Shall I call Dad to help?"

"No," Gloria said quickly. "Don't bother."

With her hips swaying from side to side, she led them down a narrow hallway to a small room next to the kitchen. It was furnished as an office with a battered desk, a steel filing cabinet and four hard chairs. The room looked like a man's and smelt like a woman's. Thornhill noticed that the cigarette butts in the ashtray were rimmed with lipstick.

"Someone back there was saying there's been a murder in Templefields," she said, her manner elaborately casual. "It's not true, is it?"

"There has been an incident." Thornhill said. "I am afraid we can't tell you any more than that at present."

Gloria sat down behind the desk and waved them to chairs. "Now what can I do for you?"

Thornhill was sure that she knew why they had come. She was too clever to seem wary, but her lack of surprise gave her away.

Kirby leant forward, holding out his cigarette packet. "Smoke?"

"I don't mind if I do."

Kirby took one as well. He lit both cigarettes before continuing: "Nothing to worry about, Gloria – we're interested in one of your customers."

She blew out smoke through her nostrils. "Oh, yes?"

"Chap called Charlie Meague."

Gloria frowned. "I'm not sure I know who you mean."

"Don't give me that," Kirby said sharply. "He's been in here the last couple of nights. I saw him myself. But maybe we should ask your husband. Perhaps he can tell us more."

Thornhill glanced at Kirby and realised with distaste that the sergeant was enjoying himself.

"There's no need to disturb Harold," Gloria said. "You mean Charlie, don't you? I always think of him just as Charlie. That's why when you said Meague it didn't register straightaway."

"Funny, that," Kirby said, drawing deeply on his cigarette. "I understand you remembered his surname on Friday afternoon, and where he lived. Because you went to visit him, didn't you?"

Gloria's face twisted. "Ma Halleran. That cow."

"Now, now, Gloria," Kirby murmured. "We understand that you and Charlie had one of those boy-and-girl romances. Long ago, when the world was young."

She shrugged. "That's one way of putting it."

"Tell us about it."

"There's not much to say, is there? I knew him when we were kids. I hadn't seen him for years until a couple of days ago. There was this bloke asking for him. Little chap with a beard."

"And did he find Charlie?" Thornhill put in, knowing the answer but wanting to test Gloria's attachment to truth.

She nodded. Her eyes darted from Thornhill to Kirby and then to the cigarette in her hand. "Listen, what's all this about?"

"When did you last see Charlie?"

"He was in last night. So were you, Mr Kirby."

"Have you seen him today? Or maybe your husband has?"

"I told you, there's no call to bring Harold into this. Charlie came round this morning just before opening time."

"What did he want?"

She stabbed the remains of the cigarette into the ashtray. "This needn't go further, need it?"

"Put it this way, Gloria," Kirby smiled at her. "If we're not satisfied with your answers, we're going to have to talk to Harold. Is that what you want?"

Gloria stared across the desk, not at Kirby but at Thornhill. "He wanted to borrow Harold's car. He looked awful, Mr Thornhill – like he'd been sleeping rough."

"And did you let him have it?" Thornhill asked.

"Of course I didn't. Harold would bloody murder me." Her eyes flickered. "Anyway – Charlie frightened me. He flashed all this

246

money at me – at least a hundred quid. He wanted me to run off with him. Then and there. God, he was acting like we were kids again." She hesitated. "And there was blood on his hand."

19

Through the thin November air came the sound of St John's clock striking the first quarter. Charlie thought it must be either a quarter past one or a quarter past two. It didn't bloody matter.

He sat in the little yard with his back against a wall and the whisky bottle between his legs. At this time of day, when the sunshine reached the court, it was warmer outside than in one of the tall, ruined buildings. Long ago, when they were young, he and Gloria would meet in this yard. Here she had let him make love to her for the one and only time: she had her back against the wall; both of them had been alert for approaching footsteps; and afterwards she had been furious because of the mess and the discomfort.

Charlie had not made a conscious decision to take refuge in Templefields. He had not needed to think. Once there, he realised that he had nowhere else to go – or not until nightfall. He guessed that the police would be watching the roads and the railway by now. He wouldn't have a chance of getting away. After dark, however, it might be different. Stealing a car offered him his best chance.

He had gone through the contents of the sack and the kitbag concealed in the chimney. All that effort for next to nothing – the pathetically inadequate haul of items he had stolen from Masterman's the jeweller's, the King's Head and Chandos Lodge. He was cold and hungry. The only thing that had any real value to him now was the bottle of whisky from Ma Halleran.

He had known it would be stupid to have a drink. But he was so cold that his teeth rattled on the neck of the bottle. The whisky stung his swollen lips and warmed him down to his belly. He drank more of it. The more he drank, the more he needed to drink. It seemed to him that if only he could get enough whisky inside him, everything might be all right again. Jimmy Carn might stand up again, the back of his head as good as new. Gloria would smile and touch his hand. His mother would be back in the house in Minching Lane.

He could not believe that he had killed Carn. Charlie thought of himself as an ordinary man. How then could he have killed someone? The very idea made him feel ill and unreal. He remembered Ma

Halleran's face when she had seen Carn's body: how her mouth opened and nothing came out, not even a scream.

He didn't want to think about killing. He counted the money instead. You knew where you were with money. The first time he made the total a hundred and fifty-eight pounds. The second time it was a hundred and sixty-three pounds. The third time he gave up after he reached a hundred. He put the notes down on the flagstone beside him.

The wind made the notes twitch like dead leaves. One of them half slid, half floated across the yard. Charlie drank more of the whisky. By now he had almost finished the bottle.

Jesus, I'm getting as bad as old Harcutt. But it didn't matter. He thought of poor ugly Tony and how she used to follow him around in the garden at Chandos Lodge; and he wondered why she'd been so stupid as to come home. You couldn't go back. Charlie realised that now. He'd been a fool to let Gloria get under his skin again.

The sky was bright blue, and floating overhead was a convoy of small, sunlit clouds. But the shadows were lengthening, crawling further and further along the flagstones. Charlie shifted his bottom along the cold stones to keep himself in the diminishing patch of sunlight.

Soon the sunshine dwindled until it filled only one corner of the yard. He watched the banknotes skittering to and fro in the wind. He noticed with resignation that he'd finished the whisky. The church clock chimed again.

Charlie heard footsteps coming down the alley from the direction of Minching Lane. He did not move. His eyes drifted in and out of focus. He shut them because he felt tired.

When he opened his eyes there were four men standing in the archway which led from the yard to the alleyway. He blinked and the four men became two. The two policemen moved cautiously towards him.

The older man – Thornhill? – said something which Charlie heard but did not understand. Charlie's head fell forward on to his chest. He knew that Gloria must have told them where to find him.

20

Williamson directed a hostile stare at Thornhill. The superintendent was standing by the window with his hands in his pockets. He was dressed for relaxation in a yellow tweed jacket over a bright green jersey; grey trousers and brown shoes added touches of sobriety to his off-duty plumage. There was a poppy in his lapel.

"Where the hell were you?" he said to Thornhill. "I wanted to see you as soon as I got here. Didn't you get my message?"

"Yes, sir." Thornhill shut the door of Williamson's office behind him. "But we were just on our way out. We've made an arrest."

"Have you, indeed? I'd prefer to have been consulted. Charlie Meague?"

"Yes, sir."

"I just hope you haven't jumped the gun. It's a pity that Halleran woman didn't actually see him do it. Murder charges can be tricky."

"We can take our time on that. We can hold him for burglary."

"What do you mean?"

"When we found Meague, we also found things taken from the King's Head, Masterman's and Chandos Lodge."

Williamson sniffed in a way that implied disapproval, an odd reaction to what should have been good news. His eyes were bloodshot – perhaps he was still feeling the effects of the Masonic dinner at the Bull. Thornhill also remembered how sure the superintendent had been that Charlie Meague was not the type to take to burglary.

"Is he talking?" Williamson asked.

"He's sleeping. He's drunk as a lord. Threw up in the patrol car, I'm afraid, mainly over Sergeant Kirby's trousers. I don't think we'll get much out of him until he's sobered up. Dr Bayswater's having a look at him now."

"Has anyone remembered to tell Meague's mother?"

"The doctor says she died last night. Meague had only just heard the news. Maybe that's what drove him over the edge."

Williamson grunted. "Then the odds are he won't hang. Pity." He rummaged through the change in his trouser pocket. "Well – it could be worse," he went on. "There's a murder, but at least the victim's a man from London, and we've got the killer. And we've also wrapped up the burglary case." He stared blankly at the window. "Straightforward police work always gets results," he murmured. "Essentially it's a team job – a matter of firm leadership, method and organisation. I must ring the chief constable."

Williamson paused. Thornhill guessed he was trying out phrases in his mind, phrases for the chief constable, phrases for the gentlemen of the press.

"You seem to have – ah – kept on your toes, Thornhill. Good work. Of course, I'll need to have a report on my desk as soon as possible." Williamson pulled out a pipe and toyed with it. "But that reminds me, I'm sorry to say that I had a complaint about you last night. It's always painful to have to pass on something of this nature. I imagine you know what I'm referring to."

"Mr George?"

"Exactly. I emphasised to him that you're new to the job, and I hope we can deal with this on an informal basis. I don't think you quite appreciate Mr George's position in this town. There's a distinct possibility that he may fill the next vacancy on the Standing Joint Committee. And then, of course, there's the real point at issue: we have a responsibility to protect our citizens from the unwanted attentions of stray drunks. Don't you agree?"

"I got the impression that Mr George wasn't exactly sober himself."

Williamson jabbed his pipe stem towards Thornhill. "Don't get clever with me."

"Do you know who the other man was, sir?"

"Of course I don't."

"His name's Oliver Yateley. He's a Labour Member of Parliament." Thornhill watched Williamson's face.

"Yateley? Yes, now I come to think of it, I have heard the name."

"I understand he's on the wireless a good deal. We talked for some time, afterwards. Interesting man."

Williamson glanced almost furtively at Thornhill. He sat down and began to fill his pipe. "Well, I always say there are times when the man on the ground has to make the decisions," he said with the air of a man making a concession. "Every officer must be able to act independently if need be."

"Yes, sir," Thornhill said.

"I'll have a word with Mr George. I am sure he'll understand. Circumstances alter cases." The superintendent put his hand on the phone and nodded a dismissal. "Well, sort out that report, and let me know when Meague's fit for questioning. I'll want to be there."

"There's something else I'd like to mention."

"Can't it wait?"

"I think not. It's Major Harcutt."

"Tragic accident," Williamson said, speaking in newspaper headlines. "Respected war hero from old Lydmouth family."

"But was it an accident?"

"I imagine that's what the inquest will come up with. I know suicide's a possibility, but I understand it's no more than that."

"There are still one or two points to clear up."

"Later. We're in the middle of a murder enquiry. I want you to concentrate on the Carn business."

Thornhill began to speak, but Williamson held up a large, square hand.

"Get that report done," he said, "talk to the witnesses. No ifs, no buts. Give Meague a damn good grilling. What I'd really like is to prove premeditation. Then there wouldn't be any nonsense about a reprieve and Charlie Meague would get what he deserves. There's only one way to deal with a killer in my view. Hang him."

21

The telephone rang as Edith was doing the washing-up and the children were squabbling over a board game called 'Journey Through Fairyland'.

Wiping her hands on a tea towel, she went to answer it. The house smelled of roast beef. She felt a little too full and pleasantly sleepy. She would have liked to go to bed for an hour or so.

"Darling, it's me," Richard said. "I'm sorry, I'm not going to be able to get back this afternoon."

"Well, if you can't, you can't." Edith thought of his lunch drying up in the oven. The afternoon shut in with David and Elizabeth stretched uninvitingly before her. "I might take the children out," she said. "Up to the park perhaps, or down to the river."

"I wish this could have happened on any other day."

She recognised the note of misery in his voice. "I thought it was just a burglary."

"It's a little more than that."

Her hand tightened on the phone. She knew better than to ask for details now. "So we'll expect you when we see you, shall we?"

"Yes," he said, sounding very far away. "Don't wait up."

He rang off. She put down the phone and smoothed her skirt over her hips. The familiar dread settled over her. She began to shiver. It was the recurrent fear, the one that never went away and often slipped into her dreams: Richard having to deal single-handedly with a murderer who was probably armed and by definition ruthless.

He was so proud of his job and she tried never to show him how much it worried her. *Be careful*, she had wanted to say to him. *We need you.*

22

"Damn," Charlotte said when the doorbell rang. She prodded her husband with her toe. "You get it, dear, will you?"

Philip rubbed his eyes and yawned.

"The door, Philip. Someone's at the front door."

He tore himself away from his armchair and left the room. It was a little after three o'clock. This was the dead time of a Sunday afternoon – after lunch and before tea time. On Sundays, once lunch was out of the way, Susan was off duty for the rest of the day.

"Such an inconvenient time to call," Charlotte grumbled. "Whoever can it be?"

Jill already knew that Nemesis had arrived at Troy House in a small Austin. She could see out of the window from where she was sitting at one end of the sofa, with Antonia pretending to read a book at the other. The sight of Thornhill getting out of the car had brought her to the edge of panic. She felt powerless to avert whatever was going to happen: as if all of them were at the mercy of a huge and passionless machine.

She heard Philip's voice in the hall and then Thornhill's. The door opened.

"Antonia," Philip said. "Mr Thornhill would like a word."

Charlotte was already on her feet and advancing towards the doorway. "Inspector, what a terrible business this is. Would you like to use the dining room? You'd be quite undisturbed there."

There was a soft thud. Jill glanced round. Antonia had let her book fall to the carpet. She was sitting with her hands on her lap, staring straight ahead.

"Just a few loose ends, Miss Harcutt," Thornhill said.

"Would you like me to come, too?" Jill asked Antonia.

"Yes," Antonia said.

Jill glanced at Thornhill, daring him to argue. But he nodded as if her suggestion were the most natural in the world. Antonia stuffed her cigarettes into a pocket of her cardigan, stood up and shuffled towards the doorway.

Charlotte led them into the dining room where she fussed over the seating arrangements, tried without success to separate Thornhill from his overcoat and briefcase and offered them tea. Thornhill got rid of her with a courteous efficiency which Jill couldn't help but envy.

The three of them sat down at one end of the large mahogany table. All the furniture in the room was heavy and of ample proportions. A three-quarter-length portrait of Grandpa Wemyss reading his own newspaper hung over the fireplace.

"I have some news for you," Thornhill said.

Antonia stared at him.

"I don't know whether you've heard that a man was killed in Templefields this morning?"

She gave no sign that she had heard.

"Well, in connection with that, we have arrested a man, and when we found him, we also found a number of items which we think may have come from Chandos Lodge. I've got a few of them here. I wonder if you can identify them."

He lifted the briefcase on to the table and unpacked some of its contents. One by one he laid on the table two gold watches, three rings and a pair of jade earrings. Jill stared at them. The rings were old and very grubby; and if their stones were real, they would be valuable.

"I remember my mother wearing those earrings – and that ring, I think, the one with the diamonds in it." Antonia's voice trembled. "Who stole them?"

"Someone you used to know, Miss Harcutt. Charlie Meague."

"No. Please, no."

"Why do you say that?"

Antonia shook her head and took refuge once more in silence.

Thornhill waited a moment and then went on: "Shall I tell you what we think happened? And I'd appreciate any help you could give me with the details." Again he paused, but Antonia said nothing. "Charlie Meague needed money for reasons which needn't concern you. So he turned to burglary. But burglary's a specialised trade and he wasn't very good at it. His mother used to work at each of the houses he tried. But Chandos Lodge was rather different. For one thing, he had a grudge against your father. I understand that he sacked Meague and his mother in 1939. Can you confirm that?"

"Yes. And he shouldn't have done it. There was no reason."

"You probably won't have heard that Mrs Meague died in hospital last night. Pneumonia. She was delirious towards the end. According to Dr Bayswater, she said something about poor Miss Tony. And she also said, more than once, 'It wasn't you, was it, Charlie?' What do you think she might have meant?"

"How do I know? It was so long ago. I haven't seen the Meagues for years."

"I think Charlie Meague had seen your father more recently. Just before his dog was run over, Major Harcutt was seen talking to a tall man outside the gates of Chandos Lodge. In fact, there's a suggestion that Milly was chasing the man when she was run over. There again, we found the remains of a clock in the dustbin this morning. Rather a nice clock, as it happens."

Antonia hugged herself.

Thornhill smiled at her. "Can you tell us when the clock was broken?"

"Yesterday morning." Antonia frowned. "It seems like months ago. I think my father knocked it off the mantelpiece while Jill and I were out doing the poppies."

Thornhill glanced at Jill who nodded in confirmation. "We've just had it fingerprinted," he said. "It's got Charlie Meague's prints on it."

"I don't understand," Antonia said.

"It suggests that Meague visited Chandos Lodge between his return to Lydmouth and before the clock was broken – in other words, before the burglary." Thornhill hesitated. "In fact it confirms what Meague told me today. He was so drunk I wasn't sure he knew what he was saying. He also told me he recognised something when he found the bones at the Rose in Hand. The box they were in. Apparently it used to be in the garden shed at Chandos Lodge." Thornhill turned back to Jill. "You and Mrs Wemyss-Brown surprised him looking for it on Friday evening. He was making sure."

"But that's impossible." Jill thought her voice must sound shrill and false to the others. "It can't have been the same box. It—"

"Where *is* Charlie?" Antonia interrupted, her voice shrill. "He's not dead, is he?"

"No, of course not," Thornhill said. "When I last saw him, he was snoring away."

"But he killed this man in Templefields?"

"That's for a jury to decide, Miss Harcutt."

"But it's what you think."

Thornhill leant forward. "I'm afraid this may be painful for you. You see, I do have to bear in mind the possibility that Charlie Meague also killed your father."

Antonia stared at him. She opened her mouth and tried to speak. In the end all that emerged was a whispered "No".

"Do you feel all right?" Jill asked her. "Now you've identified the jewellery, I'm sure the inspector wouldn't mind if we postponed the rest."

Thornhill was still staring at Antonia; he ignored Jill's suggestion.

"We're pretty sure that Meague was in the house last night. He might easily have found your father in a very deep sleep because of the whisky and the barbiturates. It would have been a simple matter for Meague to turn off the gas fire and then turn it on again without relighting it. He could have done it in the room or at the mains. If it were done carefully, there would be no fingerprints."

"But why?" Jill said. "Or don't you bother about motives?"

"They aren't as important to a policeman as you might think, Miss Francis. In this case, however, I think Meague hated Major Harcutt because he believed that he and his mother had been sacked unreasonably. We have to remember that Meague was in an unsettled state of mind because his mother was seriously ill. He also had very pressing financial problems. There's a strong possibility that he tried to blackmail Major Harcutt yesterday morning. If the major refused, that would have given Meague an additional reason to hate him. And finally..." Thornhill broke off. "If you'd prefer, Miss Harcutt, we could ask Miss Francis to leave the room for a moment at this point."

Antonia shook her head. "It doesn't matter. Jill knows."

Thornhill glanced at Jill and raised his eyebrows. "Knows what?"

"Don't say anything," Jill said to Antonia. "This is all speculation."

"Not entirely, Miss Francis. For one thing there are the bones from the Rose in Hand."

"Amelia Rushwick's baby?" Even as she spoke, Jill knew it was no use.

"The baby which Major Harcutt encouraged us to associate with Amelia Rushwick."

"But the brooch – and the newspaper."

Thornhill looked steadily at Jill. "Easy enough to plant that sort of evidence. On forensic grounds, it's impossible to tell whether the bones are fifteen years old or fifty years old. Indeed, it's something of a miracle there's anything left of them at all, once the rats and the cats had had their fill. And the brooch raises an interesting point: Major Harcutt knew that it was made of silver. Do you remember my asking you if you or Mrs Wemyss-Brown had told him that? And you said you hadn't."

"Perhaps he heard from someone else."

"Very unlikely – on your own admission, you and Mrs Wemyss-Brown were the first to tell him about the discovery."

"Perhaps he simply assumed it was silver. Many brooches are."

"Perhaps. But there's another possibility, isn't there? By the way, Miss Harcutt, did you know that your father considered taking out a lease on the Rose in Hand yard from the Ruispidge Estate in 1939?"

"For Christ's sake," Antonia muttered, "must you go on and on?"

"I'm sorry to upset you. Would you rather leave this till later?"

"An excellent idea," Jill said.

"No, let's get it over with." Antonia's hands struggled with her cigarette packet. "Has anyone got a match?"

There was a moment's pause while Thornhill lit her cigarette and found her an ashtray. He stared at her for a second.

"I'm sorry to have to ask this, Miss Harcutt, but were you pregnant in 1939?"

Antonia nodded slowly. She kept her head bowed. A few flakes of dandruff drifted down to the table.

"What happened to the baby?"

"My father took him away. He was going to be adopted. That's what my father said."

"We have to consider the possibility that the Templefields remains were those of your baby and that they were put there by your father. Furthermore, that he took care to ensure that if any traces of the body were found some years later, they would be assumed to be the work of Amelia Rushwick, or at least to have had something to do with the Rose in Hand in the last century. Charlie Meague guessed or knew all this, or enough of it to make it worth his while to try blackmail."

"But he couldn't possibly have known anything about it," Jill pointed out.

"He could if he were the baby's father," Thornhill said. "I think his mother suspected it. That would fit in perfectly with what she said to Dr Bayswater. And, of course, it explains why Major Harcutt sacked the Meagues. He couldn't go to the police without his daughter's part in it coming out. It wouldn't have been just the social stigma. Technically, you see, Miss Harcutt had committed a criminal offence."

"This is sheer fantasy," Jill said. "And I don't like the way you're trying to browbeat Miss Harcutt." She knew as she spoke that the accusation was unfair.

"We should have a few more facts after we've talked to Charlie Meague again," Thornhill said. "But it seemed wiser and kinder to talk to Miss Harcutt first."

It was a reprimand, and Jill felt herself flushing. For an instant there was a look of triumph on Thornhill's face, and in that instant she hated him.

"There's another reason why this is important," he said to Antonia. "It could affect the case against Meague."

Jill sat up sharply. "He's already on a capital charge, isn't he? So this could mean the difference between a prison sentence and being hanged."

There was a crash as Antonia's hands hit the table. She dropped the cigarette which rolled across the gleaming wood. Her mouth was open and her lips were drawn back as if in a silent scream or snarl. She began to pant. She tried to speak and failed. The others waited. Thornhill picked up the cigarette and rested it in the ashtray. It had left a small burn on the otherwise immaculate surface of the table.

"But it wasn't Charlie," Antonia gasped. "He never touched me. And he didn't kill my father either. It was my father who made me pregnant. It was my father who took away my baby. And do you know what I found out yesterday? He didn't have my baby adopted as he said he would. He killed him and tossed him in a cesspit in Templefields and left him for the rats. *That's* why I killed him."

The room was silent, apart from their breathing. Thornhill was looking at Antonia. Jill was conscious of a fiercely maternal urge to protect her from his eyes.

"Miss Harcutt, I shall have to ask you to come to the police station with me. Perhaps you'd like to ask Miss Francis to come with you. And you may like to telephone your solicitor before you leave."

"I haven't got a solicitor," Antonia said. "Anyway, I'm not sure I could afford one."

"You needn't worry about the money," Jill said.

Antonia stared at Thornhill, her face puzzled, almost disappointed. "Why don't you just arrest me?"

"I'd like you to make a statement. Then I'll need to talk to my superiors."

Antonia put her head in her hands. Jill pushed back her chair and stood up.

"Mr Thornhill, may I have a word with you in private?"

He nodded. They went out into the hall together. To Jill's surprise, the drawing-room door was closed: Charlotte, or possibly Philip, must be exercising a superhuman control over her curiosity. Nevertheless, both Jill and Thornhill automatically stood close together beside the big chest and kept their voices down. As they whispered, Jill watched their blurred and unrecognisable reflections moving on the polished wood.

"Why don't you let it alone?" Jill said. "Does it really matter?"

His shoulders slumped. "It matters to Charlie Meague. I don't want him charged for a murder he didn't commit. Nor does Miss Harcutt, I think."

"That's not what I mean. Why does Harcutt's death have to be murder? Everyone else seems to think that it was an accident. He was an ill and lonely man. Nobody liked him. And he died peacefully in his sleep. Wouldn't it be kinder to leave it like that?"

He shook his head. "I can't do that."

"Why not, for God's sake?" She came a little nearer to him, aware

259

that something in him was unsettled by her nearness. "Does anyone else know about this? Is there other evidence that you haven't mentioned?"

"I can't discuss that with you."

"Don't be such a damned stuffed shirt." Almost at once, she added, "I'm sorry. I shouldn't have said that."

"It doesn't matter."

"Listen. Your job's all about justice, isn't it? And justice should be concerned with the spirit of the law, not its letter. Isn't one of the principles of justice that the punishment be proportionate to the offence? Antonia's been punished enough already. And she'll go on punishing herself, too. Don't you agree?"

"What I think doesn't come into it."

"Of course it does. It's up to you whether this goes any further."

Thornhill raised his head and stared at her. He looked like a man who had failed, she thought, not like a hunter who was on the verge of tracking down his prey.

"I don't think in the long run there's anything to be gained by tinkering with the truth," he said slowly. "And I think Miss Harcutt wants to tell the truth. That's partly because she doesn't want Charlie Meague to be prosecuted for something he didn't do. And it's partly just to be honest. She's been living a lie, you know. It can be a great relief when you start telling the truth."

"That's cant," she said. "The next thing you'll say is that you're only doing this for her own good. And that's only one step removed from what Harcutt probably told himself when he raped her: that she deserved it, that she was asking for it."

"I know."

"I warn you, this won't be easy for you. I don't think you've got much of a case, and we'll fight it all the way."

He looked at her without saying anything. She noticed the dark smudges under his eyes: his skin was tinged with grey. His face is hungry, she thought irrelevantly, and so terribly sad. He turned away and opened the dining-room door.

"Miss Harcutt?" he said. "Is there anything you need to do before we leave?"

23

The dark blue Rover slid along the kerb and drew up outside police headquarters. The engine died and the headlights faded. Philip Wemyss-Brown opened the driver's door and got out. He went quickly up the steps into the station.

Sergeant Fowles was on duty. "They're in Mr Williamson's office, sir. Shall I get someone to take you up?"

"That's all right. I know the way."

Fowles opened the flap to let him past the counter. Philip walked up the stairs. The big building was quiet. Sunday was usually the most peaceful night of the week. The first floor had been partitioned into offices before the war. Williamson had one of the larger ones – half of what had once been a bedroom; the window overlooked the High Street. Philip tapped on the door and went in.

"There you are," Williamson said. "Take a pew."

The superintendent's face was pink. Jill and Thornhill, on the other hand, who were sitting as far apart as possible on the other side of the desk, looked tired and drawn. As Philip came in, Jill glanced at him and the relief on her face was obvious; something which Philip was accustomed to identify as his heart lurched within his ribcage.

"I think this calls for a drink," Williamson said. "We all deserve one. It's been one hell of a day." He slid open a drawer in his desk and took out a bottle of whisky. He opened another drawer, fished out two glasses and stood them on the blotter beside the bottle. "Thornhill, would you get a couple more glasses from the kitchen? And maybe a jug of water. I like it neat myself, but some people prefer to dilute their pleasures."

"I don't want a drink, thank you," Jill said.

"I'd rather not either," Thornhill put in. "Not on an empty stomach."

"Well, that's all right." Williamson pulled the cork out of the bottle and began to pour. "I was just saying to Miss Francis that if the chief constable agrees, we'll have a press conference tomorrow. The sooner the better, of course. There are enough rumours flying around town already."

Philip took the glass which Williamson gave him and turned to Jill. "How's Antonia?"

"As well as can be expected in the circumstances," Jill said. "Mr Williamson says I can see her tomorrow morning."

"Of course you may, my dear," Williamson said, beaming at her; she looked at him with loathing; he appeared not to notice. "Miss Francis has been a great help," he said to Philip. "Hasn't she, Thornhill?"

"I'm sure Miss Harcutt thinks so," Thornhill said.

Jill glanced quickly at him and then down at her lap.

"We're not ogres, you know," Williamson went on. "It's always awkward when a lady like Miss Harcutt is in this sort of position. Not that it happens often, I'm glad to say. But when it does, we like to smooth the way as much as we can."

"Charlotte sent her love to Antonia," Philip said awkwardly. "And of course if there's anything we can do, you must just let us know."

Williamson cleared his throat. "I know we all feel deeply moved by the tragedies which have recently occurred," he said. "And on Remembrance Sunday, too. It's a sad business." He sipped his whisky. "Still, I think we have cause for a little celebration. Don't you agree? At least this business hasn't been allowed to drag on. There's every chance that the guilty will be dealt with as soon as possible. I think the force has responded magnificently."

He looked round the room. Perhaps, Philip thought, Williamson was hoping that someone would respond with "Hear, hear!" or a toast to the county's glorious CID.

Jill picked up her handbag and stood up. "Don't think me rude, but perhaps we'd better be getting back to Troy House. I'm sure Mr Williamson and Mr Thornhill have work to do."

In an instant, all three men were on their feet. Philip swallowed the rest of his whisky and put the glass on the desk. Jill moved towards the door which Thornhill was holding open for her. As she passed him, Philip could have sworn that the pair of them stared at each other for an instant longer than was normal; and she didn't acknowledge his courtesy in any way. But the moment passed so quickly that he decided that he had imagined it. He knew from experience that he was inclined to read too much into Jill's behaviour, especially where other men were concerned. Not that it was any of his business.

Williamson escorted them downstairs. "The chief constable's over the moon, you know. He's got the Standing Joint Committee next week, and this is just the sort of thing he likes to tell them. Feather in our cap – not every County CID could deal so promptly with a case like this."

The superintendent stood at the front door waving to them as they went down the steps and got into the car. He was pink-faced and triumphant, like a Dickensian host waving farewell to the last of his guests.

Philip started the engine, and drove slowly down the High Street.

"I've never met such a stupid, conceited man," Jill said.

"Which one?"

"Williamson, of course," she said, sounding surprised that he'd needed to ask.

"He's conceited, all right. But he's not stupid. If he thinks he's got the case wrapped up, he almost certainly has."

"Antonia made a statement," Jill said. "She insisted. They were very good about it – made sure she had a solicitor and so on. And they tried to be terribly considerate – endless cups of tea. But she's admitted everything. And she's piled on the detail, too. I think she feels it might help Charlie Meague. Do you know what she said to me? 'Charlie's the only male who was ever really kind to me.' Christ, it's a mess."

"What did you do to Williamson? He practically tried to kiss your hand as we were leaving."

"I rather overemphasised my contacts in the national press."

They drove through the deserted streets. It was another cold night and a fat moon was hanging in the sky. Philip liked the smell of Jill's perfume, and he liked knowing she was in the seat beside him. Happiness took him by surprise – just for second and then it was gone.

"Thornhill was very quiet, I thought," he said.

"Yes." Jill hesitated. "Have you got a cigarette?"

"I didn't think you still smoked."

"Sometimes I do. Could we stop for a moment?"

He pulled over at once. They were near Lydmouth's war memorial, a stone pillar surmounted by a life-size statue of a soldier in helmet and leggings, with a rifle slung over his shoulder. There were wreaths stacked around the base of the column.

"I just need a moment to calm down," Jill said. "Sort things out in my mind."

"There's no hurry." Philip felt for his cigarette case.

Jill nodded at the memorial. "The book was right. November is the month of the dead."

"What book?"

She took a cigarette. "Something a man was reading on the train."

"It must have been bloody awful for you, all this."

"How's Charlotte coping?" Jill asked, taking him, as so often, by surprise.

"She's rather upset, actually." Philip flicked his lighter and lit their cigarettes; the flame brought colour to her face. "A lot of people don't realise that she's really quite sensitive. It's not just that Antonia's someone she knows and someone who was staying in her house. In a funny way, she blames herself for the whole thing."

"But that's nonsense."

"She says it wouldn't have happened if she hadn't dragged Antonia back to Lydmouth. And she also feels bad about sacking Mrs Meague. You remember? She tried to pinch a snuffbox? The poor woman must have already had pneumonia then. She can't have been responsible for her actions."

"Charlotte did everything from the best of motives," Jill said. "You could just as easily say it was my fault because I drove Antonia back to Lydmouth. If you leave out guilty intent, where do you draw the line?"

"You're right," Philip said, staring at Jill's darkened profile. "There's no rational reason for her to feel guilty. But guilt isn't an altogether rational process, is it?"

"No." She drew on her cigarette and turned her face towards his. "Philip," she said suddenly. "You've got a job going on the *Gazette*, haven't you? Would you consider me, if I applied for it?"

"Is that a joke?"

"No. I have to do something, you see. And I'd like to work down here."

"Something happened in London, didn't it?" Philip felt a hot rush of jealousy. "Something to do with that chap who rang up?"

"Yes. I'll tell you about it sometime. Not now. But that's not why I want the job. What about it?"

"Are you really sure you'd want to do it? You'd spend half your time checking the names of the bridesmaids."

"I realise that. And I am sure."

"Makes one think of racehorses pulling carts. Still, if you're really serious, I'll think about it." Philip leant forward and fumbled for the key in the ignition; his jealousy had vanished and he felt enormously cheerful. "Of course I'd have to have a word with Charlotte about it, too."

24

It was half past eleven by the time Richard Thornhill let himself into his house. Victoria Road was cold and silent. As he twisted the key in the lock, he glanced up at the night sky. It was sprinkled with stars.

A light was burning on the landing. He went through to the kitchen and checked that Edith had banked up the boiler. She had left him some cold beef sandwiches and a Thermos flask of coffee. He ate half a sandwich and took a few sips of the coffee. He felt too tired even to swallow. He drank some more coffee in the hope that it would warm him.

There were footsteps on the stairs. A moment later, Edith came into the kitchen. She was wearing a quilted dressing gown which stretched to her ankles. Her face looked scrubbed and very young.

"I thought I heard you." She sat down beside him. "Are you all right? You look awfully tired."

"Fine. Thanks for the sandwiches."

She gripped his hand. "Don't shut me out, Richard. I need you."

He pulled his chair towards hers and put his arms around her. "It's all right. I'm sorry this has been such a ruined day."

"I met this woman when we were up at the park," she said. "She told me there'd been this terrible murder in Minching Lane. Someone had his head bashed in."

"That's more or less what happened, I'm afraid."

"But I've been so worried. Can't you see?"

His arms tightened round her. She moved nearer to him. Her body was warm and soft.

"It wasn't like you'd think," he said. "I arrested two people today and both of them will probably end up on murder charges. One was so drunk he couldn't stand up by himself. And the other was a woman who came up to my shoulder. She looks like a rabbit and she was absolutely terrified. Poor kid."

"Would it help to tell me? I'd like to know."

He told her about Charlie Meague and Antonia Harcutt. He began reluctantly, but as he went on talking it became easier; his professional experience had taught him that confession had a momentum of its own.

"It's the girl that worries me, you see. If I'd kept quiet, no one would ever have known that she'd killed her father."

"No one except her. Will she hang?"

"Almost certainly there'll be a reprieve. So she'll go to prison instead. For someone like that, it will be living hell."

"You had to do it."

"That's just it. I didn't have to."

A few minutes later, they went upstairs. When Thornhill came back from the bathroom, Edith was sitting up in bed with a book in front of her. As he slid into bed beside her she turned towards him.

"Richard," she said.

She moved a little towards him and twisted her face up to his. They started to kiss. He felt her hand running down his body and turned towards her. Their lovemaking had an urgency to it, a compound of desire, guilt and relief. For Thornhill, it was over too quickly. His urgency had defeated itself, leaving him with a sense of futility, of soured hopes.

Edith stroked his hair. "It's all right," she murmured. "It's all right."

Afterwards, they settled down to sleep beneath the mound of blankets and the eiderdown. Thornhill was very warm. He felt Edith's body shaking slightly under his arm.

"What is it?" he asked. "Are you crying?"

"Yes, but it doesn't matter. I'm just so glad that you're safe."

The trembling stopped and gradually her breathing acquired a slow regular quality. Thornhill stared, dry-eyed, into the darkness. The events of the day trekked through his memory towards an unknown destination.

Jill Francis loomed up in his mind. He didn't want her there: she was an intruder and her very presence made him feel disloyal to Edith. He plucked words out of the darkness to describe Jill Francis. The words were like incantations and their purpose was to drive her away. She was cold, he thought. Remote. Arrogant. Irrational. Snobbish. And she had lovely eyes.